W9-BVF-711

Harlequin Books

TORONTO • NEW YORK • LONDON
AMSTERDAM • PARIS • SYDNEY • HAMBURG
STOCKHOLM • ATHENS • TOKYO • MILAN
MADRID • WARSAW • BUDAPEST • AUCKLAND

Harlequin Historicals first edition February 1993

ISBN 0-373-28762-3

KNIGHT'S LADY

His hands tightened on her. "You could have been killed!"

Ari smiled up at him. "There is no need to shout at me."

"I'll do more than shout!" he roared. "I'll turn you over my knee and paddle your sweet little—"

"You are not my father!" she cried, struggling in his grasp.

"And you can thank heaven I am not." He hung on tighter. "I'd not have coddled you."

"Coddled? Coddled!" Her voice rose to a wail. "I work right alongside my grandfather." She clenched her fist and swung at his belly.

Gareth caught her wrist in his left hand, twisting her arm behind her back and slamming her flush against his body. "You little witch."

"It is your fault," she cried, tossing her tangled hair from her face. "You make me so angry I could..."

He stilled. "Could what?" His breath fanned her cheek, as his eyes burned into into hers....

Dear Reader,

This month we bring you the first book in a delightful trilogy by author Maura Seger. Set in Belle Haven, a fictional New England town, *The Taming of Amelia* is an adventurous tale of two people destined to forge new lives for themselves in the Colonies. It sets the stage for stories of the town's future generations—right up to the present day, with a tie-in book from Silhouette's Intimate Moments line.

Prolific newcomer Kit Gardner is sure to please with *The Stolen Heart,* a high-spirited romance between an aristocratic English girl and the Pinkerton detective whom she thinks is an outlaw.

New to Harlequin Historicals but certainly not to romance, Virginia Nielsen has written a moving story about a privateer and the Creole woman who rescues him in *To Love a Pirate.*

Knight's Lady, Suzanne Barclay's new book, features another of the irresistible Sommerville brothers. Introduced in *Knight Dreams* (HH #141), Gareth is the eldest sibling and heir to a fortune, yet the granddaughter of a lowly goldsmith holds the key to his heart.

Look for all four titles at your favorite bookstore.

Sincerely,

Tracy Farrell
Senior Editor

Books by Suzanne Barclay

Harlequin Historicals

Knight Dreams # 141
Knight's Lady # 162

SUZANNE BARCLAY

has been an avid reader since she was very young. Her mother claims Suzanne could read and recite " 'Twas the Night Before Christmas'' on her first birthday! Not surprisingly, history was her favorite subject in school and historical novels are her number-one reading choice. The house she shares with her husband and their two dogs is set amid fifty-five acres of New York State's wine-growing region. When she's not writing, the author makes fine furniture and carpets in miniature.

To Mom and Dad,
for making sure I learned to be a lady—
despite my protests

Prologue

East Anglia Coast, Britain
May, 1358

'Twas just past midnight, with a line of leaden storm clouds crowding the night sky, when Hugh Harcourt and his two cohorts slunk across the wet crescent of sand left by the retreating tide and slipped into the gaping black maw carved into the sheer stone face of Tyneham Cliff.

Hugh glanced back at the lights of his cousin's ship bobbing at anchor in the choppy cove. "There's bad weather brewing, so we'll make this quick." He strode arrogantly ahead of them through the maze of tunnels to a cave set high in the cliffs.

As he stepped through the entrance, the light of his torch caught on the piles of golden coins littering the scarred worktable. They winked at him, their lure more seductive by far than the promise in a harlot's hot stare.

"Ah!" Hugh crossed the room in two strides, his hand trembling as he picked up a coin. Though he knew the pieces had been wrought from baser metals, and merely covered with a thin coat of gold, the overall effect was remarkable. "It even feels real," he whispered.

"I told you I was good." Charles Beck smiled smugly.

"The last ye made were too bright," Walter Beck grumbled. Pushing his bulk past Hugh's slight frame, he snatched up a coin and turned it in the light. "Better," he told his half brother.

"Better?" Charles screeched, abandoning the cultured air he'd put on since being apprenticed to the goldsmith, William Marsden. "Why—why this coin is good enough to fool my master!"

"Everyone knows old Marsden's goin' blind," Walter sneered. "Besides, yer other coins caught Richard de Clerc's eye."

"And instead of stealing them back from him, you had to close his eyes permanently, didn't you?" Charles demanded hotly.

"Aye, I did, lest he run to the king and bring a charge o' counterfeitin' down on *our* heads instead o' Marsden's."

"'Twas not my coins that roused de Clerc's suspicions about you. It was your scheme to set yourself up as Sir Neil Westover's steward." Charles's eyes narrowed. "I told you the Sommervilles were Westover's overlord and he'd be bound to recall 'twas you Lord Ruarke had turned out of your position at Wilton Castle. Everyone knows of it. 'Tis why you can't get another post, and we're both livin' off the little I make."

Hugh smiled as Charles's gibe struck Walter dumb. Physically Walter reminded Hugh of his father, though Lord Edmund Harcourt was far smoother, far more clever than Walter. It pleased Hugh to hear Charles attack Walter because Hugh dared not speak up to his father. Not until he, Hugh, had gotten the one prize that had obsessed and escaped the old man for years—the Sommervilles' title. Aye, he'd show his father he was cunning and resourceful enough to succeed where Edmund had not.

"Bring up that business wi' the Sommervilles again, and I'll blacken both yer eyes," Walter growled, fists clenched.

"You started it," Charles whined. "And if my eyes swell up, I won't be able to see to make the rest of the coins."

"An excellent point," Hugh smoothly interjected. "How long will it take you to finish?" he asked to divert them.

Eyeing his brother, Charles shrugged. "A week or so."

Walter lowered his fists, his wet lips split by a wolfish grin. "One week and I get me money."

"And I get Arianna de Clerc for my wife." Charles added.

"Things won't happen as quickly as that," Hugh warned. "'Twill take time for our merchant friends in Tyneham to get the coins into the hands of the townspeople. What good is it to accuse the Sommervilles and Marsden of counterfeiting if the coins aren't in circulation?"

"But Sir Neil plans to marry Arianna next week," Charles cried. "I'll not have that old man beddin' my Arianna first," he added fiercely. "You'll have to speed things up."

"Aye, me creditors are breathin' down me neck. I need the gold now," Walter pointed out, fixing Hugh with a hard look.

Hugh suppressed a shiver. He wasn't afraid of Walter, exactly, but his sire's efforts to *toughen him up* had instilled in him a great respect for beefy fists. "Have patience," he cajoled. "After the coins have been passed out, I'll bring the matter to King Edward's notice. His majesty will send someone to investigate the matter. The trail will clearly lead back to Marsden and the Sommervilles. They will be accused of treason and hanged, of course, but it'll take a few weeks for all to happen as I've planned."

"But Arianna'll be married by then! It isn't fair," Charles grumbled. "I've run all the risks. I stole the metals from Marsden. I spent my nights in this bloody cave making the coins." His lower lip stuck out. "I don't care about ruining the Sommervilles. I only agreed to this scheme because you said Arianna would be mine after the king hanged her grandsire."

"So she will be." Hugh slipped on the oily smile that was all he had from his sire, except mayhap his cleverness; but Edmund saw nothing but Hugh's small size. "Charles, you'll have years to enjoy your little wife. And Walter," he added, turning to the big man, "I'll loan you a small sum to tide you over."

"Done," Walter said at once.

"'Tis all your fault, Walter," Charles groused. "If you hadn't killed Arianna's father, Sir Neil wouldn't have claimed he'd promised Sir Richard he'd wed her."

"I'm tired o' things always bein' my fault," Walter snarled. "If it'll shut ye up, I'll kill Westover fer ye."

Charles's eyes bugged out. "Nay, Walter. S-Sir Neil's never done aught to me," he sputtered.

"He's marryin' yer woman. 'Tis reason enough." Walter smiled slowly. "Besides, I fancy creepin' inta the keep and slitting the throat o' the man who said he'd no ha' me as his steward."

Chapter One

"Ransford Castle looks as dark and forbidding as usual," remarked Gabrielle Sommerville, shifting in her saddle as they waited for the wooden bridge to be lowered over the moat.

Drawing rein beside his sister-by-marriage, Gareth Sommerville pulled off his helm and shook the sweaty, sun-streaked hair from his tanned forehead. As he lifted his head, the last rays of afternoon sun fell across his face, softening the harsh planes of his high cheekbones, aquiline nose and firm jaw. Under slashing brown brows his midnight eyes skimmed the thick stone walls looming ahead of them with a loving gaze. "I think you had to be born here to appreciate it," he murmured.

Four round towers, each over a hundred feet tall, anchored the corners of the castle's outer defenses, encircling approximately two acres of land and buildings. Pride and a fierce feeling of belonging surged through him as he thought of the vast estate it commanded and the people it supported. His lands. His people. For when Lord Geoffrey, his father, died, 'twould all be Gareth's, along with the earldom of Winchester.

"To me, Ransford is home," Gareth said softly. "The only one I shall ever want. What say you, Ruarke?"

His younger brother squinted against the late-afternoon sun. "'Tis a strong fortress. Just what the Sommervilles have needed to keep those greedy Harcourt bastards from swarming over them," he said, seeing the castle through a warrior's eyes.

Though he was more farmer than fighter, Gareth nodded readily. The two families had feuded for three centuries. In all that time, Ransford had kept the Sommervilles safe. Nay, the castle wasn't pretty, but it felt good to be home. He frowned, thinking of the pain and disillusionment that had driven him away from Ransford three months ago when his wife had died.

"Does it hurt you still to think of Emilie?" Gaby asked.

"Nay," Gareth said grimly. It was anger he felt when he thought of his wife. Anger at his own stupidity in marrying her. He should have guessed a woman as beautiful as Emilie had had an ulterior motive in choosing him. "I thank you and Ruarke for proposing I come to Wilton with you after her funeral."

"'Twas selfishness on my part," Ruarke said. "I needed your help with my destriers. How did Apollo behave on the ride?"

Smiling faintly, Gareth leaned forward and patted the young stallion's thick neck. His dark gray coat shone with sweat, yet he held his head high, eager to move should Gareth give the signal. "He'll do well in battle, I think, for he heeded well my commands and tired not at all despite the weight of my armor."

"I knew he'd be strong enough for a war-horse, but the grays have a streak of wildness, too, and I'd not the patience to temper it." Lifting his visor, Ruarke grinned at his brother. They were similar in build if not in temperament, both big men with wide shoulders and muscular limbs. Their thick hair was streaked with blond, their faces bronzed from long days in the sun. "Gaby was right in saying you were the man to train him and Gladiator's other get."

"Gaby was right about a lot of things," Gareth muttered.

"If only I had expressed my reservation about Emilie *before* you wed her," Gaby said, forehead furrowing beneath her sleek black hair.

Tight-lipped, Gareth raked a hand through his dark blond hair and stared at Ransford's walls. "I'd not speak of her."

Ruarke exchanged troubled glances with his beautiful wife. Damn Emilie and her poisonous ways! Gareth had ever been the quieter of the three Sommerville brothers. "The Rock"

Alex had nicknamed their brother in their youth. Patient. Stolid. Stubborn. In the two years since wedding Emilie, Gareth had grown steadily more withdrawn, stern and dispassionate. Except when he worked with the horses.

"You were lucky to have found Gaby," Gareth said suddenly and with deep appreciation.

"She's a tyrant," Ruarke replied fondly, winking at her.

"Careful, my lord," Gaby warned, her violet eyes dancing. "You are speaking of the mother of your daughters *and* the woman who prepares your food."

"Then I must be certain to make amends to her—later." The spurt of laughter and the hot look Gaby shot her husband as the party clattered over the drawbridge made Gareth burn with envy. Even when Gareth and Emilie were first married and she was pretending she loved him, his wife had never looked at him as if she couldn't wait to get him alone and out of his clothes.

Don't yearn for what you can never have, Gareth warned himself. He urged Apollo ahead with the pressure of his thighs, his thoughts diverted by the quickness of the young horse's response. While at Wilton, he'd discovered he had a knack for training the great war-horses bred from Ruarke's stallion. Their matchless size and endurance made the grays valuable to a knight in battle, but without the discipline Gareth had taught him, Apollo would lash out at anything that came within his range.

"Good, Papa has arrived," Ruarke called back, pointing to the earl's pennant flying from the top of the castle tower.

An icy wave of something very like fear rolled through Gareth. *What if his father refused his request?* Feeling his master tense, Apollo sidestepped. In the time it took him to bring the horse back in line Gareth composed himself. He had always done his duty by his family, asking little for himself. His father had to approve his plan.

As they entered the inner bailey, they became aware of increased activity and the unfamiliar livery worn by some of the scurrying servants. "Ransford has guests," Ruarke grumbled.

"Papa will take time to listen to my proposal if I have to barricade us inside his damned library," Gareth said grimly.

"Gently," Gaby admonished. "Your father is more likely to listen to reason than threats. Ruarke, do wake Cat so she has a moment to sweeten up before your family descends on us."

Gareth's harsh expression softened as he watched his brother murmur to the bundle of blankets held in his arms.

A plume of fair hair shot out of the rumpled wool, followed closely by a cross red face. The pretty two-year old had inherited her mother's violet eyes, but at the moment they were stormy.

"See, here are your Grannie and Grandpapa," Gaby cozened as a herd of silk-clad people thundered down the stone steps from the castle and swarmed across the courtyard to meet them.

Cat frowned for a minute, cranky from being awakened, then spotting the earl, squealed with delight. Holding her arms wide, she cried, "Gran'papa! Play horsey!" The noble advisor to King Edward promptly set her up on his wide shoulders and began galloping back toward the castle, neighing loudly.

"It's a good thing they can't see him at court," Ruarke said, laughing.

Averting his gaze, Gareth dismounted stiffly, trying not to think about the babe that had died with Emilie.

"'Tis good to see you, my son." Catherine gave Gareth a hard hug. She stepped back, probing the midnight eyes he'd inherited from Geoffrey. What she saw dimmed her welcoming smile. How sad and grim he still looked. "Gareth, if only I could—"

Apollo screamed in protest at the confusion, and Gareth turned away, grateful for the need to ease the horse into his new setting. By the time he'd finished, the family had gone within. They were in the Great Hall, a passing servant told him.

Which meant there were guests, Gareth thought darkly; otherwise the family would have gathered in the privacy of his mother's solar on the third floor. At the door he hesitated, recognizing two of the men conversing with Ruarke and the earl.

'The short fat one was Lord Peverell, the fox-faced one was Lord Craven. Both were puffed-up fools. He didn't know the others, but likely they were men his father knew from Edward's court. It was unusual for his father to invite such men here, because he enjoyed an occasional respite from their intrigue.

"Come," Geoffrey called, motioning for him to join them. "We are discussing those gray destriers of Ruarke's.

"And mine," Gareth declared. Taking the ale a servant had poured for him, Gareth began to outline his plans to breed warhorses at Ransford. His father's smile became a scowl after a few minutes, but Ruarke silently urged Gareth on.

"What do you think?" Gareth asked his father when he had finally run out of points to make.

"It seems you've already decided to do this," he grumbled.

"I've thought it over carefully. It's something I want," Gareth added firmly. He wanted it more than a man like him could put into words. Working with Apollo had given him a new purpose in life at a time when he badly needed it to stay sane.

From the time he had taken his first steps, Gareth had been raised to assume his father's place. Geoffrey being a man of diplomacy, Gareth had learned to ride and fight from Ransford's master-at-arms. From his mother he had learned to care for their lands and dispense justice to their people. Less eagerly he had added the rudiments of reading and writing the Norman French of the court to the English he used daily with his vassals.

Gareth had been content with his life, performing his task out of love and a deep sense of duty. Yet as he grew older, he longed for someone to love, someone to share his place at Ransford. Ruarke had Wilton, a loving wife and two children. Alex, the middle brother, captained a fleet of ships and had a score of women chasing after him.

For a time, Emilie had seemed the answer to Gareth's yearnings, but that dream had swiftly become a nightmare from which he had yet to recover. Inside he felt bruised, torn. Working with the horses salved the deep wounds Emilie had inflicted. He'd not give them up. "I would raise the grays here," he repeated, his low baritone uncharacteristically hard.

"Above all, I want your happiness," Geoffrey said slowly. "But how would it look for me to espouse peace, while my son breeds instruments of war?"

"I will do this," Gareth repeated flatly.

Geoffrey hesitated, uncertain how to deal with this cold-eyed stranger who had replaced his warm, loving son. Silently he damned the witch of a woman who had wounded Gareth so.

"Speaking of breeding," Lord Robert Peverell put in. "'Tis time Gareth gave thought to producing an heir. Your family once had an impressive record in that regard. But recently..."

Ruarke's low growl caused his lordship to fall silent, yet his point was well made. For centuries, the Sommervilles had bred only sons, so there was never any shortage of males to carry on the title. But in two years of marriage, Ruarke and Gaby had produced the unheard-of—two daughters. Cat, and Philippa, barely a year old. Though the whole family loved them dearly, the Sommervilles needed an heir.

It was Gareth's duty to provide one.

Which meant taking another wife. Gareth shuddered.

"My Margory would make a good wife and future countess," Lord Robert said. Turning, he bellowed, "Margory! Come here."

There was a stir on the stairs leading to the upper floors, and a young girl materialized. Lifting the skirts of her blue silk gown, she hurried across the rush-strewn floor. One look at her hair, blond like Emilie's, and Gareth's blood ran cold. But he saw as she curtsied to him that her eyes were brown, not blue, and she had inherited her sire's homely round face.

"This is unfair," exclaimed Lord Craven. "We agreed to wait until after dinner and introduce the girls all at once. Alice! Come here to me," he roared.

"Edith!" screamed a second man. And, "Mary!" still another. The names came so close together Gareth couldn't keep track. Young females of all descriptions squirted out of the stairwell and into the hall. Fat, thin, short, tall, fair, dark, pretty, plain, they rushed him like hounds after a fox. Behind them came their mothers, shouting, "Lord Gareth, look at my daughter."

Ruarke moved in front of Gareth. "Stop!" he bellowed in the voice he used to control his men in battle.

As the word rang off the high rafters, the girls and their mothers skidded to a halt, trembling like frightened rabbits.

"Since when am I not man enough to protect myself from a few maids?" Gareth snapped, stepping around Ruarke, who shrugged. Yet they both knew Ruarke thought his older brother inept as a soldier. The reminder didn't improve Gareth's temper, already frayed by thoughts of taking another wife. "What is going on?"

His mother hurried over, her hands fluttering. "This was not supposed to happen. It was meant to be orderly."

"What was? What is going on?" Gareth demanded again.

"Good, here you are," chirped Gaby, emerging from the buttery. "I was about to have the horn sounded for dinner, but you've saved me the trouble." She winked at Gareth and herded the guests to the tables. There was grumbling, and a backward glance or two, but not even Lord Robert dared cross Gaby.

Catherine sighed. "Thank heavens for Gaby. We'll talk later, Gareth," she said, moving toward the high table.

His father tried to escape with her, but Gareth took his arm and turned him aside. "What the hell was that all about?"

"It was a…a misunderstanding," Geoffrey said slowly. "I was at court when your message reached me, and I mentioned to Craven and Peverell that you were coming home to discuss some sort of breeding program. They assumed I meant . . ."

"You!" Ruarke slapped Gareth on the back. "This is rich. Here you come proposing to breed horses, and find yourself with a stable full of mares to choose from." Laughing harder, Ruarke announced that the long ride and the entertainment had given him a monstrous appetite and headed for the table.

Geoffrey hesitated, half expecting Gareth to smile at the jest, as he would have of old, but his son's expression only grew more grim. "I'm sorry, Gareth. After Robert introduced me to his Margory, who is a quiet, shy girl, I saw no harm in your meeting her. I had no idea so many others would come. The last thing your mother and I want is to hurt you further."

"I'm not hurt. I'm—indifferent." Aye, that was what he felt. Nothing.

"Are you saying you won't marry again?"

Gareth shook his head. "Nay. Lord Robert was right about our needing an heir. If aught should happen to me, neither Alex nor Ruarke is suited to manage Ransford." He took a deep breath to ease the tightness in his chest. "It is just that I had not thought about a wife since Emilie's..." *Death? Betrayal?*

"And you need not do so until you are ready."

"I'll never be *ready* to wed again, but it must be done," Gareth said with a trace of bitterness. "Only this time I will chose a wife the same way I would chose a mare for Gladiator. By her bloodlines."

"Nay, Gareth," his father exclaimed. "We Sommervilles have always married for love."

"I have no use for such foolishness," Gareth said tightly. "And to assure you I speak truly, I will wed a woman so homely I couldn't possibly be attracted to her."

"Homely? But, Gareth, how will you get a child on a woman you can not bear to look at?"

"In the dark and likely drunk," he said crudely. "The Sommervilles require an heir. Very well, I will marry and beget one, but I would do it in my own way."

Geoffrey swallowed, moved by his son's dedication to duty.

"And I would raise the gray destriers at Ransford. 'Tis not just a matter of wanting to," he added as his father made to object. "We need the monies the grays could bring in to supplement our rents and tallages."

Painfully true. The last outbreak of the plague had killed so many laborers that planting and harvesting were down, and with them, revenues. That the Sommervilles and their people had not suffered unduly was due to Gareth's efforts to find other sources of income. Geoffrey sighed. "Very well. After dinner, will you meet the maidens that you might choose one?"

A muscle in Gareth's cheek flexed as he clenched his teeth. "Nay. I couldn't bear to court another woman."

"Oh, Gareth." There were tears in Geoffrey's eyes as he hugged his son. The Sommervilles were an emotional family, but Gareth had always been more reserved, slower to anger than Ruarke, less inclined to roguery than Alex, yet quick enough to laugh. Since marrying Emilie, he'd stopped laughing.

Gareth longed to lay his head on his father's shoulder and weep, for all he was nine and twenty. But he kept a tight rein on his emotions as he'd learned to do these past two years.

"What do you want to do?" Geoffrey asked in a choked voice.

Raise my horses in peace. "Truth to tell, I'd have you pick a bride for me, preferably while I'm not here."

"That might be arranged," his father said thoughtfully.

Gaby rushed up, trailed by two servants bearing trays loaded with food. "You'll have more privacy if you sup in the library."

"What a wonderful idea," Geoffrey said at once, conscious of the anxious parents and daughters waiting to leap on them the moment they sat down at the high table. "'Twas a lucky day for this family when Ruarke married you, my dear." He lightly touched one of her neat black braids.

"And I am glad to be his wife—now." Pain flickered briefly in her eyes, reminding Gareth that Gaby's marriage to Ruarke had not always been as blissful as it now was. But their love for each other had seen them through. He hadn't been as fortunate. But then, Emilie hadn't really loved him.

Deep in thought, Gareth trailed after Gaby and his father. Much as he hated the idea of marrying again, Ransford needed an heir *and* a chatelaine. Emilie had enjoyed being the Lady of Ransford, but her preoccupation with her beauty and her clothes had left her little time for running the castle, and her petulance had made her a poor mistress.

He hadn't realized until now, seeing Ransford in contrast with the cleanliness and order Gaby insisted on at Wilton, how things here had deteriorated under Emilie's care—or lack of it. His next wife would have her work cut out for her. She must be as efficient and capable as Gaby, he thought as he watched his petite sister-by-marriage direct the servants to rebuild the fire and set out the food.

"Don't be pushed into a hasty marriage," Gaby whispered to Gareth. "Wait to find a woman you love and who loves you."

"Ransford and my horses are enough for me."

"Nay, they are not, and you know it." She frowned up at his stony expression then shook her head and left the room.

"That is the kind of wife you should have," the earl said.

"Aye, but I fear Ruarke wouldn't give her up without a fight, and we both know I am no match for him in arms."

"There are more important things than swordplay."

"But fighting is the measure of a man," Gareth said softly. How did others measure him? he wondered. Did they see, as did he of late, a man overshadowed by his father and brothers?

"Let us eat, my son, then I have a task I would set you to."

When they had taken the edge off their appetites, the earl fetched a parchment from his desk and scanned it briefly. "Sir Neil of Tyneham Keep is getting married."

Gareth started. "Sir Neil? But he is older than . . ."

"Older than me?" Geoffrey raised a graying brow and smiled ruefully. "'Tis true. I will turn fifty this year, God willing. Neil is closer to sixty."

"You both seem younger," Gareth offered. He was fond of Sir Neil, who had been his father's vassal forever. Tyneham's villeins were among the most productive on the Sommerville estates, and since Gareth had been so busy improving the farms hardest hit by the plague, he had not visited Tyneham in years. It struck him then that Sir Neil was childless. "Sowing the last of his oats, and hoping for a crop at this late date, is he?"

"Nay. He'll father no children. He confided to me long ago that his seed was damaged in some childhood fever."

"The girl has a son from an earlier marriage, and Sir Neil will make it his heir?" Gareth asked. If Sir Neil died before the child matured, they'd need a strong warden to run the keep until the boy was old enough to rule himself.

Again Geoffrey shook his head. "Though she is eighteen and some years past marriageable age, she's not been wed. She is the orphan of Richard de Clerc, the captain of Tyneham's guard. Sir Neil had promised his knight he would care for the daughter if aught happened to him."

"Why not just dower her?"

"The girl lives with her grandsire and great-aunt and refuses to be parted from them. Sir Neil feared no man would want take all three for the dowry he could afford to offer."

"Sir Neil is certainly zealous in fulfilling his promises. Mayhap he lusts after her." Gareth paused, considering. "Nay, if she's so old and unwed, likely she's as ugly as a hedgehog. Mayhap I should consider wedding her myself."

"Gareth," his father warned, but seeing his son smile slightly for the first time in months, he relaxed. "The girl is beneath you, in any case. Sir Richard was but a landless knight and her mother the daughter of Tyneham's goldsmith. Her grandsire Marsden is an admirable man, according to Sir Neil, but in failing health."

Gareth lost interest and sat back in his chair. "So, you'd have me attend Sir Neil's wedding?"

"Aye, thus you can absent yourself from Ransford without causing offense, and I can be about selecting your bride. But there is another reason I'd send you to Tyneham. A month ago Sir Neil wrote to inform me Richard de Clerc had been slain—perhaps by wool smugglers rumored to be operating in the area."

"A month ago?" Gareth straightened. "Yet this is the first I've heard of it? If you thought me too frail to discharge my duty and go to Tyneham's aid, why did you not send for Ruarke?"

Geoffrey held up a placating hand. "The fault is mine. I've been so preoccupied arguing against these cursed labor statutes, that I fear Sir Neil's message went unopened, buried in a stack of correspondence I didn't read until my return to Ransford today. But I'd remedy that at once. Much as I dislike violence, I'd have you hunt down the wretches and punish them."

"That sounds like work for Ruarke," Gareth said tightly.

"Nay, 'twill require your patience and cleverness to flush out the guilty parties, not brute force."

"Arianna?" Dame Cicily called, pushing open the door to William Marsden's workroom. "Oh, there you are, child."

Arianna de Clerc started guiltily, her bedraggled blond braids flying as she turned from the silver reliquary she had been working on. "I'm sorry. I—"

"Forgot the time," her great-aunt finished for her. Despite her age, the woman crossed the room as swiftly as a galley running before the wind, her plump breasts thrust out, her white wimple fluttering behind. "Oh, you've burnt another hole in your second best gown. How could you? Today, of all days!"

Easily. Her normally merry blue eyes glum, Arianna sighed and looked down. "As usual, I paid no mind to my clothes." She ran her fingers lovingly over the smooth reliquary, reluctant to leave it. Even her indulgent aunt found it difficult to understand Ari's fascination with shaping inanimate lumps of brass and silver, the wonder she felt each time her creativity and dexterity merged to produce a thing of beauty. The process so absorbed her, it blocked out the rest of the world. "I'm sorry, Aunt Cici, I just—"

"Wanted to finish the reliquary so Master Hollton would have a place for that sliver of Saint Simon's shinbone he bought last month." Frowning, her aunt peered at the engraved piece. "Stupid man. I told him that merchant wasn't to be trusted. Why, he has sold so many pieces of Saint Simon over the years 'twould seem that poor saint must have been blessed with six legs!"

"Aunt Cici. You didn't say that."

"I did." Dame Cicily's faded blue eyes danced above her full, flushed cheeks. "Told Master Hollton it was probably from some poor ass no smarter than he is."

Arianna shook her head wisps of pale hair shimmering like a halo around her face. "Aunt Cici. He's—"

"A paying customer. But we'll have no need of his money once you're married to Sir Neil."

Just once I'd like to finish a sentence, Ari thought in exasperation, running a hand over her burning eyes. She'd gotten up very early to work on the intricate reliquary. Shaped to resemble a man's arm from the elbow to fingers, it had a bubble of polished rock crystal set in the forearm. Behind that window, encircled with fat, blue carbochons, the priest would set Master Hollton's saintly fragment. Another hour's work would . . .

"You do not have time to finish it now. We're due at Tyneham Keep in two hours, and you're not yet ready."

I'm as ready as I'll ever be, Ari thought unhappily.

"No use hiding your eyes," Dame Cicily admonished. "I know your heart is not in this, but it was your father's wish, and your grandfather and I would see you settled ere we die."

"Oh, Aunt Cici," Ari murmured.

"No tears, now. William and I have lived a full life."

Ari summoned a smile. "Aye, that you have." Her voice shook a bit at the thought of losing what remained of her family.

"Though it does prick William's pride that he can no longer provide for us."

Pride was only part of it, Ari knew. Bad enough her grandfather could no longer support them, but William Marsden's creeping blindness was gradually forcing him to give up the craft he loved almost more than life.

Ari knew exactly how he felt. Well almost. She had inherited his artist's eye, and her indulgent grandfather had taught her the goldsmith's trade, even though she was female. Decreased vision prevented William from creating the fine pieces that had once been his hallmark; her sex prohibited her from carrying on for him. Women couldn't belong to Tyneham's Goldsmith's Guild.

For the past few months, however, Ari had been adding the finishing touches on her grandsire's pieces. 'Twas not strictly ethical, but her work was as delicate as her grandfather's, and they were desperate. There were commissions like Master Hollton's to complete, and they badly needed the money.

The reliquary would be the last piece they'd do, her grandfather had sworn. He felt guilty enough completing his orders in such a way; he'd not undertake any new work under false pretenses.

"If only Charles didn't have a year yet to serve on his apprenticeship," Ari murmured.

Her aunt snorted. "People hereabouts wouldn't pay much for his things, I fear. Why, his work isn't nearly as fine as yours and likely never will be. Thank God for Sir Neil's offer. We might well starve if we had to live on what little I make from the herbs, lotions and such I sell in my shop."

"Aye." Ari sighed heavily.

"Is it Sir Neil's age that makes you reluctant, child?"

"Nay." Ari glanced around. She supposed there was little to recommend the cramped room. The benches were scarred and scorched beneath neat rows of tools; the sharp smells of sulphur and hot metal hung in the air. To her, it was the best place on earth. "I'd rather live here always with you and Grandfather."

"So you've said since you passed your twelfth year and we first talked of marriage." Dame Cicily tisked softly. "'Tis an unrealistic wish. Women grow up, wed and go to live with their husbands. You should be glad Tyneham Keep is scarce a mile away and Sir Neil in his kindness has promised you can come each day to visit."

"I know, and I am grateful to him." Ari managed a smile.

Her aunt saw through it. "You are afraid of something."

"I have no skill as a chatelaine, nor do I wish to learn the duties," Ari said, her jaw set.

"'Tis my fault for not insisting you were trained in the domestic skills," Dame Cicily muttered. The whole family had spoiled Ari shamelessly after her mother's death.

The Black Plague had taken Alys Marsden de Clerc, and would have killed Ari, too, if not for her great-aunt's skill as a healer. Reeling from the loss of his wife, Sir Richard had prayed at his small daughter's bedside until she was out of danger. When Ari finally recovered, there was nothing her bereaved family could deny her, including an upbringing different from that of any girl in town.

"Sir Neil's household seems to run quite smoothly without a chatelaine," Ari ventured, eyeing her aunt hopefully.

"Bah, his steward is so old he creaks. When Jamie finally dies, you'll have to take over."

"Sir Neil says he is a simple man, with modest wants."

"Who is willing to cosset you by letting you ease into your new responsibilities. Truly, he is heaven-sent."

Best of all, Ari mused, Sir Neil had no family living. Ari's own father's cruel, aristocratic family had ruined the marriage between her father and mother. Ari had no wish to see history repeat itself. Aye, a kinless man suited her.

Conscious of her aunt's concern for her happiness, Ari said, "Truly Sir Neil is a good man. How many others would take in a mute maidservant and a crippled stable boy?"

"Aye, 'tis something else to be grateful for. Neither Grizel nor Sim would find work with another family in Tyneham did Sir Neil refuse them a place at Tyneham Keep."

"Sir Neil and I will get along very well." Once she got past the wedding night, that is. Ari could imagine herself living at Tyneham keep as his wife. In the daydreams she had woven while her hands were busy polishing the reliquary, she saw herself talking with him much as she did with her grandfather, taking meals with him, walking in the gardens. But mating with him . . . Arianna trembled.

"Come along, dear. No dreary thoughts about married life."

"Aunt Cici! Please stop poking about in my mind."

The old woman blinked, a hurt expression creeping into her eyes. "I can not help sensing things. You know that, dear."

Ari sighed, cursing her hasty tongue, but before she could apologize, the door opened and Charles entered. His usually thin mouth became even more pinched when he spied her. "I thought you'd be getting ready for your *splendid wedding*."

"And so she should be," Dame Cicily said briskly. "Charles, do clean up here. We will leave for the keep in two hours." With that, she whisked Ari out of the workroom and upstairs.

"What do you suppose has gotten into Charles?" Ari asked as they entered her small bedchamber. "I'd thought him a friend, someone who shares my love of metalworking, but ever since I agreed to wed with Sir Neil, Charles has been acting strangely."

"Harrumph. That one has ideas above his station. Now we must see to your bath. Hurry and get undressed." Motioning Arianna into the tub of steaming water set before the fire, she reached for a chunk of the soothing chamomile-scented soap she made herself. When Ari had finished washing, Dame Cicily slathered her niece's face and hands with a slimy green substance.

"Ugh. It smells like . . . a bog."

"Nonsense, it's nice, clean moss mixed with the juice of a cucumber." She tsked as she massaged the mess into Ari's hands. "'Tis terrible what that metal does to your lovely skin. But I'll have it soft and smooth for Sir Neil in no time."

The remark made Arianna sit up straighter in the tub, sending rivulets of water over the side.

"What is it, dear?"

"I had forgotten about—that."

"'That'? Which 'that' do you mean? Oh . . ." Dame Cicily's face flushed red, and it wasn't from the steam.

Ari cocked her head. Aunt Cici had been like a mother to her since her own had died when she was seven. She had never seen the older woman at a loss for words. "Well?" she pressed.

"Well, what?" her great-aunt replied in a choked voice.

"Now is not the time to pretend you *cannot* read my mind," Ari teased. "What happens after the wedding ceremony?"

"There will be a fine banquet. Sir Neil asked me to choose all your favorite dishes, and—"

"I mean, after we are through eating?"

"Er, there will be a bedding ceremony, I suppose," Dame Cicily said, washing the moss mixture from Arianna's fingers with rapt concentration. "The women and I will take you up to Sir Neil's chamber and remove your gown. The men will bring Sir Neil up, minus his clothes."

"Really?" Ari giggled, trying to imagine him without his tunic and the long gown covering him from neck to spindly shins.

"You need not be frightened. 'Tis just so everyone can see that you are unblemished. So he can not repudiate you in the morning for some imperfection. Not that you have any...so you need not worry."

"I'm not worried." *Exactly*. Ari trailed her hand through the cooling water. "Though that part does sound..."

"Humiliating?"

Ari grinned. "Cold." Then her smile faded. "It's the part that comes next that I can not quite imagine. Grizel believes it will hurt me, but since Sir Neil is old, he will not likely be too vigorous..."

"Oh, I will box that silly maid's ears for frightening you so with her nonsense."

Sighing, Ari stepped from the tub and dried herself on a linen towel. "What am *I* supposed to do?"

"Sir Neil will tell you what you must know." Dame Cicily's eyes darted about as she sought some avenue of escape.

"But, what exactly happens?"

"I have never been wed, so I could not help you," her aunt said lamely. "But Sir Neil would not cause you any hurt."

Ari tried to find comfort in that as she pulled on the gown her aunt had stitched for her. From Grizel's description, the marriage act sounded vile and disgusting anyway. Not at all the sort of thing kindly, formal old Sir Neil would do.

Instead, she began to worry about the changes marrying even so minor a knight would likely make in her life. There were the meals, for instance. Sir Neil might not understand when she became immersed in a project and simply did not appear at the table, as her aunt and grandfather did. And what if his steward did die and she was expected to run the keep?

Oh, Papa, I miss you. Tears stung the back of Ari's lids, but she ruthlessly blinked them away.

"'Tis all right to cry for him, dearling," Dame Cicily said gently, greatly worried because Ari had not shed a tear for her father, though she'd loved him deeply.

Ari shook her head, "He'd not want me to cry. Remember how he called me his Sunshine? 'Always smiling, always laughing,' he'd say," Ari added, her throat full, her chest aching with suppressed tears. She dared not let even one fall. Once started, she feared she'd never stop. Nay, her mother had cried her life away; she'd not follow that same wretched, senseless path.

Yet, it seemed impossible that her father was gone. That he would never again stride into the room and sweep her into his arms. That he would never again call her his Sunshine.

Dragging in a shallow, ragged breath, Ari swallowed the lump in her throat. "I'd not have Sir Neil see a red-eyed bride and think I regretted the marriage."

Dame Cicily's concern mounted as she watched Ari conquer her grief. Eventually the tears would come, a lifetime of them, for Ari had not cried since her mother had died. Mayhap today was not the day for tears. She summoned a ghost of a smile and sought a happier subject. "Your bridal clothes fit well."

The surcoat was of blue silk with a pattern of flowers and trailing leaves sewn in gold thread at the neck and hem. A false sleeve fell from her shoulder to the floor, revealing the fitted white tunic she wore underneath.

"Grandfather wouldn't recognize me in such finery."

Indeed, it was hard to see the ofttimes bedraggled sprite beneath this sleekly brushed and finely garbed young woman. "You look beautiful, my dear. As bright and shining as this fine May morn." Opening the door, Dame Cicily led Ari down the stairs.

The lump rose again in Ari's throat as she saw her grandsire waiting at the bottom of the stairs for them, a sad smile deepening the creases in his face. She knew he was thinking about her father—and her mother, too, his beloved daughter, Alys.

How old he looked, Ari thought, suppressing a shiver of fear for him. His long white hair brushed his shoulders, stooped from years of hunching over his work, and his eyes, once a clear, bright blue like her own, seemed cloudier than ever today. She smiled, trying to tell him without words that everything would be all right once she had married Sir Neil.

Chapter Two

Behind Gareth, a horse screamed. Whipping around, he was stunned to see an arrow protruding from its neck.

"Beware, ambush!" he cried as a horde of armed men leaped from the concealment of the rocks hugging the sides of the trail, war whoops pouring from their throats, the late-afternoon sun glinting off their upraised weapons.

Thirty of them, at least, to his twenty.

Gareth drew his sword and hauled in Apollo's reins. Shouting for his men to close ranks and protect each other's backs, he turned to face the enemy. The moves were as instinctive as Apollo's response to his nonverbal commands. Thanks to the training both he and the stallion had recently gotten from Ruarke, Gareth didn't feel completely useless.

The first blow struck Gareth's sword and reverberated up his right arm, nearly numbing it. "Damn," he gasped through clenched teeth. Though he practiced daily with a sword, it had been some time since he had actually fought in battle. Guided by reflexes alone, he parried the next thrust and slipped in under the man's guard. The wail of agony, the sickening crunch of steel cracking bone turned his stomach.

Dimly, he heard Apollo's nervous snort, felt the young destrier's muscles bunch between his thighs as the horse tried to sidestep the fallen man. He should have ridden another horse. Apollo was not yet ready for a trial such as this. Neither of them were, but it mattered little, Gareth thought as another enemy rode up to challenge him.

Curiously, he was not afraid. Hell, he was too busy trying to stay alive. Fury at himself for falling into this ambush fired his blood. Roaring the Sommerville battle cry, he cut and slashed his way through the attackers, his right hand welded to his sword grip, his left holding the shield close to his body.

Gareth lost count of the number of men he faced. Both arms ached with tension and strain. Sweat dripped from beneath his helm into his eyes, yet he dared not take time to wipe it away.

Beside him, a man screamed, and Gareth looked away from his current opponent long enough to see Enrich, the master-at-arms who had been his teacher, go down. With a bellow of fury, he disengaged and slashed out. His blade sank deep, slicing through the enemy's padded leather and into muscle, drawing a satisfactory cry of anguish. But before he could withdraw his sword, Gareth felt pain shoot through his right side.

Pulling back sharply, Gareth freed his blade and brought up his shield, which absorbed a vicious blow that might have severed his head. Even the blunted impact was strong enough to unsteady him; his shield drooped a fraction, and the sword's backswing caught him in the side of the head. Black dots danced before his eyes.

Gareth made a convulsive effort to stay in the saddle, but Apollo, terrified by the unfamiliar movement, chose that moment to rear. Unseated, Gareth reflexively kicked his feet free of the stirrups as he fell in order to stay clear of the horse.

He landed on his back, the initial shock jarring the breath from his body. Before he could do more than roll onto his stomach, a tremendous weight slammed down on him. As the rest of the air hissed from his lungs and darkness reached out to enfold him, he dimly realized a horse must have fallen on him. Apollo? Sorrow stabbed him. He had loved that horse. What a waste, his mind cried out, then all thought was swallowed up in a gray mist.

Gareth awoke to silence and the knowledge that he was alive. He smelled the dirt his face had been mashed into, felt the pain in his side and head. The screams of the dying, the grunts and shouts of those who had fought were gone. Was the battle over? Who had won? Shuddering with apprehension, he opened one eye.

The lower half of him still lay under poor Apollo. His right arm and sword were trapped, too. Without help, he'd not rise.

Gareth heard footsteps approaching and started to turn his head, but their words, spoken in coarse English, stopped him.

"Which one's Sommerville?" asked a gritty voice.

"Does it matter? They're all dead," grumbled a second. "Their armor and weapons were so plain I wouldn't ha' thought they were Sommervilles if not fer the banner they carried."

Gareth blessed the cautious nature that had prompted him to travel simply so as not to attract undue attention. He'd left his personal standard at Ransford and ordered his men to set aside their Sommerville colors. All, including himself, had worn ordinary chain mail beneath plain woolen surcoats.

"Have ye stripped them o' whot they did ha'?"

"Aye. And hidden the bodies in the brush as ye ordered. All but this one, 'cause we've got ta get that dead horse off him."

"Wait. I hear someone comin'. Leave him and get mounted."

No sooner had the men ridden off than Gareth heard the jingle of harness and the creak of wagon wheels approaching. Cautiously lifting his head, Gareth saw it held two old people, a man and a woman. Normally he'd have called out for help, but vulnerable as he was, they could finish him off and take his possessions. The profits from selling even Gareth's plainest gear would be more than a villein earned in a lifetime.

"I told ye there was trouble ahead," moaned the woman. "But would ye listen? Nay, but ye had to go and capture that infernal wild beastie. Dinna stop, whoever killed this man may be back."

"I have to see if he's alive and in need of help," replied the old man.

Despite his fears, Gareth fought to remain limp as the man leaned down and felt along his neck for a pulse.

"He lives, Bertha, but he's trapped." The man hurried back to the wagon. "We must find a way to help him."

That was all Gareth needed to hear. Old as they were, the couple couldn't lift Apollo off him, but the promise of a coin should induce them to go to Tyneham and bring back Sir Neil. "Wait," he called in English, surprised at his weak voice. He moved his free hand, dislodging the shield with a clatter that had the old woman shrieking loudly enough to raise all who had died here this day. Would that such a thing were possible.

Farmer Owen turned out to be a very resourceful man. He unhitched his team and used them to drag the horse from Gareth's numb lower body. As Gareth half sat, drinking the water the old woman offered him, he saw a third horse tied to the back of the farmer's wagon.

It was nearly dark, yet the shape and size of the beast were hauntingly familiar. "A-Apollo?" Gareth croaked.

The horse nickered and swung his head in Gareth's direction, revealing a cloth tied over his eyes and another slung around his muzzle.

"Ah, he's yours. I knowed he were too good a piece o' horseflesh ta be just wanderin' on his own," said Owen.

"He must have run from the battle when I fell." Gareth pushed himself to his feet with a groan and stumbled over to Apollo. "He's a war-horse, trained to come only to me. How on earth did you manage to capture him?"

Owen cackled at Gareth's incredulous expression. "He were worn out when I came upon him and in no shape ta argue. I quick clapped a bag o' feed o'er his nose so he couldn't smell me."

"Don't fret yerself o'er it," his wife said. "Just lie yerself down in the wagon, here, and we'll take ye ta—"

"Tyneham Keep," Gareth interjected. "I must reach Tyneham Keep as soon as possible." His first thought when they'd been attacked had been to blame the treacherous Harcourts. 'Twas their style to creep about and strike from ambush instead of meeting a man in a fair fight. But a more likely possibility had occurred to Gareth while Owen was working to free him.

The smugglers. Somehow they'd learned Sir Neil had sent to his overlord for help, and they'd simply waited on the trail to kill the Sommerville who'd come to Tyneham's aid.

Gareth's eyes narrowed. Which could mean someone at Tyneham was in league with the smugglers. Sir Neil must be warned, and plans made to hunt down and punish the lot of them.

"'Tis a far piece ta Tyneham," Owen protested.

"And yer side's bleedin' again," added Bertha.

Used to being obeyed without question, Gareth brushed aside their objections, but the old couple stood firm on his riding in the wagon.

A grueling hour later, the wagon rolled over the wooden drawbridge and jolted to a halt in the courtyard of Tyneham Keep. Groaning and holding his right arm close against the makeshift bandage wrapped round his throbbing side, Gareth crawled from the back of the wagon.

The courtyard was awash with light from dozens of smoking torches and filled with laughing people dressed up in silks and velvets. It was such a far cry from the death and violence of the past few hours that Gareth blinked in dazed astonishment.

"I've a wounded man here in need of aid," Owen told the nearest woman. She looked at Gareth, gasped and fled.

Startled from his stupor, Gareth yelled, "Fetch Sir Neil to me at once." He shouted his demand twice before a big, surly-faced soldier stomped over.

"See, here, what's this?"

"Who are you?" Gareth demanded. "What is your rank?"

"Farley, captain o' the guard, and responsible for Tyneham Keep's defense since Sir Richard's death. And you?" His gaze raked Gareth's mud-caked face and bloody, ripped clothes.

Unused to censure of any kind, Gareth ignored the question and glared at the cup of ale the man held. "I doubt Sir Neil has given you permission to drink on duty, Farley."

"I doubt he cares, since this is his weddin' day," Farley growled, shoving his face into Gareth's. "An' believe me, the fact that my lord invited all comers ta sup wi' him this day is all that's keepin' me from throwin' ye out o' Tyneham on yer ear. So mind that an' keep yer smart mouth closed."

Gareth blinked and looked around him. Sunk deep in the pain and the guilt of having survived while his men had perished, he had forgotten Sir Neil's wedding. "I must speak with Sir Neil."

"Yeah?" Farley rocked back on his heels, his scowl deepening. "Who the hell are ye ta be givin' orders, anyway?"

Gareth Sommerville, Winchester's heir, he nearly shouted at the lout of a captain, but a thin thread of common sense yet remained in his battered brain. If there was a spy at Tyneham, he had best discuss his business with Sir Neil in private.

"Who the hell are you?" Farley demanded again. The guests had moved away, replaced by a group of hard-faced soldiers who crowded close, ready to beat this troublesome stranger black-and-blue and throw him into Tyneham's moat with the garbage.

Ah, damn. Gareth dug deep into himself for some of that cleverness his father had credited him with, looking for a ruse that would bring him to Sir Neil with the minimum of fuss and damage. "I'm the knight come to take Sir Richard's place."

Farley straightened, and the men around him exchanged startled glances. "Are ye, now?"

"Aye. I'm Sir Gar..." At the last second, some deep-seated instinct prompted him to lie, and he went with it. "Garvey."

"Ye look a bit the worse fer wear, Sir Garvey."

"'Tis nothing to how I feel," Gareth growled, the whole of what had happened sweeping over him in a wave of dizziness. Clenching his teeth against it, he added, "I was attacked on the road, and nearly killed. Now, if you will take me to Sir Neil."

"Could have been those bloody smugglers. Did you get a look at any of them?" Farley demanded, while around them men gasped and whispered nervously among themselves.

Gareth weighed the reactions of Farley and the soldiers as best he could under the circumstances. Woolen masks had hidden the faces of his attackers, but the voices of the two men were burned into his brain. So far, he'd not heard them here. These men seemed genuinely surprised by his arrival and his account of the attack, yet they were strangers all. Not one did he recognize from his visits years ago.

Farley moved up in Gareth's estimation when he turned aside and instructed one of the soldiers to see the drawbridge was raised and the guard on the walls doubled. "Do ye be quiet about it," he added. "No sense alarming Sir Neil's guests if it was naught but a few raggedy thieves."

Gareth stiffened, insulted at the implication that he and his men had been beaten by a few "raggedy thieves." But then, Farley thought he'd been alone. And the captain's concern with not spreading panic among the guests was valid. "Still, I'd present myself to Sir Neil," Gareth said firmly.

"It's near time for the beddin' ceremony. Ye best come wi' me and ha' yer wounds tended to."

"Now," Gareth said, low and tight. If he delayed, Sir Neil's ear would be lost to him for the rest of the night, and maybe part of tomorrow morn, as well, depending on the elderly knight's eagerness for his young bride.

Sir Neil's bedchamber was a reflection of the man himself, Arianna thought as Aunt Cici and the other women led her inside. Spare and spartan. Far larger than her room at home, but with none of the comforts showered on her by her doting relatives. She had grown so used to that room she scarcely even noticed the rich velvet hangings that kept the drafts from her bed, or the tapestries that lent warmth and color to the walls, or the thick carpets underfoot.

Here, there were none of those luxuries, just a bed, a pair of chairs at the hearth, and three trunks piled between the two narrow, shuttered windows. Arianna recognized them as the ones she had brought with her and felt a small spurt of normalcy. Tomorrow she would unpack the things her aunt and Grizel had made for her. Then this place would seem more like home.

"Drat the maids," her aunt snapped. "I asked them to get out your chair cushions and put your hangings on the bed instead of those. Likely the lazy wenches are off eating and drinking. Tomorrow, you'll have to take them in hand."

As if she'd know how, Ari thought dismally. She glanced at the bed just long enough to see that the heavy green hangings had been pulled shut, effectively sealing off the interior of the bed. Soon she would be shut up in there with Sir Neil. Apprehension sent a shudder through her.

"We've not time to change the hangings now," Dame Cicily said to the two women who had started toward it. "The men will be here shortly with Sir Neil."

Ari shivered again, and her aunt herded her toward the fire crackling in the hearth. Kneeling on the cold, bare stone, Ari extended her hands nearer the fire flames. Their heat did not penetrate to the cold center of her being, nor did it relax the knot in her stomach, but it gave her something to do while the women pulled off her veil and loosened her braids.

The pleasure she had taken in her fine gown and the deliciously prepared food, the unexpected delight she had found in chatting with Sir Neil had all evaporated the instant her aunt whispered that it was *time*.

Time! But she was not ready. Before the protest could pass her lips, the women had swept her from the room. Ari had felt as bereft of will and control as a . . . a leaf caught in the current.

"The ceremony was lovely," said Madame Drusie, Alderman Peter Arley's wife. She was a bit younger than the other women, which was to say she was elderly, not ancient.

As Ari prodded her dazed brain for an appropriate reply, Madame Eadda, the shoemaker's plump wife, launched into a complete recital of every dish that had been served.

Ari sighed in relief. It had been a chore to converse with the strangers she'd met at the wedding feast, but she could relax among these women she'd known all her life. Relax? Nay, in a few moments Sir Neil would come and the dreadful bedding would take place. If that was not enough preying on her mind, she had the worry over Sir Neil's offer to take her to London.

"I have not been to court in years, but I will take gladly take you should you wish it," Sir Neil had said when she'd exclaimed over his description of the fine pens, the colored inks and drawing materials to be had at the London market.

"Nay," Arianna had gasped, thinking of all those nobles looking down their long aristocratic noses at her. Remembering what had befallen her poor mother in London had made Ari's stomach cramp. "N-nay, I could not."

Sir Neil had frowned. "Your grandsire tells me you spend too much time cooped up in his workroom, when you should be occupied with the things young women enjoy."

"But I enjoy goldsmithing," Ari had blurted out, oblivious to any who might overhear her secret. "You'll let me continue?"

Sir Neil had patted her hand. "Of course, but think on what I have said about getting out more. There are many things in this world to see, if you will open your mind to them."

Ari had grudgingly agreed, but she had been grateful when Sir Neil was called from the table to take a message and could not press her further on the subject.

A draft of cold air across her skin as the last of her clothing was removed roused Arianna from her thoughts. Shivering, she reached for her bedrobe.

"Nay," Madame Drusie exclaimed, dragging Ari to her feet. "I hear the men on the stairs."

"Oh, the sheets have not been warmed," Dame Cicily cried.

Someone else made a ribald comment about the couple warming their own sheets, and another said it was too late, anyway.

Arianna was propelled to the foot of the bed, and her hair hastily draped forward over her shoulders, so it covered her, however thinly, from neck to hip. As the ladies stepped back, the door burst open, and the male guests streamed in. Their boisterous laughter pierced the last of Arianna's reverie. Instinctively flinging one arm across her breasts and the other hand over the juncture of her thighs, she eyed the men warily.

Red faced with drink, the town's leading merchants were in the front. Those who could not fit into the room crowded around the doorway. They stared at her as though they had not known her most of her life. All but Charles, whose expression was a strange mix of anger and possessiveness. He looked at her almost as though he, not Sir Neil, would be sharing her bed this night.

Ari shuddered, whether from the cold or fear of what was to come, she did not know.

"Where is Sir Neil?" William Marsden asked his sister, edging around the crowd.

"Why... is he not with you?"

"Nay. We waited for him at the foot of the stairs, but when he did not come, we assumed he had snuck up here early."

"Perhaps he has not finished dealing with the message that came for him during dinner," Madame Drusie suggested.

William shook his head. "We searched downstairs before coming up. He is not in his counting room, nor anywhere else."

"Who saw him last?" cried Peter Arley.

William's expression grew more concerned when it became obvious that no one had seen Sir Neil since he had left to speak with the mysterious messenger. Mysterious, because no one had seen him, either.

"A b-boy brought word S-Sir Neil had a v-visitor waiting for him," Ari said, her teeth chattering now, but she did not think to ask for her robe, did not realize she wrung her hands instead of hiding behind them. "H-he thought it might explain why the S-Sommervilles hadn't come to the w-wedding."

"Where is Sir Neil?" demanded a deep voice from the hallway.

All heads turned in Gareth's direction, and the crowd parted to let him through. As he passed among them, the people told him Sir Neil was missing.

"Who saw this note?" Gareth asked of Alderman Arley, whom he remembered having seen once before, but had not met.

"Arianna did."

Gareth turned to look where Arley pointed, and his next question died in his throat.

The vision standing at the foot of the draped bed looked— otherworldly. Like a fairy sprite, all white skin and spun-gold hair. Unreal. Yet he could see the rapid beat of her pulse at the base of her slender neck. And more...

Her high young breasts rose and fell with each breath she took, the rosy crests playing hide-and-seek among the silky strands of hair. He longed to push it aside, to see more fully the taut belly, narrow waist and gently flared hips he could only glimpse beneath the cascading golden mass. And her face...

Gareth had seen more beautiful women, but surely none more extraordinary. None with features as delicate, eyes as bright, or mouth as kissable as this one.

Who was she?

Who *was* he? Arianna thought, as she felt the impact of his hot dark eyes all the way to the soles of her feet. His gaze roved over her as palpably as a caress, chased the chill from her skin faster than if she'd been thrust into the fire. Her heart jumped, then beat so rapidly she thought it might burst from her chest. Indeed, who was he?

"Arianna...cover yourself, dear," intruded her aunt's voice.

Dear God! Here she stood, naked but for her hair, staring at this stranger and letting him do the same to her.

Ari whirled, parted the bed curtains and dived into the blessed darkness. Her face hot with shame, she crawled toward the head of the bed. "I can never face them again," she muttered, feeling her way along with her hands. Not her neighbors, not her family. Certainly not the bold-eyed stranger.

"It is all his fault," she seethed. "If he hadn't stared at me like . . ." She stopped as her hand touched something odd. A wrinkle in the blanket? Heart pounding, she reached out, touched it again. Nay. 'Twas a solid, bony thing, covered with velvet.

What on earth could Sir Neil be keeping in his bed? Cursing the lack of light, and the people whose presence in the room made opening the curtains impossible, Ari felt along the length of the bony thing. The velvet stopped abruptly, and she felt something cold and hairy. Something that felt like . . . a hand?

A hand!

Ari screamed and snatched open the bed curtains.

In the flood of light, she saw Sir Neil laid out beside her, his eyes closed. His throat gaped open like a second mouth, dripping dark, red blood onto the pristine white pillow beneath his head.

Chapter Three

Dead. Sir Neil was dead.

Gareth could scarcely believe it. Oblivious to the shrieks of the girl being led from the bed and the shocked murmurings of the other witnesses, he crossed the chamber on rubbery legs and sank down beside the bed.

One look told him it was true. Sir Neil was dead, his face whiter than the pillow, his lips pulled back in a grimace of fear. There was blood everywhere. Terrible... terrible that so gentle a man should meet so violent an end.

A strangled groan worked its way up from Gareth's throat. His eyes closed on a wave of dizziness so strong he swayed where he knelt.

"Did you know Sir Neil?" asked a hushed male voice.

Gareth looked up into the kindest blue eyes he had ever seen. "I..." Dazed, he struggled to recall the part he had set himself to play. "He was a friend of my father's." *True enough, as far as it went.*

"You came late for the wedding, then?" the man asked.

"Aye." Weakness washed over him again; he fought it.

The deep lines etched around the blue eyes tightened. "You look a little the worse for wear."

"He says he was set upon on the way here, Master Marsden." Farley's voice.

"These are evil times we live in," muttered Marsden. "Come away, lad. There's aught we can do for poor Sir Neil now, and your own hurts want tending."

"Have to find the ones who did this. Make them pay for their crime," Gareth rasped.

"Tomorrow. You've stretched yourself to the limits this day," Marsden argued, gently urging him to his feet.

Gareth wanted to disagree, but he knew the old man was right. His head rang with dizziness, and his limbs grew weaker by the minute. For the second time that long, terrible day, he knew the sharp ache for revenge and could not satisfy it. Tomorrow. Tomorrow he would set all to rights.

Pain lanced through Gareth's side as Farley eased him into one of the high-backed chairs set before the hearth.

"Cici, leave Arianna be a moment," Master Marsden said. "She is stunned, but will recover. While this young man..."

"Has taken a sword thrust to the side, and a blow to the head," observed a soft voice.

By the gods, how could she know that? Gareth's eyes flew to the other chair flanking the fireplace. A young woman sat in it. And not just any woman, but the golden-haired temptress he had seen when he first entered the room. Only now a dark robe covered her pale curves, and she stared into the fire, her delicate profile so still she might have been carved of marble.

Her hair was the only thing about her that showed a hint of life, tumbling over her slight shoulders and down her back like a flaxen river, shooting off golden sparks in the firelight.

He should know who she was and why she had been standing in Sir Neil's chamber clad only in that magnificent hair, but his mind couldn't quite grasp the reason.

"It is because you are tired," said that same melodious voice, and he realized with a start that it was an old woman who addressed him. "Things will look clearer in the morning, if you are not fevered." She advanced on him with a determined expression, faded blue eyes boring into his so keenly it seemed she must see clear to his soul.

Not a comfortable feeling. "Who are you?" he asked warily.

"Dame Cicily Marsden is my name. The rest of your questions will wait until you are better." Her hand was cool on his brow, her fingers gentle as they probed the lump on his head.

Gareth flinched, as much from suspicion as from pain.

"Easy," she murmured. Her tone reminded him of his own when he wanted to gentle a horse. Despite his natural reservations, Gareth felt the strangest urge to trust her.

"I can do little for him here without my chest of medicines," Dame Cicily announced.

"We best take him back to town with us, then," said Marsden.

Dame Cicily frowned, then glanced at the bed. "Of course, with Sir Neil gone, there is no place for us here."

Marsden grunted. "I am afraid you are right." With the marriage unconsummated, Ari had no claim on Sir Neil's property. Not that there was much left. In these lean times, the knight had shared what he had with others. "In any case . . ."

"The Earl of Winchester will name another castellan for Tyneham Keep," Dame Cicily concluded unhappily. They withdrew a few steps to confer with Farley.

At the mention of his father, Gareth's brain came halfway alert. The golden-haired girl, Ari-something, was Sir Neil's bride, and these two old people her relatives. Now he understood why she had been standing naked in the old knight's bedchamber.

No wonder Sir Neil had wanted to wed her, Gareth thought as he stole another glance at her, but this time her beauty repelled instead of fascinated. She was no better than Emilie, he thought, his jaw clenching. A whore of the worst sort. One who sells herself into marriage by convincing some poor man she loves him, while all the while she plots his downfall.

An icy finger swept down Ari's spine. Shivering, she glanced around and saw *he* watched her. He was larger than she had supposed, dwarfing the chair even though he slouched in it, but her other hasty impressions of him had been correct. Midnight eyes, tanned skin. Filthy. Mud caked, bloodied and hard eyed. Those eyes were fixed on her with disturbing intensity.

"Do not stare at me as though you are picturing me without my clothes," she said defensively.

"'Tis not difficult, since I have already seen you thus," Gareth snarled.

Ari matched his scowl, sitting straighter in her chair, welcoming the challenge glittering in his dark eyes as an antidote to the horror she had witnessed this night. "You are a lecher of the worst sort, slipping in uninvited to peek—"

"Peek? Nay, 'twas not necessary. You stood boldly before my gaze, not even bothering to cover yourself with your hands, but waving them around in the air so your hair took flight and bared your rosy breasts to tempt mine eyes."

Ari's cheeks went hot with shame and something else that made her nipples tighten at the implications hanging ripe in the very word. *Tempt*. "I-I know nothing of such things."

"Women are born knowing such things."

"Nay, they are not," Ari assured him quickly. "And I have had no time to learn domestic skills."

Gareth raised one brow. "Domestic skills ... is that what they call whoring in this part of the country?"

Whore! "How dare you speak thus to me!" Her thick lashes fluttered about her wide blue eyes like a pair of startled black moths.

Gareth rasped out a mirthless laugh. "Try your wiles on some other poor bastard. I am immune."

"Wiles?" Ari sputtered, her fingers clenching into tight fists. "If you weren't already mad, I'd take pleasure in knocking you senseless."

William Marsden materialized between them. "Ari, 'tis time to leave."

She rose from her chair with the grace of a queen, giving Gareth a small, defiant look before exiting, head high.

"Witch," he muttered under his breath. She must have cast a spell on him, one that made it impossible for him to ignore the seductive sway of her hips.

"Can you walk downstairs, or shall we carry you?" Farley asked at Gareth's elbow.

"Where would you take me?"

"I'd take you home so my sister can bind your wounds and nurse you when you get the fever," Marsden answered.

"Nay, my place is here," Gareth said, fighting a surge of panic at the thought of being in the same house with the fairy-haired witch. "Someone must look to Tyneham's defenses."

"Sir Neil charged *me* with that duty when Sir Richard died," Farley snapped.

Gareth blinked. "Yes, but..." Old habits died hard. This was his family's holding, and he had a duty to defend it.

"Even if you have a paper from Sir Neil offering you Sir Richard's place here, your contract died with him," Farley reminded him. "There is no guarantee that the new man Lord Geoffrey sends to Tyneham will need or want your services."

True. Gareth was half tempted to shout his name and connections, but again self-preservation stayed him. He'd be the madman the little witch had called him if he proclaimed himself a Sommerville before he knew who had ordered the ambush.

Master Marsden touched him on the shoulder. "Sir Neil was my friend for many years, and I understand your need to find his killer. But you had best come back with us. There will be time enough to learn what happened when you are whole."

Time to learn what happened. Gareth stared at the chair where Arianna had sat. *Time, and proximity to the person who stood to gain the most from Sir Neil's death.* Of all of them, Arianna had appeared the least affected by the heinous crime. Such a tiny woman wasn't strong enough to overpower a knight, but if Gareth's own experience with Emilie was any guide, she could well have had a hand in it.

Gareth clenched his fist. Aye, he would go to Marsden's house and submit to the care of the strange Dame Cicily who saw too much, if only for the chance to uncover Arianna's part in her bridegroom's murder.

Betrayal. Emilie's betrayal. The pain of it exploded deep inside Gareth, lancing through him like a red-hot poker.

"Pick up the sword," he growled, gesturing at the length of naked steel lying on the wooden deck of the ship, gleaming in the fiery sun.

The man Emilie had betrayed him with, the man Gareth had loved and trusted all his life, shook his head. "I won't fight you, Gareth."

The words echoed hollowly in Gareth's mind, mocking him as Emilie had mocked her wedding vows when she'd lain with this man. The sword wavered in the heat radiating from the oaken planking, and Gareth swayed, dizzy suddenly with hatred. "Damn you, Emilie, for what you've driven me to," he cursed. But he couldn't allow his determination to waver. "If I have to, I'll kill you in cold blood," he told his wife's lover.

But when the man shook his head no, Gareth's blood wasn't cold. It ran hot. So hot. He lunged, aiming his sword at the pale, vulnerable curve of his enemy's throat, thinking the man would move away, protect himself, at least.

He didn't.

A thin red line welled up in the blade's wake.

"Nay!" Gareth screamed, jerking upright in bed. Pain spiked through his right side, stealing his breath. Dizzy. So dizzy.

A door opened. A woman stood silhouetted in a wedge of pale light, fair hair billowing about her ghostly face.

"Emilie?" he rasped. "Damn you. Damn you for the whore you are!" He screamed at her until his voice went hoarse and black dots danced before his eyes. Swaying, he struggled to stay upright, but the bed drew him back, sucked him down into a thick gray mist.

Arianna hesitated outside the door to her bedchamber, reluctant to enter. For two days the hireling knight had lain on her bed, racked by fever from his wounds. For two days, and three nights, Dame Cicily had tended him herself. This morning, she'd asked Ari to take a turn in the sickroom.

"I know nothing of such things," Ari had protested.

"That lack, as well as several others in your training, must be remedied immediately."

Arianna blanched. "Nay... I can't tend him."

"You must. Grizel will not come within twenty feet of the man. Besides, she has her hands full seeing to the customers in my herb shop. Aye, we'll begin your lessons with care of the sick, since we have someone for you to practice on."

"I'd have nothing to do with *him*."

Dame Cicily's gaze narrowed. "Why?"

"What if he starts raving about murder, again? What if screams and swears at this Emilie?"

"He won't. Sir Garvey's fever has broken, and he is on the mend. In a few days, you can have your room back, and things will get back to normal."

Things would never be normal. Arianna drew rein on that thought as she noticed how tired her aunt looked. "Very well, I will sit with him, but I won't touch him."

Dame Cicily cocked her head and gave Ari one of her strange, knowing looks. "I have a feeling there is more to this knight than meets the eye."

Ari snorted.

"I'm afraid we've spoiled you terribly. 'Twas a dream world we let you live in, your grandsire and I," her aunt muttered. "Goldsmithing." She shook her head, then added more forcefully, "From now on, there will be little time for that. All your efforts must go into learning the skills you will need to secure a husband."

Ari had gasped at this, but her aunt kept talking. "The brethern of the guild have sent over food enough to feed us today. Tomorrow we will begin your cooking lessons." With that dread pronouncement still hanging in the air, she had gone to take a well-deserved nap.

Arianna sighed, then squared her shoulders. Pushing open the door as quietly as possible, she peeked in. Ah, blessed relief. His eyes were closed. Mayhap she could get through this if he remained asleep, she thought as she tiptoed to the bed.

He didn't look very fierce now, she decided as she studied his relaxed face. The dark stubble of his beard emphasized both his pallor and the hollows gouged beneath his eyes. She had trouble equating him with the man who had so boldly mocked her on her wedding night. His hot dark eyes were shuttered now by mauve lids. The thick lashes fluttered as though some nightmare yet pursued him, and she shuddered, remembering the anguish in his voice as he'd struggled to escape his demons.

Poor man. Her expression softened. 'Twas likely the fever that had made him rail at her in Sir Neil's chamber. Determined to do her duty, Arianna reached for the cloth and basin of water on the table beside the bed.

How wet should the cloth be? More was probably better than less, Ari decided. Wringing a tiny bit of water from the cloth, she turned toward the bed and plopped the wet rag down on her patient's wide forehead. Water streamed out in all directions, running into his sweaty dark blond hair, pouring over slashing brown eyebrows to pool in the sockets.

"Emilie, dammit! Art trying to drown me now?" he shouted. His eyes flew open, and one hand came up to grab her wrist.

"Nay, I—I am not Emilie," she stammered.

"You," he rasped, flinging water from his eyes with the other hand. "*You'd* like to drown me, too."

"I am nursing you." She tried to free her hand, but his grip on her only tightened.

"The hell you are." He blinked furiously, the muscle in his jaw twitching as he ground his teeth together. "Get away from me." He cast her arm aside with surprising force, spilling her off the bed and onto the floor.

"Ouch!" Arianna scrambled to her feet. "Why did you do that?" She faced him hands on hips, eyes brimming with wounded outrage. He glared back at her so fiercely she stepped back. "I was only trying to help."

If anything, his scowl became blacker. She *felt* something emanating from him. Something dark and mean. It crept over her, leaving goose bumps in its wake, and the strange sensation that he hated her. Why should he, when he didn't even know her? Bah. She was getting as bad as Aunt Cici.

"Don't want your help."

"Why?"

"I see that amazes you, no doubt you are used to men falling at your feet." His eyes still blazed with unholy fury.

"'Tis the fever speaking," she said, partially to reassure herself. "If you will lie quiet and let me bathe your face, you will soon feel more like yourself."

An odd smile twisted one corner of his dry, parched mouth. "But I am not myself . . . and can not be until this is over."

How strange. "If you will let me help . . ."

"I don't want your help," he said, low, hard and frosty.

Her frayed nerves snapped. "No more than I want to be here, I assure you, Sir Knight."

"Hah! I have had experience with she-devils like you."

"Why do keep saying such things about me?"

"Because you would marry for wealth and position."

"Shows what you know," Ari spat back. "Those are the very *last* things I want. I was marrying Sir Neil because . . . because I am not male."

He blinked. "What does that mean?"

"If I had been born a male, I could do as I want."

"Shows what you know." His eyes closed.

Ari scowled at him. Was he so arrogant he always had to have the last word? "Which brings us back to why *I* am tending you. My aunt has sat with you for several days and needs a rest."

His eyes flew open. "How many days have I been here?"

"Two. And three nights."

"Impossible." He levered himself a half inch off the bed, groaned and sagged back, his breathing ragged. "Damn, I'm weak as a babe. What drug have you fed me?"

"Drug? My aunt is a skilled herb woman, you ungrateful wretch. She nursed you . . ."

"Spare me the hysterics," he growled. "Just bring me my clothes and assist me to dress."

"You can't order me around, and you can't get up. Your wound will suffer damage if you move about."

"Don't snap at me, my uppity little burgher."

Ari winced, his barb striking more tender flesh than he could have guessed. "Strong words from a knight with no post."

Gareth blinked away the angry red mist swimming before his eyes. What had come over him? Even when Emilie had shown him her worst side, he'd not lost his temper so completely.

Damn, but he'd learn nothing from this vixen if he roused her ire whenever they were in the same room. Gritting his teeth, he fought to regain his composure. "Your concern is misplaced," he said coolly. "My desire to avenge Sir Neil will give me the strength to ride to Tyneham Keep."

Ari sucked in air, amazed at the change in him from hot anger to icy disdain. "Damn you, Sir Knight, if one as rude

and churlish as you really *is* a knight. You'll not undo my
aunt's hard work in saving your worthless life. She bade me
tend you in her place, and so I shall. If you will not lie quiet,
I will send for the servants and have you tied down." Ari shook
with anger, but also with a little fear. Could he know Grizel
was frightened of men, or that Sim's one good arm would not
be equal to the task?

"Woman," Gareth growled. "Do you know who you are
ordering about in this fashion?"

"A rude man who forgets he nearly died but a day ago."

Gareth grunted something foul under his breath.

Again Arianna was swept by a knowing feeling. "You are
angry because you know I am right to keep you here," she
breathed, amazed by the connection she felt to his thoughts.
Dear God, she hoped she was not developing some of her
aunt's skill at "sensing" things.

"How like a woman to gloat," he snapped.

Arianna let the topic drop. Retrieving the wet cloth, she
wrung it out in the water again and dropped it over his face,
taking special care to cover his expressive eyes.

"You are supposed to wipe my face with a cool cloth, not
just let it lay there getting warm," her patient grumbled.

Ari glared at his mouth, visible below the edge of the cloth,
the full lips compressed into a thin smirk of superiority, as
though he knew what a novice she was. Never had she felt such
an overwhelming urge to strike another person. Nay, 'twould
only make matters worse. She snatched the cloth away, refreshed it in the basin and squeezed it nearly dry. Taking care
not to touch him, she bathed his face.

Looking up at Arianna as she bent to a task she obviously
hated, Gareth tried to find some sign of treachery in her delicately formed features. The expression in her downcast eyes
was guarded by a fringe of brown lashes. She had drawn her
hair back and braided it, but a few rebellious gold tendrils
curled around her face, further softening its oval shape. She
looked younger than her eighteen years, and freshly innocent, her unblemished skin even paler than he had remembered. Was it fear? he wondered. If so, her lovely mouth was
not pinched with it, but relaxed.

Just then, her pink tongue stole out between her lips to wet them as she concentrated on wiping the sensitive skin around his mouth, and suddenly the caressing motion of the cloth fired his imagination and heated his blood instead of cooling it. Would her lips taste as sweet as they looked?

She gasped as though he had spoken the words aloud, her gaze lifting to tangle with his. What passed between them was like nothing Gareth had ever felt before. Wariness. Curiosity. Recognition. A heightened awareness of her femininity, and of his own masculinity. She sensed it, too, he knew because her eyes widened with a shock to match his own.

The air thickened until Gareth could scarcely draw breath or move to break the spell, but he knew he must or lose himself to it. Wrenching his head aside with a groan, he closed his eyes. When he could breathe again without shuddering, he opened them and asked, "Has Farley sent word of Sir Neil's death to Lord Geoffrey Sommerville, yet?"

Arianna shook herself. The fire that had blazed in his eyes until she thought it would scorch her was banked now. And so must she control herself or look the fool standing here gaping at him. "Who is Lord Geoffrey?"

"He is overlord of Tyneham Keep."

"What is an overlord?"

Gareth started in astonishment. "You claim to be the daughter of a knight, yet ask such a foolish question?"

"So, now I am stupid as well as a liar, and—"

The door opened, and her grandfather walked in. He smiled at both of them, his poor eyesight making him oblivious to their tense expressions. "Ah, I thought I heard voices within. How are you feeling today, Sir Garvey?"

Gareth blinked. *Garvey*? Then he remembered his lie. "Like hell," he muttered, wishing it was not true. "I am as stiff and sore as though I'd been dragged behind my horse, but I understand I'll recover, thanks to Dame Cicily's care."

"She is a wonder," William allowed. "I knew your fever must have broken or she would never have left you to Arianna."

"Grandfather," she exclaimed in a hurt tone.

He looked surprised. "Well, you are usually the first to admit you have no skill at tending the sick."

The knight made a satisfied sound in his throat.

Ari scowled at him, then at her grandfather. "Well, since I am not needed here, I will go down to the workroom."

"Prickly thing," Gareth said as the door slammed shut.

"Not usually. In fact, I have not seen my granddaughter behave rudely to anyone until now." William gazed after her thoughtfully, then turned his attention back to Gareth. "What will you do now that Sir Neil is dead?"

"First, I intend to find out who killed him. Has Captain Farley had any luck locating this messenger?"

"Nay. 'Twas a potboy who put the note on the table. He said the man who bid him do it was big and dressed in black, his cowl pulled close around his face, his voice deep and muffled."

"By the sounds, the deed was carefully planned. I heard some there that night say it must be the work of the smugglers who had killed Sir Richard," Gareth said to test William's reaction. The man did not act like a killer, but his family stood to gain from Arianna's marriage to Sir Neil.

William's cloudy blue eyes narrowed as he considered the question. "'Tis possible, I suppose. Sir Neil and poor Richard both had their throats slit." He shuddered at the memory. "Richard was out on the cliffs when he died, and many believe it was because he had stumbled upon these smugglers."

"You disagree?" Gareth tried to lever himself up against the pillows, but pain sliced through his side, so he subsided.

"I am not certain what to think. The rumors of smugglers operating in the area came about because the townspeople saw lights on the cliffs in the dead of night," William said slowly. "But Richard felt that did not necessarily mean smuggling. He *did* think something suspicious was going on out there, though. He told me so just before he went out that last night."

"What did he suspect?" Gareth asked, frowning.

"Alas, he did not confide in me."

"Could he have told Sir Neil?"

"Nay, Sir Neil knew no more than I."

"Strange that he would not confide in his lord."

"Sir Neil trusted my son-by-marriage," William said with a smile. "Between them they had divided up the work so Sir Neil saw to the farms he loved, and Richard kept the peace."

Gareth nodded. He and his father had a similar arrangement. Gareth's management of Ransford left the earl free to pursue the politics he loved and spend time at King Edward's court. "These smugglers, or whoever they are, would not know that. Perhaps they thought Sir Neil knew something."

"It has been over a month since Richard's death," William reminded him. "Why would they wait so long to silence him?"

"I do not know," Gareth said dispiritedly, wincing as he sought to find a more comfortable position.

"I am tiring you," William said at once.

"One more question. Has Farley sent word of Sir Neil's murder to my—to Lord Geoffrey?"

"Aye. A messenger left yesterday." William pursed his lips. "Will you stay and see if the next man the earl sends to Tyneham will have need of your services?"

"I will stay until I find Sir Neil's murderer."

Sir Garvey's quiet determination made William smile to himself. Cici had the right of it; here was a likeable lad, he thought before he spoke. "How do you propose to succeed where Farley, who knows the area and the people, has not?"

"I won't know that until I have studied the situation for myself—perhaps even poked about the cliffs." Under his soft voice could be heard the steely ring of tenacity.

Pleased, William squinted to better make out the blurred features of the young knight. Handsome, Cici had said, even hinted he might make a match for Arianna, had he any property or prospects of a post.

"Is aught wrong?"

William flushed at the direction his thoughts had taken. "I fear my eyesight fails me, and I would see you better."

Gareth felt an unwelcome frisson of compassion for the man. *A blind goldsmith had about as much chance of survival as a toothless wolf.* In the aftermath of Sir Neil's murder, he had tried to paint all three—Dame Cicily, William and Arianna—with the same black brush. Now he was not quite so certain of his strokes. The old man and woman seemed harmless enough. "Step closer, if you like," he said easily.

"Nay, I have tired you enough with so much talk. My sister will flay me if you worsen. Just tell me, is there anyone you would have me write to say you have arrived, wounded but safe?"

"No one," Gareth said, thinking his father would soon have Farley's message and either come himself or send someone to Tyneham Keep in any event.

"You are alone, then?" At the knight's nod, William sighed in disappointment. Likely the lad was penniless. Ah, well. "Someone did a good job of raising you. Art patient, cautious and loyal beyond your years."

"I am nine and twenty." It felt good to speak the truth. Damn, he disliked this lying more and more.

"Ah, ancient, to be sure." William's eyes danced briefly. "I wish Ari had a bit more of your patience and . . ."

"Sweetness of temper?"

"Usually she is . . . well, not sweet. She is too lively and impatient to be called that, and we have indulged her, I fear after her dear mother, my daughter, died. But she is usually happy and quick to smile. I have never known her to snap as she did at you. It must be the strain she has been under since Sir Neil's death," William said defensively.

Indeed, Gareth sneered to himself. "She must be upset to find herself widowed and so soon in need of another who can provide for her as . . . handsomely . . . as Sir Neil."

William frowned at the bitterness in the knight's voice. "Certainly Ari can not hope to find another husband as kind and generous as Sir Neil," he said, thinking of how pleased she had been at being able to continue with her goldsmithing. No other man would be so understanding. "And she is not anxious to marry, but I would see her comfortably settled before I die."

I bet you would. The easiness and pleasure Gareth had felt in the old man's company evaporated.

Later that evening, Charles found Walter at The Forge and Anvil, the alehouse he usually frequented. Walter sat at his favorite corner table, a woman on his knee. She was cleaner and prettier than the usual sort Walter could get.

"Walter. I have to speak with you, alone."

Walter grumbled in disgust, but sent the woman away with a pinch on her ample rump and a promise to join her upstairs. "This had better be good," he said when she had gone.

"Sir Garvey is going to live."

"That is what sent ye scurryin' here like a scared rabbit."

"You said you wanted information on him." Charles bristled and rose from his chair. "I came to tell you that he was hired by Sir Neil to take Sir Richard's place."

"Oh, sit down, ye're sensitive as a nun's tit." Walter scowled at Charles until he sat, then he rocked back in his own chair. "Garvey's oath to Sir Neil died wi' the old man, and Farley'll not have the authority ta give him a place at Tyneham wi'out the great Lord Geoffrey's leave."

"I forgot how well versed you are in such matters."

"And a good thing I am," Walter snapped right back. "Neither ye nor the high-and-mighty Hugh thought ta stop that messenger from bringin' Lord Geoffrey word of Sir Neil's death, did ye?"

"Nay," Charles said grudgingly. He expected his brother had enjoyed killing Farley's messenger almost as much as he'd enjoyed ambushing the Sommerville men and killing Sir Neil.

"Thought not. Same as neither o' ye thought Lord Geoffrey'd send someone ta Sir Neil's weddin'. Wonder who it was we killed?" Walter mused.

"If it had been one of the sons, or the earl himself, we'd have heard by now," Charles muttered.

"Ye're probably right. Shame, that. Now, find out everythin' ye can about this Sir Garvey and report back ta me." Walter polished off his cup of ale in one swallow, wiping his mouth on the back of his hand.

"Now see here . . . I am not your slave."

"Do it," Walter growled, pushing his face into Charles's. "We are gettin' close on this one, and don't need another knight poking into things what don't concern him. I'm fer killin' him outright, but Hugh's afraid that if another knight turns up wi' his throat slit, the king'll hear o' it."

Charles reluctantly agreed and stood to leave, but Walter stopped him with a look.

"No thanks fer clearin' yer way ta the fair Arianna?"

"Shh." Charles looked around to see if anyone had heard.

Walter's grin twisted into an angry grimace. "Don't ye *shh* me. And see ye keep a close eye on that hireling knight. If he learns somethin' he shouldn't, I'll open him ear from ear, and the king be damned. This time, I get my due."

Chapter Four

Cooking was not fun.

It was hot, disagreeable work.

From across the kitchen, which was as close as Arianna could get to the roaring fire she'd built in the huge kitchen hearth, she scowled at the iron pot slung over the cook fire. The bottom of it glowed red, nearly engulfed in the dancing flames; above it writhed a curtain of steam.

The wretched knight's dratted gruel probably needed stirring again. Grabbing up a long-handled wooden spoon, she reluctantly sidled closer. The heat was so intense, she threw her left arm over her face and turned it partially aside as she hastily dipped the spoon into the bubbling liquid.

One swipe. Two. Arianna cried out in pain and leaped back, examining her right hand to see if it had been burned off. It was still there, but the skin was shiny and apple red. The hair on her arm had been singed. She turned and plunged it into a bucket of water, dirty spoon and all.

"Ahh . . ." Arianna drew in a grateful breath, and smelled something burning. The gruel? Nay, this had a hint of yeast.

"Not the bread." She sprang toward the door of the bake oven built into one side of the hearth, taking a moment to wrap her hands in her skirts before she pulled the door open.

A wave of gray smoke rolled over her. She coughed, fanning it away with her skirts, then reached for the loaf she had gotten up at dawn to make. "Please don't let it be . . . Burnt."

Wait. The top was dark brown, not black. Which meant it was not really burned, she told herself, just *well done*.

Ari rapped on it with her knuckles to test its doneness as Grizel had instructed. Hard. Was that good? Drat, she could fashion as difficult a piece as the reliquary from a lump of metal, remembering her grandfather's intricate instructions in minute detail. Why couldn't she remember how the bread was supposed to sound?

"Bah, people eat bread, they do not listen to it."

Ari dropped the bread on the tray alongside a crock of butter and one of honey, then poured a cup of ale. This time she wrapped a towel around her hand before dipping a bowl of gruel from the pot. It was thin and unappealingly gray, she thought as she set the bowl on the tray. But then, she hated gruel.

Now came the worst part—carrying the food up to the knight, maybe even feeding it to him if he was not strong enough to manage on his own.

"Do not look on this as punishment," her aunt had said when she'd set Ari to this task while she sorted out a new batch of herbs. Curiosity about what had happened to the Marsdens had sparked a brisk business in the herb shop. Many of the jars were empty now and must be replenished before the shop opened that morn. "Look on this as valuable training."

Ari had looked on it as an opportunity to serve in purgatory, and that was before she had known the cook fire would be hot enough to melt lead. "Why can Grizel not make the bread and feed the knight?"

"Grizel must help me, then see to the wash. We are behind in the work and need your help. You need to learn."

What she needed was to find the knight had either gained the strength of Samson over the night, or was still sleeping, Ari thought as she crossed the solar. How would she find him? Ari wondered, balancing the tray on one hip as she eased open the door to her bedchamber. Hot with anger, or icily arrogant?

He was sitting on the edge of the bed.

Ari was so surprised to find him awake, so startled by the broad expanse of naked male flesh, she nearly dropped the tray. Jesu, he was magnificent, his skin deeply tanned, stretched tight over a thick chest sprinkled with dark hair and arms that bulged with muscles. She had never seen the like of him. Her fingers itched to capture his likeness in bronze.

"Well, are you going to stand there all day, or bring me something to eat?" he snapped.

She stepped completely into the room, her enchantment with his physical appearance dulled. "Are you always this rude?"

"Oh, it's you." If anything, his expression became more grim. "I thought it was the maid."

"She won't come in here." Determined not to let his mood intimidate her, Arianna lifted her chin and started for the bed.

"You might wait until I'm decently covered," he growled, twitching the blanket to cover his lower body.

Ari stopped midstride, her cheeks flaming. "I—I did not realize you were . . . bare all over."

"Oh?" One brown brow arched in disbelief. "More like you wanted to sneak a peek at me."

"Why would I want to do that?"

"Never mind. I am starving. Set the tray there." He waved a hand at the bedside table.

As if she were a serf! Ari controlled the urge to throw the tray at him. Barely. "Can you move the basin aside?"

"Not without getting up," he challenged.

Bait her, would he? "Do not trouble yourself. I have not yet broken my fast and would not want my stomach turned by your crude display."

Gareth mouthed an oath. *Crude* had been a word Emilie used to describe everything that happened in their marriage bed. He'd thought her cold, until he'd learned she'd taken a lover. Ari's sharp, choppy movements as she set the tray on the floor and cleared the table betrayed her anger and kept his own bubbling.

Sweating and muttering under her breath, Arianna dragged the small table closer to the bed. "There," she panted out, snatching off the cloth napkin.

"What is that awful smell?" he exclaimed.

"It is not awful. It's . . ."

"Burnt!" he cried. "The damned bread's burnt to a cinder." He grabbed up the knife and hacked off a piece, or tried to. The blackened crust broke open, and raw dough oozed out of the center. "I'll be damned."

"Oh . . . how did that happen?" Ari said in a small voice.

"Obviously it was not baked properly." His tone was as crisp as the crust on the bread.

"I did not do it on purpose."

"Really?"

His gibe cut through her remorse and struck a spark of fury. "Why did I go to all the trouble of making the unholy bread for you?" she demanded, hands on her hips. Before he could answer, she rushed on. "You can not know how much work it is to make bread. First I was dragged from my pallet in my aunt's room when it was still dark outside and my muscles were all stiff from sleeping on the floor instead of my nice soft bed where some lout of a knight is curled up sound asleep. Then I had to mix all these complicated ingredients together and let them rise. And knead the dough, which is sticky and awful and . . . and the fire in the hearth is so hot you can scarcely stand to get near enough to put the loaf in the bake oven . . . and—"

"I see," Gareth managed. His traitorous lips twitched with nearly forgotten urge to grin.

Arianna drew herself up. "Don't you dare laugh at me."

"I haven't laughed in two years," Gareth mumbled, but she looked so comical he could barely control himself.

"You *are* laughing." Ari snatched up the roll of parchment she'd left on the floor the day before and raised it over her head.

Gareth lifted a hand to ward off the blow and groaned as pain tore through his side.

Instantly contrite, Ari dropped the parchment. Laying a hand on his shoulder, she stroked gently. "Have I hurt you? Shall I fetch my aunt?"

Gareth sucked in air between his teeth and shook his head. The fire in his side had subsided to a dull ache, but the muscles lower in his body were tightening in a familiar but unwelcome response to her touch.

"Damn my hasty temper, but I have never made bread before. And it was so dratted hot." She continued to stroke his shoulder, enjoying the feel of his warm skin and the play of the taut muscles beneath. "Grizel's instructions seemed so simple. Perhaps I built the fire too high."

"Stop that," Gareth said through gritted teeth.

Ari blinked. "Stop? Stop what? Oh, the talking." She smiled wryly. "Grandfather says I have a horrible tendency to babble except when I am working on a piece of…" She bit off the rest and looked away from his hypnotic eyes. 'Twould be too easy to trust this man, too easy to say too much.

"What else have you brought for me to eat?" Gareth shrugged out from under her hand and leaned closer to the table. The sooner he ate, the sooner she would go. Maybe then his breathing and pulse would return to normal.

"Gruel." Gareth made a face, and she chuckled. "I hate it, too, but my aunt says it builds strength."

He picked up the spoon and stirred, peering suspiciously into the murky grayish liquid. "Burnt."

"Nay." Arianna leaned closer, watched in horror as Gareth lifted a spoonful and sniffed.

"Burnt," he affirmed.

"Oh, no. I stirred it, just as Grizel said. I can not think how it could have burned. Now what will you eat?"

Her disheartened tone brought Gareth's head up, and he looked at her closely for the first time that morn. She did indeed look as though she had had a terrible morning. Her beautiful hair had come undone from its braid and straggled down her back. A few tendrils stuck to her flushed cheeks. Smudges of flour were streaked across her nose and her forehead where she had rubbed them with her hands. To top it off, the dismay in her eyes reminded him of young Cat's when she'd tried to master running before walking.

Gareth smothered another smile. The fever must have weakened him, for he couldn't hang on to his anger, no matter how little he thought of women in general, no matter what he thought this one might have done. "Mayhap it's not too burnt." He took a spoonful and swallowed it as quickly as possible. "N-not bad." Grimacing, he took another spoonful.

"Oh, I am so glad. Mayhap you could eat the bread if I scraped off some of the crust."

"And the raw part?" He tried not to gag on the gruel.

The smile she gave him was dazzling, dangerously infectious. "I'll put lots of butter and honey on it." She seized the loaf and began whittling on it with far more zeal than skill.

The spoon suspended halfway between bowl and mouth, Gareth watched, expecting at any moment to hear her cry for a cut finger. Again he cursed himself for a fool for caring what she did, but he breathed a sigh of relief when she held up a mangled hunk of bread. That treacherous pink tongue of hers crept out from between her teeth as she concentrated on dressing up the bread. The sight of it wiggling back and forth drove Gareth's pulse crazy.

"There." Ari held it out her offering, piled high with golden butter and dripping honey from all four sides. "Oh," she added at his look of consternation. "Let me hold it so you will not get all messy."

She leaned across the table, and he smelled on her hair the incongruous mix of lavender and burnt bread. The motion pulled the bodice of her simple gown tight across her breasts. He remembered them from that first night, full, pale globes teasing him through the curtain of her hair. Desire washed through him again. His lips parted on a hungry moan; it was not warm flesh that filled his mouth, but hot sticky bread.

"Good?" she asked as Gareth struggled to chew the large piece he had bitten off.

"Not bad," he managed to mumble. Chewy, with a slightly charred aftertaste, but the honey made it tolerable.

"Good. I am going to fix myself some. All this hard work, and I am hungry as a wolf." Plopping the rest of his piece onto the tray, she hacked off another section of bread and prepared it has she had his. Oblivious to her sticky fingers, she then pulled the chair closer and sat with a sigh. "*Dieu*, my feet are tired. I am not used to so much standing."

"Why did you have to work in the kitchen?" he asked when she had eaten the bread and washed it down with the rest of his ale.

"Because no one will marry me if I can not cook."

"Sir Neil did," he said grimly.

Pain filled her eyes. "Poor Sir Neil. He only wed me because he had promised my father he would take care of me."

"Why did you accept?"

"Because he was willing to give us all a home."

Emilie had defended her actions by claiming her family had pressured her, Gareth thought darkly. "And Sir Neil was wealthy. Is that what you look for in a husband?"

"Nay, only a willingness to take us all," she repeated.

"Meaning your grandfather and great-aunt."

"And Grizel and Sim, too."

"Who are they?"

"Grizel is our maid, and Sim does whatever he can to help."

Gareth frowned thoughtfully. It was doubtful that the maid had killed Sir Neil, but this Sim was a possibility. "Why have I not seen these two about?"

Arianna smiled that sweet, easy smile of hers, the one that made his breath catch. "Grizel is afraid of you."

"Why? She doesn't even know me."

"There is no need to take offense. She fears all men because she was abused when she was a child. She is a mute, as well." Ari clapped a hand over her mouth. "She will be embarrassed that I have told you of her past. But since she is wary of men, you are unlikely to see her."

"How does she accomplish her tasks if she is mute? How does she see to your grandsire's needs if she hides from men?"

Ari shrugged. "Grizel is a hard worker and a good cook. She can write down simple questions and make signs. Over the years she has lost her fear of Grandfather, but when he has male guests, he must serve them himself."

Gareth tried to imagine his father or brothers serving their own guests so that a mute maid could cower in her bed. "Why do you keep her?"

"Where else would she go? Who would hire her?" she said patiently. "You see why I cannot marry just any man."

Gareth grunted. What he saw was that instead of one bloodsucking female, such as he had wed, the man who married Arianna would get five. A wife who could not cook, a blind goldsmith, a strange old woman who might be a witch, a maid who feared men, and a... Gareth had no idea what this

Sim's story was, but the odds favored his also being defective in some way.

"I would rest now," he growled.

Ari felt the knight withdrawing from her. The air between them, which had been warm, and at times charged with the strange tension she had felt the day before, was cold, now. She regretted the loss of that closeness. And, too, the longer she was with him, the stronger grew the urge to capture him in bronze. "Could I draw you?" she asked in a rush.

"What?"

"Please don't be angry. All I wanted to do was sketch you."

"Sketch me? Whatever for?"

Ari couldn't answer that. Bending, she retrieved the parchment and unrolled it for him to see. "See. It's a sketch of a drinking cup." She waited for his words of praise.

"Why does this boar have horns?"

"'Tis a stag." Ari moved to the side of the bed and traced the charcoal lines with her fingers. "See."

"Nay, but you have drawn a hog."

Her first reaction was indignation. "It is not."

"Art thou blind or ignorant?"

"Oh. Of all the mean things to say! I was willing to forget the awful names you heaped on me that first night because I knew you were in pain, but I need not stand here while you criticize something precious to me."

Turning from him, Ari ran across the room. Behind her, she heard the knight call. Without stopping, she dashed out the door, nearly colliding with Grizel, who was passing through the solar with an armful of linens.

"Wait!" Gareth shouted again. Wrapping the blanket around his waist, he struggled to his feet and went after her. His legs wobbled as they had the first time he'd stepped foot on the deck of his brother Alex's ship. At the door, he stopped to catch his breath, clutching the door frame for support.

A short, dark-haired woman stood a few feet away, watching Arianna's retreating back.

"Arianna," Gareth croaked.

His quarry did not pause, but the other woman spun in his direction. She was young and passably pretty, he saw, as her eyes widened with fear. Was this Grizel? Gareth wondered. Before he could frame the question, she made a high, keening sound and fainted dead away at his feet.

"They'll pay for this," Gareth muttered as he snuck from the bedchamber. The "they" being Dame Cicily, who had refused to give him his clothes until he was well, and Master Marsden, who had upheld the dame's command.

Dammit, he was well. Hadn't he gone meekly back to bed while Arianna and Dame Cicily revived Grizel? Hadn't he eaten every mouthful of the stew the old woman had brought him at dinner? Hadn't he slept away the afternoon?

He felt fine. Well, a trifle weak, but it certainly wouldn't kill him to ride to Tyneham Keep, consult with Farley and ride back. Apollo, who Marsden had assured him was safe in a hut behind the house, needed riding anyway. And Gareth needed answers to the dozens of questions buzzing in his brain.

Crossing the solar, Gareth noticed vaguely that the room was well furnished, with a table and chairs set for the evening supper, and a thick carpet underfoot. There were colorful hangings on the walls, and the gleam of silver plate on the sideboard. Marsden could not be in such dire straits or he'd have sold such things to raise money. What other lies had they told him? Gareth wondered as he pulled open the door.

The sweet smell of herbs wafted up the stairs, reminding him that Dame Cicily was supposedly an herb woman. She must have a shop in her home.

So! Gareth grinned as he hiked up the blanket he had wrapped around his waist. It would serve the woman right if he ran into some of her customers clad like this. His smile faded. The rest of his clothes had better still be packed in his saddlebags, and the bags had better be in the hut with Apollo. Anxious as he was to meet with Farley, he had no desire to ride naked through the town and up to the keep.

"Did ye get it?" asked a female voice from below the stairs.

"Aye," another, even younger sounding woman replied.

Though it was dark at the top of the steep stairs, Gareth flattened himself further into the shadows.

"Can I see?" The voices came from the front of the house.

"It's done up in a pouch. I'm ta soak Harold's feet in it three times a day."

"And that'll cure his warts?"

Hah! He'd known the old woman was a witch.

"Dame Cicily thinks they're sores caused by those old boots o' his. She loaned me a few pennies so as we can buy new ones."

Frowning, Gareth ignored the rest of their conversation. *Dame Cicily could still be a witch,* he reasoned. It helped him to think of her as such; it justified his lies. He stood in the dark wrestling with his conscience until he heard a door close, cutting off the women's voices.

Momentarily Gareth sagged against the wall. Jesu, he hated being here, and the sooner he left, the better. He crept down the stairs and out the back door.

The hut Marsden had spoken of stood at the far edge of the herb garden. Gareth glanced at the varicolored clusters of plants as he passed by, the varieties neatly set off from each other by narrow rows of stones. The effect was pretty, as well as functional. 'Twas obvious Dame Cicily took great care with the herbs and such that were her livelihood, he grudgingly admitted. In fact, the gardens at Ransford could have profited from the old woman's touch, neglected as they had been during these past two years.

Resecuring the blanket around his lean waist, Gareth slipped up to the door of the hut. The wooden building was larger than he had expected, and in very good repair. The door squeaked a little as he swung it open, and Gareth instinctively looked back over his shoulder.

Something cold touched his stomach. "Stop right there."

Gareth's head whipped back, and he stared incredulously at the youth holding him at bay with a sword. His own sword. "What the hell . . . ?" Gareth started to reach for it.

"Don't move." The youth enforced the command by pressing the sword point into the soft flesh just below Gareth's linen bandage. From the boy's height and gangly limbs, Gareth guessed his age at near twelve, but the black eyes that stared at him down the length of the blade could have belonged to a seasoned warrior of fifty.

"Who are ye?" the boy asked.

Gareth glanced around. The hut had been partitioned into two sections. Judging by the kegs and crates piled neatly along the walls, the part they were standing in was used for storage. Light spilled through the half-open doorway to the right, and he saw there was straw on the floor. That must be where Apollo was being kept. "Sir Gar...vey, come to check on my horse."

The boy grunted, his grip on the sword unwavering, but admiration flickered through his eyes. "He be well, 'ceptin' fer a cut on his fetlock. I been tendin' it."

Gareth's fists tightened on the blanket. "I'd see him."

"The missy's wi' him. Can't be disturbed."

"Who?" The sinking feeling in the pit of Gareth's stomach had nothing to do with the sword leveled there and everything to do with the certainty that Arianna was "the missy."

"Mistress Ari. Said she mustn't be bothered."

Fury and alarm flooded Gareth, but he showed neither. "Sim. You are Sim, aren't you?" At the boy's nod, Gareth continued, "Well, Sim, Apollo has been trained as a war-horse. Do you realize how dangerous a destrier can be?" God alone knows how this boy had managed to win Apollo's trust and treat him. "But your mistress could get hurt if she comes too close to him, or alarms him."

"He were right skittish when she came in," Sim allowed, casting a quick glance at the open door. From within, came a nervous neigh and the sound of heavy feet striking packed earth.

"Mayhap we had better check on her," Gareth ventured.

Sim's grunt was noncommittal, but he lowered the point of the sword and walked slowly to the door. Gareth followed him, starting in surprise at the tableau inside.

Apollo's halter had been tied to a ring set in the wall of the hut. He stood there calmly munching oats. A few feet away— certainly within striking distance of the stallion's dangerous hooves—sat Arianna. She was perched on a high stool, her feet tucked up on the top rung, a parchment spread on her lap.

"Arianna! By all that's holy, come away from there," Gareth hissed, advancing on her.

Arianna turned, her eyes widening at the sight of him striding toward her in nothing by his bandage and blanket. "Shh. Dark Shadow does not take to strangers."

"His name is Apollo, and he's mine." Indeed the horse neighed a greeting, tossing his head so he nearly tore the ring from the wall.

Ari marveled at the affection she felt flowing from them as the horse tried to bury his nose in the knight's chest.

"Easy, Apollo. Easy, boy," he said softly, running practiced hands over the great stallion's neck and shoulder, then bending to examine the cloth wound around his leg. "Looks like we each have a remembrance of that battle."

Sim came up and handed Gareth the sword, hilt first. "'Tis plain ta see he's yours. So must this be."

Gareth took it with a nod of thanks. "How were you able to get close to him?" he asked as he continued to stroke the stallion's neck.

Sim shrugged. "I've a way wi' beasts." He reached with his left hand to scratch Apollo's nose. He wore no shirt, and the terrible scars running the length of his arm were clearly visible. "Mayhap they know I'd do them no harm." He flexed the arm, showing Gareth that he could only extend it partway. "A man whose own pa would beat him so is not like ta harm another poor dumb creature." Sim turned and walked away, giving Gareth a clear view of his back, ridged and disfigured from the mark of the lash.

"Dear God, how could any man do that? And to his own son?" Gareth muttered.

"Grandfather says Sim's father drank," Arianna whispered.

Gareth remembered his own father, his face flushed from too much ale on a feast day, telling stories and laughing with his kinsmen. There were drunks, and then there were drunks.

"Some men have a lot of anger in them," Arianna said. "The only way they can feel better is to make someone else feel bad."

This unexpected bit of wisdom brought Gareth's gaze to hers. His heart lurched as he stared into her upturned face. She looked so young, so innocent, no more capable of committing murder than a newborn babe. Aye, there was a spark inside her, even when she was still and grave, as now, that caught fire on something deep inside him. Each time he was with her, it burned higher, hotter, melting the defenses he had built against all of her sex, kindling a desire the likes of which he had never known—did not want to know. And yet...

The sudden warmth in the knight's eyes spilled through Ari like molten honey. No one had ever looked at her in such a way, as though he were starving and she his last meal. Aye. Hunger, but not for food. For something else. Something he wanted so much it made him shiver with longing, yet at the same time, he rejected it. Aye, she sensed his need as though it were her own, and wondered how that could be. "What is happening?" she asked.

Gareth started, shook himself free of the spell she had cast. Aye, spell. Mayhap she had sprinkled one of her aunt's powders in his gruel this morn, and that was why she affected him so. His eyes fell on the parchment on her lap. "This is what you were working on?" It was Apollo, and not a bad likeness.

Smiling ruefully, she nodded. "Grandfather said you were right about my stag looking like a boar. He said they looked much more like horses. So I came to sketch your horse."

Gareth surprised himself, and her, too, by laughing. "Apollo is a war-horse. They are larger than a normal horse, and many times larger than a stag."

"Oh." She frowned down at the drawing. "Where would you suggest I find a stag?"

"Since I doubt one will wander into town, you had best go into the woods."

"Ah. Where in the woods?"

"I do not know exactly, being unfamiliar with these parts, but near a stream where the stag comes to drink is a good place to see one."

"Near a stream. Thank you. I will find one."

"Sir Garvey!" Dame Cicily exclaimed from the doorway. "You are the worst of patients and like to end up fevered again." She swooped across the straw-covered floor and planted herself in front of him. Scowling fiercely, she said,

"Added to that, here you stand in nothing but a blanket, compromising the reputation of my niece. I am half tempted to fetch the priest to wed you."

She was probably bluffing. Nonetheless, Gareth beat a hasty retreat back to the house. He'd not relish trying to explain to his father why his eldest son and heir had married Arianna, the goldsmith's granddaughter.

Chapter Five

Gareth greeted the call to supper that evening with the enthusiasm of a condemned man facing the gallows. It was happening again. Despite his determination to remain aloof, he was slowly, inexorably being drawn in by an alluring face and a pair of bewitching blue eyes.

Nay, his growing captivation went beyond what his eyes feasted on, he morosely admitted. He bent to pull on his boots, groaning half in frustration at the damnable situation, half at the strain on his unhealed wound.

If only she wasn't such a contrary little witch, returning his caustic gibes with smiles sweet enough to rock a man's soul. Not that she didn't have a temper, and flay him with it when roused. But her anger came and went as swiftly as her quicksilver moods. Damn, but she fascinated him.

Nay. Gareth clenched his fists in angry denial. He'd not open himself up to that kind of pain and danger again. Emilie's perfidy had taught him well that women were not the weaker sex. Underestimating her manipulative powers had nearly cost him a brother, to say nothing of his own life.

Squaring his shoulders for battle, Gareth snatched open the door to Ari's chamber and saw the others waiting in the solar.

Ari jumped as the door jerked back on its hinges and the knight strode out. A man of strength and vigor, her aunt had pronounced him. Watching from her place at the table, Ari could not help but agree and admire him as he crossed the room and took the place her aunt indicated. He carried himself proudly, head high, his stride smoother than that of his prized Apollo and more assured than Alderman Arley's when he presided over town court. Truly there was much to enjoy in just watching him. Again she longed to capture his likeness in bronze.

"Do not stare at me, mistress," he growled as he slid into his seat across the table from her.

"I am sorry." Ari felt her cheeks flame but couldn't look away from his mesmerizing gaze. "You look rested."

"What I am is starving," he grumbled. "I hope you did not have a hand in this meal, for my ribs are fair knocking on my backbone." Scowling, he looked away from her.

Rude ingrate. After she'd burned her fingers and singed her hair preparing his dratted food. She reached for her pewter trencher with the intent of denting it on his arrogant head.

"Good evening, Arianna," Charles said, taking the seat beside her. "I missed you in the workroom today."

Arianna smiled and loosened her grip on the trencher. Dear, safe Charles, who had been like a brother to her these past five years since he'd come to train with her grandfather. Charles even praised her work when she knew he secretly envied her abilities. Now, *that* was knightly courtesy. "Today I began my training in housewifely things," she said sweetly.

"About time, too. You will need such skills when you marry."

Ari groaned inwardly. This just was not her night. But when Charles went on to praise her capacity for learning, saying she'd catch on quickly, she felt a little better.

"Sir Garvey," William broke in when he could. "This is Charles Beck, my apprentice."

Gareth frowned. *Beck? The name was familiar, yet the man's face was not.* He prided himself on remembering names and faces, but shrugged off the feeling he should know Charles and growled a greeting. He did not like it that the man sat so close to Arianna, nor did he like the way she smiled when she talked to the apprentice. Mostly he did not like his own reaction to these things.

The door opened, and the maid came in carrying a tray. She cast one terrified glance in Gareth's direction, set the tray on the sideboard and scurried out. His empty stomach rumbled, and he looked longingly at the steam rising from a thick meat pie. There should be another servant to cut the pie and serve it so we don't have to wait, he thought.

Across the table from him, Arianna suddenly shifted in her seat. Gareth looked up to see her staring at him, her head cocked as though she worked on a puzzle.

Anger. Impatience. These Ari sensed radiating from the knight. "One servant is all we can afford," she said softly.

Gareth started. "Why do you say that?"

She met the intensity of his gaze without flinching, yet there was something so knowing, so intimate deep in her blue, blue eyes that he wondered if she *had* read his thoughts. Her great-aunt had seemed to the night Sir Neil had died.

Ridiculous. Gareth shook his head. Miraculously, the feeling passed. 'Twas the lingering effects of the fever, or a lucky guess on her part, he assured himself. Yet it took several minutes for his heartbeat to slow. Around him, life went on as usual. William and Dame Cicily exchanged news of the day. Charles asked Arianna a question and she responded. He must have imagined the whole thing, Gareth decided.

The maid returned bearing a tray of cheese, bread and fruit. Sim followed, a pitcher of ale in his good arm. He poured a cup for each of them, the process slowed by his deformity. The boy knew his way around horses, but was uncomfortable serving.

Knowing what it was like to be judged and found lacking, Gareth's heart went out to young Sim. His respect for William and Dame Cicily rose, also. Arianna had spoken the truth when she'd said no one else would want either Sim or Grizel, even given the current labor shortage. Their kindness put him in mind of Gaby, who had a soft spot for wounded creatures.

The pie tasted as good as it smelled—the meat spicy and tender, the crust flaky. Gareth fell to eating with the gusto of a large man who hadn't eaten a full meal in nearly five days. In minutes, he had cleaned his trencher and drained his cup. He hadn't eaten with so much relish since . . . since Emilie's death. He signaled to Grizel to serve him another slice of pie.

She shivered, casting a desperate glance at the other heads bent over their trenchers.

"I am sorry I frightened you this morn," Gareth said in the quiet voice he used with the horses. Still she didn't move. He tried a rusty smile. It must have turned out well, because she crept forward, eyes wary, and snatched up his trencher.

Whirling away, she cut another slice of pie with jerky movements, shoveled it onto the trencher and sidled back. She set the trencher down an arm's length away from him.

"Thank you," he said gently. "The pie is very good."

She gasped, turned and fled the room. No one else remarked her leaving.

Gareth sighed. Ah, well, her behavior was none of his concern. At least the mouse of a maid could cook.

"From where do you come?" Charles blurted out.

"My sire had a small keep near Shelby," Gareth improvised. Lying to Charles was easier than lying to the others, and Shelby was not too far from Ruarke's castle at Wilton, so he knew the area should questions arise.

Charles's pasty face grew paler. "What is your surname?"

"Smythe." It was a common enough name.

"Ah. Do you know the Sommervilles of Wilton?"

Gareth frowned. "When last I was home, that place was held by a family named de Rivers." True enough. His maternal grandsire, Roger de Rivers, had held Wilton before dying and willing it to Ruarke. "Are you from that area?"

"Nay," Charles said quickly. "I had heard tell of the family, is all."

"Not surprising," William interjected. "Geoffrey Sommerville, the Earl of Winchester, was Sir Neil's overlord. I met the earl once many years ago and found him to be a wise, kindly man—for one of his station."

"What do you mean by that?" Gareth demanded.

William's milky eyes widened. "Why, only that so few nobles take an interest in the people who work their lands, other than to wonder how they might get more work or more money in rents and tallages from them. But the earl was different. He seemed genuinely to care for the welfare of the merchants and the villeins who work the fields."

"As did Sir Neil," Dame Cicily remarked sadly. "I only hope the earl will send another like Sir Neil to hold Tyneham Keep."

To this, everyone nodded but Arianna. "What is an over-lord?"

William glanced at Dame Cicily. "I see we have indeed ne-glected your education. An overlord is the person to whom a castellan such as Sir Neil owes fealty. A portion of what is grown on Tyneham's farms goes to Lord Geoffrey. We in town are pledged to him, too, and give him a tallage for our busi-nesses."

Arianna's frowned deepened. "In order to raise money to pay that, the townspeople must oft pledge you their valua-bles. What does the earl do for the people in exchange?"

"He provides protection from attack."

"Where was his grand protection when the smugglers killed my father and Sir Neil?" she exclaimed.

Gareth felt compelled to defend his family's honor. "As soon as Farley's message reaches him, the earl will send men to—"

"To what?" Ari cried. "Nay, his help comes too late."

"Then *I* will find the ones responsible and make them pay."

"That won't bring back the people I loved." Tears welled in her eyes, and Gareth reluctantly had to admire the control with which she fought them back. "This great earl should have come when the lights were first spotted on the cliffs."

"The earl is not God," Gareth said tightly. "And catching smugglers is chancy. Being a girl, you don't understand how—"

"Aye, I am female," Ari snapped, her teeth grinding to-gether in frustration. "Though lately I've had cause to regret not being born male."

Gareth looked to William and Dame Cicily for support, but they merely shrugged, seemingly amused by his predicament.

Charles broke the tension. "When will you be leaving, Sir Garvey?" he demanded.

"Charles," William chided. "The man is scarce healed, and welcome to stay until he is."

It suddenly occurred to Gareth that the Marsdens had never asked him about his family origins, nor had they demanded coin to pay for the medicines and food he had consumed. If they were as greedy as he'd imagined, they might have let him die of his wounds, kept the coins in his purse and sold his sword, armor and horse. Instead, they had taken him into their home and nursed him through the fever, even given him their granddaughter's bed to sleep in.

Shame filled him. No matter his suspicions, his parents had raised him better than to repay their generosity with treachery. Yet he must go on lying until he could discover who had murdered Sir Neil. The sooner he got down to that business, the better. The sooner he left Marsden's house, the better. Twice he had come close to kissing Ari, and God alone knows what insanity that would lead him into. Even watching her eat stirred and tightened his body, desire making a mockery of his customary control.

He had tried likening her to Emilie. Both small, blond and beautiful, but there the comparison ended. He simply could not relate Arianna's fresh, bright spirit to his dead wife's treacherous nature. Nor could he rid himself of the unwanted yearnings he felt every time he looked at her. Mayhap if he gave in and lay with her once it would cure him . . .

Nay, he'd not repay the kindness of the two old people smiling at him from across the table by ruining the girl. For that's what it would amount to. Even did he wish it otherwise, which he did not, he hastily assured himself, Arianna could never be more than a dalliance for him. 'Twas his duty, his destiny, to wed a lady of his station.

"I must leave in the morn," Gareth announced curtly.

"Nay!" Dame Cicily exclaimed. "You are not strong enough."

"I go only as far as Tyneham Keep, to hunt for Sir Neil's murderer," Gareth said. He saw Arianna's face go white, and suspicion again reared its ugly head. Did she fear what he'd find at the keep? Even the Holy Church said women were natural-born liars, after all. And he'd been taken in by a deceitful woman before. Perhaps it was a failing in him.

"Your wound will need redressing each day for the next week," Dame Cicily reminded him.

"Someone at Tyneham can see to it," he said shortly.

"Bah, there is not a clean strip of linen in that place."

"Come back and stay the night with us, at least," William pleaded. "My sister can rebind your wound."

Gareth stiffened. Every word they uttered heightened his distrust, strengthened his determination to leave. "I may remain at the keep past the hour when the town gates close, so do not expect me."

The dame held up a plump hand. "Only know you are welcome."

"Thank you," Gareth muttered. "I return your chamber to you, mistress," he added, avoiding Arianna's blue eyes.

"We can set up a cot in Charles's chamber," William began, oblivious to the venomous stare his apprentice directed at him.

"I'd not dream of crowding Master Beck," Gareth said evenly, though his belly clenched at the thought of spending the night breathing the air Charles exhaled. There was something about the man's tone and manner that reminded him of a viper. A well-oiled viper. "I will sleep with my horse that I may start early."

"And undo all my hard work by taking a chill? Absolutely not," exclaimed Dame Cicily. "You will sleep on a pallet here in the solar where 'tis warm."

Much as Gareth disliked being ordered about by a woman, agreeing with her was easier than arguing. And he did not really care where he slept as long as it was not with Charles, or between the lavender-scented sheets that made him wonder what it would be like to taste Arianna's skin.

Soon afterward, Dame Cicily and William retired to their separate chambers opening off the solar.

While the knight prepared his pallet before the hearth, Ari trailed after her aunt. "Aunt Cici, what do you know of men?"

"Men in general, or Sir Garvey in particular?"

Ari sighed. "He is not like anyone I have ever known. Most times he makes me so angry I could spit. And I do likewise with him, I think. But sometimes . . ."

"Sometimes?" Dame Cicily echoed, smiling gently.

I have the strangest urge to touch him. Only she couldn't say that. "He would make an interesting subject for a statue."

"Oh?" her aunt said knowingly.

"Never mind." Ari shook the thought away, kissed her aunt's wrinkled cheek and went off to bed. But not to sleep. The lingering feeling that something precious was growing between herself and the cold, remote knight persisted.

After bidding everyone good sleep, Charles went downstairs. Normally he waited a few hours to make certain everyone was asleep, then he snuck out to the caves. The guard at the little-used gate in the worst section of town was only too eager to accept a coin in exchange for letting a man out. His orders, after all, were to keep unwanted intruders from getting in.

Purely by rote, Charles checked to make certain the doors were locked and the windows barred. Crime was not a large problem in town, but people assumed a goldsmith kept a fortune in his strongboxes, so Marsden liked everything shut up tight. Fortunately for Hugh Harcourt's scheme, Marsden had entrusted Charles with the keeping of the inventory.

Charles crawled under the workbench and pulled out the locked boxes until he came to the one shoved way in the back. Unlocking it, he carefully counted the small bars of gold and silver, though he knew he'd have heard of it if Marsden had discovered the shortage.

As he worked, Charles chewed on the problem of Sir Garvey. The hireling was the opposite of what Charles had expected. Young, handsome, polished and assured. Charles had long studied the habits of his betters in order to mimic them, and Sir Garvey fairly stank of wealth and noble breeding. If the man had been thrust into the role of mercenary, Charles would bet his last, albeit false, coin it was a recent development.

Not that he cared why Sir Garvey had fallen on hard times. He had only one worry. What if Sir Garvey took an interest in Ari? Hell, the bastard had cast his eyes on her at supper. Charles's blood ran cold as he recalled the terrible moment. Knights, even penniless ones, were an arrogant lot who thought all females fair game. Ari was so naive she'd not even know what the knight was about until her skirts were up and the deed done.

Charles's gaze narrowed. Knights were not the only ones who could play at that game. His mind churning with plans of his own, he hid the bit of gold he'd use tonight in his tunic, put the boxes back as they'd been and hurried off to the caves.

The sun had been up an hour when Gareth approached the gates of Tyneham Keep and demanded admittance. A head poked over the top of the wall, sunlight glinting on a round steel helmet. "State yer name." Behind the man, Gareth saw several more.

In such troubled times, the show of strength and caution pleased Gareth, but his admiration had worn thin by the time he'd yelled his name—his assumed name—twice more to two different soldiers. "Farley will know me," he shouted at last.

"Farley's on the cliffs at Grassy Point," the man replied.

"I know the way," Gareth called, and turned Apollo around.

Tyneham Keep was virtually unassailable, situated as it was on a rocky promontory, its back at the lip of the cliff, facing the sea. The only approach was a path atop a narrow causeway. A few hundred feet beyond the keep, a trail ran down one side of the causeway, then along the edge of the cliffs.

Gareth took the trail, thankful he'd given Apollo a chance to run off some of his energy earlier. Used to a daily workout, the stallion had been frisky after his long confinement in the hut, and the cliffs were no place to take a spirited mount.

Hundreds of feet high, Tyneham Cliffs ran for miles, curving in and out to form small bays. Near the keep the cliffs presented a sheer rock wall to any who came from the sea. Had the smugglers somehow found a way up it?

Gareth knew how treacherous conquering the cliff could be. On an earlier visit here, he had leaned over the edge to pluck a young hawk from its nest, lost his footing and nearly fallen into the sea. Pausing, he looked over the edge and caught a dizzying glimpse of the narrow beach and the surf frothing around half-submerged rocks. Landing a boat here, even a small fishing boat, would not be easy, he thought as he rode on.

Grassy Point faced the keep across the neck of Tyneham Bay. At the point, the lay of the land was very different, level and grassy as the name implied. No keep had been built here, but there was a large demesne farm belonging to Tyneham.

Gareth found Farley on the cliff, gazing at the keep across a stretch of choppy gray water. With him, pointing and talking, was Rob Elgen, the shrewd old man whose family had held Grassy Point farms of the Sommervilles for six generations. Gareth had spent time here on a visit seven years ago.

Dismounting and keeping his helmet on to hide his face from Elgen, Gareth walked up to them. "Farley..."

The captain whirled, his hand falling to his sword hilt. "Ah. Master Marsden said ye were like to live. What do ye here?"

"I have come to help you find Sir Neil's killer."

Farley grunted, his expression as he assessed Gareth's dented helm, torn mail and stained surcoat saying how little value he thought Gareth's help would be. It rankled as surely as the look Ruarke wore when Gareth entered the training grounds.

"My mind is clear, even if I'm not back to fighting strength," Gareth said tightly.

"Ye were a fool ta tire yerself riding all the way here," Farley grumbled. "We've nary a clue."

"What about the messenger?"

"The potboy was the only one who saw him—big man in dark clothes, a stranger."

"Did the boy not think it odd a stranger would demand to see Sir Neil on his wedding night?"

"Ye did," Farley reminded him with a hard stare.

Great, next he'd find himself accused of Sir Neil's murder.

"Besides, potboys take orders, they don't ask questions. Speakin' of which." Farley's gaze sharpened. "How came ye to Tyneham just in time to find Sir Neil dead?"

Gareth felt tired suddenly, remembering all that had happened that day. The air inside his helmet was stifling. He longed to remove it and lift his face to the cool wind coming off the bay, but Elgen watched him as closely as Farley did.

Gareth stepped to a huge rock a pace away and leaned his mailed back into the cool surface as he spun an altered version of the attack. "When I regained my wits, I found myself under a dead horse," he said at the end of the telling. "I'd be there still if Farmer Owen had not come along."

Farley nodded and relaxed his stance slightly. "Do ye think those who ambushed ye could have been smugglers?"

"They were trained fighting men," Gareth replied. *Looking for a Sommerville.* He wondered again if they'd been Harcourts. Nay, fighting, even from ambush, wasn't the style favored by Lord Edmund Harcourt or Hugh, his whelp. Deceit and treachery were their weapons of choice.

Two years ago, Edmund had tried to use both to bring down the Sommervilles. It had taken his brother Ruarke's brawn and Gaby's wit to thwart Edmund's efforts. The flames of the feud had died down after that, but they glowed like a banked fire in the minds of every Sommerville and Harcourt.

Nay, the Harcourts were likely far away in their stronghold, counting their ill-gotten gold and plotting to get more.

"Are you certain there are smugglers operating here?" Gareth asked. "William says Sir Richard was not convinced of that."

"Aye." Farley looked across the bay. "Elgen and his people have seen lights on the cliffs."

Gareth straightened. "Sir Richard was looking into that the night he was killed."

Elgen spoke up, "Aye, one o' me boys found his body the next morn. Saw a speck o' color on the rocks near Tyneham Keep that didn't look right. Poor Sir Richard lay wi' his throat cut."

Just like Sir Neil. "Where were these lights?"

"It's hard ta say exactly, but they look ta be halfway down the cliff," Elgen said slowly.

Gareth stared at the seemingly impregnable wall of rock rising from the sea. "I recall the keep was built on the ruins of an ancient Danish fortress. Are there any passageways leading down inside the cliffs?"

"Nay, the old storerooms and dungeon the Danes dug beneath the fort are still in use," Farley said. "But no tunnels, nor any trails down the face of the cliff, either. I had men lowered over the edge on ropes. They found nothin' but birds' nests."

"Tyneham is near smooth," Elgen interjected. "But Grassy Point, here, is pockmarked wi' handholds and trails so a child could walk down it. Which is why the ancient ones built their fort across the way instead o' here. The only caves I know of on the Tyneham side are down on the beach," Elgen added. "In my Da's time, the local lads used ta play in them. A pair o' them tarried too long—got caught by the tide and dragged out ta sea. No one goes down there now."

Apparently someone did, Gareth thought. And what better place for smugglers to lurk than in caves the locals avoided. But that still didn't solve the riddle of the lights on the cliff face. "Have there been lights since Sir Richard's death?"

Elgen nodded. "Aye. Every night. Sometimes they're dim, sometimes they move, like someone was walkin' about on the face of the cliff."

"In the dark?" Gareth studied the sheer rock. "That seems impossible, even if they had ropes tied around their waists."

"It's spirits," Elgen murmured.

"And spirits sailin' the ship we've seen in the bay, too?" Farley asked in disgust. "It's come each week since Sir Richard died. Always on a Monday, between ten and midnight. Sir Neil asked Elgen and his people to keep this quiet," the captain added. "Didn't want to alarm everyone till we knew what was up."

"What about tracks?" Gareth wanted to know. "Smugglers would have to have wagons to move the wool." Wool being the most obvious and lucrative item to smuggle from this area.

Elgen shook his head. "Nary a sign o' horses or wagons. Not before or since Sir Richard got himself killed."

So, why had Richard and Sir Neil been killed? And by whom? Gareth wondered. His heart contracted at the memory of Arianna's pain when she'd talked about losing the people she'd loved. Pain but no tears. Oddly her bravery made him more determined than ever to catch and punish whoever had killed the two knights.

"Tyneham isn't a good place fer smugglin' anyway," Elgen said. "There's safe anchorage and an easier way to the beach a mile down the coast. A man'd be plain stupid ta risk these cliffs and the tides around the rocks."

"So, what do you make of all this?" Gareth asked slowly.

Farley shrugged. "Damned if I know. Show me a wall to defend, a hill to take, and I will tell ye the best way to go about it, but this . . ."

"Could someone at Tyneham Keep be involved?"

"Nay. When we first saw the lights, Sir Richard bade me watch the men and servants closely. We used the excuse of the increased danger to close everyone in the keep at night."

"How about the town?"

"Ah, that is another matter," Farley growled. "I wanted to conduct a house-to-house search, but Sir Neil and Sir Richard were both against it. No matter their instructions, soldiers ofttimes become . . . overeager. They rough up a man for not answering their questions, kiss a likely wench, steal a flagon o' wine, and next thing ye know, Alderman Arley is banging on the gates o' the keep demandin' retribution. Sir Neil did not want the people overset."

"You think the townspeople know something?"

"They always do," Farley grumbled. "The merchants know who has extra coin to spend. Neighbors see who is away at night. And the trash, the whores and thieves who roam around at night know everyone's business. True, a troop of soldiers would disturb the peace, but one man . . ." He glanced at Gareth. "Especially a man livin' wi' one o' their own whilst his wounds heal . . ."

"Ye could find out more'n Farley, that's sure," Elgen said. Gareth groaned like a man doomed. "Then I guess it's back to Marsden's house for me." And back into Arianna's web.

Chapter Six

"Ari will never agree to wed him," Dame Cicily said firmly.

Though she didn't normally stoop to eavesdropping, Ari couldn't resist pausing outside the partially open door to the workroom. Were they discussing Sir Garvey? Despite her efforts to remain calm, her heart beat a little faster.

"He's a likely suitor," her grandfather huffed. "Not too old, and with his future secured."

That eliminated the knight, Ari thought glumly.

"Aye, but she'll not want to leave us and move to Norwich."

Nay, she would not. Ari could stand the suspense no longer. Bursting into the room, she blurted out, "Who is it?"

"Why, John Woolmonger," her grandfather replied.

Arianna recoiled. She opened her mouth to protest, but no sound came out.

"Why your look of fear, child?" he quickly asked, gathering one of her cold hands in his large, callused palm. "John seems a gentle man. Nor are his prospects easily dismissed. He will inherit his sire's prosperous wool and cloth trade."

"Not if he weds me, he won't," Ari cried. "I'll ruin him. His sire will disinherit him."

"Who told you that?"

Ari cast desperate eyes at her aunt. "No one had to."

Dame Cicily frowned. Though Ari had never voiced her fears aloud, the old woman knew what troubled her niece. "The Woolmongers are *reasonable* people."

"But arrogant. When Master Woolmonger and John came to purchase household items and jewelry for Madam Woolmonger, the old man looked down his nose at us."

Dame Cicily snorted. "He's very tall."

"Ari? Cici? What is this all about?" William asked.

Unwilling to hurt her grandfather by bringing up the past, Arianna studied the pointed toes of her shoes.

"'Tis because Richard's family treated Alys so badly when she and Richard went to live with them," Dame Cicily said.

William winced. "I'd not excuse what the Baron de Clerc did to Alys, and to Richard, too, his own son. Nay it turns my stomach to recall my dear daughter's pitiful condition when she and Richard finally made their way back to Tyneham. But the case with John is not the same at all. Richard's sire was a baron, and Richard angered him by wedding Alys without permission. John's father knows of his intention to wed Ari."

"I should think Master Woolmonger would want his son and heir to choose someone from their own guild," Ari retorted.

Her grandfather shrugged the comment aside. "'Tis not unknown for a man to marry outside his craft."

I don't love him, Ari wanted to shout, but she hadn't loved Sir Neil, either. "What could I bring them besides the ability to bear children?" she cried in despair. "They'd not let me continue with my goldsmithing, nor could I keep house. And I don't know the first thing about cloth or sewing." She'd be nothing, a valueless thing. "Please don't make me wed him."

"Oh, child of my heart." He wrapped her in his arms. "You know I'd not force you did you not wish it, but . . ."

"Thank you, Grandfather." Ari burrowed her face into his stiff old work apron, inhaling the familiar scent of metal. "I'd not move so far away from you and Aunt Cici, either."

"'Tis just as well, then, that I did not encourage John when he came to the workroom yesterday and asked how long you would mourn Sir Neil," her grandfather muttered.

Ari gratefully seized on the change of subject. Leaning back in his arms, she asked. "How long *should* I mourn?"

"I don't know," her aunt replied. "You were only married for a—a few hours. I will ask Dame Arley for her opinion."

It was William's turn to sigh. "Our funds are running short, and I'd see you settled afore long. If no other prospect presents itself soon, I may ask you to reconsider young John."

"Please don't."

"Nothing need be decided this morn," Cici said soothingly. "Come with me while I open the shop," she bade Ari.

Ari kissed her grandsire's leathery cheek and fled.

"Is there no one who has taken your interest?" her aunt asked when they had reached the shop in the front of the house. "Not Charles, perhaps?"

"Charles is like a brother to me," Ari replied, pacing the confines of the small room, her finger idly touching a crock of salve here, a string of dried herbs there.

"What of Sir Garvey?"

Ari whirled, her heart pounding, her chest tight with that strange yearning feeling she experienced whenever she thought of the knight. Nay, but she must not think of the knight. "Sir Garvey is gone now."

"Only as far as Tyneham," Cici drawled. "He could return at any time." She chuckled as Ari's eyes flew to the door. "Sir Garvey seems unlikely to terrorize you by suddenly becoming wealthy and powerful."

"Don't mock me!" Ari cried.

Cici sighed. "I am sorry, child. I'd not hurt you for the world, but you must see your fears are groundless."

"What happened to my parents was real. My earliest memories are of my mother crying endlessly for having ruined my father."

"You are stronger than your mother, and not all people are like the de Clercs," her aunt insisted, but Ari was not soothed.

What they needed was money enough to see them through until she could find someone she could safely wed. But where to get the money. *The cup.* She perked up, the drinking cup she had been sketching earlier suddenly becoming a set of twelve. With a large matching bowl to hold spiced wine. If Master Hollton did not want the set, mayhap they could take it to Norwich to sell at the Great Fair. Was there enough raw metal, silver, gold and bronze in the strongboxes for her purpose? she wondered.

One last project produced under her grandfather's mark. Why had she not thought of it sooner?

"Where are you going, Arianna?" her aunt called.

Ari turned at the door, not having realized she had moved. "I . . ." Her grandfather wouldn't approve. She agreed with him—in principle. But these were desperate times. Besides, if she said she was going to the forest to sketch a stag because the knight had laughed at hers and the cups must be perfect, her aunt would protest and remind Ari she'd never been to the woods, never been far from her own neighborhood or outside the town walls except to go to the keep. And then never alone. "I thought I'd take a walk and think on your words," she said lamely.

Her aunt raised a skeptical brow. "See you don't go far."

"Aye." The lie hung heavy on Ari's conscience as she darted away. Grabbing her cloak from a peg in the hall, parchment and charcoal from the kitchen table, she left by the back door. As she rounded the corner of the house, she ran into Charles.

"Sorry," he muttered, taking her elbow to steady her. "Where are you going in such a hurry?"

"Going?" More questions, more lies. She wasn't good at this.

Charles gave her a little shake. "Pay attention. I asked where you were going in such a hurry."

Ari smiled, determined to brazen this out. "To the woods."

"To the woods? By yourself?" He frowned his disapproval.

"Aye. By myself." Stubbornly.

An odd expression flickered in Charles's eyes. "Interesting. Aren't you afraid you might meet up with some man who'd try to force his attentions on you?"

"I hadn't thought about that," Arianna said slowly. Her aunt and grandfather were always accusing Ari of leaping before she looked. This time she would act cautiously. "Would you come with me, Charles?"

"Of course," Charles said silkily. He offered her his arm, smiling smugly when she took it. *And by the time we return we will know each other a great deal better, and I'll not have to wait weeks to have what I want.*

"I appreciate your doing this. Let me tell you why we are going." Ari glanced over her shoulder at the house, then back to whisper, "I want to sketch a stag." She started to tell him the rest, but Charles hurried her toward the street.

"I am more than happy to accommodate you in any way I can." He chuckled as though he had made a jest.

Arianna saw nothing funny in his words, but smiled because his feelings were easily hurt. Remembering how annoyed he had been when she'd married Sir Neil, she decided to keep her project secret from him, too. If, God forbid, she couldn't get enough for the pieces, Charles would be almost as upset as she'd be herself when she was forced to marry John Woolmonger.

That decided, Ari started to notice her surroundings. The street was narrow and rutted with dried mud, crowded on either side by houses and shops that slumped against each other for support. Drab and tired best described the area and the people, she thought, watching the townsfolk trudge by, eyes on the ground, shoulders bent beneath heavy bundles.

Over everything hung a cloud of misery thicker than the dust kicked up by a passing cart. "How much goes to the earl?" she asked Charles.

"How much what?" he asked without stopping.

Arianna repeated her question, but Charles still did not understand, and she ground her teeth in frustration. Charles's brain often trod a different path from hers. She reminded herself that few people had the perception she and her aunt had, remembered instead that the knight had been quick enough to follow her thoughts on more than one occasion. But he was gone.

She sighed with regret and stopped in the middle of the street to repeat last night's conversation about Lord Geoffrey and the tallage.

"The earl leaves only enough to keep the people alive so they can earn more," Charles grumbled.

Surely that couldn't be true. Her grandfather had said good things about the earl. "But the aldermen have fine homes." Her grandfather had a fine home—for the moment.

"Bah! The merchants are as bad as the nobles. Though this labor shortage has made them all notice the peasants for the first time, if only to pass those bloody labor statutes."

"What are they?"

"Laws that say workers will only be paid what was given before so many of them died, not what they can get now that there is greater demand for their skills." He took her arm and hustled her along. "Such things don't concern a woman, anyway."

"Why not?"

"Because everything belongs to her father or her husband."

"But a woman's sweat goes into earning the money," she said hotly, remembering how hard she had worked. If she had known even a small portion went to some fat, greedy earl . . .

"It belongs to her husband."

"That's not fair." Ari stopped again.

"You are right, of course," Charles said smoothly. "I have just told you what most men believe."

"What do you believe?" she asked sharply.

"Why, that a couple should share the work and the profits," Charles lied. His smile widened when she relaxed and resumed walking. *Naive as a sheep being led to the slaughter.* "There are the woods," he said silkily, pausing just outside the gate.

A quiver of excitement went through Ari as she stared at the dark green mass in the distance. "How far is it?"

"About half a mile, I think."

"Have you ever been there?" she asked, hearing a hint of uncertainty in his tone.

"Nay, but it lies directly ahead. We can't get lost." He started down the road.

"Do you think we'll find a stag?" Ari asked as she skipped along beside him.

"I think we will find everything we need." Had the glint in his eyes intensified, or was it the reflection of the sun?

Arianna chattered all the way to the woods, but Charles seemed not to mind. He patiently answered her questions as best he could, though she suspected he knew no more than she did about the world outside the town.

"Oh, it's so cool and dark," she said as they stepped inside the tree line. "Look how deep and intense the colors are."

Charles muttered something about sitting down, but Ari walked deeper into the woods, still following the trail that had led from the road into the forest. "We need to find a stream."

"Arianna, stop a moment," he called after her.

"Nay. I think I hear water up ahead." Clutching the parchment tighter, she hurried along. Overhead, birds squawked and winged away; in the thick brush bordering the path, twigs snapped and leaves rustled. She paid no attention to the sounds, her attention focused on drinking in the colors and shapes.

A few minutes later, she burst through the trees into a small clearing. In the center was a huge water puddle as smooth and shiny as a polished silver mirror. A fat brown bird floated on it, followed by a half-dozen tiny yellow creatures. "Oh. What are these beautiful little birds?" She whispered so as not to disturb the tranquility of the scene.

Charles came up behind her and slipped an arm around her waist. "You are the beautiful little bird." His breath fanned her cheek, reeking of stale ale.

She shuddered and tried to move away, but his grip tightened. "Please, Charles, we have to find the stag."

"I'll be the stag and you my little doe," he murmured. "Shall we frolic in the stream?"

"What a silly thing to say." She frowned at him over her shoulder. "You can release me. I'm not in any danger of falling into the water."

"I have no intention of releasing you until—"

The rest of Charles's words were drowned out by an angry, high-pitched squeal. Turning toward it, Ari saw the biggest, ugliest pig she had ever seen, glaring at them from the forest's edge.

"My, God, it's a boar!" Charles cried.

"Sir Garvey was right. My stag did resemble this creature. Mayhap I'll draw it." She began to unroll the parchment.

"Draw it," Charles shrieked. "We've no time for that. Run before the damned thing attacks."

As if to punctuate his statement, the boar pawed the ground with sharp-looking hooves. Lowering its head, it took several prancing steps toward them.

"Run!" Charles screamed. "It'll rip us to pieces...." Without waiting to see if she followed, he fled back down the path.

The pig took two steps after Charles, then stopped, swinging its head at Ari and snorting loudly.

Fear raised the hair on her arms, sent her heart racing. "Mayhap if I stand still it will go away," she murmured.

It didn't. For what seemed like hours, she and the boar stared at each other, neither blinking. Its tiny red eyes probed her as though looking for some weakness. The leaf-filtered light shone faintly on the wickedly curved tusks protruding from either side of its long hairy snout.

Charles's departing statement about the boar ripping them to pieces rang over and over in her head, making her shiver each time. She didn't blame him for leaving but wished he had waited a second for her. Had he gone for help? How long would it take?

The boar snorted and shifted its stance. Ari backed up a step. The boar stalked closer; she retreated until she slammed into a tree. With a porcine squeal of triumph, it charged.

Screaming in terror, Ari dropped the parchment, lifted her skirts and ran for her life.

Gareth groaned as he reined in beside the Marsden's hut. Jesu, but he felt weak. His side ached; his head ached.

Sim ran out and reached for Apollo's bridle. "Ye're back. But ye don't look so good, Sir Garvey," the lad observed.

"Just tired," Gareth grunted in reply and slid down off the stallion. "Did too much, but don't tell Dame Cicily I said so." He was not sorry he'd gone. Having *some* plan of action made him feel better. Good thing he hadn't burned his bridges with the Marsdens by storming off last night. "Is Master William within?"

Sim shook his head. "Him and Dame Cicily went to Alderman Arley's. Mistress Arianna and Master Charles left near an hour ago, and ain't back yet," he added darkly.

Gareth tried to ignore the sudden, possessive tightening in his chest. "So?" he demanded sullenly.

"The mistress never goes out."

"Never?" What was she, a hermit? 'Twould explain her unusually pale skin, though, he supposed.

"Nay, she never goes out. Stays inside, she does, makin'..." Sim frowned. "Well, never ye mind that, she just stays in."

"Perhaps they've gone to the market." That jumped up apprentice was probably buying her trinkets while *he* was trying to find out who had killed her late husband.

"Nay. Followed them as far as the South Gate."

Gareth straightened. "Were they going to Tyneham Keep?"

"Nay, that's the *North* Gate. Out the South Gate's the road to Norwich. There's naught between Tyneham and Norwich but fields and woods."

"Woods." An icy finger touched the back of Gareth's neck. "Could they have gone to pick herbs for Dame Cicily?"

Sim snorted. "Mistress Arianna would not know mint from mistletoe, and him..." The boy made an even ruder sound. "The farthest *he's* gone from the house is the ale shop where he meets that brother o' his. He were there this noon."

"You followed him there?"

"Smelled ale on his breath."

It occurred to Gareth that Sim might prove helpful in locating these smugglers. But that was for later. "I have an idea Mistress Arianna may have gone into the woods to see if she could find a stag."

"A stag?"

"She wants to draw one for some cup."

Sim's scowl deepened. "She shouldn't ha' gone off into the woods wi' just *him*."

Gareth could not have agreed more, though he guessed their reasons differed. "I'll bring her back." He pulled himself up onto Apollo, the air whistling out between his teeth as the ache in his side became a lancing pain.

Sim wanted to come, but Gareth left him behind with orders to send help if he had not returned in an hour. Jesu, but he hoped he had another hour in him, Gareth thought.

The woods were dark and cool after the heat of the afternoon sun. Gareth had put his helmet on when he left the town, but he removed it now the better to hear and smell. His sword, he left unsheathed, lying at the ready across his thighs. Birds cried overhead, gliding from branch to branch like advance scouts. In the brush that crowded the narrow trail, small animals scurried out of the way.

His eyes moved constantly, following each noise and movement, his nerves and muscles on alert. Even though he didn't know these particular woods, the familiar scents and sounds boosted his confidence. The woods were his domain; he was as at home in the fields and forests as Ruarke was on a battlefield, as Alex was on the deck of a ship. If Arianna and Charles had come here, he would find them.

Following Sim's directions, Gareth located the pool in a secluded glade. For a moment he remained inside the tree line, scanning the area with a practiced eye. All was quiet. On the far bank, a mother duck led a line of ducklings to the water and hopped in.

As Gareth kneed Apollo into the clearing, the ducks scrambled for the rushes. He smiled at the downy yellow faces peering out at him. How they'd have delighted Arianna.

Apollo made to put his head down for a drink, snorted and shied back two steps.

"Whoa, boy...what is it?" Gareth signaled him ahead, but the stallion balked. As he leaned down to see what had unsettled the horse, Gareth saw cloven-hoof marks on the muddy bank.

Boar. Fresh tracks by the look.

To dismount would be suicide. He stood in the stirrups. The tracks led to the left. Gareth followed, noting two spots where the beast had pawed the ground. Not a good sign. The boar was after something.

A quarter of the way around the pond, he saw something white in the grass. Leaning down, he speared it with his sword. A piece of parchment, torn and muddied by the boar's hooves.

Arianna.

For an instant, his mind went black and his body iced with fear. Apollo snorted and shook his head, responding to the tension in his rider's body.

Gareth straightened in the saddle and called her name at the top of his lungs. The trees before him swallowed up the sound, and the birds took flight, flapping and shrieking.

"Easy," Gareth said, more to himself than the horse. This time, Apollo responded when Gareth urged him on, realizing the stink in his nostrils was the enemy and they were on the hunt.

The trail of grass flattened and earth ripped up by the boar's furious passage was easy to follow. He imagined Ari's terror as she fled before the maddened beast, and his gut coiled tighter. Briefly he wondered if Charles knew how to use a sword, if he even had one with him.

Dear God, he once had seen a pack of hunting dogs torn apart by a boar. He dared not even think what this one might do to small, defenseless Arianna.

Ahead, the trees thinned, and they burst into a small clearing. Gareth had a quick impression of grassy meadow and a towering tumble of black rocks.

"Here," a voice called, muffled by his pounding pulse.

Gareth pulled the stallion to a halt, twisted to the right.

"Here," Ari cried again, waving to him from atop a rock.

Gareth could scarcely believe his eyes. He kneed Apollo into motion, clearing the distance and dismounting in an instant. In the same moment, Ari had scrambled down and threw herself into his arms. To Gareth, it seemed a lifetime. It seemed his heart had stopped beating when he found the parchment and only started again when he had her safe. He wrapped himself around her, drawing in gulps of air. She felt so tiny, so vulnerable, trembling in his embrace. His own body shook with delayed reaction. Relief. Fear. And something else he dared not examine too closely.

Ari raised her head from his chest, a pink dent in her cheek where it had been pressed into his mail. "I am glad to see you," she said shakily.

"Art thou all right?" His own voice was none too steady.

"I am now." She smiled that rich, dizzying smile. "Jesu, but I was frightened."

"As well you should have been. What were you thinking, going off like that?"

"You said my stag was terrible. I needed to see one."

His hands tightened on her. "You could have been killed!"

"But I was not." Ignoring latent tremors of fear, Ari smiled up at him. "And there is no need to shout at me."

"I'll do more than shout," he roared. "I'll turn you over my knee and paddle your sweet little—"

"You are not my father to be speaking to me so," she cried, struggling in his grasp.

"And you can thank heaven I am not." He hung on tighter. "I'd not have coddled you as they have."

"Coddled? Coddled!" Her voice rose to a wail. "I work right alongside my grandfather." She clenched her fist and swung at his belly.

Gareth caught her wrist in his left hand, twisting her arm behind her back, and slamming her flush against his body. "You little witch."

"It is your fault," she cried, tossing her tangled hair from her face. "You make me so angry I could . . ."

He stilled. "Could what?" His breath fanned her cheek, his eyes burned into hers. "What could you do?" His voice was low now, husky, with a silky note she had never heard before.

The sound ran through her like hot wind through the trees, rustling her insides. The pressure of his arm holding her so close she could scarcely breathe no longer imprisoned but embraced. "I don't know." she murmured, dazed and confused by the changes he had wrought in her.

"Don't know what? Don't know why we tear at each other?"

Ari nodded, watching the fire build in his midnight eyes, feeling it warm her clear to her toes. "But you do."

"Aye, I do." Tossing the sword aside, he brought his right hand up. The tips of his fingers brushed up her bare neck, then tunneled into her hair, cradling her head. "I know, but I don't know what the hell to do about it." His thumb massaged the sensitive skin below her earlobe.

Ari moaned and trembled, her eyes drifting shut. "You make me feel all shivery inside," she murmured.

He groaned, his left hand releasing her wrist to rub her back. "You shouldn't tell me that," he said without censure.

"Why? It's true."

"We both wish it weren't. It can lead nowhere." He caressed her neck until her head fell back and her knees turned to water so she had to grab hold of his shoulders to keep from falling.

"Only I can't stop wanting you, nor you me. That is what this is all about." His words whispered across her lips, their flavor mysterious and seductive.

The touch of his mouth on hers was light, fleeting, but it made them both shudder, and Ari felt the tension build in him as though he held himself back. She knew exactly how he felt, though she had no words, nothing in her experience to describe the hot, needful hunger building inside him...inside her, coiling so tight she could barely breathe.

"This is a mistake." His voice was as aching and raspy as her skin.

"It feels right being here in your arms."

"God, how I want you." His grip tightened. "More than I knew it was possible to want anything." His mouth closed over hers, warm, moist and incredibly stirring. She parted her lips to the first touch of his tongue, moaning at the seductive entanglement of texture and taste.

"Ari," Gareth growled into her mouth as he sank to his knees in the soft grass. It wasn't right, but it was what he needed, what they both wanted. She murmured something—assent? He wasn't sure, could barely hear her over his pounding pulse.

Nay, not his pulse...hooves. Thudding rhythmically. A maddened porcine squeal sounded nearby.

Gareth's head snapped up just as the boar stormed into the clearing. "Run for the rocks!" Scrambling to his feet, he shoved Ari behind him and reached for his sword. It lay several feet away, between himself and the hard-charging boar. There wasn't time to retrieve it and defend them against the boar's charge.

On instinct, Gareth crouched low. One eye gauged the distance to the sword, the other watched the boar. He'd wait until he could count the hairs on its ugly snout and smell its hot, foul breath, then . . .

"Run," Ari screamed. Moving so quickly he was a blur, Gareth dived out of the path of the speeding boar, tucked his body, rolled and somehow came up with the sword in his hand. "Watch out. He's coming again," Ari cried.

Gareth turned, chest heaving. Damn. His side felt as if it were on fire. Fighting desperation and his own abused body, he gripped the sword hilt in both hands and gathered what strength he could. The blow had to be perfect.

The earth shook as Apollo, forgotten in the heat of battle leaped between Gareth and the boar.

The pig halted, tiny eyes narrowed, nostrils flared to assess this new threat. That instant cost the boar its life.

Apollo screamed a challenge and struck out with a heavy hoof, catching the boar in the ribs and lifting it into the air. Legs milling, the beast hit the ground and bounced once. The stallion kicked it on the rebound, then jumped on it with all four hooves as it landed again.

Chapter Seven

Apollo stood quietly in the shallows of the pond as Gareth cleaned the gore from his legs.

"He seems very calm now," Arianna called from the bank.

"Looks can be deceiving." Gareth straightened and looked over at her. She sat on a rock in her torn green gown, her knees drawn up and her arms fastened about them, watching him with grave curiosity, apparently unconcerned with her smudged face and the leaves in her hair. She looked like a guileless urchin. Yet he remembered how seductively that slender body had melted against his, how sweetly that pink mouth had parted for his searching thrust.

Groaning, Gareth turned away. Looks could be as deceiving in a woman as in a horse, and just as deadly. "You mustn't forget that Apollo's trained to kill," he said harshly.

He was angry because he'd kissed her. The kiss had upset her, too, but it wasn't anger that warmed her blood every time she looked at his mouth and remembered the dizzying sensations that had surged through her at his touch. Would that it were. "You're very good with him."

"I raised him from a colt."

"And trained him to kill."

"It wasn't necessary." He patted Apollo on the rump and waded from the pond, water squishing from his boots. He should take them off, but it required more energy than he had at the moment. Lord, he was tired. Trembling slightly, he sat down on the rock farthest away from hers.

"Why wasn't it necessary?"

"Because he was sired by my brother's destrier. The grays are a fierce breed. Fighting is in their blood." *Just as cruelty is in a woman's.* "It takes a strong hand and a determined man to keep such an animal under control." *The same could be said for a woman.*

He had a brother. Ari stored the information away and got on to a more important question. "Why don't you like women?"

Gareth started. "What makes you say that?"

"Just a feeling," she said, shrugging.

He grunted and looked away from her.

Change of subject. "You are large and beautifully formed."

"And you are blunt, mistress," Gareth growled.

She didn't pretend to misunderstand. "You know I admire your body. I asked if I could sketch you."

"You must not say that to a man," he sputtered, wavering between insult and astonishment. The body she praised knew exactly how to react. Every muscle below his belt tightened.

"Oh? It seems a silly rule, but it is the horse I intended to discuss. As I said, you are large." She grinned teasingly. "Yet the horse dwarfs you. It must take courage and patience to curb such a beast without breaking its spirit."

Gareth seized on the compliment like a lifeline. "Gabrielle, my sister-by-marriage, says I have the temperament for training them that my impatient younger brother has not."

He disliked women, yet he spoke Gabrielle's name fondly. "I think it is your gentleness. I felt it when you held me in your arms and kissed me. Even when you put your tongue in my—"

"Mistress!" he exclaimed, his face red as fire.

Ari blinked, startled by the shame radiating from him. "Are tongues another thing I may not mention to a man?"

"Aye," he growled, propelling himself off the stone. "We must leave."

"Is it because of Emilie?" Ari blurted out.

"What?" he exclaimed, nearly stumbling in his shock. His gaze narrowed to a wary squint. "Where did you hear that name?"

His anger remained, but it had been joined now by pain and some deeper emotion she couldn't read. "You screamed it in your fevered ravings and cursed her for a foul bitch. Then you called to someone named Alex, begging him to raise his sword ere you be forced to do murder—"

"Enough!" he cried in an anguished voice. The word rang around the clearing as he turned away, shoving both hands into his hair and holding his head as though it might fly to pieces.

Drawn by his suffering, Arianna went to him, wrapped her arms around his trembling body and held tight. "I'm sorry. So sorry you were hurt," she whispered.

Spitting out a ripe oath, Gareth flung away from her. "You know nothing. *Nothing,* do you hear?" He stood with his back to her, trembling as the stallion had in the wake of the pig's death. "What else did I say?" he rasped, turning on her.

His eyes were terrible, dark, haunted pools of suffering. Ari shuddered and reached out her hand to him. "Let me help."

"Nay." More than pride made him shake off her offer. He never wanted to think on that horrible day again. Fists clenched, he growled, "Tell me what happened."

"Your shouts roused me from my pallet in the solar. I dashed into my room to help, but you were unconscious again."

"And your aunt?"

"She had stepped away to get fresh water, returning only as I left your bedside. I swear," Ari added fervently. Damn, her hasty tongue. "I had nearly forgotten the incident until a few moments ago when you looked so wretched."

Aye, wretched. Gareth drew in a deep, steadying breath, then let it out slowly. It didn't ease his pain, but, then, nothing did. "We'll speak of this no more. Come, 'tis time we returned."

"But you are still tired."

"I'll get no rest here," he snapped.

Ari raised a brow. Clearly another change of subjects was needed. "Have you been a breeder of horses all your life?"

"Nay." Curtly. He stalked toward the horse.

She scrambled to keep pace. "I am sorry that you only recently learned you were suited to it, but . . ."

His head swiveled around, fixing her with a stare that had shaken grown men. "Did I mention that when I was fevered, too?"

"Nay, you did not." She trembled but held her ground.

Gareth tried to ignore the growing respect he felt for her. "Then, why did you say that?" he demanded, hands on hips.

Arianna shrugged. "It was a guess."

The way she had *guessed* what he was going to say the night before? Gareth didn't like this at all. "You will stop guessing things about me, and stop digging into my past."

"Surely talking about the horses is safe enough."

"Has anyone ever told you that you talk too much?"

"Aye, frequently." She tipped her head and smiled up at him. "Grandfather says I stood in line twice when they were passing out curiosity. But there is so much to learn, and how will I find out anything if I don't ask questions?"

Gareth hated it when her inane comments made sense. "Stand aside while I lead Apollo from the water," he commanded, reaching for the stallion's reins.

"Shouldn't we wait here for Charles?"

Damn. He'd nearly forgotten about the apprentice. "Where is he? Why wasn't he with you?"

"When the pig charged, Charles ran one way, and I another. I suppose he has gone for help," she added lamely.

"Humph. More like he is still running." Gareth supposed it was too much to hope that the boar had finished the apprentice off before coming after Arianna.

Apollo stepped from the pond and shook like a large hound, sending water in all directions. Arianna backed away from the spray, absently wiping the droplets from her skirt.

"I fear Charles is not very reliable. I'll have to take him from my list of marriage prospects," she joked.

Gareth's eyes narrowed. "Because he is not wealthy?"

"Nay. In fact, that is in his favor." The knight grunted in disbelief, but Ari hurried on lest he question her statement. "I'd not wed a man who runs off at the first sign of trouble."

How easily she spoke of marrying again. How heavily the same prospect weighed on his spirit. "Which brings us back to why you were here afoot and unarmed?"

"Why, looking for a stag to sketch," she replied as though it should be perfectly obvious.

Gareth raised one brow. "Why this obsession with sketching?"

"Because..." *Think. Think.* "Because I am an artist," she said with a dramatic wave of her hand.

"What do you do with these drawings?"

"Do?"

"What purpose do they serve?"

"They...they are beautiful to look at, and are religious in nature," she added, thinking of the reliquary.

"Impractical," he announced.

Arianna bristled. "Everything need not be practical."

"If it isn't, why have it?"

"To look at." She thought of the silver medallions inlaid with lapis she had made to decorate Master Arley's Bible. "To simply enjoy."

He made a sound of disgust as he swung into the saddle. "Gaby has a weakness for bright colors and pretty things, but at least she weaves them into wall hangings to keep out the drafts. Come here, and I will lift you up."

So, this Gabrielle was perfect. "I do not wish to ride with you." She crossed her arms and glared up at him.

"How like a woman to sulk for a criticism."

'Twas on the tip of her tongue to ask if that had been Emilie's crime, but she was not such a fool. "I am not sulking. I am trying to decide which I hate worse, your unfair attitude toward females or your lack of appreciation for beauty."

He scowled blackly. "'Tis a long way back, and I am too weary to ride beside you while you walk."

"No doubt Gabrielle's wall hangings are ugly, but useful."

"Some people account them pretty," he allowed.

"But not you?"

Gareth shrugged. "I am too busy to take note of such things. Now let us go back. Your family will be worried about you."

It was the one inducement Arianna couldn't ignore, though she thought it sad that he had no time to notice the beauty around him. Once he had her settled before him, she told him so. They were still arguing the merits of practical versus beautiful when they emerged from the forest and ran into Charles and a rescue party armed with knives and stout sticks.

Gareth's nagging concern with how he was going to worm his way back into the Marsden household he'd so ungraciously left dissolved the minute he drew rein beside the hut.

"Ye found her!" Sim cried, hurtling down the garden path with Dame Cicily and Master William in his wake.

Their exclamations of joy ringing in his ears, Gareth lowered Arianna to the ground. As her feet touched the ground, she looked up at him, and their eyes met, locked.

"Thank you," she murmured. There was gratitude and more in her steady blue gaze, soft things that drew on him as keenly as the beauty he mistrusted. "Don't worry I'll say anything about—well, you know. Despite what you may think, I do understand what it's like to have something too terrible to share."

Too terrible to share. Gareth opened his mouth to ask what she meant, but she was immediately surrounded by her two elderly relatives. They clucked over their chick so they reminded him of his own parents waiting at Ransford.

Three days had passed since Farley had sent word to Ransford of Sir Neil's death. Why hadn't his father sent someone to Tyneham? As though sensing his agitation, Apollo shifted his feet nervously.

Sim sprang forward and took the bridle, dragging down on Apollo's head with his good arm, his other hand stroking the stallion's neck to quiet him.

"He needs rubbing down," Gareth said as he swung from the saddle, his teeth clenched to keep back a moan. His knees nearly buckled, and he steadied himself with a hand to Apollo's flank.

"What's this?" Sim said. "There's blood on his shoulder."

"Not his, the boar's, I think," Gareth said.

"Boar!" Dame Cicily and William exclaimed together.

"A boar chased me, and Sir Garvey rescued me," Arianna explained, the smile she sent her champion dazzling.

"Apollo deserves the credit," Gareth protested weakly, the pounding in his temples and the weakness in his legs increasing as swiftly as his discomfort over the incident.

Ari countered his denial, her words flowing so swiftly as she described the incident he felt dizzier still. It wasn't true. He hadn't been quick or brave or any of the things she claimed. It was his fault she'd gone to the woods in search of a stag, and thanks to his uncontrolled lust, they would both have been injured or killed if not for Apollo. The thought of her slim body mangled by the boar's hooves made him sway.

"Easy, lad, you're pale as new snow." William slipped his shoulder under Gareth's armpit. "Ari, take his other side."

Gareth started to protest again, but Dame Cicily shushed him with a fierce word. "You should have been abed," the old woman scolded as the other two struggled to bear Gareth's weight down the garden walk. "Not out rescuing foolish girls with no better sense than to go to the woods alone."

"I wasn't alone," Arianna grumbled. "Charles went with me."

"And where is he now?" William demanded.

"He said he'd promised the men from the alehouse a keg of beer if they helped rescue me," Ari replied. "There was no need for their services, but they expected payment just the same."

"And he was no doubt ashamed to show his face here after running off and leaving you," Dame Cicily muttered.

"He did attempt a rescue," Ari said, tightening her grip on Gareth's waist.

How odd to be leaning on a woman, Gareth mused. Emilie had thought only of her own well-being. Yet after their conversation in the woods, he felt vulnerable to Ari and wanted to refuse her help, even though it was all he could do to put one foot before the other. Abruptly he stopped walking. "I'm too heavy for you."

"No. No, you aren't." Lifting her chin, she urged him on.

Despite his reservations, he hadn't the strength to argue. Somehow they managed to get him up the stairs and into Ari's bed. He protested that, too, and was shouted down by all three of them. Between them, William and Dame Cicily unarmed and undressed him while Arianna went off to fetch her aunt's medicine chest. By the time she returned, he was decently tucked beneath the sheets. Another blessing. No matter his exhaustion, he couldn't prevent his body from stirring at the sight of her.

He closed his eyes to shut out the adoring smile he ill deserved, and fell asleep between one troubled breath and the next. When he awoke he was alone, with a candle burning beside the bed and the sounds of clanking cutlery filtering in from the solar. Judging by that and the darkness outside the window, he guessed it must be supper time. He'd slept three or four hours and felt curiously refreshed.

And hungry. Absolutely starving. He struggled into his clothes, which someone had brushed and left neatly folded on the trunk beneath the window.

The maid was just lifting the tray of dishes when he opened the chamber door. She started, her eyes wide with fear. Gareth winced, anticipating a scream and a crash when she dropped the tray. Neither came. Instead, she lowered the tray to the table, uncovered a bowl of stew and a plate of cheese and bread, setting them at the place that had been his the night before.

Gareth blinked. "You saved that for me?"

Grizel nodded, smiling shyly but with unmistakable gratitude.

Damn. He didn't deserve this, but the girl watched him with the wariness of a fawn ready to bolt, so instead of arguing, he thanked her in his softest voice. Her smile broadened, but when he started forward, she paled, snatched up the tray and fled.

Gareth shook his head. What a strange girl. He had supposed all mutes were witless freaks. Yet, despite her fears, Grizel seemed intelligent, and the food she turned out was every bit as tasty as the meals Gaby's excellent cook prepared.

Mayhap he could induce the maid to return to Ransford with him when he left, Gareth mused as he swallowed a mouthful of stewed chicken. The food served up by the castle's kitchens was terrible by comparison, but Emilie had insisted on keeping the man because he had once served in the king's own kitchens.

"'Twould not work," Gareth muttered, pushing away the empty bowl and standing. Even supposing Grizel would leave the Marsdens, her fear of men would make working at Ransford impossible. Besides, he was supposed to be finding Sir Neil's killer, not hiring a new cook. And even though Gareth had so far not found evidence they had profited by the old knight's death, the Marsden family still had the most to gain from it.

Still, Gareth couldn't help feeling guilty as he snuck down the stairs like a thief and crept along the dark corridor. Some spy he'd turned out to be, he thought, yet he pressed on toward the faint murmur of voices coming from the front of the house. He'd learned at an early age that duty almost always pinched. The older he got, the more severe the pinch.

Through a partially opened door, he smelled the pungent aroma of herbs and glimpsed shelves lined with neat rows of pottery jars. Great bunches of dried stuff hung from the rafters overhead. Ari sat on a high stool, her head bent over a ledger.

"Now, then," Dame Cicily said briskly. "If you've finished copying the directions for the soap, we'll start on the lotion."

"Don't you think I should check on the knight?"

Gareth's heart stopped.

"Such devotion to your patient is commendable," the older woman said dryly, "but he's in no danger. Just a foolish man who tried to do too much, too soon. The lotions . . ."

"Aye, Aunt Cici," the girl replied dully, dropping her gaze to the book in her lap. Almost, Gareth felt sorry for her, but this *foolish man* had questions that needed answers, and while these two were occupied, he'd best be about them.

He found the goldsmith's workshop by smell and process of elimination. William was within. "Might I have a word with you?" Gareth asked from the doorway of the workroom.

William turned from the bench, seemingly unsurprised to see him there. "Of course, come in."

Gareth did, closing the door securely behind him.

"I was trying to decide which of these things to give you for saving Ari's life," William said, gesturing at the pieces lined up before him on the workbench.

Gareth's eyes widened at the gleaming display. A pair of silver candlesticks shaped like intertwined dolphins, so beautifully carved they seemed almost real, a silver salt dish of incredible delicacy, a cup of gold and silver set with blue stones, and a gold medallion on a heavy gold chain. Though he was no judge of such things, Gareth realized each was a masterpiece in its own right and likely worth a fortune. "I can't accept anything so valuable."

"My granddaughter's life is worth far more."

God, he had never felt so unworthy of anything in his life. "I am certain it is, but . . ."

"Have you great wealth that you can afford to turn down what I offer?"

"Have you so much you can afford to give it away to the first man who does you a favor?"

Sadness flickered in the old man's cloudy eyes, making Gareth regret his sharpness. "Nay. Sit down," he said, gesturing toward a stool. "You can not be fully recovered, and my legs are still shaking from Ari's close brush with death. She is precious to me. All I have left of my dear daughter, Alys, and Richard, who became like a son to me. Even though I did oppose their marriage, at first, I finally gave in because they so loved one another."

From what Gareth could tell, Sir Richard had been a good man, much loved. If that was so, why would a burgher not want his daughter to improve her station by wedding a knight?

"We lost Alys to the plague when Ari was but seven. Little wonder we spoiled Ari after that. She was all we had left." William cleared his throat. "Which piece do you like the best?"

Gareth hesitated, his mind was on Ari as he tried to imagine her loneliness growing up without a mother, her grief at losing her father, too. Still she managed to smile. "The dolphins are well done and very unusual," he said absently,

"You've a good eye. The candlesticks are my best pieces." William ran one scarred finger over the head of one of the dolphins. "Mayhap because so much love went into them. I made them as a bride's gift for my wife. When it comes time to sell the rest of my things, they will be the hardest to part with."

"Sell? Why would you sell them?" Gareth asked, already knowing the answer. It was hard sitting here, listening to William tell him in a voice gritty with emotion that he was going blind and would soon be forced to give up his craft. Far harder than it had been to sit in his father's library a week ago and listen to the same tale. Before, he hadn't known the Marsdens, hadn't been involved in their lives. Now he was much more involved than was wise.

"I have already sold a few of the lesser pieces at the Norwich fair," William went on, still stroking the dolphin. "To sell too much, too quickly, is to shout your need to the world. A desperate man gets a far poorer price. I must see Ari settled before I am reduced to that."

The ache at the base of Gareth's throat intensified. "I wish I could help."

"You already have by saving my Ari's life. I couldn't go on if something happened to her."

Gareth groaned. "'Twas Apollo who saved her life, both our lives, really."

"I doubt Apollo would have a use for any of these things."

And I am not worthy of them. "What I would really like, is to find Sir Neil's killer," Gareth muttered.

William's hand fell away from the dolphin. "Has Farley had any luck?"

"Nothing so far. He told me about the lights on the cliff." Gareth stroked his chin thoughtfully. "You mentioned that Sir Richard had gone out to investigate. Would you remember what day of the week that was?"

"I'd not soon forget. 'Twas a Monday. I wanted to go with him, but he refused. Said it was a cold night, and he was just looking about."

"For what? Did he give you any idea?" At William's negative shake, Gareth stood to pace. "Damn, why couldn't he have confided in someone, left a clue or a note behind?" He stopped suddenly. "Did you search Sir Richard's things?"

"I—I never thought to go through them. It was such a shock," William stuttered.

"Did he have a room here?"

"Nay, he stayed most nights at Tyneham Keep in case he was needed. He did keep some things here, though, and the rest Sir Neil brought to us after Richard was..."

"Where are they now?"

"In a trunk beneath Ari's bed.

"I'll see what I can find." Gareth turned to leave.

"What about the candlesticks?" William called after him.

"Such beauty would be lost on me," Gareth replied. "Besides, I have no place to keep them."

He found the trunk with no difficulty, was on his knees lifting a pile of clothes from it when the door burst open.

"Grandfather said I'd find you here. What are you doing with my father's things?" Ari demanded. Light from the candle he'd set on the floor wavered, spilling gold and shadow over her angry face.

"Looking for a clue to his murder and Sir Neil's."

Her eyes bored into his, sharp and searching. The back of his mind tingled with a strangeness he'd come to associate with that particular look. Could she really read his mind? He wanted to look away from her, yet found he couldn't.

She smiled sadly, breaking the spell. "You aren't certain you'll find anything, are you?"

"Nay." Warily. Uncomfortably.

"I'll help." Crossing the room, she knelt beside him in a graceful swirl of green wool.

The sweet scent of lavender wrapped itself around him. He fought against its sensual lure. "I suppose I should have asked your permission to go through his things."

"I suppose." She met his gaze with her unblinking candor. "But you aren't used to asking for anything, so I forgive you."

Too close to the mark. "Do you feel up to the task?"

"Nay. But 'tis necessary."

Gareth respected both her courage and her control. It must be difficult sorting through the possessions of a loved one. He'd ordered the extravagant gowns and tinted face powders with which Emilie had spun her web of deceit piled in the middle of Ransford's courtyard and burned the day of her funeral.

"Where shall we start," Ari asked him, conscious he had drifted from her to some dark scene from his past.

Blinking away the bitter memories, Gareth nodded at the clothing on the floor. "We need to go through them carefully."

"What are we looking for?" The smiling sprite of this afternoon, the adoring damsel of this evening were both gone. Her face betrayed only determination.

"I wish I knew."

They searched in silence. The knight went through the clothing with grim efficiency; Arianna carefully folded the garments he was done with and piled them to one side. Sorting through the remnants of her father's life was almost harder than burying him had been. Like a final farewell. She bit her lip to keep the tears at bay.

They found a few odds and ends, a bit of twine, a few pennies left in the leather purse he had worn at his belt, a hunk of peppermint candy, fuzzy with pocket lint. This last brought a lump to her throat. "Papa was a quiet man," she murmured. "His weakness for sweets made him seem more..." She choked and looked away.

The knight's large hand cupped her arm, warm and oddly comforting, where this afternoon his touch had ignited a heat of a different sort. "I can finish this alone, if you wish."

His gentleness, on top of everything else, nearly undid her. Ari battled the urge to bury her face in his shoulder and let go the dam holding her bitter, strangling tears at bay.

Gareth felt the convulsive shivers run through her body and into his. Her struggle not to cry moved him more poignantly than a river of tears would have. "Cry. You have every right."

She stiffened beneath his touch and drew in a ragged breath that caught on a sob. "Nay, I never cry."

"Never? Surely when your father died."

She shook her head. "Papa would not have wanted me to cry. He said it made my eyes red as a rabbit's. 'Tis true," she added, looking up at him through spiky lashes, the blue of her eyes magnified by unshed tears, the pain and sorrow in them at odds with her faint smile.

What he saw was a brave girl with little artifice. It scared him. "I'd finish this alone and spare you," he said gruffly.

Again she shook her head, bending to the task with a will and a determination that made his respect less grudging.

At the bottom of the trunk was a small, locked chest. Gareth was surprised at her reaction when he asked for the key.

"'Tis just my parent's marriage lines and such."

If that was true, why did she look frightened? "The perfect place to hide an important clue," he drawled.

Reluctantly Ari got the key from the bottom of her own trunk. "I ought to know the contents by heart," she babbled as she handed it to him. Her hands fluttered nervously. "My father had few things of value, but he enjoyed showing them to me. There, that is the silver spur given him when he was knighted," she said as the knight lifted it out and set it on the floor.

"'Tis richly wrought. Who was his sire?"

"Guy de Clerc," Ari mumbled. "Ah, and here is their marriage contract." She snatched the rolled parchment from the chest before the knight could touch it and clutched it on her lap.

Odd. Gareth's fingers itched to unroll it, if only to satisfy a small niggle of curiosity. But she had willingly let the matter of Emilie drop. Could he do less?

Ari breathed a sigh of relief when he didn't press, her emotions too raw to bear the telling of her parents' story.

"What is in these?" He withdrew two small leather pouches from the chest.

"I've never seen them before."

He undid the ties on the smaller one. A dozen or so gold coins and a scrap of folded parchment spilled out into his palm.

"Oh, what are they?"

"For shame," he chided lightly. "That from a goldsmith's granddaughter? They are gold florins."

"I handle few coins myself, and then only a shilling or two."
She traced a finger over the raised pattern struck into the gold.
"How much are they worth?"

"Your grandsire must not be a moneylender, then, else
you'd know the latest exchange rates down to the nearest
ha'penny." It didn't surprise him that William avoided such a
low, mean business. "I should say each is worth three
pounds."

"I see." Her shoulders drooped.

"You were hoping for more."

"Aye." She slanted him a rueful glance. "Saying so will no
doubt enhance your opinion that I am a greedy woman, but
the money would be most welcome."

Gareth winced at the memory of the goldsmith offering him
a choice from his pitiful store of treasures. "Did Sir Neil leave
you nothing?"

"Nay, the marriage was not consum..." She blushed.
"There wasn't much. Grandfather says Sir Neil gave most of
what he had to feed others."

Conditions at Tyneham were worse than he'd imagined.
Deep in thought, Gareth opened the first scrap of paper.
"Forge and Anvil," it read.

Arianna frowned. "What does it mean?"

"It could be the name of a shop or smithy."

While they puzzled it over, he opened the second bag. It
contained two piles of coins, each wrapped in a twist of
parchment. One read, "Reece," the other, "Bentwood."

"Do you think these are shops, too?"

Gareth stared at the coins in his palm—six from Reece, another four from Bentwood. They looked right, they felt right,
but something about them was wrong. Something that set his
teeth on edge and jangled his nerves.

"Are new coins worth more than old ones?"

"Nay," he said slowly. Then the pieces of the puzzle slid into
place. *The coins were all new.* What, he wondered, were the
odds of finding twenty new gold florins in a town the size of
Tyneham? Obviously Sir Richard had thought it strange

enough to separate the coins and mark them.

Mark them with the names of the places where he had gotten them? It was a lead worth pursuing.

Hell. It was the *only* lead he had.

Chapter Eight

"Are you awake?"

The whispered question jolted Gareth from a sound sleep. He opened his eyes to a pale face suspended above his in the murky dimness of early morning. "Arianna?" he croaked.

"I found out about Bentwood." She leaned closer, the movement dislodging a cascade of bright hair.

It slid over his bare chest, as soft, silky and seductive as a lover's caress. Desire rushed through him so swiftly it stole his breath.

"You do remember about Bentwood, don't you?" she asked.

He barely remembered his own name. "What the hell are you doing here?" he managed.

Her smile faded. "I came to tell you about Bentwood."

"It isn't even dawn yet."

"Aye, it is. I've been up for an hour—baking bread." She wrinkled her nose in disgust, drawing his gaze to the smudge of flour at the tip.

Gareth fastened his attention on that endearing blemish with the desperation of a drowning man snaring a lifeline. She looked like a messy child. He couldn't want to draw her down beside him and lose himself in her softness.

He couldn't—but he did.

Arianna watched in stupefied fascination as his lids lowered and the pulse at his temple quickened. Such a simple thing, but the promise glittering in his dark eyes, veiled only by the thickness of his lashes, made her heart skip, then pound. *Come closer,* he urged silently.

Kiss me. I'm dying for the taste of your mouth.

Had he said that? Ari wondered. Had she? It didn't matter, it was true. She swayed closer, touched her lips to his, gasping as the unexpected thrill of his mouth opening under hers sent a wave of liquid heat spilling through her body. He groaned, tunneling a hand through her hair and cupping her head to hold it still as his tongue slipped between her parted lips. All her senses exploded at once, leaving her deaf and blind to everything but the magic of his kiss. She gave herself up to it, her mouth merging with his, the flames leaping between them like a wildfire. The pleasure built and built, gathering inside her until she thought she'd burst.

"Oh, God." Gareth wrenched his mouth away from her, his breathing fast and ragged, his desire stretched so taut it seemed it would rip him apart. He dragged his hand from her hair, threw it across his eyes. "I... we can't."

Ari sat back on her heels, her fingers pressed to her still-tingling mouth. "I know." She was naive but not stupid. Much of what happened between a man and a woman was a mystery to her, but she was fairly certain the knight had been about to give her a lesson—with her complete, nay, very willing cooperation. "But I ache inside from wanting to be near you," she whispered miserably.

Gareth lowered his hand, winced at the sight of her bowed head and softly shaking shoulders. "I know." He managed to sit up, started to reach for her, then thought better of it. "I know it hurts." He half thought, half dreaded the ache wasn't entirely physical. A nagging voice in the back of his mind told him things might be different for him with a woman like Arianna. Someone open, honest, caring. "But we cannot be together."

She slowly raised her head, her eyes wide with questions he hoped she wouldn't ask. "Why not?"

Damn. Because I'm not what I seem. "You said yourself that you must wed a wealthy man who can care for you and your family. I can not be that man. This... this desire we feel will pass."

"Desire?" she said in a small voice.

That she looked so heart-wrenchingly young reinforced all the differences between them. "Aye, 'tis desire, nothing more," he added gruffly, firmly.

Arianna nodded, not because she agreed, but because she sensed her unhappiness increased his. Strange, she had always associated that kind of closeness with love. "Will you still be my friend."

"Aye." His voice sounded a little choked.

Maybe the idea of settling for mere friendship between them seemed as impossible to him as it did to her. It helped her to think so, but her heart still ached.

The catch at the end of her shuddery sigh went through Gareth like a sword thrust. "What did you come to tell me?"

"I came to tell you that Bentwood has a shop at the Market—selling cloth."

"Cloth. There is a good deal of money to be made in that trade." Which meant many coins changed hands there. Did Bentwood know the coins were fake? "What about the other two names?"

"Grizel didn't know anything about The Forge and Anvil, but she says Reece is the blacksmith."

"Dammit. I told you not to mention this to anyone."

"I asked Grizel because she does our marketing and knows the town best of any of us, but Grizel is loyal to me. Because she was a mute, her parents abandoned her at the town gates. If not for Aunt Cici, the townspeople would have left her there to die. I was only a babe myself when my aunt brought Grizel home to raise alongside me. So you see, she would never do anything to harm this family."

Gareth sighed. "Well, don't tell anyone else." He had intended to make a circuit of the town himself the night before. But he had made the mistake of lying down on his pallet in the solar while waiting for the others to fall asleep and had slept straight through until Arianna had wakened him.

"What will you do now? Will you go to Bentwood and confront him with the false coins?" Arianna asked in a rush.

"How did you know...?"

"I looked at one again this morning. I know you said not to, but it bothered me so I couldn't sleep."

"What did?" he asked suspiciously.

"That they all looked so... perfect." She glanced over her shoulder at the deserted solar, then leaned closer. "There is a thin layer of gold on top, underneath, they are base metal."

"I suspected as much."

"You did?" Her eyes narrowed. "Why didn't you tell me?"

"This is men's work," he muttered. "Now if you will leave, I would like to dress."

Ari stood and shook her skirts. "It was *my* father, and *my* husband who were killed. That makes this *my* business, too." Before he could think up a reply, she swept from the room.

Gareth set out for Bentwood's after breaking his fast. The longer he walked, the bleaker his expression grew and the heavier his heart. Everywhere there were signs that Tyneham wasn't half as prosperous as Gareth had assumed. Some buildings were in poor repair; a few had even tumbled down. Scrawny children struggled to perform adult tasks; the adults, meanly dressed and dull eyed, scurried about like overworked ants.

Why hadn't Sir Neil asked him for help? Gareth thought grimly. Nay, 'twas his responsibility, he who had failed his people. No matter that conditions were worse elsewhere, he should have found time to visit here. By the time he reached Bentwood's, Gareth was coldly furious with himself.

The shop faced the bustling market square. Though the wood-and-lath structure was nicer than the small wooden stalls of the bead maker, pin seller and others that dotted the square, it was not nearly as fine as the flanking stone buildings belonging to his competitors.

Gareth was no merchant, but he found it odd that those two shops stood idle while Bentwood's crawled with eager buyers.

A stout woman gave him a black look as he attempted to edge into the crowded shop. "Wait yer turn," she snapped.

Gareth stiffened, yet common sense forced him to nod compliance and wait in the doorway.

The florid-faced little man in a garish yellow tunic must be Bentwood. Everything about him, from the oily way he ogled the female clients, to the imperious way he snapped at his two skinny helpers, grated on Gareth's taut nerves. He found it easy to believe Bentwood had knowingly passed the false coins.

Gareth curled his hands into fists, wishing he had them around Bentwood's fat neck. He was glad the king's new Statutes of Treason made counterfeiting a treasonable offense. He'd enjoy seeing Bentwood stripped of his property and hanged for further depressing Tyneham's fragile state with his worthless coins.

When this was over, he'd order all the counterfeit coins collected, Gareth decided, and somehow find the means to reimburse his people for their loss.

"May I help you, sir?" inquired one of Bentwood's clerks.

"I—I, er, I was looking for..."

"A length of blue velvet," chirped a familiar voice. Laying her hand on his arm, Ari described the cloth she sought.

The clerk bobbed his head and darted away through the crowd.

"What are you doing here?" Gareth demanded into her ear. "You didn't wait for me."

"Because I told you you couldn't come."

"I thought you would change your mind."

"You thought no such thing, you little witch."

"Is this what you had in mind?" asked the clerk. Glancing nervously at Gareth's scowl, he proffered a bolt of blue velvet.

"I'm not sure. What do you think, Sir Garvey?" The glance Arianna slanted him through her lashes was as bland as milk.

"You don't want to know," he grumbled.

Bentwood appeared at the clerk's elbow. "Is aught amiss?"

"Nay." Ari coyly fanned those same long lashes at the cloth merchant. "How much for this beautiful cloth?" She simpered sweetly.

"Ah, how kind, dear lady," Bentwood oozed. He named a price.

Arianna nodded. "Very reasonable. I will take this bolt and another of white velvet. Be certain it is of the same quality."

Bentwood started as though insulted. "But of course. If you are not perfectly satisfied by my goods, I will *personally* bring round another bolt."

Gareth's lip curled in disgust at the oil dripping from the man's tongue, but Arianna only offered another dazzling smile. "I understand your terms are payment in cash," she said quietly.

"'Tis how I can offer such good prices," Bentwood replied.

"Ah, so that is your secret." Arianna opened the pouch she carried on her belt, extracted two gold florins and dropped them into Bentwood's sweaty pink palm.

The man gaped at them as though she had put down two dead frogs instead.

"Is aught wrong?" she asked innocently, nearly choking on the urge to laugh.

"Nay. Gold florins." He poked at them with a pudgy finger.

"I believe you owe me two shillings."

Bentwood ran a finger around the neck of his tunic as though suddenly finding it too tight. With the other hand, he gestured for the clerk to bring her change. "I will have the cloth sent round to you. Now, if you will excuse me, mistress." Bentwood bowed and turned to tend another customer.

Chuckling quietly to herself, Arianna accepted her change. "Did you see…?" Her words ended in a squeak as Sir Garvey grabbed her by the elbow and hustled her outside.

"What the hell do you think you're doing?" he shouted when he had her on a side street well away from the shop.

"Helping." Ari wrenched her arm free. "Grizel said Bentwood's business had teetered on the brink of ruin, until recently when he suddenly took to undercutting the prices charged by the other merchants—providing customers could pay at once and in cash. This seemed very strange to me."

Gareth grunted in reluctant agreement.

"Did you see his face when I paid? He knew the coins weren't real. He knew." She took his hand to emphasize her point.

"Aye." Gareth's frown deepened. "I wish you hadn't done it."

"Why? Now we know—"

"All we know is that Bentwood recognized those coins for what they were. That doesn't prove he made them, or knows who did." Gareth grabbed her shoulders and gave them a little shake. "Don't you see? If he is guilty, you've tipped our hand."

Ari hung her head. "I—I didn't mean to ruin things."

"I don't give a damn about ruining things," he growled. He started to shake her again, but the fear for her safety was too great. Even knowing he shouldn't, he pulled her close, wrapping both arms around her. She stood still and stiff in his embrace, yet he savored the feel of her slim body. "Bentwood, or whoever is behind this, may think you know about the coins."

"You're afraid for me?" she asked in astonishment. At his nod, she melted, molding the softness of her body into the hard planes of his. "I guess you'll have to rescue me again."

Her assumption that he could both warmed and alarmed Gareth. "I'm no hero," he muttered, tightening his hold on her.

She tilted her head back and gave him a dazzling smile. "I think you underestimate yourself. What do we do now?"

"We take you back home to your great-aunt." He reluctantly dropped his arms and stepped away.

She bit her lip and wrapped both her arms around herself. The gesture was not lost on him. She was as cold without him as he without her. "I'd rather be with you," she said softly.

Gareth drew in a long shuddery breath and looked down the crooked street hedged with narrow, crooked houses. 'Twas a bleak neighborhood, but suitable to his mood. He'd have liked nothing better than to stand here holding her all day, but that would solve nothing and only add to their mutual misery. "People are staring, and I'll not have your reputation ruined."

Her sigh echoed his. "Mayhap we should try to find Reece's, first," she whispered as he turned her toward home.

"Nay!" he barked, drawing several strange looks. It would seal the suspicion of whoever was behind this to have the two of them, or even Gareth by himself, show up at another place where Sir Richard had found false coins.

As soon as he had Arianna safely home—and her assurance she'd stay there—he'd send Sim down to the blacksmith's on some suitable errand.

"Where is Sir Garvey?" Arianna muttered for the dozenth, nay the hundredth time that long, tedious afternoon. The silence in the empty solar mocked her growing concern. The supper hour approached and still he hadn't returned from his mysterious errand. Mysterious, hah! He had probably gone to Reece's, or to The Forge and Anvil. Even now, he could be lying in some ditch with his throat—

Nay. She couldn't bear to think of losing someone else she...loved. Nay, she must not love him, for that way lay pain and sorrow. Not of the sort that had mired her mother in grief and cheated her father of his birthright, but pain nonetheless. Biting her lip, Arianna jabbed the needle into the linen pillowcase she was making, took a generous stitch and dragged the needle out the other side. She'd think instead of the drinking cup she intended to start on that night.

Heavy footsteps pounded up the stairs. The door opened, and the knight strode in, his mail and sword tucked under his arm.

Her heart soared from the depths of despair, thumping wildly at just the sight of him. "Oh, I'm so glad you're back!" The words were woefully inadequate to describe her feelings. She needed to touch him, make certain he was all right. Jumping up, she ran across the room and flung her arms around his waist.

"Ari...mind my sword." His tone was cool, his body stiff beneath her touch.

"I was worried about you."

He frowned and glanced away, but not before she had seen the yearning in his eyes, the slight softening of his lips as a sigh of regret slid past them. "You should not have. I am well used to caring for myself."

"I can not stop what I feel," she replied quietly.

His head snapped around. "You must try," he said in a husky voice with no pretense of misunderstanding the true meaning of her words. Then even lower, "We must both try."

A desperate denial filled Ari's throat, but seeing him frown, feeling his pain as clearly as her own, she swallowed it. Unclenching her fists from his tunic, she stepped back. "You are right, of course." It was a lie, and she saw by the tightening of his jaw that he realized it, too. "Have you learned aught?"

He sighed harshly, yet she sensed his relief at her acquiescence. That almost made her own pain bearable. Almost.

"The others will be up in a moment." He set his sword and mail in the corner with his rolled-up pallet. "We should not discuss this where they may overhear. You must trust me to take care of things."

"It isn't lack of trust. 'Tis my cursed curiosity," she replied, smiling wryly. "And I'm also worried about you."

"I can take care of myself," Gareth repeated, yet her concern warmed him more than he wanted it to.

Ari nodded, longing to share her other feelings with him. Like a person awakening from a long sleep, she began to see that she had drifted through life, allowing her relatives to direct its course. Partly this was because females had no say, but she had been more passive than most, her head buried in her craft.

The time for such thinking, or lack of thinking, was past. If she didn't take charge of her life, she would end up married to John Woolmonger, and that she couldn't bear.

"Remember you promised not to go back to Bentwood's, or attempt to visit the other places," he warned.

Ari scuffed a toe on the floor. "Aye." Grudgingly.

His lips twitched, then he threw back his head and laughed. It was the first she'd seen him abandon his guard and relax enough to enjoy himself. She watched, fascinated by the transformation from formidable knight to carefree lad.

"What is so funny?" she wanted to know.

"You," he gasped, wiping tears from his eyes. "You've stitched your sewing to your skirts."

Ari looked down and blushed. "Oh, drat. Here I had thought sewing so much easier than cooking." Surprisingly she laughed.

The door opened, and the rest of the family trooped in. "At least I'm in no danger of burning down the house," she told them all between bursts of laughter.

Watching her, Gareth ached with wanting her. Not just the tempting little body shaking now with mirth, but the bright, eager, ofttimes-provoking spirit burning inside. He didn't know which hurt worse, the ache of longing or the pain of denial.

Harcourt House, the Harcourts' London house was luxurious, but tiny compared to Harte Court, the grand estate a day's ride to the north. Still, Hugh spent all his time here. Why not? He was allowed no say in running the castle, the city provided more pleasurable diversions than the country and greater distance from Edmund, his despised father.

The house Hugh considered his had come into the family when Hugh's grandsire had kidnapped the wealthy Marshal heiress and impregnated her with Edmund. Young Maude had refused to marry him, but this first Hugh wasn't called "The Cruel" only for his abilities to squeeze every last ounce of work from his wretched vassals and every penny of profit from his vast estates. He broke Maude's arm and beat her until she gave in, Edmund was fond of telling his own children.

After Edmund had been safely born, Hugh The Cruel had challenged his wife's sire over the matter of her dowry. He bested the man in the lists by substituting a weakened lance for Marshal's whole one, killing the man before Maude's own eyes as she watched with her babe in her arms. That was Edmund's second favorite tale.

"How long do you think Father and his bride will grace us with their unwanted presence?" Jesselynn Harcourt muttered.

Shrugging, Hugh turned his brooding gaze from the fire in the hall hearth to his sister. Dressed in baggy brown hose and a long green tunic belted with a strip of leather, Jesse leaned one hand on the carved stone mantel, her booted foot propped on a low stool. The male attire and pose were so at odds with her slender, delicate beauty, yet so typical of his twin's nature, that Hugh smiled fondly. "Not long. He hates coming to court and bowing to the earls and dukes above him."

"It's because of *her.* He always tries to impress them at first. Then when they don't get pregnant . . . After six wives, you'd think he'd give up."

"Not until he has an heir to replace me," Hugh muttered.

Jesse snorted, blowing a corkscrew of red hair from her freckled nose. "If they stay much longer, I'm going back to Harte Court," she grumbled, green eyes icy with hatred. "Jesu, but my nerves are jumping. Spar with me, Hugh."

"Aye, I've naught to do before Cousin Parlan arrives."

Jesse made a face at Parlan's name, but whirled away to retrieve a pair of wooden swords leaning against the sideboard.

They were identical in looks if not in temperament, but on her the oval face framing wide green eyes, the fine bones and lithe grace spelled beauty. They made Hugh look small and weak.

"En garde," Jesse cried, tossing him the heavier of the two swords and lunging forward.

Hugh raised his blade to counter her first stroke, and the force of it jarred his teeth. "You've been practicing, Jesse," he praised as they circled the room, parrying and thrusting.

"I was taught by the best swordsman in London—you. And I've had time on my hands whilst you've been off with Parlan."

Don't ask why. Hugh missed a step. But his sister's cry of anticipation as she closed in became a grunt of defeat as Hugh recovered. Deflecting her blow with the flat of his blade, he sent her sword flying with a clean backstroke.

"Damn," Jesse grumbled, massaging her numbed hand.

"Let's see what you can do against a real man," roared a horribly familiar voice.

Hugh turned just in time to stave off a blow to the throat from his father's sword. The gleaming steel bit into Hugh's wooden blade, hacked a chuck from it before Hugh could disengage and dance out of range. He felt no fear, only an old rage.

"Aye, you're quick, but you've no backbone," Edmund snarled, his green eyes glittering maliciously, his jowls quivering.

"He's not properly armed," Jesse cried, throwing herself between her brother and father.

"Hiding behind a woman's skirts," Edmund growled, his smile ugly. "Except, you don't wear skirts, do you, daughter?"

"Nay," Jesse retorted, chin high.

Leave her be. 'Tis your fault she's like this. But Hugh knew speaking would solve nothing. If only Edmund would die. *If only I could kill him.* Hugh despised himself for that weakness, too.

Patience. Hang on a little longer and you'll have something sweeter even than his death. Think how low your mighty sire will be brought when he bows to Hugh, new-made Earl of Winchester. "'Tis all right, Jesse," Hugh murmured, squeezing her arm as he stepped around her. "You left the court early, sir."

Edmund grunted. Casting a scathing glance over his two children, he sheathed his sword. "Blanche felt ill." At the snap of his fingers a plain, plump blonde sidled up to him. Never taking his eyes from Hugh's, Edmund pulled her close, his wide, fleshy hand splaying over the girl's stomach. "With luck, your successor already rests here. Think on it," Edmund rasped. "And just to make certain..." His smile became a leer. "I'd plow the field again." Laughing at Blanche's shocked gasp, he took a handful of her ample rump and prodded her from the hall.

"He's usually nicer to them than that at first," Jesse said.

Hugh smiled faintly. "Mayhap he's getting desperate."

"Parlan, my boy, you are well come," Edmund's voice boomed from beyond the carved wooden entry screen. "I'd visit with you, but my new mare wants servicing."

Jesse winced. "First Edmund, now Parlan. I'm going out."

"Nay. I'd not have you get into trouble again."

"Damn you, Hugh, 'twas two years ago, and I wasn't hurt."

"Not hurt! You fell into a gorge, knocked your memories from your head and were seized by our enemy."

"Hardly seized," Jesse said stoutly. "Gaby Sommerville rescued me, nursed me back to health, and helped me to get home again when I finally remembered who I was."

Hugh didn't want to hear anything good about the Sommervilles. "It's night, Jesse. Please stay inside."

"What if I told you I didn't trust Cousin Parlan and asked you not to see him." When Hugh didn't answer, she sighed. "I'm going, but I'll take a guard with me."

Arianna bent over the workbench, her file moving with swift precision as she shaped the hardwood into the bowl portion of the drinking cup. This would become the mold. Over it she would layer the silver, painstakingly beating it with a small hammer until the pattern of the mold had been transferred to the metal.

It was late, and her eyes burned from concentrating on the task, still she was determined to complete the mold tonight. She hadn't been able to sleep, anyway. Sir Garvey had gone off after supper. Concern for him out chasing after a horde of murdering smugglers on his own had kept her tossing in her bed. She had waited until her grandfather and great-aunt were asleep, then snuck downstairs and begun work on the cup.

So intent was she on her work, that she didn't hear the door open behind her, nor see a dark figure slip in. It glided closer, drawn to the circle of light cast by the single candle flickering on the workbench.

"You're the one," growled a low, furious voice.

Ari gasped and turned, the file flying, the wooden mold rolling across the bench. "Garvey? What do you here?"

"I'd ask you the same," he grated out. "But it's obvious." The light turned his face into a mask of primitive fury, stark planes and deep hollows from which his eyes blazed down on her. "Sir Neil—and your own father. I can scarce believe it, yet 'tis plain you are not different from other woman. Nay, you are as full of treachery as any of your sex. Call me a fool."

"You're a fool," Ari spat. "Any fool could see I'm making a drinking cup, not minting florins," she added with asperity.

"You could make a cup?"

"Hah, you think I have the skill to make coins good enough to pass for real, yet I couldn't fashion a cup?"

He blinked. "I hadn't thought..."

"That's plain to see." Retrieving the mold, she slapped it against his mailed chest. "Does that look like a coin?"

"Nay." A trifle sheepishly. "But what was I to think?"

"The worst, apparently." Tossing her bright hair defiantly, she jumped down off the stool and opened one of the strong-boxes. She dragged out the brass candlesticks she had made when she was eight and told him in rapid fire detail how long it had taken her, and what techniques she had used. Next she placed before him the silver reliquary her grandfather had not yet delivered to Master Hollton and repeated her explanations.

He laid a hand on her arm as she turned to get out another piece. "I believe you. I'm astonished by you."

"You are?" she asked warily. "Because I am a woman practicing a man's craft?"

"Partly," Gareth said in all honesty. "I have never known a woman who was a crafts—craftsman—and belonged to a guild."

"Women aren't allowed in this goldsmith's guild."

"Then you make these things for yourself?"

"When I was young my grandfather indulged me by letting me do just that, melting down many of the pieces so I could reuse the metal. Since his eyesight is failing, I've been completing what he can't." Ari covered her mouth with her hand. Too late she realized she had handed this man who mistrusted her a weapon that could bring destruction to her whole family.

Gareth sighed. "I see this is a night for misunderstandings. I'd not harm your grandfather or you." He took her hand and sheltered it between both of his. "Your secret is safe with me, and I most humbly beg your pardon for thinking ill of you."

"I cannot imagine *you* humble," Arianna said, chuckling. "But I accept and apologize for screaming at you like a shrew."

Gareth was almost as surprised by her quick apology as he'd been by her unusual talent. Emilie had sometimes raged for hours, then sulked for days over an imagined slight. He squeezed her hand in silent understanding before letting it go. "Why are you down here so late?"

Ari decided to risk telling him about the cups and unrolled the sketches she'd made. A cozy sort of intimacy sprang up between them as they leaned their heads together over the workbench. It was different from the hot restlessness she felt when he kissed her, but warming just the same. "Grandfather won't like it that I'm making something, but..."

"I understand." It was on the tip of his tongue to tell her he would buy them from her, at whatever price she deemed fair, anything to ease the fear in her wide blue eyes. But he didn't dare tell her the truth about himself.

"If I don't get enough, I may have to wed John Woolmonger."

The air hissed out between Gareth's teeth as sharply as though he'd been punched in the gut. "So soon? Who is this man?"

"He's the heir to a wool merchant from Norwich." She sighed and rerolled the parchment.

Gareth's belly clenched tighter. "Wealthy, I presume?"

"Aye."

"Sounds like the answer to your family's problems."

"I'd not wed him," she declared. Nay, she'd not have her life poisoned as her mother's had been by her husband's venomous kin. "'Twould mean moving to Norwich and leaving everyone I love behind." *But I'd wed you.* Sir Garvey would be perfect. He had no family, and even though he had called these feelings they shared desire, she knew for certain 'twas love she felt for him.

The soft expression that stole over Arianna's face tore at Gareth, made him want things that were impossible. Damn her for having wormed her way past his defenses. "Most women leave their home when they wed," he said, picking up the thread of conversation again.

"I am not most women, and I'll not live in his grand house with his wealthy, arrogant family." Ari set the mold down on the bench. "Now, wilt thou keep my secret so I can save my family?"

Gareth wanted to offer her more than just money. 'Twould satisfy the desire raging between them even now, below the surface as they talked of other things. But there was no honor in being a mistress, and Arianna was a woman of honor. "I'll keep your secret."

Ari shivered at the tension behind his words and turned away to clear off the workbench. "Did you go to The Forge and Anvil?"

"Aye," he said, so strangely she whirled to face him.

"You found something?" she asked breathlessly.

Gareth forced a bland expression. "Nothing, really." From outside the crowded tavern, he'd watched Charles argue with a man Gareth knew by sight and reputation. *Walter Beck.*

If that greedy slime was Charles's brother, mayhap Charles had made the false gold florins. The question was, how to prove his suspicions? And how did the mysterious lights and the ship fit in?

Even more pressing, why hadn't his father sent someone in response to Farley's message?

Chapter Nine

Arianna jumped out of bed the next morning fired by new determination. She would marry the knight.

It shouldn't be hard to overcome his hatred of women, she reasoned as she pulled on her clothes. He liked her, after all. Well, he liked her when she hadn't done some foolish, impulsive thing and made him angry. And he desired her. The desire that blazed to life in his midnight eyes whenever their gazes met, gave Ari courage and hope.

Over the next few days, Ari applied herself to her domestic lessons so she could learn to feed her knight. During the mornings, she followed Grizel, learning how to bake bread that wasn't charred on the outside, and how to roast meats on the spit until they melted in the mouth. In the afternoons, she either practiced her mending or sat with her great-aunt, copying down instructions for making candles, soap and such.

On Monday morning as they prepared chicken for the noon meal, Grizel cocked her head, her eyes silently asking Ari if she was happy.

Arianna shrugged. "More like resigned." Eyes crossed, she blew a feather from her sweaty nose. If she married John Woolmonger, she probably wouldn't have to pluck chickens, but his family would pluck her of her self-respect as the de Clercs had her mother.

Garvey was a better choice. He liked her family, and he had no home, so they'd live here. Best of all, he had no carping relatives to poison their love and kill their marriage. "Your lessons will be a great help to me when I marry Sir Garvey."

Grizel made a growling sound and shook her head as she poked at the chicken in the stew pot.

"I know you think I'm making a mistake, but I do love him." But would he let her continue smithing?

Ari had wrestled with that question each night as she'd secretly worked on the cup. There would be little time for such things, and likely no money to buy the necessary metals. Ari frowned, recalling that the strongbox she'd raided for the silver to make the cup had contained less precious metal than she'd thought it should. She'd have to find a way to ask her grandfather if he'd sold some of it to pay their bills.

Grizel tapped her on the shoulder, her face screwed into a fierce, forbidding scowl.

"I'd be the first to admit Sir Garvey has not been in good humor these past few days," Ari allowed. "He's had a lot on his mind," she added with a touch of anger. He spent all day and all evening out walking about the town, doubtless pursuing the trail of the false coins.

'Twas unfair that he excluded her. She had an even greater interest in finding these murderers. He should be willing to overlook her impetuousness in going to Bentwood's. After all, she was far from stupid, and she could help—even if he didn't think so. Yesterday she had cornered him as the family walked back from mass and told him about her latest finding.

"The silver coins are not silver, either," she'd whispered.

"What?" His head whipped around, and he blinked as though his mind had been many miles away. "Wait until we are private."

Ari scowled at him. They were as alone as they were likely to get. Charles had remained in bed this morn, and her grandfather and aunt had stopped to talk with the Arleys. "There's no one to hear, and we may not get another chance to talk—since you are *never* private with me," she snapped.

"You know why we are not," he shot back, the hunger in his midnight glance speaking volumes.

Arianna suppressed a shiver of longing, finding it harder to deny what she felt for him. Couldn't he see they belonged together? She knew she could get a good price for the cups. Why shouldn't they wed and use that money to support them all until Garvey established himself?

Even she was not bold enough to propose marriage, however. And the middle of the street with the last of the worshipers rushing past on the way to their homes was no place to bring *him* to a proposal. Conscious of his hard stare, she whispered, "The coins I received in change at Bentwood's are coated with silver, as the florins were with gold."

He nodded and resumed walking, but his hand came up to grip her elbow as he steered her around a mud puddle left from last night's rain. She relished that brief contact. "Yesterday I sent Sim on an errand to Reece's," he said, his voice low. "The coins he received in change were likewise coated."

Arianna sucked in a quick breath, then let it out slowly. "So, Papa must have made the same connection." *And died for it.*

"Please be careful," she beseeched him.

He nodded. "I am. Always."

Arianna could think of a few ways in which she wished he was *less* careful. "Are you any closer to finding out who?"

"Nay, but by tomorrow I should be."

"How?" she had whispered, chilled by his tone. He had a plan; she knew he did, but he had shaken off her question and turned as her grandfather called for them to wait.

Grizel's hand on her arm startled her out of her reverie. The maid's eyes were questioning.

"I am worried that Sir Garvey will come to some harm."

Surprisingly the maid nodded in sympathy.

Sighing, Ari pushed an errant strand of hair behind her ear. "He mistrusts women as you do men. How am I to make him trust me?" A surge of panic swept her. What if his hate went too deep? What if she couldn't change his mind?

Grizel smiled sadly, then turned to lift the pot of bubbling stew from the fire.

The meal was ready. Ari took a deep breath, but it didn't ease the ache in her chest. "I'll tell Grandfather he should wash up for dinner."

The sound of her grandfather's angry voice stopped Arianna at the door to the workroom. "I still say you will be in danger if you go."

"I know what I am doing," rumbled Sir Garvey's deep reply.

"So Richard said when *he* went to investigate the lights on the cliff."

Ari's hand came up to cover her pounding heart. Nay, he could not be going to the cliffs.

"I haven't said that is where I am going," Sir Garvey said blandly. "Only that I will not be joining you for supper."

"And you have a letter you would leave with me to be opened in case you do not reappear by morn," her grandfather said with a mix of concern and exasperation. "I do not need my sister's gift to hear apprehension and grim determination in your voice."

"I vowed to catch this murderer."

"Aye, so you did."

Garvey was going to the cliffs. That was what he had meant yesterday when he'd said that by today he'd know who the killer was. Surely he could not mean to go alone. But who was there to go with him? Certainly not Charles, or her grandfather. Captain Farlcy? Nay, if that was so, why had he not admitted as much to ease her grandfather's concern?

Ari did not like the conclusions she reached. He was going. *Alone.* Fear surged through her, and an anguish so sharp she nearly cried out. Stuffing a fist into her mouth, she battled the urge to burst in and beg him not to go. He'd not listen to her any more than he had to her grandsire.

Nay, she must find another way to keep him safe.

It was ten and dark by the time Gareth secreted Apollo in the trees behind Elgen's stables and began to make his way down the path to the beach. Moonlight painted the cliff side in stark relief, silvering the rocky outcroppings and draping the hollows in deepest black. The path was steep, narrow and deceptive, his balance made awkward by the need to keep one hand on the hilt of his sword to prevent it from scraping on the rocks and betraying his presence to anyone who might be listening.

He went slowly, picking his way along. When he reached the beach, he stood still for a moment, glad of the solid feel of sand beneath his boots. The breeze blowing in off the sea dried the sweat from his face as he scanned the light swells for some sign of a ship. Nothing. Good, he'd counted on arriving early.

Beginning at the base of Grassy Point, Gareth walked along the crescent of sand left by the retreating tide between the water and the cliffs. The sea had cut small caves into the face, nothing large enough for a man to stand upright in, but echoing with the scuttling sounds of night creatures, crabs and the like. As he neared the sheerer face of Tyneham Cliff, he saw the large cave Elgen had mentioned.

It gaped above the pale, moon-bathed sand like a dark, toothless maw ready to gobble anyone foolish enough to venture inside. No wonder it had attracted the attention of the local lads, he thought—and the smugglers.

Drawing the short dagger from his belt but leaving the sword sheathed for the moment, Gareth slipped up to the entrance of the cave and peered inside. Black. He could see nothing beyond the few feet of filtered gray moonlight. From inside his tunic, he drew flint and a candle.

The huge lake of seawater that filled the floor of the cave reflected the golden glow of the candle he held aloft, sent it bouncing off the wet surfaces of the domed cavern. Its far wall came down sharply to meet the water, but a narrow stone ledge ran along the near side, where he stood. A coating of slick green moss made walking along the ledge even trickier than coming down the cliff, but it also muffled his footsteps.

Nerves taut, senses probing the darkness beyond the reach of his light for the slightest hint of trouble, Gareth slowly made his way down the gullet of the cave. There was no sound but the rhythmic beat of his pulse against his ears and the steady drip of water from the stone spikes overhead. Nor were there any signs that others had come this way the week before.

Mayhap the smugglers weren't using the cave to hide their coins or do whatever they had killed Sir Richard to conceal.

The cave narrowed suddenly and bent sharply to the left. Easing around the corner, he saw the lake ended abruptly at a low stone wall. Ten natural steps led to the top of the barrier, then down a short passageway. He traveled to the end of it, made another turn and found himself in a stone hall twice the size of Marsden's solar. The ceiling rose so high above him it swallowed up the light. There was a floor of hard-packed earth underfoot, with no moss to muffle his steps as he made his way around the perimeter of the hall.

Gareth counted three other tunnels leading off from the hall, and in the wall near the one through which he had entered, he found a pair of iron grommets of the type used to hold a torch. On the ground beneath them were piled several torches and a small chest containing flint and candles.

"Hah," he muttered with a smile of satisfaction. As he bent to close the chest, he heard the sound of muffled steps in the tunnel leading from the beach.

Gareth slewed his head around, frantically judging the distance to the relative safety of the other tunnels. Too far. Blowing out his candle, he crouched, his dagger clenched in his right fist, his body tensed to spring.

A single bar of light suddenly spilled from the tunnel into the cavern, followed closely by a dark figure. Gareth rose up from hiding, grabbed his pursuer around the throat.

His prisoner gasped and dropped the candle, plunging them into darkness.

"Don't move," Gareth growled. His senses registered the slightness of the body he held, the softness of the throat he threatened, and the faint scent of lavender. *Lavender?*

"Arianna?"

"Oh, Garvey, thank God, it's you." Heedless of the knife, she turned and pressed her face into his chest.

Cursing roundly under his breath, Gareth grabbed her and shook her, wishing for light so she could see his fury. "Arianna. What the hell are you...?"

"You'll have to shout at me later. There is a ship in the bay, and men rowing toward the beach." Her disembodied voice trembled slightly. "I—I fear they mean to come in here."

His hands tightened on her. "How far behind you?"

"Not far. I dared not run through the cave to find you for fear of slipping on the moss."

"Good girl," he said reflexively, then remembered. "Nay, you are not," he growled. "But I will punish you later." *Pray God there is a later.* Releasing her, he pulled the flint from his tunic with fingers that shook, located the fallen candles, lit one and pocketed the other. "Come, we must shelter in one of the other tunnels," he commanded in a hoarse whisper.

She wore men's breeches and a shirt, probably Sim's. Her face was deadly pale, her eyes wide with terror, but she took the hand he extended without a murmur or a whimper, raising his admiration for her. Damned if he'd tell her, though, foolish, impetuous little witch.

Arianna started to enter the first tunnel they came to, but Gareth pulled her back. "Wait, there are footprints leading in there. It's impossible to say how recently they were made," he added. "But we'll not chance it." He cast a quick look at the beach tunnel before herding her to the next one. He thrust the candle into the opening. "Looks unused." He pulled her in after him. They hurried along in silence for fifty feet or so, then ran into the reason why the tunnel had not been used.

A rock slide blocked it completely, cutting off any exit.

"Damn," Gareth muttered under his breath.

"I—I think I hear voices," Arianna murmured.

Instantly Gareth pinched out the candle. The sounds grew louder, echoing in the hall they'd just left.

Arianna trembled so violently Gareth wrapped his left arm around her and hugged her close against his side. His right hand tightened on the knife. "They can't see us in here," he breathed into her ear. She shuddered, but mercifully didn't ask what he'd do if anyone came into the tunnel. He had no idea. Fight, he supposed, like a cornered animal, with a vengeance but little hope of victory.

He wet his lips, tasted the bitterness of despair and thrust it aside with a determination that surprised even him. Arianna was depending on him; he couldn't let her down.

Tentative fingers of pale light crept slowly into the tunnel where they hid. Ari tensed, but the light stopped before reaching them. The men from the ship must have paused in the cave instead of continuing into the tunnel with the footprints.

A minute passed, then another. Ari's heart beat so loudly she thought the smugglers must hear. Beneath her ear, Garvey's heart echoed hers, yet the rock-hard muscles she clung to and the strength of the arm sheltering her made her feel oddly safe.

"Sit down here on these rocks," he said softly as he let go of her. "I'm going to move closer and take a look."

Ari shivered as much from the withdrawal of his warmth and support as from fear for his safety. "Don't go."

"You'll be all right here."

"But what about you?" she whispered.

Gareth smiled faintly. They made a fine pair, each more concerned for the other's security than their own. "I'll be careful. Stay here and don't make a sound."

In the harsh glow cast by the pair of smoking torches, Gareth saw three men in dark clothes talking together at the entrance to the cave. Two were soldiers, by their hard, weathered faces and rough garb. Each wore a sword and a brace of daggers.

The third man, big, blond and well dressed, spoke up. "Jem, go up to the workroom and see what's keeping the Becks. Step lively, now, our merchants'll be here soon."

As the soldier started toward the tunnel Gareth had nearly hidden in, a fourth man was revealed. Smaller than the rest, but more elegantly dressed, the cowl of his fur-lined cloak was thrown back to reveal a narrow face in a thicket of red hair.

Hugh Harcourt. Gareth almost gasped aloud as he recognized his family's enemy. He'd only seen the fox-faced Harcourt heir once before, but the occasion was burnt into his brain.

Edmund, Hugh's father, and a mad Sommerville cousin bent on vengeance, had plotted together, maneuvering the Sommervilles into fielding an army. It was the first time this generation of Harcourts and Sommervilles had met in battle. Edmund then convinced Geoffrey to meet him in single combat, to the death, winner take all. If Gaby had not arrived with proof of the Harcourt's treachery, Gareth's father would have been killed, and Edmund would have confiscated the Sommerville estates and the title that had obsessed the Harcourts for centuries.

Mightily displeased, King Edward had forced the Harcourts to slink back to Harte Court, but clearly they had not given up on their quest.

Hatred filled Gareth as he studied his enemy. Harcourt must have been behind the ambush that had taken the lives of the Sommerville men and nearly cost Gareth his own. And it was likely no coincidence the false coins had turned up in a town pledged to the Sommervilles. What devious scheme had Hugh and his sire hatched? How could Gareth prevent them from succeeding?

"Go back to the entrance and wait for the good townspeople," Hugh commanded. The remaining soldier nodded and left.

"Well, cousin, we are nearly there," the blond man said.

"We are nearer our goal than you think." Hugh propped a foot on the chest. "I have a slight change of plans in mind," he continued, eyes gleaming in the flickering light.

His cousin flashed a matching smile. "One that will come as a surprise to the Becks and our greedy merchant friends, I'll warrant. I have always said that my esteemed Uncle Edmund underestimated your talents."

Hugh preened under the praise. "What I want to do..." He paused. "The Becks are coming. You'd best conceal yourself."

The cousin tied on a black mask with thin eye slits and cloaked himself in shadows.

"Charles, Walter," Hugh said, smiling as the two entered the stone chamber. "Have you the coins?"

"Aye." Charles handed Hugh a leather sack.

Walter moved in behind him and dropped a larger bundle at Hugh's feet with a resounding clank. "This is the last o' them."

Air hissed through Gareth's teeth. 'Twas a voice he'd have recognized in hell ... Walter had led the ambush. Hatred and fury crackled though Gareth like a lightning strike, goading him to avenge his fallen men. If he rushed in, could he kill Hugh and Walter before the soldier or the cousin retaliated?

Nay, he was one against four, with Ari to protect. Gareth's blood cooled, his brain cleared. *Bide your time; get them all.*

"Who's this?" Walter demanded, pointing at the blond cousin.

"You'll meet him soon," Hugh said. "Is all quiet in town?"

"Nay," Walter growled. "Sir Richard's daughter's been passin' some o' the coins."

"What?" Hugh's voice rang hollow in the cave. His frown deepened as Walter spilled out the tale of Ari giving the coins to Bentwood. Charles struggled to assure them that *he* would see the girl caused no trouble. "Not good enough," Hugh ground out, pacing in the circle of light. "We'll have to get rid of her."

There was a soft gasp in Gareth's ear, and he turned to find Arianna crouched behind him, her eyes wide with fear. He started to rebuke her for having moved, then swallowed it. 'Twas her life, after all, that they were discussing so dispassionately in the next room. Well, Charles was not exactly dispassionate in his defense of her.

The blond cousin cut through the arguments. "Let it lie. Here come our merchants."

Hugh scowled at Charles. "For the moment, we will trust you to see the girl does nothing to endanger our project."

A fierce tremor shook Ari as she leaned into Gareth's back. He didn't dare utter a whisper of reassurance, but he reached around and squeezed her hand where it gripped his upper arm. She whimpered softly and brushed a quick kiss across his knuckles.

"Ah, good sirs," Hugh said heartily as the soldier returned with three men.

Gareth was not surprised to recognize Bentwood, Reece the blacksmith, and George, the short, squat man who owned The Forge and Anvil. Smiles and bits of news were exchanged all around as Hugh divided the coins Charles had made into three pouches, giving a portion to each of the men.

Bentwood told them about Arianna paying for the bolts of cloth with the false florins. He was upset to be out payment for the fabric but didn't really think Arianna knew anything. "'Tis likely old William got them in payment from a customer who had purchased goods from him."

"Aye, John Miller came in and paid fer his ale wi' one o' Charles's silver coins," George grumbled. "I was some put out, till I recalled all I saved meself when I gave me customers the coins in change, and I felt better about the matter. I've a mind ta pay me tallage ta Lord Geoffrey wi' some o' them.''

Gareth frowned. Did Harcourt hope to bankrupt the Sommervilles by filling their coffers with worthless coins?

"We will see you next week," Hugh said. As the three merchants hoisted their bags of coins, he added, "Would you like to meet the man responsible for this profitable scheme?"

"I thought it was you," Bentwood replied.

"Me? I've not the resources," Hugh said with just the right shade of modesty. "Nay, I give you..." he paused dramatically as the blond cousin stepped from the shadows. "Gareth Sommerville.''

Gareth's gasp was drowned out by those of the merchants. He stared at the blond man in stunned disbelief. Surely they couldn't believe ... but the imposter was big and blond and masked, and none of the townspeople knew Gareth Sommerville. If they had, they'd have known the real Sommerville heir had been living in their midst for over a week.

"I wasn't serious about payin' yer sire wi' the false coins," George stammered.

The imposter chuckled. "He would not have accepted them. Who do you think is the real power behind this?"

The merchants gasped even louder at this, but Hugh gave them no time to ask how the earl hoped to profit by cheating his own townspeople. "Escort the merchants to the cliff path," he bade the waiting soldiers.

"I've decided my share's not large enough," Walter announced when the merchants had left.

Hugh glared at him. "You agreed..."

"That was before I knew a Sommerville was involved," Walter began, then he cocked his head at the imposter. "I've nothin' agin ye. Why, we scarce even met whilst I was at Wilton. My quarrel's wi' yer brother, Ruarke."

"Ruarke is a hasty man," the imposter said evenly.

Walter grunted and turned back to Hugh. "Ye said ye wanted ta punish old Marsden because he'd cheated ye, but now I wonder. 'Tis strange, a Sommerville and a Harcourt workin' together."

"Mayhap I tire of waiting to inherit," the imposter replied.

"Then the earl's not really in on this?" Walter demanded.

Hugh stepped up to him. "Does it matter to you?"

"Nay." Slowly. "But I want more . . . I want The Forge and Anvil," Walter growled. Hugh readily agreed.

"I'm satisfied with William Marsden's business and Arianna," Charles claimed.

Gareth felt Arianna start and clapped a hand over her mouth to absorb her shock. Her trembling tore at him like sharp claws. Damn. He'd find a way to stop Hugh and his cousin.

After promising to meet Hugh and the fake Gareth Sommerville next Monday, Walter and Charles took their leave.

"You see why we must speed things up," Hugh said.

"Aye." His cousin whipped off the mask and raked a hand through his blond hair. "Chances are the girl doesn't know anything, but Walter could be trouble. We should leave a man here to deal with things until we return."

Hugh smiled grimly. "I've no intention of waiting until Monday. We sail tonight for London to lay our findings before the king. A few days, at most, should put us back here with a royal command to gather evidence."

"And when they see the coins, and hear the testimony of the Becks and the good merchants, a summons will be sent out for Lord Geoffrey's arrest for high treason." The cousin chuckled and shook his head. "You are a marvel, cousin."

One of the soldiers hurried into the cavern. "M'lord, the tide has turned." Hugh and his cousin left swiftly.

As their footsteps died away, Gareth eased his hand from Ari's mouth. Wrapping one arm around her, he lit a candle. "We have to go," he whispered.

She shuddered once, then leaned back to study his face in the dim, shifting light. "They'll accuse my grandfather of making the coins, won't they?"

"And the earl with him." Hugh planned to frame Gareth's father for treason. The reason was obvious. In cases of treason, the crown could confiscate the Sommerville estates. Likely the Harcourts intended to claim them as reward for uncovering the plot. And King Edward, though he had long been Geoffrey Sommerville's friend, would be forced to comply.

"I'll see that doesn't happen," Gareth promised. "But we have to get out of the caves before the tide comes in." He rose slowly, taking Arianna with him. He groaned as an agonizing rush of feeling flooded his numbed legs.

"My legs have gone to sleep." Arianna leaned on him for support, echoing his moan of distress.

"I know, but we have to get moving." Their arms wrapped around each other, they stumbled from the tunnel like wayward drunks and crossed the cave. As their limbs warmed to the task, they walked faster, along the short tunnel, then down the stone steps, but the water rose faster. It had reached the third step and was climbing by the time they arrived.

Arianna hung back, watching the dark water surge into the narrow tunnel leading to the sea. "How deep will it get?"

"I don't know. Wait here a moment." Gareth felt his way down the rest of the steps until he could stand on the ledge. The water swirled about his knees; the undertow tugged back, trying to dislodge him from the slippery moss underfoot. "I don't know if we can reach the mouth of the cave without falling and being pulled out to sea." They couldn't swim to Grassy Point in any case. The pounding surf would smash them to bits on the rocks before they were halfway there.

Close behind him, Ari said, "We can do it." The water lapped at her thighs. She swayed precariously with its ebb and flow.

"Ari, for God's sake, go back." He started for her.

"I can make it." Her foot slipped, and she lurched forward.

Crying her name, Gareth lunged, hands outstretched, but it was too late. She went down with a gasp and a gurgle.

Chapter Ten

"Arianna!" Gareth's frantic cry rose above the rush of water, ringing hollowly from the cave walls. Holding the candle high, he struggled to pierce the treacherous black tide undulating all around him. She'd been under only seconds; it seemed like hours. More than enough time for her to have been swept beyond his reach and out to sea.

Suddenly a cloud of something pale and frothy flickered just below the surface. He sank his fingers into a silky mass and yanked hard. She erupted out of the water, spitting and coughing and gasping his name.

With a glad cry of his own, Gareth braced his feet wide and hauled in his catch. "Hold tight to me." He nearly lost his footing when she latched onto him.

It was dark, so dark, but he had her. Dragging her into his arms, he staggered backward. His ankle struck the steps, and he lurched up them, collapsing onto the first dry one he came to. Relief swept him, so profound it brought tears to his eyes and robbed him of speech.

"I—I could have drowned," she sobbed into his throat.

"Shh..." He couldn't talk about it, couldn't even think about it. God, he had almost lost her. How much more precious she seemed, how much smaller and more vulnerable the body trembling in his arms. He gave thanks to God, the God he had stopped believing in when Emilie had told him that the child she carried—the heir he had been longing for—was not even his. Not his, but sired by a man he had once trusted.

Arianna stirred. "The light's gone out."

"So it has," he said unsteadily. "I must have dropped the candle." He wondered when, and how in hell he'd found his way to safety without a light. "I have another one inside my tunic." It felt strange to talk of candles when she'd come so close to death. He found the candle, and the flint, mercifully still dry.

Ari blinked against the light and shyly lowered her eyes. "I—I'm sorry to be so much trouble." Her hair was slicked back, her lashes darkly spiked against wet, colorless skin, her lips blue and trembling. She shouldn't have looked desirable shivering there on his lap. And he had a dozen things he should be doing instead of staring at her. Like finding a way out of here. Yet, none of them seemed more important than Ari-anna.

He wanted her so badly, had tried so hard to resist her. Trembling with the force of his tangled emotions, he set the candle down. "You're alive . . . that's what matters."

The heat of his breath fanned her lips in the instant before his mouth came down to warm hers. Ari tasted desperation and thanksgiving on his tongue as it stole between her teeth. She met it with a moan, understanding both. It was good to be alive, and they celebrated it together, touching, stroking, their bodies straining to be closer. Liquid fire spilled through her veins, warming from the inside out.

"Ari," Garvey groaned against her mouth. "Oh, Ari." He lifted his head, staring at her with such intensity she shivered in anticipation. "I . . ." He groaned again and buried his face in her wet hair.

"W-what is it?"

"Nothing. Everything." He sucked in air, then let it out slowly. "I—I was afraid I wouldn't find you in time."

"I knew you would." She hugged him closer. "I knew . . ."

He kissed her temple, then laughed shakily. "You have more faith in my abilities than I do. A second longer . . ." A shiver racked him, and though she sensed it wasn't from the cold, she belatedly tried to push herself from his lap.

"I'm getting you wet."

His grip tightened possessively. "Nay, let me share what heat my body has until I can find a warmer, drier place." He picked up the candle and thrust it into her hand. "Hold this, and I'll carry you back up to the cave."

"Then what?" she asked as he walked up the steps.

"We'll try the tunnel Charles and Walter came out of. Maybe it leads to another exit." He doubted it, or the Becks would have left that way instead of risking the cliff trail. More like, it led to the room where Charles had made the coins.

Some twenty feet back into the tunnel, he found a set of stairs leading up into the impenetrable blackness. Shifting Arianna's slight weight, he bid her hold the candle higher and started to mount.

"Nay, I—I can walk," she said through chattering teeth. "Y-you may h-have n-need of your s-sword."

Gareth nodded. "I doubt it, but you are sensible for thinking of it," he said gruffly, setting her down.

Ari wrapped both arms around her shivering body, sorry to be deprived of his warmth. "If I were p-practical instead of f-foolishly impulsive, I'd not have f-followed you."

"I'll not deny I'd prefer you safely tucked in your bed to here, wet and cold," he replied, taking the candle and starting up the steps, his sword drawn and ready. "Yet if you hadn't come when you did, I might have been caught in the cave by Hugh and his men."

In spite of her blue lips, she smiled cheekily. "Does this mean I'm forgiven?"

"Nay, merely that I am postponing punishment until I have you safe and dry." He tried to sound stern, and failed.

"I'm glad we came or we'd not have know what they planned."

"Aye." He sighed. "Quiet, now, till we know what's up here."

Shivering in her wet clothes, Ari followed him up the short flight of steps and down a corridor. It seemed the whole night had been a series of dark places illuminated only by the narrow circle of candlelight. She tried not to think about the other shocks the night had brought—Charles's involvement in making the false coins, the implication that her grandfather would be blamed—but her mind returned to Harcourt's vil-

lainous scheme again and again like a moth drawn to deadly
flame.

"This explains why Elgen thought he saw lights on the face
of the cliff," Gareth said softly. He had stopped before a chest-
high opening in the tunnel wall through which spilled a pale
swath of moonlight.

The wind whistled through the natural window, tugging at
Arianna's hair as she joined him. In the distance, she saw the
outline of Grassy Point; below she caught a dizzying glimpse
of phosphorescent froth breaking over dark rocks. "D-do you
th-think this t-tunnel leads out?" Her teeth chattered together.

Gareth swore under his breath and hurried her away from
the drafty opening. Arianna's skin was clammy, and she shuf-
fled along like an old woman. If he didn't get her warm and
dry soon, she'd sicken for sure.

Endless minutes later, he found the cave.

A blanket had been hung over the entrance. To keep out
drafts, he supposed, but it also prevented him from seeing
what lay in store for them within. Gareth turned to tell Arianna to keep back until he was certain it was safe, but she was
already slumped against the wall, both arms wrapped around
her body. Damn. She seemed to be fading away before his eyes.
"Hang on just another minute," he whispered.

She nodded slightly, her eyes glazed and staring.

Damn. Gareth pushed the blanket aside with the tip of his
sword, then shouldered past it, the candle held aloft. The cave
was small. A quick glance told him it was deserted. He
breathed a sigh of relief as other things registered in his mind.
Coals still glowed in a brazier. A pallet and a jumble of blankets lay in one corner. It was going to be all right. He would get
her dry and warm, and she'd be all right. She *had* to be all
right. "Arianna. You can come in."

A second passed, then another. Still, she didn't come. Dread
tightened Gareth's gut. Lifting his sword, he ducked outside.

Arianna lay in a sodden heap on the ground.

Ari awoke with a start as an icy draft pierced the warmth
that had enfolded her. She opened her eyes to darkness and

confusion. Slowly her sleep-befuddled brain made sense of her surroundings. She lay—naked—on her back under a coarse, musty-smelling blanket. The pallet of straw crinkled beneath her head as she turned toward the growing light.

A fire burned close by. Silhouetted in its golden glow, Garvey bent to tend the flames. Firelight gilded his lean, muscular body and grave profile, licking provocatively over his bare bronzed chest and corded limbs. The breath caught in Arianna's throat as he stood, naked but for a white cloth slung low around his hips.

He was beautiful. She wanted to touch him. As though sensing the greedy need building inside her, he walked to the pallet and knelt beside it.

"I'm sorry I woke you," he said huskily.

Wordlessly she reached up. His shoulders were incredibly warm and smooth beneath her hands. He shook at her touch, the shudder moving through him and into her, racing along suddenly sensitized nerves. Deep inside, she felt something pull tight. "I need you." It was all she could think to say.

"Ari..." He leaned forward, bracing a hand at either side of her head, his eyes locked on hers. "We shouldn't..."

"You're wrong. We belong together. I feel it. I know it as surely as I sometimes sense your thoughts."

He stiffened. "You've been through a lot tonight."

"Maybe that's why I need so badly to touch you, to be held by you." Her hands glided up his neck, framed his face.

Gareth groaned, swaying above her, a heartbeat away from kissing her and throwing a lifetime of doing what was right out the window and doing what he wanted, needed more than his next breath. After hours of holding her, first to ward off the terrible cold, then because he couldn't bear to let her go, one kiss was all it would take to send him over the edge into the complete and utter insanity of making love with her.

If only he hadn't been forced to remove her wet clothes, he might have been stronger. He had seen her naked before, and lain awake nights dreaming and wanting. This time there'd been no curtain of hair to hide her silky white skin, lush curves and tempting hollows from his ardent gaze. If only he didn't know how soul-wrenchingly good her beguiling little body had felt pressed against his as she slept. If only... But it was too late for that, as he had known from the start.

"I love you," Arianna murmured, her fingers tunneling through his thick blond hair as his mouth closed over hers.

And I love you, God help me, was Gareth's last coherent thought before he gave himself up to fate, or whatever force had brought them together. Her lips parted at his first touch, her tongue tangling eagerly with his in an erotic prelude of what was to follow. She matched the urgency of his desire, her heart pounding against his chest. Small whimpers came from her throat as he took the kiss deeper, and she shivered in his arms.

Slowly. Dimly he realized he should go slowly with her. Emilie had always complained of his unbridled haste. Wrenching his mouth away, he buried it in her sea-scented hair. "Ari... I don't mean to frighten you."

"I'm not. I love it. I love you." She nuzzled her cheek against his, then rooted around until she captured his mouth again. This time it was she who led, luring him to further madness with each sensuous swirl of her tongue. When he finally dragged his lips from hers, Ari took a gulp of air and laughed throatily. "I—I forgot to breathe."

"Me, too." Gareth chuckled, unable to remember if he'd ever laughed in bed but charmed by the way it made him feel. Light, free and giddy. As though she were the first woman he'd ever touched, and he had all the time in the world to explore her. He started at her neck and kissed his way down, pushing the blanket aside as he went, marveling at each new treasure he uncovered. The vulnerable pulse at the base of her throat, the delicate curve of her collarbone, the tempting upper swell of her breast.

Ari moaned as Garvey's tongue laid a trail of fire across her skin, gasped as it lightly laved her nipple and moved on. Unembarrassed by the intimacy of the unexpected gesture but dazzled by the heady sensations spilling through her, she reached for him, her hands closing over tousled curls and warm, damp skin as she drew him back to her breast.

"Do you like that?" he growled.

"You know I do." Her soft words became a whimper of unbearable excitement as his hot, wet mouth closed over the sensitized peak and gently suckled. Her every sense came vividly alive, her skin tingled as though it had been brushed by fire, her pulses pounded in thunderous discord, but nowhere more tumultuously than at the juncture of her thighs.

His hands roamed over her with possessive familiarity, finding each pleasure point and awakening it with breath-stopping caresses, coming lastly to the hidden center where the longing and the need had built to a sharp ache.

"Oh," she gasped at the intrusive slide of his fingers along a secret passageway.

The fingers withdrew, pressing lightly over the coiled focus of her desire before leaving entirely. "Shall I stop?" His voice was as dark and compelling as the wanting inside her.

"Nay," she said quickly, her eyes flying open. He lay beside her, propped up on one elbow, his gaze intent, glittering beneath heavy lids. The hunger in that look stoked the fire in her blood. "If you do I think I'll . . . I'll shatter."

On a low growl of agreement, he twisted free of the linen that had hidden the proof of desire, giving her a brief glimpse of rampant power in the dim light, before he stretched full-length beside her and pulled her against him, letting her feel the taut strength of him pressed hotly on her thigh.

His drugging kisses, the provocative slide of his hands over her breasts gave her no time to fear what she'd seen. He loved her, she felt it in his touch, knew it in her heart.

When he rose up above her, she parted her thighs on instinct. Arching her soft body into the hard planes of his, she welcomed his weight and even the sharp pain that accompanied his first swift thrust, because beyond she found there was more. A golden, magical place that lay just past the sensual storm of giving and taking, of bodies joining and souls merging so closely, so thoroughly, they were almost one.

Arianna cried out as the last plateau was reached, and everything around her simply exploded. Colored lights danced behind her tightly closed lids. Dimly, she heard Garvey shout her name, felt him tremble in her embrace.

                              *   *   *

Still half-asleep, Arianna shivered and reached out for the
body that had warmed her while she slept, though in truth they
had done little sleeping. She smiled, remembering the last time
he had wakened her. Or had she wakened him? No matter,
they had loved so sweetly, so tenderly that she had cried for the
wonder of it. When she'd told him why she cried, Garvey had
squeezed her so tight she couldn't breathe and had made love
with her again. Fiercely and urgently, this time, as though he
feared someone would come and snatch away their newfound
happiness.

So why was he gone from their bed? Ari sat up, wincing at
the ache in secret, untried muscles. But it was a delicious ache,
one she relished as she glanced around the cave. A fire crackled in the brazier, a fat candle burned on the table, and a skin
of water lay close at hand.

Warmed by his thoughtfulness, she took a quick drink, then
washed the stickiness from her thighs. Her borrowed clothes
had been left to dry before the fire. Stiff with salt, they abraded
her skin, especially her sensitive nipples. As she struggled into
them, she noticed the tools on the table, and the flecks of gold
glittering in the light. Reminders of Charles's betrayal.

Sir Garvey burst through the blanket at the doorway. "'Tis
not yet dawn, but the tide's out. We have to leave."

Arianna blinked. "Good morn to you, too."

He didn't return her smile. "Are you all right?"

"Of course." She cocked her head, judging his mood. "You
are upset that we found such pleasure in each other's—"

"Arianna, stop guessing what's in my thoughts."

"'Tis not guessing. I can . . . feel your anger." She paused,
considering. "But it's yourself you are angry with, isn't it?"

He shoved an exasperated hand through his hair. "Aye."

"Well, I refuse to leave until you explain why." She plopped
down on Charles's rickety stool.

"The tide will not wait."

"Then you had best speak quickly."

"Stubborn wench."

"You did not find me stubborn last night," she reminded
him.

Shame flamed in his face. "There are things you don't understand, reasons why we can not be together."

"Nothing we can not overcome." She bit her lip. "Or is it that you have had your fill of me?"

Gareth drew in a shuddery breath and expelled it slowly, his eyes never leaving her beautiful face. Just remembering the feel of her body, the smell of her skin, the sound of her laughter sent a wave of joy washing over him, followed swiftly by an even stronger wave of longing for what couldn't be. "I doubt I'd have my fill of you if I lived to be a hundred."

She pleated Sim's stiff tunic with trembling fingers, her eyes troubled. "But you still see no future for us."

"I am not what I seem," Gareth said bluntly.

"You are good and kind and brave. And I love you. I need no more than that." She squared her shoulders. "Between us, we will find a way to make a living. The sum I get from the sale of the drinking cups should keep us until you find a post."

If only it were that simple. Gareth wanted to fling himself down on the cold stone and weep. Instead, he said, "We have more than money to worry about."

"Aye, the tide." Arianna picked up the candle and brushed past him. In the tunnel, she slowed her steps and began to think. It had hurt her unbearably that he wanted to deny their love, but he was right about them having other concerns.

"We must find a way to save my grandfather," she said, glancing over her shoulder.

His expression remained closed and distant, but he nodded as he stepped around her to take the lead. "We'll alert my...Lord Geoffrey to the problems here, and get your grandfather to a place of safety."

"Bah! The earl didn't send help before when my father was killed. And he has been predictably slow in answering Captain Farley's message about Sir Neil's death."

Nay, if his sire had received Farley's message, the whole of the Sommerville clan would have been here by now. Nor was Farley at fault. Tyneham's priest had confirmed writing the message and sending a soldier away with it the day of Sir Neil's funeral. Gareth suspected Hugh had somehow waylaid the

man. "The earl will respond this time. I'll see to it personally."

"How will we keep my grandfather safe until he does?
Those men could be back with the royal warrant any day. Drat,
when I saw my grandfather's store of gold and silver was low,
I should have realized Charles was responsible. I will scratch
out the eyes of that... that snake... when we get home."

Gareth groaned inwardly. Damn, he needed to be two people, one to stay in Tyneham and keep Arianna and her family
safe, the other to ride to Ransford and tell his father Harcourt planned to frame the lot of them for treason.

Treason. The charge was so grave, the penalty so terrible,
Gareth could scarcely think of a way around it. Perhaps if they
struck first, captured the men who were involved and took
them to London to face the king's justice.

Nay, Bentwood, Reece and George would swear the leader
of the plot had been Gareth Sommerville. And his presence in
the area, under an assumed name, might strengthen their
claim. Damn.

"Sir Garvey?" Arianna's hand on his arm halted Gareth
midway across the cave where Hugh and his conspirators had
met the night before.

As he looked down at her pinched features, his fears took a
different direction. "Are you tired? Shall I carry you?"

She smiled grimly. "Nay. I mean, I am tired, but you
needn't carry me. You've been so silent, and I'd know what
you are planning. How will we save Grandfather? What will
we do to make Charles pay for his betrayal?"

Gareth vaguely recalled her vow to scratch out the apprentice's eyes, and yet another concern surfaced. How was he to
keep Arianna from rousing Charles's suspicions? He didn't
doubt his own ability to fool Charles. He'd concealed the
heartache of his first marriage for nearly two years, but Arianna with her expressive eyes and open candor was a different matter. "I think it might be well if you went away for a
time. Have you relatives in a nearby town?"

"I see." Her gaze locked on his, as intent and probing as
ever. "You regret our joining that much?"

"Oh, Ari." Gareth opened his arms, and she came willingly, clasping him around the waist as though she'd never let go. "Never think I regret making love with you," he said softly, rubbing her back with his free hand. It was the best, most wonderful thing that had ever happened to him. Last night, as he'd held her while she slept, he'd almost let himself believe they could be together.

Drunk on her nearness and lingering memories of shared passion, he'd even dared to weave dreams of a shared future. True, she was not his equal, but her sire had been a knight. And he loved her. God, how he loved her. She was brave and clever and honest and quick to laugh. And he loved her.

Morning had brought a sobering dose of reality. He'd already promised to marry the woman his father chose for him. A lady with good bloodlines to pass on to their children and the domestic skills to run their estate. Ari's lineage was barely adequate, and she'd be hopeless as a chatelaine. Before him had risen the glum picture of himself trying to deal with the servants while his wife sat in the solar and happily turned out brass urns.

"I'm so glad you don't regret my being with you." Her misty eyes were suspiciously at odds with her broad smile.

Gareth winced, hoping she didn't see too far past his statement. "How *did* you come to follow me?" he asked before she could press him further about their relationship.

"I begged a ride in Farmer Owen's wagon. You rode slowly, so we were able to keep pace."

Vaguely Gareth remembered there being a good deal of traffic on the road from town to Grassy Point. "Where did you tell him you were going?"

She smiled mischievously. "After you. I told him I had hopes of becoming your squire."

"My squire?" he choked, eyeing her feminine features, long hair, and the curves only partially concealed by her baggy breeches and salt-stained shirt.

"I tucked my hair under a cap and borrowed Sim's things from my mending basket." She wrinkled her nose as she looked down at her clothes. "They fit a bit better before my dunking."

Gareth shook his head. "And what did you tell your grandfather and Dame Cicily?"

"Umm." She dropped her gaze to his chest. "I, er, left a note saying I was going with you on an important errand and would be back late."

"Arianna." He sighed heavily. "They are probably worried sick about you."

"Nay. They won't worry if they know I'm with you." The eyes she raised to his were wide and earnest.

Gareth's face grew hot with shame. He'd betrayed them, too, the old couple who'd taken him in, treated him like a member of the family, even thinking he was penniless. Only he was worse. A snake who had slithered into the peaceful garden of their lives and defiled their one treasure.

"Don't berate yourself," Arianna said softly, her hand resting on his heart. "We are meant to be together."

Gareth just shook his head, hating himself too fiercely to form a reply.

Two hours after leaving the cave, Gareth reined in behind Marsden's house. The sky was just turning from black to pale gray, and only the kitchen window showed signs of life. With any luck, he'd arrived before any but Grizel were up.

As he swung down from Apollo's back, Sim stumbled from the hut, rubbing the sleep from his eyes.

"I feared fer yer safety when ye didn't return last night," the boy said, taking hold of Apollo's bridle.

"I've been at Tyneham Keep," Gareth replied. Well, for most of the past hour, at any rate. Arianna had been none too happy to be left behind there. In fact, she had refused, until he'd finally told her of the plan he'd worked out as the two of them had picked their way back up the cliff trail.

Luckily she was nearly as intelligent as she was stubborn. "I think it will work," she'd said without hesitation. "But wouldn't my grandfather and Aunt Cici be safer here in the keep with us?"

"It could arouse Charles's and Walter's suspicions if all of us left. Thinking their scheme had been discovered, they might decide to silence us all."

Ari had finally promised to remain in the tower chamber that had been her father's when he was alive. Knowing she was safely beyond Hugh's reach had gone a small way towards assuaging Gareth's guilt. But he still dreaded facing William and Dame Cicily, who would probably take one look at him and know exactly what he'd done to her precious niece.

Grizel met him at the kitchen door, her eyes bruised with fatigue and full of questions he couldn't begin to comprehend. Which was probably just as well. He did manage to find out that Charles was yet abed, and the master and mistress were upstairs.

Gareth's apprehension mounted as he climbed the stairs and knocked tentatively on the solar door. It was William who answered it, dressed for the day and looking only a little worried. He smiled on seeing Gareth, and looked beyond him with hopeful eyes.

"Ari is fine, but I . . . she is not with me right now," Gareth said in a rush. "If you will let me in."

"Of course, of course," William said, stepping aside, then closing the door when Gareth was within.

Seated at the hearth across the room, Dame Cicily set down the tunic she had been stitching and hurried forward, offering cheese, ale and a slice of yesterday's bread.

Stop! Gareth wanted to shout. *Stop being kind to me.* "Just the ale," he rasped. Motioning them to take the chairs by the hearth, he sat at their feet. After cautioning them about the need for silence, he began the speech he had rehearsed for the past hour or more.

William shook his head when he heard what Charles had been doing. "I can scarce believe it," he murmured. "The boy has lived with us for five years."

Dame Cicily was not nearly as generous. "I never warmed to him, William. Imagine, thinking he could have your business and our Ari." The frown wrinkling her brow deepened.

"To say nothing of their plans to involve the earl in this mad scheme."

Gareth grunted. Farley had sent a heavy guard with the message Gareth had written to his father. They should arrive at Ransford tonight—tomorrow morn at the latest. He prayed his sire was there, and not in London attending King Edward's court. Tempted as he'd been to go himself, he didn't dare leave Arianna and her family unprotected. And, too, it was imperative he be here when Hugh returned with the king's warrant.

"Do you think you can fool Charles into believing you know nothing of what he's about?" Gareth asked.

William exchanged a brief glance with his sister before nodding. "It will be difficult, but we'll manage," he said. "'Twill be worth the trouble to see my young apprentice punished for his crimes. But Ari is another case."

"So she admitted herself," Gareth said with a ghost of a smile. "Is there a relative you might say she'd gone to visit?"

"Nay, but I have a friend in Norwich," Dame Cicily replied thoughtfully. "The woman is renowned for her housewifely skills. Many a wealthy merchant's daughter has been sent to her for training. We will say an opening became available, and she left for Norwich yester-eve. Will that satisfy your needs?"

"Aye." Then the oddness of her phrasing struck Gareth. He made the mistake of looking directly at Dame Cicily for the first time since entering the room, and abruptly wished he hadn't. *She knew.* She knew he'd lain with Arianna even when there was no hope of his marrying her. Heat flooded his face; a lump of guilt and misery suddenly obstructed his breathing.

I didn't mean to hurt her, he wanted to cry. But that wasn't entirely true. He had wanted her, dreamed of having her, until the yearning and the longing nearly suffocated him. When the time had finally come, when he'd been faced with making love to her and damn the consequences, he'd damned them. And her. And himself. He'd taken Ari, dear, sweet, beautiful, trusting Ari, without a thought to the bleak string of endless, empty tomorrows they'd both have to face alone. Or to the shame he'd heaped on her, or the shambles he'd made of her life.

"Do not torture yourself," Dame Cicily said softly, her pale, knowing eyes smiling down on him. "You are meant to be together."

You don't know the odds we face. Gareth swallowed hard, but the lump refused to move.

Chapter Eleven

Safe behind Tyneham's walls, Ari paced restlessly before the fire in the second floor tower room that had been her father's. She didn't want to be safe, she wanted to be with Garvey, wanted to be certain he didn't take any of the stupid risks men seemed prone to. She was quickly discovering that just because they were large and strong, they also thought they were invincible.

The sound of a baby crying pierced her thoughts. A babe, here in this male stronghold?

Running to the arrow slit, Ari drew aside the thin oilcloth covering it and stared down into the courtyard.

A knot of soldiers watched a two-wheeled cart lurch through the gate of the inner wall. It was a pitiful thing, the wooden sides weathered and cracked, the wheels weaving wildly. A human pulled it instead of an animal, the straining efforts of the puny thing visible beneath the tattered blanket thrown over its shoulders like a cloak. Two creatures nearly as frail slumped inside the cart. A child, and the wailing babe.

Ari's heart went out to these poor people. Her hands pressed to her mouth, she waited for the soldiers to help, but the louts merely shrugged and watched the cart's halting progress.

Midway into the courtyard, the thing pulling the cart fell forward and didn't get up. The cart tipped sideways, nearly spilling the two children into the dirt.

"That is the last straw." Ari whirled away from the window and left the chamber at a run with never a thought to the promise she'd made Garvey to remain in her father's room.

Down the narrow circular stairway she flew and out into the courtyard. Crossing it at a run, she fell to her knees beside the prostrate person.

"'Tis a woman," Ari breathed as she turned the body over. The poor thing was naught but skin and bone beneath the few rags she wore. "Do something," Ari demanded, glaring up at the circle of hardened faces around her.

Indifference became astonishment, then confusion. "L-lady Arianna?" one ventured.

Drat. Ari suffered a brief pang of regret as she remembered the care with which Garvey had smuggled her into the keep at first light. Well, there was no hiding her presence now. "Aye, 'tis me," she said with more confidence than she felt.

The man tugged respectfully at his forelock and asked what she wanted done.

Ari nibbled on her lower lip. Good question, and one she felt shamefully inadequate to answer. "Who heals your hurts?"

The man shrugged. "'Tis peaceful here, fer the most part. What damage is done in trainin' or huntin' down the odd thief, we mostly see to ourselves."

"Oh." It was up to her, then, Arianna thought dismally.

The babe's shrieks has subsided to weak whimpers. Somehow they were worse than the crying, and the woman on the ground looked half-dead. Ari thought longingly of sending for her aunt, or even the doctor whose skills Dame Cicily reviled. Common sense stayed her. 'Twas no game Charles and his cohorts played at, and many lives precious to her hung in the balance.

"Are there any wives here?" she asked.

"Nay, we're a bachelor keep, exceptin' fer two old women who clean and help in the kitchens."

"What passes here?" The crowd parted for Captain Farley. His look of violent disapproval when he saw her said it all.

Perversely, the injustice of the situation stiffened Ari's backbone. "These people are in need of our aid, Captain." Rising, she faced him with an outward display of calm. "Pray have them placed in my chamber."

"They are serfs," he growled.

"They are human beings who will die without help."

"You were supposed to remain in the tower, mistress," he reminded her.

"Lady Arianna," she retorted, seeking support from the title she hadn't wanted, wasn't even certain she could claim. "The sooner these people are moved, the sooner I will return to the tower." She kept her chin high, her back and shoulders squared beneath Sim's salt-stained garments.

A grudging look of respect flickered in the captain's eyes. "Very well, my lady." He turned and began snapping out orders to the loitering soldiers.

Surprised, nay, shocked he hadn't sneered at her, Ari stood back as a litter was fetched. When the poor woman was hoisted onto it, the child forgotten in the cart suddenly rose and cried out, clutching the now-silent babe. One of the soldiers made a grab for the child.

In a burst of unexpected energy, it ducked under his arm, jumped to the ground and dashed after the litter. The rags it wore left bare thin arms and flashing, sticklike legs.

"Halt!" Ari bade the litter bearers, dropping to her knees. "'Tis all right," she said softly. Her vision blurred by tears, she reached out to comfort the child.

The girl shrank from Ari, clutching the babe more tightly. Distrustful eyes, dark and old beyond a child's years, stared at her from a dirty, pinched face surrounded by a wild tangle of matted hair. Ari had no experience with children, but comparing this one's size to those who'd accompanied their mothers to her aunt's shop, she guessed the girl was four. Too young to have known such misery and hopelessness.

"Is this your mama?" Ari gently inquired.

The disheveled head nodded briefly.

Ari bit her lip. "I won't hurt her. I just want to feed her, and you and the babe, too."

A spark of interest kindled in the dark eyes; the bloodless lips trembled slightly.

"Are you hungry?" Ari asked softly. "Would you like some..." What did children eat? she wondered in sudden panic. What was there in Tyneham to eat now that dinner was over? The bread and chicken she'd devoured so eagerly an hour ago nearly rose up to rebuke her. She swallowed hard.

Bread. Surely there was bread. "Would you like some bread? And mayhap some milk for the babe?"

The child licked her lips, her gaze flicking to her mother's still, ashen face.

"There's enough for your mama, too, when she wakens. Will you come with me?" Standing, Ari extended her hand.

The child looked at it for a long moment before reluctantly yielding her own thin, grubby fingers.

The feel of the small, cold hand resting in her warm one shook Ari to the bone. She could tell that the exchange had affected even the hardened soldiers in the courtyard. Suddenly they couldn't do enough for her, or the strays. A blanket was draped over the child's mother. Farley offered to carry the child, but she refused to relinquish her grip on Arianna.

As they crossed to the steps leading into the keep, Ari made a mental list of what she thought she needed. "Please bring food to my chamber in the Knight's Tower," she asked of the servants clustered in the doorway. "Bread, cheese, whatever you can find, and milk. Also a tub, soap and lots of hot water. They will need clothing, too, but I don't suppose there is anything suitable."

"We've some wool we could cut and stitch into something," a stout old woman offered. "Till then, they could wrap themselves in blankets."

Ari smiled though she felt more like crying. "Whatever we give them will be better than what they have now."

It was early afternoon when Gareth finally returned to Tyneham Keep. Jesu, but he was tired and sweaty. In the past day, he'd had less than two hours' sleep. The stubble on his face itched; the salt had dried on his legs and his body itched. Since leaving the town, he'd begun to dream about taking a quick bath, falling into the nearest bed and sleeping until nightfall. Then he'd rise and stand watch. Tonight, and every night, he'd keep watch for Hugh's cursed ship.

If the vessel arrived before his father did, Gareth had resolved he'd snatch up Ari's kin and servants, and shelter them in Tyneham. The keep could hold out until his father arrived with reinforcements. By then, it wouldn't matter if their actions roused Charles's suspicions. Damned if he'd wait calmly for Hugh and the king's representatives to arrest them all.

As Apollo pounded over the lowered drawbridge, Gareth lifted his eyes toward the Knight's Tower across the bailey, and dreams of a different sort sprang to mind.

Dreams and hopes of the kind he'd never had before, even when his marriage to Emilie was new. Dreams of a woman who sometimes understood him better than he did himself. Hopes of spending a lifetime with her, basking in her sweet laughter. Foolish hopes he had no business fostering, but they refused to die no matter how savagely he had slashed at them with the sharp swords of logic, reason and duty.

In his eagerness, he spurred Apollo toward the tower, nearly riding down Captain Farley.

Apollo reared as Gareth reined him in, then trod in a tight circle as an apology was offered. The captain readily accepted, then contritely offered one of his own.

"Be damned," Gareth roared when he heard what mischief Ari had gotten herself into while he was gone. His temper completely slipped its leash the second he swung down from the saddle. "And after promising me . . ."

"The serfs were in miserable condition. A woman and her two young children."

"She endangered herself for . . . for serfs?"

Farley cleared his throat. "I brought that to Lady Arianna's attention, but she said they *were* humans and in need."

"I don't give a bloody damn if they were dying. She promised she'd stay hidden. By God, this time, she's gone too far." Chest heaving, fists clenched at his sides, Gareth stalked to the tower and took the dangerously narrow steps at reckless speed.

He slammed open the door to the second-floor chamber. It hit the wall with a satisfying crash. The sound still reverberated off the stone as he strode into Arianna's chamber and beheld the frozen tableau.

Ari crouched beside a wooden tub, a babe in her arms, a child in the tub. Firelight shadowed their frightened faces, glistened and danced on the water spilled all around them.

"You've good cause to be afraid, *Lady* Arianna," he roared.

"Oh, Garvey. Thank God you've come!" she exclaimed, and tried to rise, but the child erupted from the water. Wailing with fear, it clasped two thin arms around Ari's neck. That set off the babe. Screaming loud enough to raise the dead, it snagged Ari's hair in its waving fists and tried to pull her forward, even as the child pulled back.

"H-help," Ari choked out, struggling to free herself.

The rage drained out of Gareth in a long, heavy sigh, and his shoulders slumped in defeat. "Damn," he muttered as he waded in to rescue her.

They were both soaked to the skin by the time Gareth managed to extricate Ari from the babe's grip and pry the child from her neck. The child refused to let go of Ari completely, though, forcing Arianna to lean half into the tub as she talked to him.

"Thank God you came when you did," she panted. "Poor Rupert was crying, and Janie needed help to wash her hair."

Rupert was still crying, shrieking in Gareth's arms. He tried to view the babe with contempt, or annoyance, but the slight weight of its bony body contrasted so poignantly with his memories of Ruarke and Gaby's fat, happy little Philippa, that the attempt failed miserably.

"Could you take off his wet things and wrap him in a dry blanket?" Ari asked, staring up at him with absolute trust and faith in his abilities.

Gareth frowned. "I've little experience with babes." Truth to tell, all babes were an uncomfortable reminder of the one that had died with Emilie. The one she'd tried to pass off as his own until he'd suspected her perfidy and forced a terrible confession from her.

"I've *no* experience," Ari said cheerfully. "But we're making do. Janie has been very helpful. She's seven, though you'd not know it to...to look at her."

Gareth grunted. Rupert's squawls had muted to sniffs; still he wanted no part of this. "Are there no servants about?"

"The only two females have their hands full preparing supper for us all. Besides, Janie has not taken to them." Ari dropped her voice to a whisper. "She screams if strangers come near her, Rupert, or their mother."

"Would that she saw me the same way," he grumbled.

"Impossible. Your kindness shows in your face."

Ah, damn. "Where is the mother of these serfs?" Ari nodded towards a slight, blanketed figure lying on a pallet near the hearth. "What's wrong with her? Why didn't she respond to her children's cries?"

"She's not diseased," Ari hastened to assure him. "Just starving and exhausted. She pulled the children in a cart some ten miles from their farm to the keep. And they aren't serfs. They're villeins—free people."

Gareth frowned. "Why are they here?"

"As best I can make out from Janie, her mother came here to beg for Sir Neil's help. Mary's husband died two weeks ago. Because there was no one to work the land, they were put off it, and the farm given to a man with three sons. With no one to take them in, Mary and her children were left homeless and starving."

Ari scowled fiercely. "'Twas the Earl of Winchester's land they were thrown off. That greedy wretch caused this."

"He isn't greedy," Gareth said defensively. "There is a good reason why each farm must produce as much as it can. People in the town and people at Tyneham Keep depend on Lord Geoffrey's farms for their food, too. If the fields aren't worked, there is no harvest, and all go hungry."

"For this, three people must die?" Ari snapped. Turning her back on him, she began to soap Janie's hair.

Gareth frowned. The order to remove Mary from the farm could only have come from the earl, yet his father would never have done such a thing. "The Sommervilles are known for their just treatment of their tenants and villeins," he began, which was not boasting; it was the truth. "The men who took Mary's farm may have done so illegally. The labor shortage has caused a number of bond tenants to run away from their rightful lords and hire themselves out for higher wages than their lord would have to pay them. Not satisfied with this, some serfs have turned outlaw, taking whatever they want by force."

"What makes you think it was outlaws and not the earl who drove Mary from her farm?" Ari asked stiffly.

Because I know my father. "You should not concern yourself with such things," he muttered.

Ari cocked her head. "Because I am a female, you mean. But shouldn't the welfare of others be everyone's concern?" Before he could frame a reply, she rushed on. "I've been so consumed by my craft that I never gave a thought to others before. 'Tis as if I've been sleeping these past few years and only just awakened to what is going on around me. And I find I do not like what I see. Nay, I do not like it at all."

Rupert chose that moment to shiver violently and cry out, earning Gareth a pleading glance from Ari.

"All right," he grumbled. It wasn't, but he was used to performing unpleasant tasks in the name of duty. And it would have taken a harder heart than his to ignore the needs of so tiny and helpless an infant.

Shed of his dirty, wet rags, Rupert resembled a plucked chicken. "He still looks gray," Gareth said as he wrapped the babe in the blanket. And he was still crying, albeit softly.

"M-mayhap 'e's still 'ungry," offered Janie's small voice, muffled by the towel Ari was drying her with.

"I've been keeping a bowl of milk warm there near the fire," Ari said. "And there's a clean cloth beside it. Dip it into the milk, and Rupert will suckle."

"Surely you don't expect *me* to nurse him?" Gareth exclaimed.

Ari grinned. "Not personally. But it's either feed Rupert or tend to Janie."

There were other choices, but he was in way too deep to mention them, nor could he bear to kill her faith in him.

A moment later, Farley stuck his head in, his eyes widening. Gareth could well imagine what went through the captain's head at the cozy domestic scene he found. "What is it?" Gareth growled, feeling his face go red.

Farley blushed himself. "I, er, just wanted to make sure everything was all right. You were a bit upset."

"We are fine," Ari replied, smiling serenely and looking not the least embarrassed to be found tending a villein's child. "Sir Garvey has been a great help."

"Ah." Farley's brows rose, but he wisely didn't comment.

Gareth cursed under his breath, thinking how Ruarke would laugh if he could see him now. The only good thing about this entire episode was that it had briefly taken his mind off the potential for disaster looming on the horizon.

"Are you still angry with me?" Ari inquired hesitantly.

Gareth's shoulders stiffened, but he didn't turn from the stone battlements where he stood, his eyes facing the restless sea, his arms braced on the deep-cut crenellation.

It was dark, lacking only a few minutes until one in the morning. A pale moon rode high overhead, and a single torch flickered in the cool night breeze.

Ari shivered, wrapping her arms around her for support. "I—I am sorry."

He didn't answer for so long she shivered again. Had she gone too far this time? Would his back be permanently turned against her? And just when she'd thought things were finally going to work out for them.

"What are you sorry for?"

She let out a small sigh. At least he was still speaking to her. "I am sorry I left the tower when I'd said I wouldn't."

His sigh echoed hers. "But?"

"But what?"

"There is a but. You are going to tell me again how wretched the serf and her children looked."

"Villein," Ari corrected him, and wished she hadn't when he at last turned on her.

Torchlight caught the fury in his sable eyes and set it blazing. "Serf...villein...I don't give a damn." He bit out. "That you should endanger yourself for such as they."

"Ah, if Mary had been a lady, you would not be angry?" Ari stepped forward into the fray, her nerves frazzled to the breaking point for having spent the hours between supper and now pacing alone in her chamber. Alternately beset by contrition and righteous indignation, she had at last sought him out, knowing as certainly as she did so many things about him, that he would not come to her.

"I hate such superiority," Ari cried, forgetting her vow to be calm and objective. "'Tis cruelty of the worst sort, because a person can not help the circumstance into which she was born."

Gareth's brown brows rose at the passion in her voice. "Who flayed you with that lash?"

"Not me," Ari replied nervously. "My mother was made to suffer for who she was. But that is beside the point," she hurried on before he could question her. "I think this is not about worry for me, or whether Mary is a serf or a lady. I think you blame me for Captain Farley's announcement at supper."

Gareth grunted and raked an exasperated hand through his sun-streaked hair. That she could read him so clearly sometimes unsettled him. "You must admit his speech was unfortunate."

"Must I? What you really mean to say is that you think I put him up to saying we had run off together."

His frown deepened. "Someone gave him the idea."

"Farley explained afterward that half the people at Tyneham thought you had kidnapped me, and the other half whispered that we had wed in secret. He could think of nothing else to say that would not blacken your honor or my reputation." Ari ground her teeth together, torn between leaving the lout to think what he would and staying to resolve this.

At supper that night, the captain had asked for everyone's attention and explained to them, per Sir Garvey's request, that they must keep Lady Arianna's presence at Tyneham Keep a secret, most especially from the townspeople and traveling merchants.

The servants and soldiers gathered in the hall had exchanged puzzled glances. 'Twas the cook who voiced the question, "Why?"

Farley had frowned and looked first to Sir Garvey, then to herself for an answer. When none was forthcoming, he had formed one of his own. "Lady Arianna would wed Sir Garvey, but old William Marsden is not pleased by the match. She...er...is hiding from him."

"Good fer ye, m'lady," shouted one of old women who had been so helpful in getting Mary and her children settled. The others in the hall took up the cry, their faces wreathed in smiles.

"'Twould seem ye've won their hearts, m'lady," Farley had said to Arianna.

Ari had been pleased to hear that, for she had come to know and value the folk of Tyneham more in the past few hours than ever she had when betrothed to Sir Neil. Again, she thought it was because her mind was no longer focused inward, on herself, but outward, on the people around her.

Her smile, and her brief wave of happiness had fled at Sir Garvey's stricken look. She'd known he was thinking a marriage between them was impossible, given his lack of prospects, and her heart had ached. The longer she had paced in her lonely chamber, the more determined she had become not to lose him.

Ari raised her chin as she faced him across the moon-washed battlements, despair giving her the courage to press on. "Please don't let your pride rob us of the chance at happiness."

Gareth started, swept by a tide of old insecurities. Had she discovered who he really was? "What do you mean, *my pride?*"

"I know you are trying to do what is best for me." She paused to lick her lips, her gaze steady, beseeching. "But I am used to a simple life, and I don't care for fancy clothes. To me, there are worse things than being poor." Her voice dropped to a low, agonized whisper. "Living without you is the worst thing I can think of."

Gareth's heart twisted. *Damn.* What was he to do? Duty and desire warred inside him, like claws tearing at his vitals.

She stepped closer, so her own unique scent wrapped around him on the evening breeze. Lavender and warm skin. His head swam with the memory of how she'd tasted on his tongue. The pulse beat wildly in the vulnerable hollow at the base of her throat. He wanted to press his lips to it, wanted to savor the strength and the life flowing in her, wanted to feel her soft body melt against his, tempering its hard planes. He needed her more than the breath trapped in his lungs.

"Can you honestly say you would be happy to see me wed a man who could give me those things?" she asked, her pained tone mirroring his own anguish.

Gareth struggled to remember that his father and the rest of the family expected him to marry well and produce a leader for the next generation of Sommervilles. But duty seemed a cold, lifeless dish served up beside the warm, vibrant woman staring up at him with her soul in her eyes.

In that instant, Gareth realized it wasn't only love he felt for her, it was something too wonderful, too all-encompassing for mere words. *Love.* That word took in all the things he felt, yet expressed none of them accurately. "Nay, I'd not see you wed another," he choked out. *But.*

Ari swallowed hard, her vision blurred. Blinking rapidly, she summoned a smile. "Good, because I don't think I can live without you." The smile wobbled, and his heart with it, every fiber of his being calling out to her. "I'd work very hard on the cups and bowl, and I know the next man who comes to rule Tyneham Keep will want you for his captain. How could he not, you are all that is brave and good."

The selflessness of her offer shook him. Emilie had come to him with grasping fingers and a cold heart. Ari offered everything she had with an open heart, certain that together they could conquer the odds. Her confidence in his abilities poured like a healing balm over his self-doubts. He cupped her determined little chin, his thumb caressing her soft cheek. He wasn't surprised to discover she hadn't been crying after all. Suddenly nothing was more important than making this brave woman his forever. "I accept your proposal, my lady."

"Really? Oh, Garvey." She threw herself into his arms, relishing the dents his armor put in her waist and back as he squeezed her tight. Everything was going to be all right.

"There may be some...some hard times ahead for us," Gareth cautioned, thinking of the unpleasant task of informing his sire that his eldest son and heir was marrying a nobody. A beautiful, clever, courageous woman, to be sure, but a goldsmith's daughter, nonetheless.

Ari stretched up on tiptoe, tunneling her fingers through his hair as she drew his lips to hers. "I love you," she murmured, her breath warm, her mouth warmer still as it opened beneath the insistent pressure of his.

And I love you. More than I thought it was possible to love anyone. He wanted to tell her so, but she wouldn't let him stop kissing her long enough to say anything. Groaning, Gareth gave himself up to the kiss. How could he have thought he could live without her? His father would just have to understand that only with Ari's love and support could he be a whole man, capable of leading the Sommervilles when the time came.

Nor did Ari come to their family empty-handed. Her compassion, her capacity for helping others was a dowry without equal. In these troubled times, 'twould benefit the Sommervilles far more than money or breeding. Nay, no matter what else he had to do, Gareth was marrying Arianna de Clerc.

"I don't like it," Walter grumbled, staring morosely into his cup of ale.

Charles frowned. "What's not to like? I've finished the coins, and in a week we'll have—"

"Why didn't Hugh tell us about the Sommervilles from the start?" Walter demanded.

"Probably because he knew you'd been involved with them."

Walter raised his head and glared at his brother across the scarred tavern table. "Never ye mind throwin' that in my face again. I say Hugh's got plans he ain't told us about."

"Y-you think he'd cheat us of our share?"

"In a minute. But, I'm thinkin' it's more than that." Walter sat back and massaged his jowls. "It strikes me as queer, a Sommerville goin' agin his kin and sidin' wi' a Harcourt."

Charles shifted in his seat, his knuckles white where he gripped his cup. "What are we going to do?"

"Keep our eyes and ears open, fer one thing. Hell, I wouldn't be surprised if Hugh and that jumped-up Sommerville o' his came back here in a couple o' days, not a week."

"You think that wasn't Gareth Sommerville?"

Walter shrugged. "The man looks like a Sommerville, but the blood flows thick in that family. Nay, I can't figger Gareth Sommerville turnin' agin his kin, but neither can I figger what Hugh's game is."

"Maybe Hugh plans to accuse the earl of making the coins."

Walter straightened. "Aye, ye could be right, considerin' the bad feelings between the two families." Leaning forward, he cuffed Charles on the shoulder. "'Tis good ta see ye can use that head o' yers fer more'n holdin' yer ears apart."

"Then Marsden won't be accused of treason, and I won't get to marry Arianna," Charles whined.

Walter scowled his brother into silence, then signaled for another round of ale as he pondered the matter. "The way I sees it," he confided after the barmaid had sloshed more ale into their cups and swished away, "is that Hugh's after somethin' bigger, somethin' he doesn't want us ta know about. Mayhap he even thinks ta cut us out o' the original deal."

"Nay. What are we going to do?"

"Ah, quit yer slobberin', Charlie boy. Walter'll figure somethin' out, never ye doubt that." He downed half the cup of ale, wiping the froth off on the back of his hand. "We'll keep our eyes peeled fer Hugh's ship. When it comes in, we'll go down and ha' another talk wi' him."

"What if Dame Cicily lied about sending Arianna to Norwich to learn housewifing? What if she went there to get married?"

"Now ye're not usin' yer head. Would the girl get married wi'out the dame along? Course not." Walter's eyes narrowed to dangerous slits. "No matter whot, we're not comin' out o' this empty-handed. Nay, we're stickin' close ta Hugh and gettin' our due from him, one way, or another."

Chapter Twelve

Dawn sent slender golden fingers streaking across the sky and out over the gray sea below, gilding the ripples of the incoming tide.

Gareth rubbed his gritty eyes and turned his back on the water he had watched through a second sleepless night. If Hugh had made it back this quickly, he wouldn't be able to land until the tide went out again, so it was safe for him to leave his post and get a few hours' sleep.

Over on Grassy Point, Farley's men would watch through the day in case Hugh decided to anchor there and come overland, as some merchant ships did to unload cargo destined for the town.

Stumbling down the stairs from the battlement, Gareth bumped into Farley coming up them. "I was on my way to relieve you," the captain said, frowning. "Damn, ye look terrible."

Gareth rubbed a hand over his stubbled face. "Nothing a few hours' sleep won't cure." He wanted to ask if Arianna was up yet but held himself back. If he knew where to find her, he'd be tempted to seek her out instead of getting the rest he so badly needed to face today's tasks.

"I, ah—" Farley scuffed at the step with his boot toe "—I'm sorry for what I said at supper yesterday. A dozen people had asked what you two were doing at Tyneham and if ye'd run off together. I said what I thought they'd believe most quickly."

Gareth smiled despite his fatigue. "I apologize for my behavior. I didn't want people to think ill of Arianna for taking a husband so soon after... after Sir Neil's death."

"You mean, it's true? You and Lady Arianna are...?"

"Betrothed," Gareth finished for him, surprised at the steadiness of his voice, the ease with which the word fell from his lips given the problems he and Ari still faced. After sealing their fate with a kiss that had warmed him for hours, he'd reluctantly sent her back to her chamber. He'd spent what was left of the night staring at the restless sea and contemplating the joys and sorrows to come.

"You're a lucky man. And as to her reputation, the folk of Tyneham know she and Sir Neil wed because of his promise to Sir Richard. She's in need of a strong protector. Better you than some man not of her choosing, as ofttimes happens."

"Aye." Gareth's fist clenched at the thought of Ari carried off by some greedy man who supposed she'd inherited great wealth from her grandsire and her dead husband. Not even the church was proof against marriage by kidnapping.

"Have you given thought to whether you'll stay and seek a post with the new man Lord Geoffrey sends us?"

"I, er, haven't decided," Gareth hedged. The longer he knew these people, the harder it was to conceal his true identity. Pray God, it wouldn't be much longer. "I hope your men got my message through to the earl."

"Aye. I sent two men out a few hours later to trace their route and report back any signs of foul play. The men returned last night to say the messengers had safely left the district."

"Your precautions were well taken." Gareth sighed and ran a weary hand through his hair. "Have you a room I can sleep in? I fear the hall will be noisy this time of day."

"We've enough space here so that a knight need not bed down in the hall with the soldiers and servants. Jamie, the steward, has instructions to show you to the chamber next to Sir Neil's. 'Tis small, but there is a bed and fire."

Both were welcome, as was the tub of hot water oozing steam before the hearth. "Thank the captain for his thoughtfulness," Gareth told the steward.

The old man's leathery face split into a toothless grin. "'Twas the Lady Arianna's suggestion. Came ta me an hour ago and bade me have the water ready when the tide turned. There's bread, wine and hot soup, too." He gestured to the table. "Told her soup was a queer thing ta break yer fast on, but she said ye'd been on watch the night and it'd heat up yer innards."

Gareth smiled. Ari hated rising early, yet after getting not much more sleep than had he, she'd climbed from her bed to see to his comfort. A sweet warmth stole through him, muting his exhaustion and the gnawing anxiety of the past night. In the darkest hour just before dawn, he'd begun to wonder if in his desperate need to be loved he'd imagined Ari's goodness, endowed her with more compassion and understanding than one woman could possess. Her thoughtfulness showed him the error of his black introspection and turned his mind down more pleasurable paths.

"The lady of the manor often bathes a guest," Gareth said silkily. "Will the Lady Arianna be seeing to mine?"

Old Jamie hooted. "Ye young men are all of a piece," he said as he began to release Gareth from the confines of his surcoat and the chain mail worn beneath. The steward's gnarled fingers made surprisingly short work of the fastenings. "Dead on yer feet, and still out fer a—"

"Keep a leash on your wicked tongue," Gareth snarled.

"'Twas not me havin' wicked thoughts about the lady," Jamie retorted, eyes twinkling. He removed Gareth's padded leather gambeson and draped it over the chest at the foot of the bed before heading for the door.

"I'll not have her name sullied," Gareth called after him.

The little man turned, cocking his head. "None here'll think ill of ye and the lady if ye share a bed. Half the folk think ye're wed already, and ye're a hero to everyone fer tryin' ta catch Sir Neil's murderer. And as fer me—" the old man shrugged "—I've known Arianna de Clerc since she were a babe. I'm that glad ta see her wed so well, *m'lord.*"

An icy chill tightened Gareth's skin. "What do you mean?"

"Knew who ye were the minute I clapped eyes on ye. Ye've filled out greatly in the seven years since ye were here before, but ye've the look of the earl. Aye, and the bearing, as well. Farley's remarked to me that yer horse and trappings were too fine, yer manner too assured fer a landless knight.''

"What did you tell him?" Gareth asked tonelessly.

Another shrug. "Said mayhap ye'd recently fallen on hard times. Figured ye had a good reason fer hidin' yer name."

Gareth nodded slowly. "Several."

"Ah. Ye needn't fear I'll say anythin'. Now, yer water and yer soup are coolin', *Sir Knight,* so ye'd best be at both. The Lady Arianna'll demand a full report the minute I step foot in the hall." He chuckled. "She has a lot to learn about being a chatelaine, but what she lacks in skill, she makes up for in her, ah, enthusiasm. She's left strict instructions ye're ta sleep after ye eat and bathe. So don't ye be showin' yer face below stairs till noon."

The foolish grin stayed on Gareth's lips long after he'd climbed from the tub, dried himself on the linen towel warmed by the fire, and crept between the crisp sheets. Tired as he was, it took awhile for his mind to let go the hope Ari might join him, longer still for his body to relax enough for sleep.

Sir Neil had been a man of simple tastes, content to sit at table with his men during meals, instead of apart from them at a table on a raised dais. Out of respect for the man, Old Jamie continued to order the knight's customary chair left empty.

Seated to the right of Sir Neil's place, Ari stared at the chair as the people filed into the hall for supper that evening. How different her life would have been had Sir Neil not been killed. If he had lived, would she still have fallen in love with Sir Garvey?

Arianna shivered. Aye, to her eternal damnation, she feared she would have. From her first sight of him as she stood naked and shivering, waiting for Sir Neil, she'd felt drawn to the handsome young knight. She'd felt for him the breathless anticipation she should have felt for her new husband. How awful it would have been to be married to one man, forced to lie with him while her heart and soul belonged to another. The pain that thought brought was nearly unbearable.

'Tis all right, she reminded herself. Sir Garvey would soon be her husband. Yet, now that her heart's desire was within reach, Sir Neil's death weighed more heavily on her conscience.

As though her mind had conjured him up, the knight appeared at her elbow and pulled out Sir Neil's chair. "Good evening," he said huskily.

"You can't sit there," she cried. "'Tis Sir Neil's place."

The warmth fled his eyes. "I see," he said stiffly, letting go the chair and turning away.

Ari jumped up before he'd gone two steps and grabbed his arm. "Oh, drat my hasty tongue. I did not mean it like that. Only I feel so..."

Gareth studied her pleading face for an instant. "So guilty?" At her sad little nod, he sighed. "As do I."

"'Twas not our fault he died," Ari lamely offered.

"Nay, but we profit by it."

"What are these long faces?" Old Jamie demanded, appearing beside them. "And after everyone went to so much trouble preparin' a special meal in honor of yerselves."

"They did?" Ari looked around, suddenly realizing they were the object of many concerned stares.

"Aye. So ye'd best be seated, so they can begin servin' the food." The little old man herded them back and sat them together on the bench, leaving Sir Neil's chair vacant. "He'd ha' wanted this fer ye," Jamie whispered for their ears alone.

Ari looked up at her knight and smiled faintly. "Sir Neil *did* tell me there was more to life than goldsmithing. He thought I should go forth and see other things."

"I doubt he meant creeping around in dark caves after a pack of murdering cutthroats," Gareth grumbled, but he couldn't keep the corners of his mouth from twitching. His reward was a teasing smile from Ari. "Don't think smiling and fanning your lashes at me will save you from the punishment you deserve."

"What would it take, then?" she teased.

Lord. He'd better grab the upper hand or she'd be as unruly as Gaby. Growling, he gave her his sternest glare. "'Tis not a laughing matter. You must learn to think *before* you act."

Glancing at him seductively through her lashes, she drawled, "If I come to your chamber later, will you give me lessons?"

"Baggage," muttered. "Your aunt will never make a proper lady out of you."

Ari tensed as though he'd slapped her.

"Dearling, what is it?" he asked, instantly concerned. She trembled as he cupped her pale cheek in his hand.

"You're doubtless right." She laughed shakily. "Thank God I am wedding you and need not worry about becoming a great lady."

Gareth's fast-beating heart slammed up against the wall of lies he'd built and faltered. "Ari, there is something . . ."

"I brought yer trencher, Lady Arianna." Young Janie slipped between them and laid a slice of manchet bread on the table for Ari and the knight to share.

"I've seen little of you today. What have you been doing?"

"Eating." The gleam in Janie's eyes said it all.

"And your mother and baby Rupert?"

"Sleeping and eating. We've a room ta ourselves off the kitchen. 'Tis near bigger than our hut was." Janie's smile filled her thin face, her eyes round with the wonders of Tyneham.

Ari put her arm around the girl and patted her bony shoulder. "I'm glad you're settling in."

"Ma's scared they won't let us stay, so we've been helpin' out this eve." She nodded to her dark-haired mother darting between the tables with a tray of broken meats.

"Your mother should be yet abed."

"She told the cook she was used ta bein' busy. I helped gather greens in the garden and scraped the carrots."

"I'm sure cook was glad of the help, but—"

"Janie, I told ye not to disturb Lady Arianna." Frowning angrily, Mary took the girl's hand. The woman's color had improved, but she still looked frail.

"It's all right, really," Ari insisted. "And you don't have to work to earn your keep."

"I'll not take charity."

"At least wait till you're well and stronger."

"Nay, m'lady, we've got ta make a place fer ourselves from the start." Head high, Mary scooted her daughter toward the buttery door and went back to serving.

"I wish I could get their farm back for them," Ari mused.

Gareth snorted. "And how would a woman manage a farm alone?"

"I don't know, but that doesn't mean it can't be done. Mayhap she could find some men who'd be willing to help with the work in exchange for food."

"No man would work for a woman."

His arrogant, superior tone grated on her nerves and provoked her to answer, "Of all the foolish . . ."

"Stewed rabbit, m'lady?" Old Jamie slapped a large spoonful onto their trencher without waiting for a reply. "That should keep yer mouths busy awhile." Giving them a pointed look of disapproval, he stomped off.

"The steward is right. Arguing in public is—"

"Not ladylike?" Ari ground out. "But then, we've already agreed I'll never be a lady."

"I didn't say that," Gareth muttered, conscious of the heads turned in their direction.

"'Tis the truth. My mother was not a lady, and neither am I." Hiding her pain, Ari tossed her braid back over her shoulder and turned her attention to the meal. Spoon in hand, she poked at the mass of overcooked rabbit before her. "I'll be glad when I can stop playing at lady of the keep and go home to my family and Grizel's cooking."

"My appetite has also fled," Gareth mumbled. Perhaps because of the lies stuck in his throat.

Gareth left the hall as soon as the meal was over, returning to his room for a few hours' sleep before standing the night watch. Though it was only nine o'clock, the rest of the keep had already retired for the night. Dawn came early.

Sleep refused to come to him, however, and he paced between the window and the fire, his footsteps muffled by the thick skin covering the floor. Clasping his hands behind his back, he stared into the dancing flames, searching for a way out of the twisting labyrinth he found himself in.

He must tell Arianna who he was. The more time that passed, the worse it was going to be to admit he'd continued to lie to her. Yet he did not trust her to keep his secret, and if word of his presence here somehow reached Walter and Hugh, he'd be as dead as Sir Neil and Sir Richard were.

At gut level, Gareth knew Hugh was behind the two murders, but he had no more proof of that now than he did that Hugh had masterminded the making and circulating of the false coins.

With their own necks at risk, sweating a confession from Hugh and his cousin would not be easy. What if he couldn't? The dreadful possibilities made him shiver despite the warmth of the fire. If he and his father and brothers were all accused of treason, stripped of their estates and hanged, who would see to his mother, Gaby and the children? What of Ari and her family? It was even possible that the king would be forced to throw the other Sommerville kin off their lands, too.

Nay, the risk was too great. Like it or not, he must keep his secret from Ari a little longer.

"Garvey. I hope I am welcome," whispered a soft voice.

Gareth whirled and froze at the vision Ari made walking across the room, her hair loose about her shoulders and cascading down the front of her robe. The candle she held aloft turned her tumbled curls into a river of gold, reminding him so forcefully of her wedding night, his heart lurched. Would she lose another husband ere she truly became his wife?

She rested her hand on his arm. "I am sorry we quarreled."

"I, too." He put his hand over hers and squeezed gently to seal the apology.

"Aunt Cici says men and women view things very differently."

Gareth smiled into her upturned face, his fears fading beside the joy seeing her brought him. "She and Gaby would get along well. Gaby and Ruarke are forever at each other's throats about who will lead and who will follow."

"I could not live like that," Ari said firmly.

"Agreed. I am a man of peace, especially at home."

"Is it because of Em—never mind," she added, withdrawing hastily at the tightening of his jaw. "You were tense at supper, and I wondered if you were thinking about Hugh and the coins?" she asked as she set the candle on a nearby table.

"Nay," he lied. "'Tis the strain of keeping my hands off you." His eyes lingered with undisguised desire on the curve of her hips and the thrust of her breasts rising and falling beneath the soft robe.

"I love you." She leaned her forehead into his chest.

Gareth caught her around the waist and held her close. "And I love you," he murmured into the bright spill of lavender-scented hair. "But you shouldn't be here," he added gruffly.

"You want me here." She felt the evidence pressed into the slope of her belly.

"I'd not compromise your honor." He tried to set her away, but she twined her arms around his neck.

"If it's shameless to want you, then I am shameless," she said, looking up at him with unabashed yearning. "Besides, we are going to be married."

"Just as soon as this thing with Harcourt is over," he promised, his lips lowering to those she offered. *Sweet.* He'd forgotten how sweet she tasted, how perfectly her mouth molded to his. Nearly as perfectly as her body and his fit together, like the interlocking parts of a puzzle.

"Oh." She sighed when he lifted his head. "It seems a hundred years since last you kissed me, but this isn't why I came in search of you."

"It isn't?" He smiled teasingly. "Then there's something I'm not doing right."

She chuckled, stretching up on tiptoe to arch against him. "Everything felt right to me, but then, I am just a novice at this business. I fear I need lessons."

"You do?" His heart raced at the invitation she shot him from beneath lowered lashes. He had a sense of losing himself in her bewitchment and didn't care. For the first time in his life, he felt free and happy. A great bubble of mingled desire and giddiness rose up inside him, making him feel light as air. He twirled with her in his arms so she squealed with laughter.

He found her open mouth and welded it closed with his, delighting in the small moans of pleasure his darting tongue drew from her as he kept them spinning.

"I'm dizzy," she confided when he stopped circling and raised his head.

"Dizzy as a drunk," he agreed. "You have that effect on me. Have since the first."

"I know." Her lips brushed his; her breasts pressed softly into his chest. "I felt it, too. That's part of what makes it so right." She kissed him again, sliding her tongue into the corner of his mouth. "We have only two hours till the tide turns and you go back up on the battlements. I'd not waste all of it standing here."

"Brazen wench." He kissed her again. When he lifted his head, his smile had faded. "I love you so much it scares me."

She sobered instantly, sensing this was no idle comment, but a glimpse inside his usual guard. "What are you afraid of?"

"Losing you."

His simple statement awakened her own fears. After leaving him on the battlements the night before, she'd lain awake wondering if he'd succeed in thwarting Harcourt's mad scheme. Worrying that even when this terrible time was behind them, Garvey might not find a place rich enough to support the two of them and her family.

Mayhap she was being superstitious, but Garvey seemed too perfect to be true. A strong, handsome knight willing to live in Tyneham instead of seeking fame and fortune elsewhere. What if later he regretted his choice? What if something came between them as her father's parents had come between Richard and Alys?

"I, too, am afraid." Shivering, Ari pressed her face into his woolen tunic as his arms tightened possessively around her. Time hung suspended as they clung together, drawing strength from each other to battle the unknown, uncertain future.

Ari's spirits recovered first. Raising her head, she smiled faintly. "We can't know what the future will bring. We can only face each problem as it comes. Remember, I'll always love you . . . no matter what."

Gareth's throat grew tight. He should be the one saying that. "I'll hold you to that pledge." Bless her ability to see past the bleakness of the moment. "I love you, Sunshine."

"My father called me that," Ari murmured.

"'Tis true. Your smiles light up my life like sunshine. Until you came along, I lived in darkness."

Touched, she murmured, "Then you agree we belong together?"

"I'd show you what I feel." Drawing her into his embrace, he nuzzled her throat. At her soft sigh of encouragement, he began working his way down to the upper curve of her breast, each nibbling kiss accompanied by her hushed moan.

Her nipples peaked, hard and sensitive as he parted her robe and stood looking at her in the firelight. "Beautiful—more beautiful than I remembered." His mouth closed over one excited tip and drew down with devastating gentleness, his touch deft.

Ari cried out her pleasure and sank her fingers into his hair, urging him on. He lifted her, fitting them together. Male to female. Hard to soft. Her head fell back in abandonment, the breath quick and ragged in her throat, punctuated by gasps that stoked the heat in his veins to a fever pitch.

Slowly. He had wanted to go slowly, to initiate her in the ways of love with a finesse that had escaped him during that explosive time in the caves. Then, suppressed passions and the dangerous lure of the unknown had wrested his customary control from him and he was swept into uncharted waters. Now, memory and the sweet flesh beneath his lips spurred him to urgency where he would have preferred to linger.

Groaning, he dragged his mouth from her breast and bent to pick her up in his arms.

"What are you doing?" she murmured.

"Carrying you to the bed."

"Nay. When I walked in and saw you standing before the hearth, I pictured us making love here on the fur with only the fire for light and only your kisses to keep me warm."

She was a picture herself—a study in wanton beauty, her face flushed with desire, her hair a tangled halo backlit by the fire. The dark green robe hung loosely from her shoulders, contrasting sharply with her pale skin and wet red nipples.

"Sunshine, there are a few things you may teach me." He lowered her gently to the rug, then shed his clothes. Her heavy-lidded gaze followed his every move, widening slightly as he stripped off his hose and stood before her.

Broad shoulders, smooth muscles lightly furred with honey hair, long lithe limbs, these she had glimpsed before, but the other was a mystery now uncovered. The proof of his desire, rising thick and strong from its nest of curls, stirred Ari's senses on many levels.

"Say you'll let me sketch you," she murmured, rising to her knees and reaching out to touch him.

"Now?" He raised a teasing brow at her, but his body betrayed his eagerness, trembling as her fingers traced a fiery path down from his hipbone. The breath hissed out between his teeth as her small palm encircled him. "Easy, else we'll be done before we've scarce begun."

"Teach me," she whispered, her eyes alight with sensual promise as her gentle urging brought him down beside her.

"Everything I know, my lady, and when we've run through that we'll make the rest up as we go along."

"I like the sound of that." Ari liked it even better moments later when he thrust into her, and told him so, throwing back her head and groaning. He echoed her pleasure as she caught his rhythm and matched it. Her fingers dug into his hips as their passion intensified.

"Aye, stay with me, love," he crooned. His hands were under her, one at her shoulders, the other at her buttocks, cradling her up off the floor as he silently encouraged her. His mouth found her breasts again and suckled, sending shock waves rippling to the aching core of her. Inside her the pressure built to a frenzy, and her hips answered, rocking against his, searching frantically for surcease.

Groaning against her breast, he clasped her closer, shifting to match her needs as his own soared out of control. They clung together as the wave crested, their cries blending as the peak was reached and they floated back down to earth.

A few minutes later, Gareth stirred and turned on his side, relieving her of his weight and throwing the edge of her robe over their heated bodies. Tucking her under his arm, he kissed the top of her head and asked, "Are you all right?"

"Mmm." Warmed by his concern, Ari opened one eye. "I am fine. Nay, more than fine," she murmured, kissing his chin.

"I love you."

"And I you. Does everyone do it like this?" she asked, then blushed at his stare. "I did not mean on the floor, I meant . . . Well, I was afraid. I had heard there was pain."

"You did have pain that first time, I'm sorry to say."

"'Twas nothing. Gone in a moment and replaced by such joy that I forgot until now that it was supposed to hurt. When I wed Sir Neil, my aunt was not much help, having never been married."

"But, she is called *Dame* Cicily."

"When she opened the herb shop, she reasoned the title would inspire more confidence than if she'd called herself Mistress Cicily." Ari nibbled on her lower lip. "Are you certain they are all right alone with Charles?"

"Aye, I told you that I broke my fast with them that morning, and couldn't believe what players they were. There that betraying bastard sat at their table, yet neither by tone nor expression did your grandfather nor Dame Cicily show they knew what he'd planned."

Ari trembled. "I worry about them."

Gareth sat up and reached for his scattered clothes. "And I worry that you grow chilled here on the floor."

"Wait." Her hand closed over his. "I would sketch you."

"You should be in bed, asleep."

"I could not sleep for our quarrel. I came here to draw you and see if we might make peace between us."

"What we made was far more satisfying than peace," he murmured. "But I'll be going up on the battlements soon."

"Not for another hour or so. Your protests make me wonder if you really do not want to be with me."

He didn't answer, but his expression changed in the second before he looked away. In his eyes, she'd seen desire war with uneasiness. What had she done? Nay, 'twas not that. It was something he withheld. Something besides that dratted Emilie stood between them, preventing him from relaxing completely. Suddenly she was afraid to be apart from him. "I will dress and come with you."

His head whipped back around. "Nay, you will not."

Forcing a bright smile, she shrugged. "What else can I do if I can't sleep and want to be with you?"

"I could tie you up," he growled, but the threat lacked substance. "Oh, all right," he said after a moment under her pleading gaze. "I will sit for this damned drawing, but only for an hour. And don't think I will always be so easily managed."

"Never." Ari's smile was dazzling enough to rouse a flicker of desire in his sated body. Unwilling to let her know how much influence she had over him, he reached for his clothes again.

"I would draw you without them. I want to capture you just as you are now. An ancient god cast in gilt and shadows. Or the first man rising naked and unashamed to face his new world."

Gareth shook his head. "Women and their romantic notions."

"Sometimes you are glad I have them," she pertly replied.

The flames behind him haloed his sun-kissed hair in fiery gold as he threw back his head and laughed. He looked like a pagan god. One knee rested on the fur. The near leg, bent so the muscles of his thigh and buttock corded, displayed a subtlety of strength echoed in the arch of his back and the width of his shoulders. But there was more. Sensitivity in the curve of his mouth. Intelligence reflected in his midnight eyes.

"I'd sketch you without your clothes," she said huskily, repeating her intention.

Gareth shifted, the novel idea of sitting naked while she sketched him proving strangely arousing. Already his skin tingled at the thought of her eyes moving over it, and a familiar pressure tightened his loins. "All right."

"Oh, thank you." Leaping up, she reached for her robe.

"No clothes for you, either, Sunshine."

Ari stared in dismay. "You expect me to be naked, too?"

"Seems only fair." He grinned suddenly. "And I know how you are about things being equal between men and women."

"Fiend, to hang me so by mine own words." Ari gathered her hair around her and bent to retrieve her drawing materials from the floor where she'd left them. The heat of his gaze scorched her through the meager covering, so her skin glowed red by the time she sat down on the bed. "Happy?"

"Very." It was a pleasure to watch her work, sitting on the foot of the bed in all her naked glory. With only the sound of the crackling fire and the scratching of charcoal on parchment to break the silence, she worked for several minutes.

The movement of her head as she studied her work sent a tendril of pale hair sliding aside to reveal one rosy breast. As though sensing his interest, the nipple pouted back. His body quickened in swift response.

Damn. The explosiveness of his climax should have left him sated for a week, yet he wanted her as badly now as he had when she'd walked into the room. *Damn.* Excessive lust was Alex's province, not his. Not that Gareth had been celibate, but no woman had ever made him feel like this. Hot and restless and tense as a pulled bowstring.

"You promised to stay still."

"I am staying as still as I can," he rasped.

A small feminine smile curved her lips. "Part of you isn't."

Glancing down, Gareth guessed what she could see below the curve of his bent leg. "'Tis all your fault."

"But I haven't done anything."

"It isn't necessary for you do anything," he wryly observed.

"I see." She studied him for a heartbeat, then a speculative gleam entered her eyes. "What if I want to do something?"

Gareth rose lithely and stalked toward the bed, his dark gaze locked on hers with an intensity that sent shivers of anticipation racing through Arianna. He stopped beside the bed, his hand sliding under her hair and pushing it back over her shoulder so his hungry eyes could devour every fire-lit curve and hollow. "What would you do to me, Sunshine?"

Ari's lips parted on a sigh. "Everything."

Chapter Thirteen

Arianna opened her eyes a fraction and glared at the bright sunlight slanting in through the arrow slit. It must be nearly noon. Soon Gareth would get up to watch for the ship again. She didn't want to let go of him or the beautiful memories they'd made in the early-morning hours when he'd come back to her after completing his watch on the battlements.

Sighing, she snuggled back against the wide expanse of his hairy chest, her smooth legs sliding along the warm, muscular length of his.

"'Tis about time you stirred," came his deep baritone.

Ari rolled onto her back and stared up at Gareth. His head was propped up on one hand; his eyes glowed like the banked coals in the hearth. "Good morn," she said softly, blushing slightly.

"I would we had the night to live over."

Ari shivered at the intensity of his gaze. "I, too. Must you leave already?"

"Soon, but not yet." He slid his free hand over her hip and moved slowly across her belly, desire sweeping through him as he felt the delicate muscles contract beneath the satiny warmth of her skin. He paused just below the swell of her breast, smiling at the swiftness with which passion darkened her eyes. "How could I leave you when you look at me like that?"

"Then you will never leave me," Ari whispered. Rasping her name, he filled his hand with her breast. She closed her eyes on a moan, pressing herself into his palm, trembling as the familiar, syrupy heat spilled through her.

Gareth smiled, thrilled by the desire softening her animated little face. *Mine. All mine.* His heart expanded in his chest until he thought it would burst. "Nor will I ever let you go," he murmured. Lowering his head, he kissed her with all the possessiveness pent up inside him.

Ari welcomed him as he slid his tongue between her parted lips. Tasted his passion and possessiveness, yet she wasn't startled by either. Twining her arms around his neck, she arched closer, glorying in his groan and the shudder that shook his big body as he wrapped both arms around her and accepted her invitation to deepen the kiss. For all his size and strength, he was strangely vulnerable to her. The realization that she had such power over him made her feel humble, protective.

They were both breathing hard by the time Gareth raised his head. "I love you," he said hoarsely, his gaze dark and urgent.

"So much it frightens you." She smiled with all the love inside her, her hand shaking slightly as she pushed the sun-lightened hair from his forehead. "But you have nothing to fear from me, because I love you... and I always will."

"Oh, Ari." Gareth buried his face in her neck. "I need you so. I think I have needed you all my life."

"And I need you, my love," she whispered in his ear. "Let me show you." Running her hands down between them, she touched him.

"Temptress." Gareth's teeth clenched as he fought to maintain control of his surging desires. "You're so small, so delicate, so new to this. I'd let you rest this morn," he murmured, but her coaxing fingers were driving him mad.

"I'm not made of glass," Ari softly chided, smiling up into features tender with the love he bore her.

The teasing grin that curved Gareth's mouth covered his inner determination to protect her even from himself. "Nay, you are flesh and blood, and it pleases me you're so hot for me."

"Hot!" she cried, releasing him and taking the bait as he'd known she would. "'Tis indecent to speak so."

"Nay, it is the truth," he drawled, wagging one brow at her. "Only think how you moaned and cried my name when my lips uncovered your sweetest treasure."

"Oh!" Ari's cheeks flamed. "You think I am a harlot."

He frowned. "Never that. Remember what passes between us is right and beautiful, Sunshine, because 'tis done for love."

"I know you love me, but I'd not have you think ill of me. Nay, that I could not stand," she added fiercely.

"I fear love has made me blind to your imperfections." Chuckling at her snort, he reluctantly disentangled himself from silky limbs and sat up. "There are two things you must cure yourself of, however, my willful, disobedient little love. You must always follow my commands, and you must cease saying the first thing that comes into your head."

"Willful? Disobedient?" Ari doubled up her fist to sock the nose he looked down. "Who are you to speak so to me?"

"Your husband," he teased. Dropping a kiss on her furious brow, he climbed out of bed—and out of range. Yet she looked so adorable in her rage, he couldn't resist a parting shot. "'Tis my duty to point out your flaws and help you cure them," he added as he padded over to the hearth and retrieved his clothes.

Ari jerked upright, clutching the sheets to her breasts. "I am as I am," she snapped indignantly. "And I will not be made to feel guilty over what I can't change."

"Won't?" Gareth asked, the question was muffled as he pulled on his tunic. Free of the garment, he cocked his tousled head at her, a dangerous light gleaming in the eyes that had so recently adored her. She'd have many adjustments to make in her life when they were wed and she was mistress of Ransford. He'd smooth her way however he could, but on these points he must stand firm: He'd not have her endangering herself through heedless actions, nor could the Countess of Winchester go about spouting the first thing that entered her head. "'Tis a childish attitude to take," he warned with deceptive softness. "You could wound someone with a careless word, or come to some harm through an impetuous act."

Ari tossed her head. "So, we are back to my coming to rescue you in the caves."

"And giving away your presence at Tyneham by going to the aid of Mary and her children. I can see you have not learned your lesson about thinking before you act," Gareth grumbled, shoving a frustrated hand through his hair. "Mayhap I should have beaten you after all."

"Beaten me?" Ari cried, aghast. "No one has ever lifted a hand against me."

"Why am I not surprised?"

"Oh, you are an . . . an unfeeling man."

Both brown brows arched this time. "You can say that after what transpired between us last night?"

Hurt, Ari fought back with the first weapon to enter her mind. "Oh, you like it that I am 'hot for you', but when I say things to displease you, you become an arrogant ogre."

"Arrogant?" Gareth laughed. "Alex is arrogant, not me."

A forceful knock swung Gareth's head to the chamber door.

"Sir Garvey?" Farley called from the other side. "There is some confusion here. Lord Alexander Sommerville is come in answer to your message. But he claims it was sent by his brother, Lord Gareth. When I said there was no one here by that name, he demanded to see you."

Alex, here? They had not spoken to each other since that terrible day when Emilie's lies had nearly goaded Gareth into killing Alex. There must indeed be trouble at Ransford, to bring Alex instead of their father. Still carrying his boots in one hand, Gareth sprinted across the room, unbolted the door and swung it open. Sure enough, his middle brother lounged against the far wall of the gloomy corridor.

"Gareth?" Alex straightened, squinting against the sudden glare of sunlight. "When I heard the laughter and the shouting, I was afraid I'd guessed wrong and the mysterious Sir Garvey was not my solemn big brother, Gareth," he drawled.

Ignoring Arianna's gasp of surprise, Gareth stared at the thin pink line cutting across the hollow in Alex's tanned throat. Once, it had been red, dripping with blood. Once, he had spilled his brother's blood. Now he couldn't bear to look him in the eye.

"I know I'm the last person you want to see, now or ever," Alex said tightly, his smile fading. "But Papa is somewhere between London and Wilton, and your message sounded urgent." That mocking smile of his returned as he glanced past Gareth. "Ah, I'm happy to see you found a likely wench way out here in the wilds, though why you were shouting at her instead of—"

"Alex," Gareth roared, moving to block his brother's view of the bed and Arianna. They were of a height, with wide shoulders inherited from their sire. Yet somehow Gareth managed to avoid Alex's startled gaze. "Let us continue this discussion in Sir Neil's counting room."

Curiosity remained in Alex's dark brown eyes, but he nodded and started back down the tower stairs with an equally baffled Farley trailing after him.

Drawing in a deep breath, Gareth turned to face Arianna. Her eyes were wide with shock and a dozen questions, none of which he had the time to answer at the moment. "I can't stay to explain things, but I'll be back as soon as I can. We'll talk then," he said lamely.

Ari stared at the closed door, her heart beating wildly in her throat as she relived the confrontation between Lord Alexander Sommerville and Sir Garvey. Nay, not Sir Garvey—Gareth, Gareth Sommerville. Inside, she felt cold and hot at the same time. Her mind whirling with the enormity of what had just happened, she struggled to understand what it all meant.

Clearly he had lied to her about his name. Had he lied about loving her, too?

Ari stuffed a knuckle into her mouth to keep from crying out in her pain, her confusion. *Why? Why?*

The scratching at the door barely intruded on her chaotic thoughts, but the opening of the door caught her eye.

Grizel stuck her head in, her expression wary.

"Oh, Grizel." Glad to see a familiar face, Ari held out her arms to her friend. The maid rushed to her side and hugged her tight, understanding without words Ari's need to be held. Tempted as she was to collapse and give in to the tears burning her eyes, Ari fought to remain in control. Spill a tear now, and she *knew* she'd never stop. "What are you doing here?" she asked at last in a shaky voice.

Grizel sat back on the edge of the bed and bent her left arm at an angle.

"Sim brought you. But why did you come? To see me?" Ari interpreted as Grizel pointed to her. "To see if I was all right? Oh, Grizel. I am touched, knowing how afraid you must have been to come among so many men."

Grizel shrugged, started to gesture, then seized a piece of parchment from the bedside table. Dame Cicily had taught both girls the rudiments of writing so that they might be of help in keeping records in the two shops.

Grizel bent over the parchment, writing that the soldiers of the keep had not bothered her at all, merely pointed the way to Sim, who waited for her in the courtyard below. Was Ari all right? Grizel asked at the bottom of the paper. William and Dame Cici were worried.

"Until a short while ago, I was the happiest woman alive. But no more." Ari sighed. With little encouragement on Grizel's part, Ari told her everything. Well, nearly everything.

When Ari had finished her tale, Grizel's brown eyes were sad. With a gesture she asked where the knight was.

"Knight? Nay, Garvey is no mere knight. His name is not even Garvey. He is..." Ari's voice trailed off as a thought struck her. Gareth was a member of the wealthy, powerful Sommerville family. As such, he was not only beyond her reach, he was in danger of being hanged for treason if Hugh Harcourt's plot succeeded. Either way, alive or dead, Gareth was lost to her.

"Unbelievable!" Alex exclaimed when Gareth had finished telling him what he knew of Hugh Harcourt's plans. "Jesu, they are an evil, deceitful pack."

"Aye," Gareth said absently. He stood at the window, looking out over the wall to the restless sea beyond. His insides churned as relentlessly as the dull gray water, and with less hope of calming. He'd expected to have more time, some warning, at least, before Ari learned he'd lied to her. What must she be thinking? Undoubtedly, that he'd lied about loving her, too.

He ached with the need to go to her and set her mind at ease before she did something rash, but duty to his family held him prisoner here. "The question is," he said without turning, "how are we going to stop Hugh?"

"I like your idea of capturing him when his ship returns."

"I'd feel more assured of our success if Ruarke were here."

Alex knew his older brother too well to take offense. It was his own fitness to lead Gareth questioned, not Alex's. "There wasn't time to wait for him. I had made port three days ago, and arrived at Ransford yesterday to find our mother there, newly come from London herself. She was in such a stew over how to help you, she was nearly ready to lead a column of men here herself. I decided I could reach you the quickest by sea. After sending word to Ruarke to search for Papa, I rounded up as many of my sailors as I could and sailed here. The *Sommerville Star* is anchored some two miles down the coast, aboard are eighty men-at-arms from Ransford."

Gareth nodded. "I didn't mean to sound ungrateful for your presence here, Alex, but . . ."

"The devil would be more welcome." Shoving a hand through his hair, Alex walked to the window. "Let it go," he commanded, putting both hands on his brother's shoulders.

Gareth tensed. "I can't."

"Given the terrible lies Emilie had fed you, you had every reason to seek me out," Alex said in a low, charged voice.

"But not to kill you. God, I nearly killed you." He leaned his head against the window frame, his knuckles white where he gripped the smooth oak.

"But you didn't," Alex insisted, his fingers digging into Gareth's hard flesh. "Your blade barely broke my skin."

Nay, he hadn't done it, but he'd wanted to. In the moments after Emilie had claimed the child she carried was Alex's, Gareth had hated his brother enough to do murder.

"Let it go," Alex said softly. "I forgave you long ago."

I can not forgive myself, nor forget that a murderer lies beneath this civility I cloak myself in. "I'd speak of it no more," Gareth said. Shrugging free of Alex's touch, he paced to the hearth, poured himself a cup of wine. He drank it quickly, welcoming the raw fire that clawed its way down his throat.

Alex drew in a breath and slowly let it out, powerless to ease the bitterness eating at his brother. "Then tell me of your plan to trap Harcourt."

Gareth's sigh was one of relief. "I'd suggest we divide the men you brought with you. Some we'll add to Tyneham's soldiers, the others can remain aboard the *Star* with you. You can hide your ship in one of the smaller inlets until Harcourt's ship is sighted entering the cove. My force will wait on the beach for them to land, while you sail in to block the entrance and cut off their escape route to the open sea."

"Excellent." Forcing a smile, Alex poured himself a cup of wine and refilled Gareth's. Dropping into Sir Neil's chair, he stretched his long legs toward the fire. "So, tell me about the wench?" he drawled.

"She is not a wench. She's the woman I intend to wed," Gareth said tightly, braced for an explosion.

"What?" Alex bolted from the chair, his eyes wide. "But... but Mama said Papa was choosing a wife for you."

His brother's harsh tone made Gareth wince. "We had agreed on that before I left Ransford, but something has come up."

"And I can guess what it was. She's a tempting morsel."

"Keep a civil tongue in your head," Gareth snarled.

So. Fierce determination had replaced Gareth's usual calm, patient expression. This was serious. Not even when he'd come to accuse Alex of sleeping with his wife had this wild, possessive light gleamed in his eyes. Nay, then big brother had been out to ease his shattered pride, with blood if necessary. Now there was more than mere pride at stake. "Does she love you, too?"

"Aye," Gareth growled. His square chin came up in challenge.

"Who is she?"

"Her name is Arianna. She is ... was ... Sir Neil's bride."

"The goldsmith's daughter?" Alex exclaimed.

"Granddaughter." Even more belligerently.

Another greedy blond beauty. Alex's grip tightened on the cup until he felt the metal bend. Ruarke and Gaby had once prevented him from making a mistake where a woman was concerned. It was his duty to keep Gareth from making a similar mistake, but he knew his brother wouldn't listen to him any more willingly than he had listened to Ruarke and Gaby. "I would meet her before I return to the *Star*."

Gareth stiffened. The last thing he wanted was his charming rogue of a brother sniffing around Arianna. "We won't have time if we're to ready our trap before Harcourt returns."

Alex shrugged. But he knew for this, he'd make time.

Arianna leaned into the crenellation and stared blindly at the sea, scarcely feeling the chill of the stone beneath her arms. The sun was setting. Grizel and Sim had returned to town, and still Gareth had not come to explain away his lies. Her pride wounded, her heart aching, she'd instinctively come up to the battlements. To relive the memory of happier times?

The whispers of the wind, the pounding of the surf on the rocks below reminded her of the background sounds that had accompanied the promises they'd exchanged on this very spot two nights before. False. His declaration of love, his offer of marriage, all as false as the name he'd given her.

"Arianna?"

She turned, half dreading, half hoping to see the Gareth, but it was the other one—his brother. "You have come to explain in his stead."

"Explain what?"

"Explain why he lied to me about his name."

"I didn't know he had, but nay, that stallion of his was wreaking havoc in the stables. While he was settling the beast down, I came to see if I could . . ."

"Settle the fractious mare?" she inquired archly, quietly pleased to see his eyes widen in surprise.

Recovering quickly, he shrugged off her snide comment and strolled over to her. Negligently leaning one broad shoulder against the stone, he stared down at her, his dark eyes so like his brother's she suppressed a shudder.

There was a family resemblance, too, in his aristocratic nose and the way he cocked his head as he studied her. But where the knight was solid and compact, Alex was lean and rangy, with a catlike stride, and slow, smoldering smile. It teased the corners of his mouth as he addressed her.

"I understand you are to wed my brother."

"Obviously I am not."

"Ah, you think he lied to lure you into bed? I doubt it. That is my style, not Gareth's."

Arianna felt her face color at his implication, but she held her head high. Bad enough her heart and pride were bruised, she'd not let him humiliate her, too. "'Twas not Gareth Sommerville who offered me marriage," she said stonily. "I proposed to him."

"Now, why does that not surprise me?" he jeered.

"What do you mean?"

"I think you know. How much would you take to disappear from his life?"

Ari blinked. "You are offering me money to leave him?" Was this how it had been for her mother?

"I might have known I'd find you here," Gareth growled.

Arianna and Alex both started and turned as Gareth advanced on them. His sword remained sheathed, but the fury blazing in his eyes made Alex step back from her. "Gareth, this isn't what you think," he began, holding up a placating hand.

"Isn't it?" The muscle in Gareth's jaw jumped as he ground his teeth together.

"Jesu, Gareth, be reasonable. I was just trying to help."

"Help yourself to my woman?" Gareth grated in a terrible voice. "If you seek to repay me for taking Emilie from you, you needn't bother. The wounds she inflicted are deeper than any vengeance you could have extracted."

Emilie? Ari frowned. "Now I remember. Alex was the man you called to when you were fevered," she whispered. "The one you didn't want to kill. Were you fighting over Emilie? What happened between the three of you?"

"Ari. Go and wait for me in your chamber," Gareth said tightly. "I will follow directly."

She wanted to refuse, but the bitter, haunted pain in Gareth's eyes turned her will to jelly, and she ran from the battlements without a backward glance. Safe in her room, she paced, her nerves in shreds. Somehow, she must gird herself to resist him, to turn her back on him and all they might have had together. She must return to her grandfather's house and pick up the scattered pieces of her life.

The door opened so quietly she didn't realize Gareth had entered until he spoke her name. Whirling around, she found him standing just behind her, his hands clenched at his sides, his body tense as though to withstand a mortal blow.

"I regret lying to you about my name," he said. "But I deemed it necessary."

"Why?" That there was no anger, only curiosity in her wide blue eyes, gave him the courage to press on.

"The men who ambushed me on my way to Tyneham spoke of killing a Sommerville. And when I found out Harcourt was involved in this, I knew he'd kill me in an instant did he learn I was here alone and virtually unprotected."

"Why would he hate you so?"

Cynicism twisted Gareth's expression. "Because I am a Sommerville. The Harcourts and Sommervilles have been feuding for three hundred years. Our ancestors were distant cousins who followed William the Conqueror to England. Duke William sent the two cousins to lay siege to a castle, promising them an equal split of the spoils. Valiant warriors both, they quickly succeeded in taking the castle. The trouble started when they sat down to divide their loot. The Sommerville had fallen in love with the lady of the castle."

Gareth smiled faintly. "'Twas from that ancestor we Sommervilles inherited our possessive streak where our women are concerned. When Harcourt insisted on sharing the lady, too, Sommerville fled with her rather than agree."

His righteous fervor made Ari shiver. Surely he wouldn't insist on wedding her now. Would she have the courage to refuse him if he did? "Did the lady have no say in her fate?"

He grinned. "None. The lady loved him. She led him to a keep on the site of what is now Ransford, our castle, and fought by his side to defend it against Harcourt until the duke intervened to settle the matter. Sommerville got the lady and her family's title, Earl of Winchester. Harcourt got much money and Winchester's castle, which he renamed Harte Court.''

''But he was not satisfied with that?''

Gareth snorted. ''Not at all. No matter that they have twice our land and wealth, the Harcourts have always lusted after the earldom. Only they are sneaky, treacherous devils. Instead of openly fighting us for it, they skulk around hatching scheme after scheme in an attempt to bring us down.''

''After hearing what Harcourt has planned, I see why you were concerned,'' she said slowly. Unconsciously drawn to him, she closed the gap he'd left between them. ''But what about later, when you knew you loved me, and I you?''

Gareth's mouth turned rueful. ''Because, much as I love you, I didn't think you could keep the secret to yourself.'' She sighed, her expression so mournful Gareth couldn't resist putting his arms around her and hugging her close. At the feel of her relaxing into his embrace, the last of his tension drained away. Most women would have raged or cried, but not his Sunshine. ''I am sorry, little love.''

It scarcely mattered. What had her shoulders slumping was that she could no longer wed him. ''I wish you'd trusted me.''

''I trusted you with my heart,'' he said softly.

''Oh.'' Battling tears, Ari rested her head on his chest, her arms wound tightly around his muscular body.

''I love you,'' he murmured into her hair, dragging in the scent of her. ''So very much. About that, I did not lie. And we'll be married as soon as we've captured Hugh.''

Nay, that was impossible, now, Ari thought, suppressing a shiver as she remembered Alex's offer to pay her if she'd leave Gareth alone. Gareth's family would not want her any more than Richard de Clerc's family had wanted Alys Marsden in their midst. Less, even, for the Sommervilles were a far more powerful and illustrious family than the de Clercs.

Somehow she'd have to find the strength to leave. Once she was out of Gareth's sight, he'd forget about her and find someone else. Her heart cramped on that thought, sending an irrepressible shudder through her.

''You're cold,'' Gareth exclaimed, chafing her back with his large, warm hands. ''Let me heat you some wine.''

It would take more hot spiced wine than there was in all the world to melt the ice inside her.

Charles let himself out the back door of Marsden's house. The crushed stone in the walkway crunched beneath his feet as he hurried to the back of the garden where Walter waited. Ducking under the low-slung branches of a chestnut tree whose fruit Dame Cicily roasted in winter, he nervously faced his brother. "What's happened?"

"Plenty," Walter growled. "I was hangin' around outside Tyneham Keep when Farmer Elgen came ridin' up fair frothin' at the mouth. He sighted a ship off Grassy Point. I'm that sure it's Hugh's."

"When will they land?"

"The tide don't turn again till later tonight. They'll either come ashore then, or wait until morn."

"So Hugh *is* back earlier than he said he'd be. What are we going to do?"

"Go ta the beach and wait fer Hugh ta land."

"You're trembling, Walter. Has aught else happened?"

"Nay," Walter lied. Charles'd only whine and fret if he knew what else Walter had overhead. The hireling was none other than Gareth Sommerville. Walter wasn't certain how he could use this information to his advantage, but use it he would.

Somehow, he'd have his revenge on the Sommervilles. He only regretted it was not Ruarke and Gabrielle who had come, but mayhap he'd find a way to make them pay, too.

Chapter Fourteen

"There... a ship comes," Farley whispered.

Barely visible against the gray wall of fog lurking offshore, a white blur of unfurled canvas bobbed around the stony outcroppings of Grassy Point. The ship seemed to hesitate at the entrance to the cove, as though sensing the presence of the soldiers hiding in the rocks at the base of the cliff.

"Do you think it's Harcourt?" Gareth asked.

"I'm no sailor, but the shape seems the same, and the timing's right. He always comes between ten and midnight."

Gareth smiled thinly. "Predictability has been the downfall of more than one man." He prayed it would be Harcourt's. The watch in the tower had just cried ten. The tide had run out, exposing a narrow sliver of sand dappled with wet black stones. Across the cove, the maw of the cave was a dark smudge on the pale cliffs. The timing was right, and thus far the weather gave them an advantage.

Overhead, the sky hung low, brooding and moonless. Out to sea, the bank of fog waited for the right moment to sneak in and steal what little visibility they had. Then the fog would become their enemy; just now, it was their ally. Somewhere inside the concealment of its soupy mist the *Sommerville Star* waited, too.

"It'd be a blessing if the fog held off till they land," Farley commented in a hoarse whisper.

Gareth nodded and looked at the men around him. Alex had cautioned them that sound traveled on the water, and they must take no chances. Clad in dark wool with only chain mail beneath, but no armor that might clank or glint on a stray bit of light, they crouched in the natural cover created by a rock slide.

Gareth's gaze narrowed as the ship began to move again. A froth of white water preceded her as her bow knifed diagonally across the dark bay toward the cave.

"It has to be Harcourt," he murmured.

"Aye. What are your orders . . . m'lord?" Farley asked.

Gareth darted a glance at the captain but could see no anger for his lies in the shadow-draped face so near his own. Briefly he prayed Arianna would be as understanding when he explained they must leave Tyneham and go to live at Ransford.

She'd be upset, but she'd change her mind when he promised to take her family and servants, too. Gareth only hoped she'd be as flexible about learning to be a lady . . . his lady.

"M'lord?"

Gareth jerked his mind back to the situation at hand. "We'll let them row ashore and move away from their boats before springing the trap. Have the men wait for my signal." He was surprised at how easily the words of command came.

Farley nodded and turned to whisper the instruction to the next man. Down the line, soft murmurs could be heard as the word was passed.

Perspiration popped out on Gareth's brow as the ship moved slowly nearer on a light breeze that barely raised a chop on the water of the bay. It seemed the fog slunk in with the ship, obscuring the tip of Grassy Point. Gareth imagined his brother and crew creeping forward with it, the eyes of the lookouts straining to follow the progress of Harcourt's ship.

No matter how badly he'd needed Alex's help, having his brother rush to his rescue intensified Gareth's guilt. He hadn't intended to take Alex's woman, hadn't even known his brother was interested in Emilie until after he was already betrothed to her. Aye, she and her parents had planned their campaign well, executed it with greedy precision, and Emilie had capped off her deception by nearly forcing him to kill his own brother.

Gareth stiffened at the sound of wood scraping on stone and risked a quick look from hiding. Armed men poured from the first boat. Holding torches aloft, they fanned out on the beach as a second and third boat touched shore and were hauled from the water. Metal glinted beneath swirling cloaks; helmets made identification impossible.

Two men, one stout, one slender, drew together talking as the rest took up guard positions. The richness of their garments became apparent as they stepped into the torchlight. Hugh and the king's man, Gareth guessed. Neither was tall enough to be Hugh's cousin, who was probably staying out of sight until this was over so as not to arouse the suspicions of the king's man.

Who had the king sent? Every fiber of Gareth's being came alert. Because his father enjoyed the royal favor, there were those at court who feared him or were jealous of him. As fond as he was of the earl, King Edward surely would have sent one of Geoffrey's friends, someone who would be fair in his handling of the matter. Gareth strained to hear the snatches of conversation drifting over the beach.

"I still don't see why we couldn't land farther down the coast and obtain mounts," complained the round man.

"I have already explained that horses are not easy to come by in this godforsaken part of the country," Hugh replied.

Untrue. The merchants did it all the time, Gareth thought.

"Besides, the fog is coming in, and we might not be able to land in the morning as we'd planned," Hugh continued.

The other man tipped his head back and looked at the cliff. "Surely you don't expect me to climb that in the dark."

"Assuredly not, m'lord. We will wait here while my men go into the town and round up the guilty persons."

The man grunted but did not argue with Hugh's assertion that the people involved were guilty, as he would have had he been a friend of the Sommervilles. *Not a good sign.* Gareth tightened his grip on his sword.

"I'd prefer to wait aboard ship than here on this beach," the king's man grumbled.

"Nay, there is a dry cave a short distance away, and I can assure you we will be comfortable." At a snap of his fingers, several men staggered forward, carrying chests, blankets and a rolled-up rug. "There we can conduct our *interviews* without fear of interference from the keep," Hugh added.

Gareth's gut tightened. He doubted the townspeople would survive their so-called interviews. It was time to make their move, before any of Hugh's men got away into town. "Now," he whispered to Farley.

Lowering the visor of his helm to hide his identity as much as protect his face, Gareth rose from the rocks and headed down the beach with Farley and the others at his heels. The shouts of Gareth's men pouring from ambush rang off the cliffs. Surprise froze the tableau on the beach for a heartbeat, then Hugh's men reacted. Dropping their burdens, they reached for their swords.

The torches went out when they struck the wet sand, plunging the arena into darkness. The king's man screeched in outraged fear, but his cries were quickly drowned out by hoarse grunts and the clang of steel on steel.

Forcing his eyes to adjust to the poor light, Gareth started for the fat courtier. Whatever happened, the man must not be injured, or remain with Hugh if the ambush failed. A few feet shy of his goal, one of Hugh's men leaped into Gareth's path.

Gareth brought his sword up and made short work of his opponent, then turned back in time to see Farley's men pulling the fat courtier from the scene. Their orders were to take him up the cliffs to safety, bodily, if need be.

"M'lord . . . they flee," Farley called to him.

Sure enough, two of the boats had been launched. Hugh stood in the prow of one, exhorting his man to row faster as some of Farley's soldiers waded into the surf after them.

"Don't let Hugh get away," Gareth shouted. He started into the water, but both boats were already too far from shore.

Out on the bay, Hugh's ship made ready to leave, her masts and sails set out black as fretwork against the pale fog settled in close behind. Hugh cursed and lent his weight to the oars. In the second boat, farther from shore, two sailors worked the oars for all they were worth. A white-faced youth clung to the gunnel, shouting at Hugh to hurry.

The *Sommerville Star* materialized out of the fog in the blink of an eye, heading on a collision course with the first fleeing boat. Seconds before impact, the boy and the sailors abandoned ship. Men jumped from the rope ladders slung over the *Star*'s side and plucked the three of them from the water.

A hoarse cheer went up from Gareth's men, and seeing their cause was lost, Hugh's men on shore began to surrender. But in the time it took the *Star* to come about, Hugh's small craft reached its mother ship. Gareth cursed as he watched his nemesis scramble up the lowered ladder. The *Star* was closing on Hugh's ship, but not fast enough. With sails unfurled, the enemy vessel slipped into the billowy gray mass.

As the *Star* prepared to follow suit, Alex's voice boomed out over the water. "I'll . . . get . . . him. Nobody . . . outsails . . . me. . . ."

Gareth watched until the *Star* had been swallowed up by the fog. "God go with you," he whispered to his brother's wake. Then, squaring his shoulders, he turned back to deal with the carnage on the beach.

"Damn," Farley muttered, coming up beside him. "All we've got to show for this night's work is the king's man."

"Taken in ambush by the very people he came to investigate." Gareth frowned. "It will take some clever explaining to convince the man my family is innocent."

Farley raised the front of his helm and wiped the sweat from his face. "There's a few others that are whole enough to answer questions, and we blindfolded the king's man as you suggested. He'll not know who took him, and the men who've escorted him up top have orders to say not one word in his hearing."

Gareth nodded. "'Tis all we can do for the moment. Let's see if one of these sailors knows anything worth repeating."

His gorge rose at the pitiful cries for mercy of the first two men Farley pressed for information. *Enough. Let them die in peace,* Gareth wanted to shout, but he leaned against a rock and swallowed his aversion to the captain's methods. Lives more precious even than his sensitivities were at stake here.

The third man Farley's soldiers dragged forward whimpered and fell to his knees before the captain.

"Why did they leave me? I can't believe they sailed away without me," the wretch babbled. "My own brother left me..."

"Charles?" Gareth straightened away from the rock.

The apprentice's head came up, his eyes widening. "G-Garvey?"

Gareth flicked a glance at Farley. "How badly is he hurt?"

"Not a scratch," the captain spat. "My men pulled him out of the water ere he drowned trying to swim after Harcourt's ship."

"Be glad they did." Gareth smiled for the first time. "Charles is going to help me clear my family, aren't you?"

"I thought you didn't have one," Charles retorted.

"Ye'll keep a civil tongue in yer head and answer Lord Gareth Sommerville's questions," Farley ordered.

Charles's jaw dropped. "B-but you can't be Gareth Sommerville. He...that is...Harcourt said..."

Gareth groaned inwardly, feeling Hugh's clever scheme tightening around his neck with every word Charles uttered. "Bind and gag Charles...and the rest," Gareth ordered briskly. "We'll take them back to the keep so I can question them later." *And privately.*

"Very good, m'lord." Farley inclined his head without question then turned away to snap out orders.

Gareth only wished he felt half as confident in his abilities as Farley seemed to. *Damn.* He felt like a fish out of water. He was used to examining all sides of an issue and weighing the benefits against the problems before determining a course of action. Even the changes he'd undertaken to make the estates more profitable, the new crops, the raising of more sheep, the breeding of horses, had been approached carefully, deliberately. He simply wasn't used to making snap decisions affecting the lives of people he loved based solely on gut instinct. What if his was faulty?

"What would you have us do now?" Farley asked as they started up the cliff path, trailing the line of prisoners.

Gareth drew in a long, steadying breath and shoved his self-doubts to the back of his mind. "I'll take Charles to Wilton and await my brother and father there," he said without hesitation. Last night, he and Alex had agreed to meet at Ruarke's castle if they did not succeed in capturing all the conspirators, just in case Hugh returned to Tyneham.

"Have your men round up the merchants," Gareth continued. "From Charles's tale, I gather Walter has fled with Harcourt, but I'll take the rest with me."

"What of Lady Arianna and her family?"

"They go with me." *Willing, or unwilling.*

"You're sure the man we've captured is Lord Robert Peverell?" Gareth asked as he and Farley hurried toward the chamber where their prisoner awaited.

"Aye, he's been screaming his name to anyone who comes near. Do you know him? Is his being here good news?"

"I do...and it might be." It was possible his father had betrothed him to Robert's daughter. What was her name? Ah, yes, Margory. Shy, homely Margory.

Damn. A formal betrothal was as binding as the wedding vows themselves. Nay, his father would not have taken the irrevocable step and signed the marriage contract without informing him. But if a marriage bond were in the offing, the king might have thought to do the Sommervilles a favor by sending Gareth's soon-to-be father-by-marriage to investigate Hugh's charges.

Gareth decided he'd best not upset the delicate balance by telling Peverell he'd made alternate wedding plans.

Robert's shouts reached them even through the closed door. "I tell you, I am come from King Edward! I demand you provide me with a mount and escort back to London."

Gareth pushed open the door and nearly laughed out loud at the sight of the pompous lord lying trussed up on the bed like a fat pink pig bound for market.

"Lord Robert," Gareth said, all concern. "Whatever are you doing here?" He gestured for the bindings to be removed.

"Eh, who's that?" Robert blinked against the light as his blindfold came off. "Gareth?" he choked out, surprise and suspicion flickering across his florid face.

"Imagine my astonishment when my men told me they'd taken you with that lot of wool smugglers," Gareth said before the man could gather himself enough to voice an accusation of his own.

"W-wool smugglers?" Robert stuttered, rubbing furiously at his reddened wrists.

"Surely my father mentioned we'd been plagued with them."

"Aye." Scowling, Robert threw his legs over the side of the bed. "See here, I came from the king."

"The king is interested in my wool smugglers?"

"Of course not. He sent me to investigate you."

"Me?" Gareth's eyebrows shot up, his eyes round with innocence. "Why ever would I be smuggling wool?".

Robert impatiently brushed away the question. "His majesty thought...that is, he heard...dammit all, that scoundrel Harcourt's brought charges against you."

"Charges? You don't say? What kind of charges?"

Robert's gaze drifted to Farley and the guard who hung on their every word. "If I might speak with you privately."

Gareth wasted no time in motioning his men out and building up the fire in the chilly room. "Sorry you were treated so roughly, m'lord," he said as he handed the man a cup of wine. "We had no idea who you were."

"Nor could you have," Robert replied expansively. Settling himself into the only chair, he stretched his wet boots toward the tiny fire Gareth was feeding. "Harcourt showed up in London a few days ago with some wild tale about counterfeit coins being passed in this area. Said the Sommervilles were behind it." He slanted a glance at Gareth sitting on the stool at his feet and smiled, his pride soothed by their relative positions, as it was meant to be.

"Surely the king doesn't believe that," Gareth protested.

"Edward would rather think ill of himself than your sainted father," his lordship muttered. "And everyone is aware of the bad blood between your two families. Nay, Edward did not want to believe a word of it, but 'tis known you are looking for ways to make money." He smiled at his little jest, then added, "The king could not dismiss the matter out of hand for fear of outraging those who envy your father's closeness to his majesty."

Obviously Peverell's statement was meant to exclude himself, but Gareth remembered his father saying the man had married the daughter of an earl and struggled ever since to raise his own station in life to match hers.

"Yet, the king sent you to investigate," Gareth said, feeling his way along carefully.

"I offered to look into the business for him." His shrewd eyes narrowed to tiny slits. "The forthcoming bond between our families is not known yet, so young Harcourt was forced to agree, though he'd have preferred one of his Graham cousins."

Who would have found the Sommervilles guilty without even looking at the evidence. Much as he appreciated Robert's assistance, Gareth was determined to wed Ari, and no other. "So. Your daughter and I are betrothed?"

"The contract has not been signed."

"Ah, then we owe you a debt of gratitude for helping us," Gareth said, masking his relief.

Robert's soft features sharpened. "I would do anything to clear the name of my daughter's *husband* and his family."

Blackmailing bastard. "I would see my name cleared ere I wed," he said blandly and with perfect truth. "And now that you mention it." He scratched at the stubble on his chin. "A few of the townspeople had complained to me that some of the merchants were passing bad coin. I'll send Farley to arrest the wretches and bring them here for questioning."

"What need for questions?" Robert asked without batting an eye. "Harcourt gave me the names of the merchants and the goldsmith, Marsden, who minted the coin. You are well within your right to hang them all for conspiring against their overlord. As the king's representative, I would back you. We'll see to it come morn and leave for London immediately thereafter." He hesitated fractionally. "*If* you first have your priest draw up the betrothal contracts."

Checkmate. Much as Gareth disliked hanging men without a hearing, he'd gladly make an exception of Charles and the merchants, for their testimony jeopardized his family. The contract was another matter. "There is a priest. But the Sommerville properties are vast, and regrettably I don't recall all I am heir to." He drew satisfaction from the greedy glint in Robert's eyes. "And, too, my sire has a passion for detail. He'll want to know what your Margory brings as her dowry." Standing, he weighed his next words carefully. "Surely we can draw up the contract when we see my sire in London."

Robert rose, also, shorter by half a foot, but equally determined. "The contracts first, Lord Gareth. 'Tis treason the Sommervilles stand accused of, and I'd not flaunt so deadly a charge for just anyone. No indeed," he added, gazing up at Gareth with the self-assurance of a man who holds all the cards. "A man would be a fool to risk meddling in treason for anyone but his family."

"As you wish, m'lord," Gareth managed. "On the morrow, we will leave for Wilton, and the prisoners with us."

Let Alex sail back with Hugh Harcourt before then, Gareth prayed as he took his leave of Robert.

"You forgot to tell me you were heir to an earldom?" Ari cried, her voice rising an octave. After all the nasty shocks she'd suffered tonight, she'd thought her emotions numb. She was wrong.

Gareth's announcement that he was Lord Geoffrey's heir, and would one day be an earl himself, had lanced through her like a knife, reopening the wounds she'd so carefully sealed away.

"I assure you I did not keep my identity from you out of shame," Gareth said stiffly. Arms crossed over his chest, he glared at her from the doorway of her chamber.

Ari swallowed hard. "You should be ashamed for having lied to me when only a few hours ago you said you loved me."

"I do love you," he insisted. Hanging on to the remnants of his temper with great difficulty, he crossed to where she stood by the fire. "Most women would jump at the chance to wed an earl. Why, when I left Ransford, the castle was overrun with maids clamoring to marry me."

"Well, go home and choose one of them," Ari shot back.

"Nay, I will not." Gareth's hands clenched into fists at his sides. "I want you. You will be my wife." The dead certainty in his tone chilled her further. Though it was nearly one in the morning, he still wore the dark clothes he'd ridden out in hours ago, streaked with sand, now, and stained with salt water. If he was tired or uncomfortable, it didn't show in his face. Nothing showed there. Not weariness. Not remorse at having lied to her. Nothing save implacable determination.

"How can you say you love me and be so indifferent to *my* wants," Ari said in a small voice. "You know I would remain here at Tyneham."

"A woman's place is with her husband. Besides, have I not said your whole family could come, too? Though God alone knows how they'll fit in at Ransford," he mumbled.

"They won't. And neither will I. Don't you see, that's just the point." Panic edged her voice. "Your brother didn't like me. The rest of your family won't like me, either. They'll resent our marriage and make our life together a living hell."

Her anguish sliced through the barricade Gareth had erected to protect the feelings roiling inside himself. "Alex did not dislike you. He doesn't even know you. He was only concerned for my happiness. After what happened with..." Gareth shook away thoughts of Emilie. Now was definitely not the time to plunge into that wretched tale. "My family will like you," he growled. "Even if they did not, they'd accept you as my choice."

Ari wrapped her arms around her body to still its shivering. Gareth's words confirmed her worst fears. "I can not go with you."

"And I will not leave you here in case Harcourt returns." He raked a weary hand through his hair. "I've preparations to make for the journey, and no time to argue further with you."

"You can not make me go," Ari repeated.

"We leave at dawn," he said as though she hadn't protested. "We'll stop midway at Ransford to rest. Your family goes with us," he added, hoping to soften the blow, though God knows they would slow him down. "With any luck, we'll find word waiting for us that Alex has caught up with Harcourt, and we need not press on to Wilton."

Ari led with her stubborn chin. "Even if he does return, Hugh will not bother with me once he sees you are gone."

"Weren't you listening to what I told you about the feud?" Gareth growled. "After generations, Hugh thinks he's finally found a way to bring us down. He won't stop until he has destroyed the Sommervilles and everything, everyone, we hold dear. If he finds out what you are to me..."

"I can be nothing to you, now" she whispered.

A flicker of pain showed in his eyes before he shuttered them. "You are everything to me, and you know it. Be ready to travel at first light."

Arianna frowned, probing his hardened features in the firelight. He looked as he had the first night she'd seen him, his face seemingly carved of marble, cold, remote. But she knew him too well. Beneath the stony exterior he presented to her, she felt his suffering, his frustration. "I can not be what you want," she murmured.

"You can," he insisted. "You said we belonged together."

"Things have changed."

"Nay, you only think they have." His eyes never left hers. "You are still the woman I love, Sunshine. The woman I am going to wed. Only the timing has changed."

Ari shook her head. "There is no changing the fact that you are the heir to an earldom and I am a merchant's daughter."

He hesitated so long over his reply that her heart seemed to stop beating in her breast. "It matters not to me, though just now there are other reasons why I'd not shout our intentions to the world," he said so low she had to strain to hear him. "But never doubt that you will leave with me tomorrow...will you or nil you. And never doubt that you will be my lady wife."

His words were both a pledge and a threat. They rang in her head long after he had gone and she had lain down on the bed with little hope of sleeping for what remained of the night.

Chapter Fifteen

"Look there, 'tis Ransford!" Gareth exclaimed.

Ari started from where she had been drowsing in the saddle before him and looked up. Her first glimpse of the castle Gareth had spoken of with pride when the journey began made her shiver.

Even in the noonday sun, it seemed big and foreboding, crouched on the cliff above the small village like a great bird of prey waiting to swoop across the grassy meadow and devour all in its path.

"'Tis huge and ugly," she pronounced, forgetting her angry vow never to speak with him again.

"Ah, Sunshine, I feared you'd lost that quick tongue of yours." He laughed, his breath warm on her cheek as he hugged her stiff body. "Gaby would agree with you. I suppose you have to be born here to appreciate it as we Sommervilles do. Aye, its stout defenses have kept us safe from the Harcourts."

Ari leaned away from him, though she longed to shelter in his embrace. Ransford did not inspire thoughts of safety, it made her feel even more lonely than she already did. She bit her lip to still its trembling, and wished for the company of Grizel, who rode with Sim somewhere back in the column, or her grandfather and great-aunt, who had refused to leave Tyneham.

As promised, Gareth had taken Ari with him into town to tell her family what had happened and help them prepare for the journey to Wilton with a stop at Ransford on the way.

"I'm too old to go," her grandfather had calmly stated.

Dame Cicily had agreed but seemed more interested in Gareth's identity. "I knew you were more than a simple knight."

"But you can't stay," Ari had cried, frightened for them, panicked at the idea of going away with Gareth.

"We'll be safe inside the keep." Her grandfather grinned at Gareth. "Rich or poor, I am very glad she's to wed you."

"I am not marrying him," Ari had huffed.

"She's having trouble getting used to being a countess," Gareth had countered, his smile wider than William's. "But she loves me very much, and she'll come around."

Arrogant, infuriating man. Ari had cast pleading eyes on her aunt and announced she was staying in Tyneham. All three of them turned on her, the solar ringing with their shouted reprimands..

Gareth's quiet exterior hid a will of iron, Ari had learned when she'd wanted to ride alone. "You have no experience with horses," he'd said flatly. Defeated, Ari had spent the long hours of the journey in his arms. The unique, manly scent of him, the feel of his big body enveloping hers as they rode reminded her all too poignantly of what she'd soon be giving up.

The stout, glowering Lord Robert had not been pleased by Gareth's decision, either, but one hard look from Gareth had silenced his lordship. Still, all day Ari's skin had crawled under the older man's censorious gaze. To her, 'twas a foreshadowing of things to come. If this man hated her without even knowing her, and without being related to Gareth, how much more violent would Gareth's family's reaction to her be?

"I'd not quarrel with you, dearling," Gareth said softly.

Ari sighed, tempted, so tempted to turn her face into his mailed shoulder and cry because she loved him yet should not. She fought the urge, fought it desperately.

"Are you still angry because I wouldn't let you speak with Charles before we left?" he asked when she didn't answer.

Ari shivered thinking of Charles and the merchants. They rode in a cart in the center of the forty-man column, their hands and feet shackled, their mouths bound securely shut. Even after what he had done, or tried to do, Ari had felt a spurt of pity on emerging from Tyneham Keep and seeing Charles's white, frightened face. She'd stopped to speak with him as Gareth led her to Apollo, but Charles had taken one look at the knight and glared at her as though *she* were the betrayer, not he. "Nay, I am angry that I had to come at all," she snapped.

"The journey has tired you. Only a few more minutes, and we'll have you safe inside Ransford."

'Tis fear of meeting your family, not fatigue. Ari looked down at the ground. Was it too late to jump and run away?

"My sire is not here," Gareth grumbled as they clattered over Ransford's drawbridge. "The earl's banner would have flown from that tower had he been in residence."

The earl. Ari nearly groaned aloud. With all that had happened, she'd forgotten Gareth's sire and the Lord Geoffrey whose acts she despised were one in the same. Pray God she could keep herself from spitting on him if they did meet.

Ari gasped in amazement as they cleared the gate and came upon a huge field encompassed by high stone walls. Ringing the bailey were buildings of all sizes and descriptions. She saw a cooperage, and the smoky forge of the smith between two stables. And people. More people than she'd seen at home on market day. Men and women, servants by their plain garb, scurried about like industrious ants, their arms laden with bundles and baskets. As the column filed past, many stopped what they were doing and called out greetings. Gareth pulled off his helm and waved back, grinning like a lad and jesting with the people.

'Twas a side of him she'd never seen, yet the noise and confusion made her head ring. The stench of animals and people hanging heavy in the hot sun brought tears to Ari's eyes. "What is this place?"

"'Tis Ransford Castle," Gareth said proudly.

"But . . . but it's bigger than all of Tyneham."

"Aye." He chuckled at her incredulous stare. "It does not seem so big to me, but then, 'tis my home."

But not mine. The dark towers loomed ahead, scowling down on her in cold disapproval. *She didn't like it. She didn't like it at all.* "How long do we have to stay?" she choked out.

Gareth frowned, hurt and disappointed by her obvious dislike for the castle he expected her to run. "I've not decided when we leave. Mayhap the inner bailey will be more to your liking," he said stiffly. "'Tis quieter there. The keep and the other towers are well maintained, and the gardens are . . . well, I haven't seen them in some time, and they're not so pretty as Dame Cicily's, but mayhap . . ." *Mayhap you can remedy that when we are wed,* he started to say. But conscious of Peverell's beady glare, he swallowed the words. "Ah, there is my mother," he said as they rode into the bailey.

A slender woman in vivid blue dashed down the steps of the keep and ran across the stone courtyard. As she drew near, Ari saw her hair was fair and lightly streaked with silver, her face smooth and youthful except where lines of worry bracketed her mouth. The richness of her silk surcoat and the jewels glittering at her hips and fingers made Ari conscious of the serviceable brown gown she wore, dusty now from six hours on the road. Not even Madame Arley's feast day clothes approached the fineness of those Lady Catherine wore every day.

Ari longed to shrink from sight, to vanish into the dirt where she belonged, but Gareth swung lithely from the stallion with her in his arms. She tensed, expecting him to pull her forward to meet his mother, yet felt worse when he didn't. Setting her from him like so much refuse, he pulled off his gauntlets with his teeth and reached for his mother.

Blindly Ari turned away in search of Grizel, her self-confidence lower than the soles of her boots.

"Gareth, thank heavens you've come," Lady Catherine cried, throwing herself into his arms. "Are you all right?"

"Aye." Gareth hugged her tightly. "There's someone I'd have you meet." Over his shoulder, he saw Ari walking away. "Ari, come here," he commanded. Her face set, her feet dragging, she slowly came to him. Poor thing, she must be tired. He'd planned to ride on to Wilton directly so that Ari might meet Gaby and Ruarke, but he'd stay the night at Ransford that she might rest. "Mama, this is Arianna de Clerc of Tyneham."

"Lady Catherine," Ari murmured, sinking into what she hoped was an acceptable curtsey.

"You are well come, but I'm afraid I'm poor company today," the countess said vaguely, her attention still focused on her son. "What happened with Harcourt? Did Alex reach you in time?"

Gareth squeezed Ari's hand by way of apology, then dropped it to take both of his mother's. "Come inside and I will . . ."

"Aye, we were in time, my dear countess," Robert gushed, flipping his reins to a waiting boy and bowing before her.

"Lord Robert? Whatever are you doing here?"

His lordship's small eyes darted around the crowded courtyard. "Wait until we are private," he whispered. With the skill of a born courtier, he herded Gareth and Lady Catherine toward the steps of the keep. Over his shoulder, the portly man shot Ari a look of triumph.

It was short-lived.

Gareth stopped on the bottom step and turned back. "Ari, come into the hall and warm yourself by the fire while Lord Robert and I acquaint my mother with what has happened." Without waiting for her to agree, he escorted his mother inside.

Torn between annoyance at his arrogance and her fear of this strange place, Ari stood where he had left her. The touch of Grizel's hand on her arm shook her from her daze.

Grizel smiled faintly and stroked her cheek.

Ari let go the breath she'd been holding. "Oh, Grizel. I wish we hadn't come. I have a bad feeling about this place. Gareth was cruel to insist we come. Only see how poorly we've been treated. 'Tis obvious Lord Robert and Lady Catherine do not want us here."

Grizel's dark braid flopped over her shoulder as she vigorously shook her head in disagreement.

"Perhaps I'm quick to judge," she allowed. "But what of Gareth? He orders me about like a servant. And why are you defending him? You don't even like men."

Shrugging, the maid looked around them at the soldiers, then ahead to the knight's broad back. She signed to Ari that Gareth was an exception.

"Aye." Ari sighed. "Oh, Grizel, what am I going to do? I love him so, but I'm afraid. Even if his family accepted me, which they will not, I can't be the wife of a great lord. I was barely suited to be the wife of a penniless knight."

Grizel frowned sternly and gestured with her hands.

"So, I was Lady of Tyneham for two days. 'Twas tedious work, and I hated it."

Grizel grunted and stomped her foot.

"All right. I didn't hate all of it," Ari grudgingly admitted. "I liked helping the people, Mary and her children especially," she added, thinking of the three left behind in Dame Cicily's care. "But giving shelter to a villein family is a far cry from being chatelaine of a large castle. I can't even imagine what it would be like."

Grizel indicated her willingness to help.

"I know you would," Arianna replied, her spirits sinking further as she envisioned herself trying to run a huge estate with the help of a mute maid. As soon as the servants found out they knew more than their mistress, they'd run amok. Gareth would return after a hard day of doing whatever it was lords did to a filthy castle and terrible food. Nay, she could not do it.

"We are not wanted here," Ari said miserably.

Grizel made a sound of disbelief and touched her heart again.

"Aye, perhaps he does love me, but in time he'll come to resent me as Papa did poor Mama."

The sound of music cut across her words. Whirling around, she saw Sim leading Apollo and talking with a man wearing the Sommerville colors of red and gold. Beyond them, through the open gateway leading to the outer bailey, she saw a crowd of people and heard the lilting chords of a lute.

"Oh, what do you suppose is going on?" Ari asked Grizel.

"'Tis the players come to entertain at the castle," replied the servant Gareth had bade see to her. "Course the countess won't be much in the mood for such until this business wi' Harcourts is settled."

"Nay, I suppose not, but it seems just the sort of thing to liven up this dreary place," Ari mused. "What say you, Grizel?"

Grizel shook her head and pointed toward the keep.

"Aye, his lordship wanted ye inside," added the elderly man.

Obviously Gareth's word was law here, Ari thought, struck with the urge to flout it. "If the forbidding exterior of the castle is any sign, the inside is bound to be as dark and cheerless as the caves beneath Tyneham Cliffs. I think I will walk about in the sunshine," she replied.

Grizel, who knew well that deceptively sweet tone, frowned her disapproval. The servant merely shrugged and went back inside, himself.

The players *were* a good deal more fun than sitting inside. The tumblers made Ari laugh, the minstrel's song of love brought a tear to her eye, but it was the ropedancer who captured her attention. "Truly, 'tis the most exciting thing I've ever seen," Ari whispered to Grizel as they watched the slender girl climb the pole and walk across the rope swaying far over their heads.

Grizel's grunt of agreement became a gasp as the girl began to dance, sliding across the rope in one direction, then turning to glide in the other. She held her arms out for balance, but her eyes never looked down at the rope.

"She makes it look so easy," Ari breathed.

"'Tis most difficult," growled a deep voice at her side.

Taking her eyes from the dancer for only an instant, Ari found a dwarf garbed in the player's patchwork of bright colors looking up at her. "I'm sure it is," she said politely, trying not to stare for she'd never been this close to one of his kind before. "But I would still like to try."

"That might be arranged," he said silkily. "Course we'd ha' ta lower the rope, fer ye, But we'd do it . . . fer a price."

"So you see why I must stall for time," Gareth told his mother in a rush, turning from the window in her solar. They were alone for the moment. Peverell had mercifully gone in search of the garderobe after telling a much embellished tale of his part in capturing Charles Beck.

Lady Catherine rose from her chair by the hearth, her hands clasped at her breast, her pale violet eyes troubled. "Nay, I do not. If I read Robert correctly, he will clear your father's name if you but wed his daughter. Since Margory Peverell was also your father's choice for you, why do you not just marry the girl? She is a kind and gentle girl, and not ugly—though she does resemble her sire."

Gareth grimaced at the thought of being wed to Peverell's fat, homely daughter. Served him right, he thought grimly, for having requested, nay, demanded, an ugly bride. "Lady Margory's looks are not at issue," he said. "'Tis that I have found someone else, someone I love."

"Sir Neil's widow." His mother's usually sweet voice had a hard edge to it that grated on Gareth's jangled nerves.

"The marriage was never consummated."

"Still, she is a goldsmith's daughter."

"Granddaughter," Gareth corrected her, his fists clenching at his sides. "Her father *was* a knight," he emphasized, hurt by his mother's attitude, recalling Ari's insistence that she wouldn't fit into his world, that his family wouldn't like her, that they'd resent his wedding her and make their marriage a living hell.

Nay, he'd not let anyone or anything ruin what he'd found with Ari. Still, it hurt more than he cared to admit that Ari had been right about his family's reaction to her. Spinning away from his mother, he stalked to the sideboard, poured a cup of wine and downed it without tasting a drop. "What does this matter?" he growled, hanging onto his emotions by a thread. "Both her parents are dead, and 'tis Ari I'd wed, not them."

Catherine blinked, unable to believe her eldest son, her calm, patient firstborn, was shouting at her over some blond burgher. Swallowing the temptation to shout back, she drew in a steadying breath. "What matters, my son," she said very slowly, crossing to stand beside him. "What matters is the safety of our family. You were willing to wed the woman your father chose for the sake of breeding heirs, can you not wed her to save your father's life and mayhap the lives of all of us?''

Nay, he wanted to scream, but the voice of duty cried louder. "If it comes to that, you know I will do what must be done to protect my family," he said with a heavy heart. "But I'd put off signing the betrothal contract as long as I can. If Alex catches Hugh Harcourt and we can force a confession from him, my sacrifice will not be necessary."

"Patience is not Robert Peverell's long suit. His wife carps at him continually that she married beneath herself in taking him, and he has long hungered for more recognition at court. By forging a blood bond with our family, he eases both desires. His daughter will be a countess, and as your father-by-marriage, he will be admitted to King Edward's inner circle."

"He is anxious to see the betrothal contracts signed, but I've said I can do nothing without Papa. I'd leave Robert here and ride with Ari to Wilton to await word from Alex."

Catherine touched his arm, her eyes soft with relief. "It gladdens me that you and Alex have mended things between you."

Gareth turned away to hide his troubled expression. "Let us find Ari. I'd like you to get to know her better. She is lively and clever and I think you will like her as I do." At least, he hoped so. Much as he hated the idea of being parted from Ari, he wondered if it wouldn't be best to leave her here and spare her the half-day journey to Wilton.

"I will speak with her, of course. I'd offer my condolences on Sir Neil's death," his mother said, neatly sidestepping the issue of a marriage between them. "But I fear I am not good company with such a terrible threat hanging over our heads."

Comforting himself with the knowledge that his mother was always gracious, Gareth sent one of the maids who was sewing at the other end of the large solar down to fetch Ari.

The girl returned in a few moments. "There's no lady in the hall, m'lord."

Gareth pounded down the stairs to the hall with his mother close behind him. The hall was indeed empty, and his stomach had begun to knot with apprehension when the shouts and sounds of laughter drew his gaze to the open window. "What is going on?"

"'Tis likely the players who came here yesterday. I felt in no mood for their songs and nonsense, but I'd not send them away hungry, so I gave them leave to play for the servants and soldiers in the lower bailey." She raised a delicate brow. "Surely, Mistress Arianna won't have gone down there."

Gareth grinned and started for the door. "I'd wager any sum you say that is exactly where she is."

Ari was there, all right, only when Gareth saw her swaying precariously on a rope slung several feet off the ground, he roared her name and charged through the crowd.

Gareth's bellow brought Ari's head up and broke her concentration. "Oh . . ." Arms milling, she fought to regain her balance, then lost it. The wide-eyed servants and men-at-arms gasped as Ari started to fall the two feet to the ground. Her choked scream ended in a moan as Gareth caught her.

"Are you all right?" he demanded, hugging her tight.

"I was doing quite nicely, thank you," Ari replied, flashing him a teasing grin. "Until you came along and startled me."

Gareth hesitated an instant, scanning her bright eyes and flushed cheeks, then he laughed into her upturned face. "Ah, Ari. I feared I'd not see your sunny smile again."

The feel of his strong arms around her, the sound of his laughter melted her defenses. She couldn't wed him, but she'd be a fool to waste the few precious days they had together in sulking and self-pity. "I am here, and smiling, as you can see, but I don't think you should kiss me for it right now."

"Reading my thoughts again?" Hugging her tighter, Gareth looked up into a sea of shocked white faces—his mother's, Lord Robert's and those of the servants and soldiers he'd known all his life. They stared at him as though he'd sprouted two heads, yet he felt no embarrassment, no loss of dignity, only a pleasure so intense it made him laugh out loud again.

"I think you'd better put me down," Ari whispered.

"A good idea," Lady Catherine said weakly, her eyes wide with astonishment.

Aye, Mama, see how it is between us, Gareth wanted to shout, but Robert's presence held him back. Reluctantly

Gareth set Ari's feet on the ground. "When I was a lad, I wanted to be a tumbler," he murmured in her ear.

"That explains the quick roll you executed the day you saved me from the boar," she replied. Before he could dispute this, she added, "Can the players stay at Ransford? They told me the roads are dangerous and they fear for their lives."

"Ari, I..."

"Please. You said there was a shortage of workers."

Gareth cast a quick glance at the nervous huddle of misfits in their players' motley. "I don't know what they are suited to, but I suppose we could see—"

"Oh, thank you!"

For an instant, Gareth thought she was going to kiss him with more than just her eyes, and his heart leaped. "I expect this to be your last attempt at ropedancing," he said gruffly.

Ari grinned. "Not dignified?"

"Not safe." He gently touched a finger to her nose.

Lady Catherine cleared her throat. "Let us go back inside." As if her words had broken the spell that held them, the crowd came back to life, talking and drifting back to their duties.

"Consorting with players," Lord Robert tsked, his face settled into smug folds as he led the way to the castle. "My Margory would not disgrace her lord so, would she Catherine?"

Drat his perfect daughter, Ari thought.

"You know her better than I," Gareth's mother hedged, but she frowned as she glanced at Ari walking beside her son.

I knew it. She hates me. Ari's spirits plunged as they climbed the stairs and entered the cool darkness of the keep. She longed to look back and see if Grizel followed, but Gareth had a possessive hand on her elbow.

"Ah, here are refreshments set out for us," Catherine said as they passed through the wooden entryway and entered the deep gloom of the cavernous hall.

As her eyes adjusted, Ari saw the room was dark because the walls were black with smoke. From the timbered ceiling some twenty feet above them hung the tattered banners won in battle by Gareth's ancestors. The trestle tables had been taken down, making the hall seem even larger and more empty. At the far end of the room, several heavy chairs huddled before a cold and empty hearth.

'Twas there Lady Catherine led them, gesturing for the men to be seated and pouring wine for them herself.

Ari perched uneasily on the edge of a high-backed wooden chair. The wine was not as good as what Aunt Cici served, and the seeded cakes tasted more of mildew than spices. For several moments, no one spoke, and the tension hung heavier in the air than the smoke from countless past fires.

"Is this your maid?" Lady Catherine asked.

Ari was shamed to find Grizel standing a few feet away, her uneasiness plain. "Aye," Ari stammered. "'Tis Grizel."

"The kitchens are through that door, Grizel," Lady Catherine said kindly. "Do you go and tell the cook to feed you, also."

"Nay," Ari exclaimed. "I will go with her." Thumping her cup of wine and the uneaten cake down on a small table, she grabbed Grizel's hand and dragged her from the room.

"You can't eat in the kitchens!" Lady Catherine cried.

"She can't go alone," Ari tossed over her shoulder, nearly running in her haste to leave. She half expected Gareth to call out or come after her, but they made it through the door and into the buttery without interruption.

"Whew," Ari gasped, stopping to catch her breath. "I have never been so discomforted in all my life."

Grizel motioned for her to go back.

"Not on your life."

"Mercy, what a strange girl," Catherine murmured as the buttery door slammed shut.

Gareth gripped the arm of his chair, fighting the urge to run after Ari. And say what? Shout at her, and he'd upset the delicate balance between them again. With every moment they spent behind Ransford's walls, he felt her slipping further away from him. "The maid is a mute, and has a fear of men for having been abused when she was young."

His mother made sympathetic noises; Robert snorted.

"I'll not deny Mistress Arianna would make a diverting mistress," his lordship grumbled. "But—"

"Mistress!" Gareth leaped up so quickly the wine splashed from his cup into the musty rushes. The blood pounded so fiercely in his temples he didn't hear his mother's voice, nor feel her grasp the arm he'd lifted to strike the filth spewer.

"Gareth!" Catherine shouted, shaking his arm. "Gareth, I'm sure Robert meant no harm."

"N-nay, I did not." Robert's eyes bugged out.

Gareth blinked away the red haze of rage, appalled at himself. He'd nearly lost control as he had when he'd fought Alex, and he didn't like the feeling one bit. "Arianna is not my mistress," he ground out, chest still heaving with emotion.

Robert swallowed hard. "The way you act, I thought—"

"Don't think about her." Gareth banged his cup down on the table, denting it and spilling the rest of the wine. "I leave for Wilton."

"Now?" his mother gasped. "But 'tis six hours at least, and with the cart carrying the prisoners..."

"Then I'd best get started." Fists clenched, Gareth stalked toward the buttery, kicking the mildewed rushes from his path. After living at Wilton, Ransford did indeed seem dark and dirty. Never had he thought to be anxious to leave his home, but now it depressed him. Nay, he'd not remain here to see Ari suffer, even if it meant exhausting her further with another long ride.

"I am coming with you," Robert called after him, the distrust and determination clear in his voice.

"What took you so damned long?" Hugh demanded, rising from the rock on which he'd been sitting as Walter entered the small woodland clearing.

"Tyneham town is crawlin' wi' Farley's men." Walter dropped a sack on the ground. Casting back the cowl he'd worn to hide his features, he crouched and extended his hands to the tiny fire Hugh had coaxed to life. "It's a right raw night."

"Damn the weather. Did you get the horses?"

"Tied yonder in the trees. Didn't ye hear me comin'?"

"Nay, I was busy deciding what to do next."

"Oh, aye, Lord Hugh Harcourt, master planner," Walter sneered. "Look what yer grand scheme's brought us to. We're hidin' in the woods, my brother and the others are gone wi' Sommerville. Charles, Reece, George, and Bentwood—all gone."

"Shut up and let me think." Hugh sank down onto the stone. "Those four haven't a full set of guts between them," he muttered. "So I'd bet they'll tell Gareth Sommerville everything they know." He chuckled suddenly. "Which is lucky for us."

"Huh?"

"Reece and the other merchants only know their part of the plan. Every week they were given false coins to spread in the town, but they think Gareth Sommerville was behind the plot." His smile widened; the bleakness left his eyes. 'Twas a stroke of genius having Parlan masquerade as Sommerville.

"What about Charlie? We can't let him hang."

Or identify me as the man who asked him to make the coins. Briefly Hugh thought how Jesse would take the news that her brother was to hang for treason. His stomach clenched. Nay, he'd end his own life before he'd see that pain in her eyes, or the gloating satisfaction in his sire's.

Straightening, Hugh applied himself to the problem. "'Tis precisely because we had unfinished business here that I asked my . . . er, the captain to set us ashore once he'd eluded Sommerville's ship in the fog."

"Whot if that ship comes back here lookin' fer us?"

"It won't matter," Hugh said confidently. "I've instructed the captain to sail north and draw it away from Tyneham while we take care of things here. Now, tell me," he asked, leaning closer. "Did you find out where Sommerville is headed?"

"Nay. Those in town I dared question didn't know."

"Hmm. What about the goldsmith and his family?"

"Gone ta the keep."

Hugh nodded. "Tomorrow, I want you to get inside Tyneham and discover where Sommerville has gone. Capture me a hostage . . . preferably that pretty granddaughter Charles was so fond of. The Sommervilles are ridiculously soft when it comes to women. We'll offer to trade her for your brother."

Walter grinned wolfishly. "'Tis a sound plan . . . and sorry I am fer doubtin' ye before."

"Apology accepted," Hugh said smoothly. "You'll soon learn that I mean to win this game, no matter what I have to do."

Chapter Sixteen

Ari awoke to the sound of someone rebuilding the fire. She rolled over, groaning as every muscle in her body protested.

"Good. I see you are awake," came a brisk female voice in the French spoken by the nobility.

Ari's eyes shot open just as the unknown woman opened the chamber door and called, "She's awake. You can come in."

The woman was beautiful, delicately built with fat black braids coiled above her ears, creamy skin and eyes the color of violets. Smiling at Ari, she stepped aside to admit a procession of servants bearing steaming buckets of water, piles of clothes and a tray laden with dishes.

"What is this?" Ari asked in French. Sitting up, she clutched the sheets over the thin shift she'd slept in.

"You don't remember me from last night?"

"I don't even recall crawling into bed last night."

The woman laughed, displaying two merry dimples. "I'm Gaby."

Lady Gabrielle? Ari stared at the woman's plain blue gown, her uncovered head. "Where are your silks, your jewels?"

"Stored in my clothes chests," Gaby replied, motioning for the women to fill the small tub they'd brought in. "Silks and such are ill suited to what I do each day."

"Which is generally too much," grumbled one of the women, shaking her head so her long brown braids danced over her bulging stomach.

"I'm not the one pregnant with her first child, Felise," Gaby chided.

"Nay, but you worked just as hard when you were." The fondness shining in Felise's pretty dark eyes robbed the words of their sting.

"This impudent baggage is Felise, my sometimes friend and wife to Ruarke's captain, William de Lacy."

"Lady Felise," Ari replied, inclining her head.

"Just Felise will do," Gaby's woman said, smiling.

"Now up with you and into the tub before the water cools."

"You shouldn't have gone to so much trouble," Ari protested. "I am used to seeing to myself." Nonetheless, their thoughtfulness soothed away some of yesterday's hurt.

"Enjoy it whilst you can," Felise muttered. "She'll put you to work soon enough."

"I'd gladly help, but I have no domestic skills." Still under the covers, Ari hesitated.

"You can be about your work," Gaby told her maids, sensitive to the girl's modesty. "I'll see Mistress Arianna in and out of the tub, and you can return to clean up later."

They left as smoothly as they'd come, taking with them the empty buckets and Ari's dirty travel clothes.

Ari's grateful smile turned to a sigh of pure bliss as she slid into the hot water. "Oh, every muscle in my body aches."

"Men," Gaby grumbled. "Just because their backsides are made of iron, they think everyone can endure twelve hours in the saddle." She handed Ari the soap and a square of linen.

"What of my maid, Grizel?" Ari asked, though it was Gareth she really wanted to know about. He'd been so angry yesterday when they'd left Ransford he'd hardly uttered two words during the entire ride to Wilton.

"When last I saw her, she was in the kitchen rolling crust for the meat pies."

"B-but she can't speak." Ari made to climb from the tub, but Gaby laid a hand on her arm.

"You needn't worry about Grizel." Gaby's smile turned sad. "Gareth made certain to tell me about her, and her fear of men. I assure you no man here will force himself on her. My cook is a woman of great compassion. She and your Grizel took to each other right away."

Ari sat back in the tub. "Grizel does love to cook."

"Then she'll be doubly well come here, we love to eat."

What about me? Ari wondered. Would she be welcome also? As she soaped her arms, she watched Gaby through her lashes. Though the other woman's beautiful face was as expressionless as blank parchment, Ari sensed she was troubled about something.

"What is wrong?" Ari blurted out.

Gaby blinked in surprise, then answered just as honestly. "Gareth said he would wed you."

Ari sighed, reaching down to soap her legs while her mind whirled. "I have already told him I will not marry him."

"You have?"

"Aye." Ari shook her head. "It only made him more determined. He laughed and said I'd get used to the idea."

"Gareth laughed?" Gaby's eyes widened, then she smiled faintly. "Lean forward and I'll soap your hair for you." For several moments there was only the sound of the fire crackling in the hearth. "Gareth wasn't laughing last night. He was in such a rage as I've never seen when you arrived."

Ari nodded, tipping her head back so Gaby could pour the rinse water through her hair. "The soap smells wonderful," she murmured, inhaling the sweet scent of wildflowers.

"Mmm." Vaguely. "The flowers are from our gardens. Why don't you want to marry Gareth?"

Ari waited until she had stepped from the tub and toweled off with a length of linen set by the fire to warm. "'Tis not that I don't love him," she said slowly, unsure why she answered so openly, except that she so desperately needed someone to confide in and sensed in Gabrielle a sensitive soul. "I was ready, nay, eager, to wed him when I thought him a poor, landless knight, but when I learned he was a Sommerville, and heir to an earldom . . . then I knew 'twas impossible."

"You did? Most women would be eager to wed a future earl," Gaby said, clearly puzzled.

"Not me." Ari shivered, chilled by thoughts of Alex's and Lady Catherine's coldness, their hatred of her.

"Oh, curse me for letting you stand here taking a chill whilst I satisfy my unholy curiosity."

"'Tis all right,'' Ari quickly assured her. "I am afflicted with the same malady myself, or so my great-aunt always says.'' Nonetheless, she dropped the toweling and took the shift Gaby held out. It was soft and fine as down. "This is not mine.''

"Nay, your things are wrinkled and stink of horse. Until my women have them aired and pressed, I'd loan you some things of mine. We are of a size,'' she added as Ari started to protest. "Only you are an inch taller than I and more slender, but we'll do the laces up tighter and none will know the difference.''

What she means is that my things are not good enough to wear at Wilton, Ari thought unhappily as she combed out her hair. She'd never cared before, but suddenly she wanted to look like a lady, wanted to fit in here. She wished the yellow tunic and the green surcoat Gaby helped her put on over it were her own, not borrowed. Still, she felt better, bathed and dressed.

Over the bread and cheese the maids had left on a table beneath the chamber's only window, Gaby again asked her why she didn't wish to wed Gareth.

"I could never be the lady his station demands, chatelaine to his castle.'' Thinking of Ransford, she wrinkled her nose. "Nor would I want to live there. The castle is . . .''

"Dark and disgusting,'' Gaby finished for her, smiling. "If you think Ransford is bad, you should have seen Wilton when first I arrived here.''

Ari really looked around her for the first time. What struck her immediately was how open and bright the room seemed, its walls freshly whitewashed beneath colorful tapestries, the wooden floor covered by an intricately woven patterned carpet. "But this chamber is beautiful. I've never seen its like.''

"You'd not have thought so had you seen it two years ago. Ruarke had never lived at Wilton since inheriting it from his grandsire, but he sent the plunder he'd gained in the war with France here to be stored. When I arrived, I found the steward, that cursed Walter Beck, had let the place fall into ruin, whilst he used Ruarke's treasure for his own pleasure.''

Ari's eyes widened. "The same Walter Beck who is involved in this scheme to ruin your family?"

Lady Gabrielle nodded. "I should have listened to Ruarke and let him hang the wretch, but I did not want his blood on our hands." She took a sip of ale, then added. "I grew up in the south of France, you see, where the style of living is much different. I wanted to turn Wilton into the sort of castle I was used to. It took months of hard work to perform this miracle."

"'Twas worth the effort," Ari assured her.

Gaby eyed Ari intently over the rim of her cup. "You could do the same at Ransford, but I think your lack of skills and the castle's condition aren't the only reason you'd not wed Gareth."

"Nay." Ari shook her head, her throat tight with longing. "Lord Alex and Lady Catherine were not pleased to hear he wanted to wed me. *He* offered me money if I would leave Gareth alone."

"Men," Gaby said, frowning. "They think they can force things to turn out as they will. My Ruarke would shout his way through an obstacle, Alex, the rogue, would charm his way around it, and Gareth . . ." Her lips pursed in thought. "Until last night, I would have said he'd wait patiently to get what he wanted, but he was very impatient and very angry."

"That's because Lord Peverell said I was Gareth's mistress."

Are you? Ari could see the question lurking in Gabrielle's eyes, but then with a flick of her lashes, she shuttered them, closing off all expression with an ease Ari envied.

"I have never liked Lord Robert," Gaby said. "He reminds me of a pig . . . a puffed-up, self-important pig. And as for the others, we are Gareth's family, and we don't want to see him hurt again."

"Because of Emilie?" Ari asked on instinct.

"Aye." Gabrielle's troubled gaze focused on some distant, obviously painful, time.

"Who is she?"

Gaby nibbled at her lower lip, indecisive for the first time since Ari had met her. "Was. Emilie was Gareth's wife, dead now these past three and more," she added quickly, cutting off Arianna's startled gasp.

"Another lie," Ari murmured, shaken by the revelation.

"Gareth said he'd never been wed?"

"Nay, only he refused to discuss her with me. Don't you think he should have told me he'd been married before?"

Gaby's hand closed over Ari's cold one and squeezed gently. "Most men avoid discussing unpleasant things whenever they can, as though it will somehow make the matter disappear. But in this, I must admit Gareth has just cause to try and bury the memory. Emilie was a shallow, cruel woman. If I had known how things would turn out between them ... if I'd known her viciousness would nearly be the death of two people I love, I'd have tried anything, even murder, to see she didn't wed Gareth."

Ari stared intently into Gabrielle's eyes, trying to see beyond her words. "This has something to do with Alex, doesn't it? He and Gareth are the two who were almost killed."

"How did you know that if Gareth didn't speak of it?"

"He was wounded en route to Tyneham. My grandfather and great-aunt took him into our home to mend his hurts. He became fevered and called out one night." Ari shivered, remembering the anguish in his voice. "Called out to Alex to pick up his sword and fight with him ere he was forced to do murder."

"Aye," Gaby said hoarsely. "Emilie made trouble between the two of them. Took pleasure in it, I don't doubt. But ..." She gave Ari's hand another squeeze before releasing it. "More than that, I cannot say, for 'tis Gareth's tale to tell."

Ari reluctantly swallowed her questions and nodded.

"Enough of this glum talk," Gaby said briskly. "Much as I've enjoyed getting to know you, I have duties I must be about. If you have finished eating, let me take you on a tour of Wilton."

"I'd like that," Ari said. Standing to shake the bread crumbs from her skirts, she looked more closely at the tapestry. "Gareth told me you made your own tapestries."

"He did? I didn't think he even noticed them."

"He said they were practical."

Gaby chuckled. "How like a man.

"You say that often."

"'Tis because men and women think very differently on nearly every subject. Don't you think, mistress?"

"Please, call me Ari, as my family does, and, aye, I do think they're different. At least, Gareth and I are. But then," she added, her smile fading, "he is a nobleman and I am naught but a goldsmith's granddaughter."

Pain flickered in Gabrielle's eyes. "We are what we make of ourselves," she said softly. "I, too, once doubted I was good enough to marry into the proud Sommerville family, but Ruarke showed me we are each our own person, regardless of what blood flows in our veins."

"Easy for you to say, you were born and raised a lady."

"You carry yourself as a lady," Gabrielle countered. "And you are learned, able to converse in both English and French. Do you also write and cipher?"

"Aye." Proudly.

"Unusual skills for a burgher."

"On the contrary, such skills are important. A merchant must be able to converse with all who come to his shop—townsman and nobleman alike. Nor can he risk being cheated by having a clerk keep the records of his financial transactions."

"So you kept your grandsire's records?"

"Nay, I was trained as a goldsmith."

Gabrielle's eyes widened. "You were?"

Ari clapped her hands over her mouth. *Oh, drat.*

"Can women belong to that guild?" When Ari shook her head no, Gabrielle's smile dimmed. "Oh, how sad for you to have a craft you may not practice openly." Her expression grew thoughtful again. "Can you sketch as well as work in metals?"

"Aye. The metal is precious, so we work our ideas on parchment first."

"Excellent. I have need of your services," Gaby said, grabbing Ari's hand and tugging her from the room. "I know Felise warned against my putting you to work, but—"

"I like to be busy." Ari scrambled to keep pace with her whirlwind of a hostess.

Gabrielle stopped on the stairs. "I like you more and more, Arianna de Clerc."

"And I like you, too, Lady Gabrielle."

"There has to be a way out of this," Gareth said for the dozenth time, his steps quick and impatient as he paced the corridor of the dungeon carved deep in the stone beneath Wilton's hall. Charles and the merchants were housed here under heavy guard, each in a separate cell.

"We could try torture," Ruarke growled. "But scared as these four wretches are, I think they've already told us everything they know without our laying a hand on them."

Gareth raked a hand through his dark blond hair. "Aye, and were Robert or any other from Edward's court to hear them, Papa would be as good as hanged, and me along with them. Nay, I'd kill all four, with my bare hands if necessary."

Ruarke raised both brows. Just this morn Gaby had commented on the changes in Gareth, his restlessness, his quickness of temper. Typically, Gaby had thought the woman, Arianna, responsible for cracking Gareth's usual reserve. Ruarke had blamed the seriousness of the situation. Mayhap, it was both.

Shrugging away from the wall, Ruarke laid a hand on his older brother's shoulder and swung him around. They were of a height, but Ruarke's body was more heavily muscled from wielding broadsword and battle-axe, his hair close-cropped, where Gareth's curled at his nape. There was no denying the similarity in their piercing midnight-brown eyes.

"Say the word, and I'll kill them," Ruarke growled. "But I agree with what you said before. When Alex returns with that bastard Harcourt, the merchants and the apprentice'll be of more use to us as witnesses if they're whole and undamaged but for a few nights spent down here."

A ghost of a smile tugged at Gareth's mouth. "Wilton's dungeons are cleaner than Ransford's hall, and the food better."

"Aye, Gaby can't abide dirt—anywhere. Speaking of which, shouldn't we get back upstairs and see how fares the pretty little lady you've been fretting about?"

Gareth sighed and looked down at his boots. "I doubt Ari is speaking to me today."

"And what did you do to deserve such treatment?"

"She didn't want to come with me, and then I shouted at her and she fell off the rope she was dancing on."

"Ropedancing?" Ruarke chuckled. "She's a player, then?"

"Nay, she is not," Gareth growled. "She's the daughter of a knight, and the woman I intend to marry."

"But you said you'd have to marry Robert's ugly daughter."

"If I can't find another way to clear our name, I might have to, but I certainly don't relish the idea."

"What happened to the bargain you made with Papa?"

"Arianna de Clerc is what happened," Gareth said with a wry chuckle that even caught Ruarke's attention.

"I agree she's comely, but—"

"If you say she's only a goldsmith's daughter, I swear I'll...I'll hit you."

Ruarke grinned. "I believe you would, but I'll not put it to the test. So, you fancy yourself in love with her?"

"I am in love with her. And she with me. She's brave and clever and makes me laugh, but when she found out I had lied to her about who I was..."

"She was mad as hell. Women can be unreasonable at times," Ruarke added from the benefit of two years married to Gaby.

"Ari was angry, at first, but she understood my reasons and agreed I'd probably done the right thing. 'Twas when she found out I was Papa's heir she refused to wed me."

"Most women would sell their souls to be a countess."

"When I told her that, Ari told me to marry one of them. She was not trained as a chatelaine, and feels unequal to the task."

"She could learn."

"Aye, except for some other nonsense about being unworthy. She's convinced herself my family won't accept her because her father was only a knight, and her mother a burgher. 'Tis true some nobles have put more stock in such things since the plague killed so many lords.'' The deaths had opened the way for wealthy merchants to buy land and even manors. Alarmed by this rise of the lower classes, many nobles had become preoccupied with social status. "But I don't give a damn about such things. Why, William Marsden is worth ten of Lord Robert."

"Women live to fret over such things," Ruarke growled. "Gaby nearly got herself killed once because she thought being related to the cruel de Laurens made her unworthy to be a Sommerville."

"Foolishness. No one could be kinder or more compassionate than Gaby," Gareth insisted. "And no one could make me a better wife than Ari. True, she lacks domestic skills, but she's bright. She'll learn quickly under Gaby's guidance. I'm counting on that and on Ari's love for me to bring her around."

"It will." Ruarke clapped his brother on the back, nearly sending him sprawling. "Let us go up and rescue our women from that pig, Peverell. I'd see this Ari of yours who has made you laugh again." He started down the corridor, then stopped. "You're sure she's not like Emilie?"

Gareth shook his head. Trust Ruarke to stomp in where everyone else feared to intrude. "Nay, she is not like Emilie at all, except she is beautiful."

"Good. Gaby has yet to forgive herself for not somehow preventing you from wedding Emilie in the first place."

"I doubt I'd have listened," Gareth said, repressing a shudder as the terrible memories moved through him.

"Well, pay special attention to what Gaby says about this one," Ruarke growled. "I'd not have you hurt again."

"'Tis beautiful. Just what I wanted," Gaby said, cocking her head as she studied Ari's sketch. It was to be a scene of life at Wilton, with the castle in the background, Ruarke on his war-horse, Gladiator, in the center, and Gabrielle and the children in the foreground in a field of flowers.

"I am glad you like it," Ari replied. "Though I was afraid we weren't going to get little Cat into the picture." Adorable baby Philippa, solemn as an owl with her mother's black hair and her sire's beautiful dark eyes, had cooperated by lying quietly in her nurse's arms while Ari drew her. Two-year-old Cat, on the other hand, had refused to sit still long enough to have her likeness captured. Violet eyes snapping, fair hair flying, she'd torn about her mother's solar, into three things at once, loudly defying her poor maid and her mother at every turn.

"She has her sire's temper," Gaby had commented.

Ruarke, seated with Gareth and Lord Robert before the hearth at the other end of the room, threw back his head and laughed. "And her mother's stubbornness."

"Isn't there a horse that needs riding or one of your men who needs sword practice?" Gaby groused.

"In this weather?" Ruarke gestured at the wind-driven rain beating against the huge expanse of glass windows that took up nearly one wall of the solar. "I've fought battles in the like before, but I'd not go out willingly."

"'Tis no doubt this cursed storm that's delayed Geoffrey's arrival," Robert grumbled.

Gareth and Ruarke glared at the man, nor could Ari blame them. His lordship had been curt and surly all afternoon, muttering about unruly children and merchant's daughters who didn't know their place, until Ari had wanted to flee the room. Only pride and the steadying glances Gareth slanted in her direction kept her from leaving.

"Lord Robert, let me fix you a hot mulled wine," Gaby chirped, suddenly the fawning hostess. At his ready agreement, she bustled to her spice chest. Opening the drawers, she put a pinch of cinnamon and then one of cloves into a silver cup. As Ari watched her, Gaby turned a bit sideways, took out a small packet, unwrapped it and shook a few grains of white powder into the cup before filling it with rich red wine. A spoonful of honey, and she was ready for the poker Ruarke had heated in the fire. The air filled with the pungent scent of spices as he plunged the hot iron into the wine.

"Anyone else for some?" Ruarke asked.

Gaby glared at him, but the scowl so quickly became a smile as she handed the cup to Lord Robert that Ari might have imagined it. She did not, however, imagine the narrowing of Ruarke's eyes as he whispered his wife's name. Smiling even more broadly, Gabrielle batted her thick lashes at her husband.

"I've warned you about this before," Ruarke muttered.

Gaby shrugged and encouraged Lord Robert to drink.

What was going on? Ari looked to Gareth for the answer, but he had fallen into a strange coughing fit and was staring into the fire as though the cure rested there. For several long minutes no one said anything. Ruarke scowled. Gaby watched Lord Robert. Lord Robert drank his wine, seemingly oblivious to the tension in the air.

"Ah, that chased the chill from my bones," his lordship exclaimed. Setting the cup aside, he suddenly yawned hugely.

Gabrielle's smile broadened. Ruarke's frown deepened. Gareth coughed again.

"Damn me, but I am weary of a sudden," Lord Robert muttered. "I think I'll lie down before supper." As he heaved his bulk from the chair, Gaby summoned two maids from their sewing at the other end of the room and bade them see his lordship to his chamber.

The door had barely closed on the trio before Ruarke erupted from his chair. "You can not go around drugging people will you nil you!" he roared.

Gabrielle stuck her chin out to meet his. "'Twas either that or a knife between his ribs. I'll not tolerate such rudeness in mine own home. He insulted our children. He insulted Ari."

"Well done." Gareth put his arm around Gaby's shoulder and hugged her. With the other hand, he wiped the tears from his eyes. "Jesu, but I thought I'd split from trying not to laugh when I guessed what you were about."

"You drugged Lord Robert's wine?" Ari asked.

Abandoning Gaby, Gareth scooped Arianna up in his arms and whirled with her in a slow circle. "Aye, she did. My thanks, again, Gaby. I've been dying to do this all day." *This and more,* his smoldering gaze told Ari.

Ari shivered, knowing she should resist but powerless to tear herself from the wonderful feel of his arms around her, the pounding of his heart against hers. She wanted him to kiss her, kiss her and never stop. And he knew it. His slow, very masculine smile made her pulse race and her skin tingle.

"I feel weary myself," Gareth said softly. "Perhaps we should go and lie down, too."

"Gareth!" Gaby exclaimed. "What ails you? Only think what people will say."

"Fetch your priest, then. I'd wed her now," Gareth said, his mesmerizing eyes locked on Ari's so she could neither look away nor protest.

For once, Ruarke's was the cooler head. "Nay, but they deserve some time alone together," he said, laying a restraining hand on his wife's arm. "If any ask, we will say the journey tired them all. Do you go before Gaby's women return, none will know the difference."

Gaby nodded. "I will bring a tray of food and drink up to your chamber myself and set it outside the door."

Ari looked at Lady Gabrielle through new eyes. The woman she'd dreaded meeting had turned out to be kind, understanding and brave. An apology hovered on her lips, but how to explain without giving offense? "I thank you for providing so generously for me and Grizel. My chamber...this gown..."

"We are happy to have you here," Gaby replied, a knowing gleam in her eyes. "'Tis obvious you are important to Gareth."

Arianna took one look at Gareth's dark gaze, and the breath caught in her throat. Aye, she was important, more so than was wise for either of them.

The rope bed sagged as Gareth sat down beside her, the fire he'd built up bringing out the gold lights in his hair.

Ari drank in the sight of his handsome face, smiling in the soft light of a brace of candles. "We shouldn't be here."

"Here is exactly where we should be, Sunshine." His fingers caressed the curve of her cheek, then slid under her hair, leaving a trail of heat in their wake. "I love you too much to stay away."

Ari swallowed, her mouth suddenly dry. *I love you,* she wanted to say, but the words wouldn't come. He must have read them in her eyes, because he smiled.

"God, I've missed you. You're the sun in my life." Lowering his head, he captured her mouth in a kiss hard with wanting, fierce with desperation. For an instant, she hesitated, common sense warring with longings she was powerless to suppress. Nor could she. Moaning, she opened herself to him, body and soul, her arms twining about his neck as she arched up to meet him.

She had no memory of his removing their clothes, hadn't realized how chilled she had been until he slid under the covers and enfolded her into the hot, naked length of his body. "Oh, Gareth. I've been so frightened, so lonely," she murmured, shivering in anticipation of what was to come, glorying in the feel of him, the scent of him.

"It's all right," he whispered, his big hands stroking her as he would gentle a frightened mare. "Soon this will be over and we can be together always."

Always? Ari wasn't certain they would have an always, but at least they would have tonight. Come morn, she might regret they'd given in to their desire for each other. Tonight she needed his love to sustain her.

Because he was less well known in Tyneham, Hugh drew a hood down over his red hair and entered the keep at supper time.

Much as it pained him to follow Walter's suggestion that it was the best place to pick up information on the workings of a place, he made his first stop in the kitchens. The cook's helper thrust a bowl of porridge into his hands.

Swallowing his pride, Hugh sought out a quiet corner and wolfed down the plain fare. Gareth would pay for this latest indignity, too. He felt renewed anger every time he thought how the man had snuck into Tyneham masquerading as a hireling knight, then somehow found a way to foil Hugh's scheme just when it was about to come to fruition....

Hugh's hands shook so some of the porridge slopped onto the coarse wool rags he'd been forced to wear. Damned if he wouldn't see Gareth Sommerville in hell for this. He flung the bowl down and listened to the talk around him. No mention was made of the Marsdens, and he wondered if coming to the keep hadn't been a mistake. Scowling darkly, he sidled from the room, worked his way down a corridor and entered the hall.

Other than the few soldiers playing at dice on the stones before the hearth, the room was disappointingly empty.

"What are you doin' here?" demanded a rough voice.

Hugh spun around and confronted a face he remembered all too clearly from the nightmare ambush on the beach. *Captain Farley*. Hugh's ready tongue stuck to the roof of his mouth.

"Well?" the captain growled.

Inspired desperation struck. "Dame Cicily sent me ta see if there was word of Arianna," Hugh said in a low, garbled voice, trying his best to sound like a serf.

Farley frowned. "I told Master Marsden it could take two or three days for a messenger to come from Wilton."

Wilton. Hugh struggled to stifle his excitement. "Thank ye, yer grace," he mumbled and hurried away.

It was child's play getting out of Tyneham, but anger had replaced Hugh's earlier elation by time he'd reached the woods.

"How dare Sommerville do this to me?" he raged as he stormed into their makeshift camp, kicking leaves and twigs before him.

Walter crawled from hiding, shoving the dagger back into the top of his boot. "Ye learnt somethin'?"

"Aye." Hugh plopped down onto a blanket and reached for the wineskin. "Curse him, Sommerville's gone to Wilton."

Walter's mouth gaped open. "Wilton?"

"Might as well be the bloody moon."

"Nay, 'tis good news." Triumph gleamed in Walter's eyes.

"You're daft. Wilton's Ruarke Sommerville's stronghold. We'll not pry him from there without considerable force. And hell would freeze over before my esteemed sire would lend me an army to lay siege to Wilton," Hugh warned.

"Won't need no army." Walter smiled and rubbed his beefy hands together. "I was steward at Wilton till Lord Ruarke and his bitch of a wife turned me out. But..." his smile broadened "...I've still got the key to the postern gate."

Chapter Seventeen

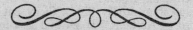

The first thing Arianna noticed when she opened her eyes the next morning was that she was alone in bed. The second was that it was late and Grizel hadn't come to wake her. Worry over the latter crowded out sorrow over the former.

Telling herself she should be glad Gareth had had the tact to leave before the castle was astir, she threw on the clothes she'd worn the day before and dragged a comb through her tangled hair, hastily braiding it as she ran down the tight circular tower stairs and along the passageway to the hall.

What she saw when she entered the hall confirmed her worst fears, a young man had Grizel cornered.

"Get away from her!" Ari cried, pushing between the pair and sending the man back a pace or two.

"What?" he exclaimed. "Oh, good morn, Lady Arianna." He bowed deeply from the waist. "I was just—"

"You leave Grizel alone, she's..."

The maid took Ari's arm and turned her around. She indicated she was all right. Indeed, her cheeks were pink, and her eyes sparkled brightly.

"Who is he? Why was he talking to you? And how?"

"I am Philippe, Lord Ruarke's squire."

"Come, Philippe," Ruarke bellowed from the doorway. "The sun's come out at last, and we've a stable full of restless horses to exercise."

Philippe touched Grizel gently on the arm to attract her attention. "I will see you later?" he asked huskily.

Grizel nodded, her color deepening as her eyes followed him.

"You aren't afraid of Philippe?" Arianna asked in wonder.

Shaking her head so vigorously her braids danced, the maid tried to assure her mistress all was well.

Ari's eyes narrowed. Her knowledge of men was limited, yet she suspected the worst of Philippe's motives. Why would he be interested in a mute maid if not to bed her? "Has he tried to touch you?"

Again, Grizel defended the lad.

"Nor will he," Gabrielle said, coming up behind them. "Even had Ruarke not forbidden his men to pursue any of my maids, Philippe was ill used before he came to us and is sensitive to others' feelings. When I first married Ruarke, I could not speak the Norman French. Philippe served as our interpreter." She smiled wickedly. "I fear we put him through some trying, embarrassing times ere I learned the language so I could shout at my lord in his own tongue."

Despite her concern for Grizel's safety and happiness, Ari chuckled at that. "You were brave to come to a foreign land where you did not even speak the language."

"'Twas not my bravery that got me here, 'twas Ruarke's stubborn insistence he'd not leave his wife behind."

"Aye, the Sommervilles are stubborn." And arrogant. Again last night, Gareth had sworn that they'd wed. *Dieu, how was she to convince him it would ruin them both?*

"Pride. The Sommerville males have it in abundance. 'Tis what makes taming them such a challenge for us poor females."

"Poor, hah. You are very adept at man taming. Lord Ruarke is big enough and loud enough to frighten even the bravest of women," Arianna said enviously. Gaby was no more than a few years her senior, yet she seemed as wise as Dame Cicily.

Gaby's smile faded. "My sire—much as it pains me to admit I sprang from his blood—was so vile a man Ruarke seems like a saint by comparison. Not that we didn't have our difficulties at first," she ruefully added. "We are both used to be-

ing in charge, and since men and women *never* think alike on
a given subject, we butt heads constantly.''

"But you love each other very much."

"Loving does not preclude fighting, I fear."

Arianna sighed. "Nay, it does not. Gareth and I are as different as two people can be. He is quiet and logical and practical, while I talk too much and rush into things without a
thought to the consequences."

"You also make him laugh. And I can see by the way you
two look at each other that you are very much in love."

The arrival of one of Gaby's maids saved Arianna from
saying it didn't matter that they loved each other.

"M'lady, can you come?" asked the maid.

It took Ari a second to realize she was the "lady," even
though she'd heard it often enough since her arrival. Everyone at Wilton treated her like the lady she wasn't, Lord Peverell's occasional digs notwithstanding. "What is it?"

"We've laid out the skeins o' wool thread. Could ye come'n
choose the colors fer the trees?"

"Aye. Will you come and see what we've been doing?" Ari
asked Grizel. Together they went up to the solar where the
frame holding the canvas for the tapestry had been set up.

Grizel smiled when she saw the sketch Ari had done, her
fingers tracing the lines of the castle. Her eyes fairly glowed.

"Aye." Ari agreed with her maid's unspoken comment.
"The love and commitment Gaby and Lord Ruarke feel for
their people shines brighter than the hundreds of candles that
illuminate their beautiful hall."

Grizel touched the figure of young Cat running through the
flowers after a butterfly, then her finger lingered on baby
Philippa. Slowly she raised questioning eyes to Ari.

"The babe is precious, is she not?" Ari said.

Nodding, Grizel's gaze skittered to Ari's abdomen.

Ari felt a flutter move through it, as though the butterfly had
come to life within her. *A babe.* Dear God, she had not
thought of that. Could she be carrying Gareth's babe? Her
skin turned cold, then hot, then cold again. Nay, surely she was
not pregnant. She couldn't be.

"Perfect," Gaby said, holding up the skeins of green and brown wool Arianna had chosen for the trees. "We will thread a needle for you, and Felise can show you the different stitches."

"Nay." Arianna backed away. "I have never tried it and wouldn't want to ruin your beautiful piece with my clumsy attempts. I'm too restless to sit still anyway. Mayhap I'll take a walk in the gardens."

"The stitches are not difficult. One with your clever fingers could master them in no time."

In truth, her fingers did itch to be creating something. It had been over two weeks since she'd finished the silver reliquary. But metal was her medium, not cloth and thread. What she longed for was to be back in her grandfather's house in Tyneham, beginning on the bronze statue of Gareth.

Thinking of him made her feel even more restless, and she fled the cozy solar with Grizel close behind. The narrow, winding stairs seemed to close in on her as she hurried down them. To fight the panic cramping her chest, she thought about Grizel. The ease with which the maid had fitted in with Wilton's kitchen staff had left Ari feeling a little bereft.

The two of them had a special relationship, the bond of growing up together strengthened by the unique way in which they communicated. It hurt to see Grizel no longer needed her, yet at the same time, Ari was ashamed of herself; she should be glad that Mave, Wilton's cook, had taken Grizel under her wing, recognized her talents with food, and given her free rein with the baked goods. She should be glad Grizel had found others to whom her lack of speech was not a problem. And mayhap even a young knight who was genuinely interested in her.

Ari had been pleased when Gareth had assured her that Sim had readily made a place for himself in the stables, his skills with the horses outshining his physical limitations.

That both Grizel and Sim had been accepted at Wilton was due to Gaby's influence. Her own page had a crippled leg, her steward was so old he had to be helped around, though his mind was still sharp. And half of the stable building housed

sick or injured wildlife being helped back to health by Gaby
and Felise, and now, Sim.

Truly Gareth had been right to praise Gabrielle. Truly she
was a unique woman, a woman worth admiring and emulat-
ing. Yet seeing how efficiently Gaby ran Wilton only served to
make Ari more aware of her own shortcomings. Nay, she was
not cut out to be a lady.

"I wish Papa would get here," Ruarke growled as he and
Gareth left the stables, hot and muddy after giving the horses
and themselves a good workout.

"I'd say he'd arrive today. Likely he sheltered in the nearest keep when the storm struck, and then set out again as soon
as the weather cleared."

"And Alex?"

Gareth gnawed on his lower lip. "I'm no sailor, but if the
storm caught them out at sea, they could have lost Harcourt . . . or worse."

"Alex has an uncanny eye for the weather, and well you
know it," Ruarke growled back. "He'll have spotted the storm
approaching and sought a safe harbor."

His brother's deep rumble soothed Gareth's nerves. His own
feelings of guilt had clouded his judgement where Alex was
concerned, made him see danger where there was none.

"I like your Arianna," Ruarke said as they crossed the bailey and mounted the stone steps to the keep.

"I'm glad." Last night, while they lay warm and sated in
each other's arms, Gareth had assured Ari that Ruarke and
Gaby liked her. She'd smiled and said she liked them, too, but
the smile hadn't reached her eyes, nor quieted his anxiety. How
could he make her see her compassion and her ready smile
more than made up for her lack of housewifely skills?

"What will you do if you can't wed her?"

Stopping at the entrance to the hall, Gareth dragged in a
deep breath, let it out slowly. "Kill myself," he said hoarsely.

Ruarke grunted. "Gaby's right, you must be in love. You're
beginning to sound as desperate as I did when I thought I
might lose her." His booming voice turned the heads of the
servants throwing a cloth over the lord's table set up on the

raised dais. "Ah, I forgot 'tis the day we hold manor court." He looked down at his filthy clothes. "I'd best wash some of this away ere I sit in judgement, or the villeins'll think I shame them. Do you likewise, and bring your Ari to our court."

"Aye." Gareth brightened. 'Twould give his little crusader a chance to see the Sommervilles *did* believe in justice.

Arianna spied Gareth striding toward her, his expression grim, his boots scattering gravel from the orderly garden path into the carefully tended roses.

"What has happened?" she asked in alarm.

He stopped so close to her his toes disappeared under the swirling skirts of her borrowed green gown. "I didn't know where you were." The slow fire burning in his eyes warmed her despite the cool breeze.

"I'm here."

"Aye, but will you always be here?"

"Here? In Wilton's garden?" Ari tried to laugh to ease the tension thrumming through her body, but the effort lacked humor.

"Here, beside me. I couldn't bear it if you weren't here, Sunshine." He gripped her upper arms, holding her still without hurting her, warming her skin, but not the coldness deeper inside. His lips brushed across hers, his breath fanned her cheek. "What is bothering you, love?"

Though she longed to fling herself into his arms and find the peace their joining had brought her last night, she knew the relief would be temporary, at best. "Only what is worrying us all. I am anxious to see this thing with Harcourt ended." 'Twas partially a lie, yet he recognized it.

"Tell me the rest, Ari. More than lack of confidence has put those shadows in your eyes."

"I would know about Emilie," Ari said, pushing the rest of her fears aside.

Gareth exhaled loudly, his hands tightening on her. "Emilie was my wife."

"She died four months ago."

"Three months, three weeks and two days ago."

For once she couldn't read his thoughts. "You loved her?"

"I didn't know what love was until I met you." Gareth's gaze locked on hers, silently pledging his love, yet also looking for some sign she was angered to discover he'd had a wife. He found only love and understanding. How could he have forgotten her capacity for caring? Knowing they would both be better off sitting down, he led Ari to a bench set back among the roses.

Surrounded by their fragrance, he began, "To Emilie I was a title, a way of life her parents had pushed her to pursue. I didn't know she had previously met Alex, and mistaking him for the Sommerville heir, practiced her wiles on him. When Emilie realized she'd erred, she quickly turned her charms on me. Poor fool that I was, I asked for her hand two days after meeting her. 'Twas only when I returned home to show my father the betrothal contract, that I discovered Alex wanted her, too."

"The two of you fought over her?" Ari asked gently.

"Like two dogs with only one bone between them. We tore at each other with words and fists, opening up wounds we can never heal." Gareth dragged a hand through his hair and exhaled, looking out over the nodding heads of roses and spiky lavender, yet seeing none of their beauty for the ugliness within himself. "Stupidity. Of the worst sort. She was already pledged to me, so there was naught Alex could do but storm off and threaten never to return."

"Did he?"

Gareth laughed, the sound as mirthless as her own earlier attempt. "Gaby drugged him and got him to Ransford for my wedding. Later, I found out that Emilie approached him at the feast. Only hours after becoming my bride, she offered to meet with my brother in secret and lie with him, claiming she loved him and had wed me for profit."

"Nay." The breath hissed out between Ari's teeth. "How awful for you."

"How awful for all three of us," he said grimly.

"You fought with him again, didn't you?" she murmured, remembering his fevered ravings.

"Aye." The anguish twisting Gareth's features was almost more than she could bear. "I had not gone to Emilie's bed for months, maybe six or seven," he said woodenly, "when she came to my chamber late one night and claimed she had missed me. She who had spurned me, called my attentions crude. Nearly two years of living with her had made me less a fool than when we'd wed. I told her to be gone, but she persisted." The muscle in his cheek jumped as he clenched his jaw.

He had bedded Emilie and regretted it. Surprisingly, she felt little jealousy. Emilie had wed him, but she had been no wife to Gareth. "Afterward, what happened?" Ari asked to spare him the telling.

Gareth smiled faintly, cupping her cheek with his hand. "Ah, Sunshine, your capacity for giving amazes me."

She nuzzled his palm and kissed it. "I would take the pain from the tale if I could."

"Nay, I no longer feel pain when I remember what Emilie did to me. Loving you has healed that wound, at least. Mayhap time will take from me the memory of how I nearly killed my brother."

"Alex?"

Swallowing hard, Gareth nodded. "Two weeks after... after she came to my room, Emilie announced she was pregnant." At Ari's gasp, his mouth thinned. "Aye, after only two weeks, she claimed to know she was carrying my child."

Ari's hand fell reflexively to her stomach. It had been only a little longer than two weeks for her, too, yet she feared... nay, she'd not think of that worry now. "Whose child was it?"

"Alex's... or so she said. I'd not have believed her even then, but she had been in London for the past six months, and I knew Alex had been there, too. Once again, she played me for the fool, washing away my doubts with a flood of tears and protests that it had not been her fault, that Alex had charmed her into his bed as he has countless others."

"So you went after him," Ari said, her hands cold, her body shaking with apprehension.

"Aye. I found him aboard his ship in London's harbor." Gareth's voice was so low she had to lean closer to catch what he said. "Alex denied Emilie's charges. Said he had not touched her since the day he'd learned she was to marry me. I persisted. Pride and fury made me deaf to the ring of truth in his words. He wouldn't fight me.'' Gareth's eyes glittered with suppressed emotion. ''I raised my sword, drew it across his throat. The tip of my blade came away red. Red with my brother's blood.''

''Oh, Gareth.'' Arianna turned and wrapped her arms around him, clung to him even as he clung to her. She could think of no words to ease his stumbling heartbeat, his ragged breathing. No balm to ease his pain. ''Yet you couldn't kill him, could you?''

He shook his head. ''Nay. I threw the sword down and left, ran before I could do something more terrible.''

''He doesn't blame you. He came to Tyneham to help you.''

''To my shame.''

''Shame?'' Ari pulled back so she could see his face. The usually impassive marble surface of his face had cracks in it, twin tracks where a tear ran down from each eye. There would be no more, but she was immeasurably moved to see a rock cry. ''You didn't hurt him. You couldn't.''

''I tried to.''

''As I am sure he tried to hurt you when he found out you were to wed his Emilie. Gaby has filled me full of tales of the proud, passionate Sommervilles. 'No one takes a Sommerville's woman and lives to tell of it,' I believe she said.''

''True.'' Gareth dredged up a smile. ''Still, I attacked my own brother over a woman's lies.''

''You could not murder anyone...least of all your brother.''

Gareth sighed, wishing he were as certain.

''Did you find out who fathered her child?''

''Nay. Rumors of her wild ways abounded at court, but no single name could I learn. When I returned to Ransford, she was dying of a potion she'd taken to rid herself of her burden.''

''I'm sorry—so sorry you were made to suffer.''

Gareth drew in a deep, cleansing breath, tipping his head back so the sun fell on his face. '' 'Tis part of the past, and I'd speak of it no more.''

Ari sighed as well, burying her nose in his shirt. ''It feels good to sit with your arms around me and the sun warming me.''

A wicked grin slashed across his face, chasing the last of the shadows from his eyes. "If you've read that much in my mind, then you know I'd much rather we were upstairs and I warming all of you."

"Sir, you are a lecher."

"Aye. But only where you are concerned," he added huskily, the wanting in his expression part desire, part something deeper, more complex. "I keep remembering how beautiful you looked last night in the candlelight without all these clothes." His lips brushed hers again, the air between suddenly so thick with the promise of passion Ari could scarcely breathe. "I keep remembering the little moan that catches in your throat when I move inside you."

"Oh, Gareth."

"Will you not put aside your foolish fears and say you'll marry me when this is over?" Gareth murmured in her ear.

Ari started. "Nay, I . . . I cannot."

"You love me, and I you. Your lack of breeding makes no difference to me."

"It will to your sire."

Gareth shrugged that aside. "Any disappointment he may have that you aren't nobly born will fade when he gets to know you."

"What if . . . what if he disowns you?" Ari asked shakily.

Gareth started to laugh, read the panic in her eyes and stopped. "You are serious? My sire would never disown me."

"So my own father thought," Ari said. Clearly the time for truth, the whole, painful truth, had come. Swallowing hard, she began, "My father married my mother without securing his own sire's permission. When he arrived at his family home with my mother in tow, and several months pregnant with me, the Baron de Clerc flew into a rage. Not only did he disinherit my father, his only son, he threw the two of them out with only the clothes on their backs. They nearly died getting back to Tyneham."

"I am sorry your father was disowned, but that does not change the fact that your grandfather was a baron," Gareth said, smiling. "See, you have no cause to feel inferior to—"

"No cause?" Ari cried. "The baron ruined my parents' lives. My mother blamed herself for the loss of my father's birthright. It drove a wedge between them, killed their love. My mother cried for that all her days until her death."

That was why she never cried. "My sire wouldn't disown me."

Ari wished she could believe him, but she knew better.

"Gareth." Ruarke called from the gate. "Court's beginning."

Gareth and Arianna sat together on a bench in the back of the hall. Many of Wilton's people had come to the court, either to have a matter heard, or to bear witness for a friend, or simply to hear their lord dispense justice.

Despite the scrubbed walls with their bright hangings, and the fresh herb-strewn rushes underfoot, the press of unwashed bodies and the heat made for an unpleasant combination. Ari refused Gareth's suggestion that they leave, pressing the orange stuck with cloves closer to her nose.

"Stubborn," he said fondly. Moving the prickly ball aside for a moment, he dropped a quick kiss on her mouth.

"Gareth, Lord Robert is glaring at us."

Turning his head, Gareth scowled back at the lord who lounged in a chair near an open window, a servant fanning him and another holding a cup of cooled ale.

"He looks none the worse for being drugged," Ari whispered.

"Aye, but Ruarke was right, she should not have done it."

"Even though we profited by her actions?" she asked archly.

He matched her grin. "Pay heed to what is going on with the court, or I'll carry you off and have my wicked way with you."

"In broad daylight?" Ari's cheeks flamed at the thought.

"Test me if you doubt it."

The challenge gleaming in his eyes sent Ari's pulses racing; it was difficult indeed to turn away and fasten her attention on Ruarke and Gaby sitting in judgement over their flock.

"Is it usual for the lady of the castle to sit in judgement with the lord?" she asked.

"Nay, 'tis the lord's business, but in this, as in many other things, Ruarke shares his duties with Gaby."

"That does not surprise me."

Gareth grunted in agreement. "Gaby is an unusual woman."

Aye, she is a lady. Clenching her hands in her lap, Ari forced her attention on the two farmers who disputed ownership of a calf sired by the bull of one on the cow of another.

"Emilie took no interest in our estates, except to spend money at a ruinous rate," Gareth went on, oblivious to her pain. "I know I need not worry you will beggar me, for you are not interested in clothing, jewelry, face powders and such."

"What makes you think I am not?" she demanded so sharply heads turned in their direction.

"Gently, love," he muttered. "I only meant you are used to plainer things, and—"

"Because I am but a plain burgher?" Her voice rose.

"Of course not, do I not tell you you are beautiful at every turn? Jesu," he mumbled, covering her knotted fists with one hand. "Let us drop this accursed subject."

"Fine," Ari snapped, wounded even though she knew it was true. She was not a great lady, used to fine things. Whipping her gaze back to the front of the hall, she saw the farmers had been replaced by the new cloth merchant from Wilton town, come to pay his "relief" on taking over the tenancy of his shop.

Perplexed by her attitude, Gareth cleared his throat and tried again. "Ransford is larger than Wilton, and we hold as fiefs several lesser keeps, a handful of towns, a mill, a toll bridge and two markets."

"I am certain the heir to a great estate has many duties," she said stiffly.

Gareth sighed but pressed on. "From the time I could walk, I've been about the business of learning to be the earl." Her interest was grudging, but it was the first she'd shown in Ransford and her role as mistress there. He'd been right to bring her to Wilton so she might learn from Gaby's example, he thought. He told her of the estate and the people whose welfare would become his responsibility when he succeeded his father. "There will be much for you to do, since Emilie took so little interest in the running of Ransford. The food, the gardens, the cleanliness, all need improving.''

The pride and love for his people in Gareth's voice moved Ari. Despite her parents' example, a part of her longed to marry him and accept the challenge of turning Ransford into the sort of place Wilton was. But would the earl and countess want her? If they didn't, Gareth would be forced to choose between his family, his heritage and his love for her.

The old steward stepped forward to read the particulars of the next case. An ugly murmur swept the hall as a woman advanced. She was the widow of the miller who had served Wilton. He had died, leaving behind this woman and one female babe. The widow had come to swear her oath of homage for the mill.

No sooner had the steward's words ceased to ring from the rafters than a burly man stepped forward. ''I am Edgar, wed to the daughter of John Miller's youngest brother. I challenge this woman's right ta the mill.''

Ruarke and Gabrielle exchanged glances, but Ari could tell nothing of their mood from this distance. ''Are you a miller, also?'' Ruarke asked Edgar.

''Nay. I work the land, as does my sire.''

Ruarke asked more questions, about the size of the farm, and how many other brothers Edgar had. ''Three,'' the man replied. Ruarke nodded. Gabrielle frowned.

''What does that mean?'' Ari asked Gareth.

''When Edgar's father dies, the farm will be divided amongst the four boys. Unless it is a large and prosperous piece of land, 'twill not be able to support them all. This man wants the mill so he can better his life.''

''Will Ruarke and Gaby grant Edgar the mill?''

''I suppose. A woman can not run a mill.''

Nay. ''But what of the widow and her child?'' Ari exclaimed, thinking of Mary and her brood.

Gareth's shrug pushed Ari over the edge.

Jumping to her feet, she cried, ''You can not put this woman out with nothing.'' Every eye in the room turned on her, some startled, many hostile; she ignored them all. ''She and her child would starve to death,'' Ari hurriedly added.

"Ari, sit down. 'Tis not your place to interfere," Gareth muttered, tugging on her arm.

She wrenched free. "Please, Gaby. . ."

"Ari." Grabbing her around the waist, Gareth yanked her down onto his lap.

"Let me go," Ari commanded, bucking and struggling against the arms that restrained her like iron bands. "I'll not let another family suffer as that dratted Earl of Winchester did Mary and her children."

"What passes here?" demanded a deep baritone.

Ari's head jerked around, and she looked up, up into the angry scowl of a man who looked suspiciously like Gareth. Warning bells went off in her head, but she was too furious, too frustrated to heed them. "Who wants to know?" she snapped.

One dusty, grizzled brow rose to mock her in a handsome face glistening with sweat, lined with the fatigue of travel. "The dratted Earl of Winchester."

The fight drained out of Arianna in a long, slowly exhaled breath. "Oh, my. . ."

The hall erupted into a hail of welcoming shouts from the assembled vassals. Gareth stood, setting Ari on her feet, but keeping one arm securely around her waist as though he expected her to attack the earl at any second.

Attack? All she wanted was to drop through the floor.

"Papa," Gareth was saying over the bedlam, "I would have you meet Arianna de Clerc, whom I brought with me from Tyneham."

"Indeed?" Again the brow went up, but this time the dark, mesmerizing eyes he'd bequeathed to his sons and used every bit as effectively as they did, narrowed. "I'd not expected to see Sir Neil's wife with you," the earl said. His expression as hard and cold as Alex's had been when he'd offered her money to leave Gareth alone, the earl looked Arianna up, then down, making her uncomfortably aware of her wrinkled dress and untidy braids for the second time in two days.

Gareth felt Ari shiver, and the knot in his stomach tightened. His first thought was to spare her feelings. "There's been trouble, Papa, and I'd speak with you in private."

Robert pushed his way through the crowd and stepped in front of Gareth. "Geoffrey, thank God you've finally arrived," he said, shooting a triumphant glance at Ari.

"Robert, I didn't expect you here, but it saves me a trip to see you. As soon as I've heard what is troubling Gareth, we can look over the betrothal contract I've drawn up between Gareth and your Margory."

Chapter Eighteen

"*B*etrothed?" Arianna cried. Whirling away from Gareth the minute he released his iron grip on her arm, she fled to the farthest corner of her chamber.

"No contract has been signed between us." He tried for calm and confident, but his voice caught on the unresolved issue of Peverell's offer to clear the Sommerville name. She turned, gazing at him across the expanse of rumpled bed linens, silent testimony to the love pledge they'd renewed the night before, her magnificent blue eyes magnified by pools of unshed tears.

"Now I see why Lord Robert insisted on coming with us."

Gareth loudly wished Lord Robert, his daughter *and* all of the Harcourts in hell. "He'd blackmail me into wedding her."

"Blackmail? How?"

"We've discussed what would happen if Charles and the merchants told their tale in King Edward's court." At her wary nod, Gareth raked a hand through his hair. "Robert will find the four men guilty and hang them without benefit of trial—as soon as the betrothal contract is signed."

Moaning softly, Arianna sank down onto the side of the bed. This was it, then. The bride fate and Gareth's family had chosen for him was here, and it seemed he must wed her. Ari had thought herself numb, resigned to living the rest of her life without him for her own reasons. If she was numb, why did it hurt so?

Gareth knelt before her, taking her cold hands in his. "You know it is you I love."

Sucking in a ragged breath, Ari nodded, her eyes squeezed shut in a valiant effort to hold back the stinging tears.

"And it is you I will wed," he continued grimly.

How? Gareth had a duty to his family... a duty to wed this well-bred lady and save the Sommervilles from ruin.

"Alex will find Harcourt and bring him here. Together, we'll force a confession from the bastard that will satisfy even the most virulent of my father's detractors." His voice hardened; his grip on her hands tightened with every word. "Then you and I will wed and live happily at Ransford, raising war-horses and fat little Sommervilles."

Ari's lip quivered. *I will not cry.*

"Ah, Ari." Gareth pressed her face into his shoulder and tried to absorb the shudders racking her slender body. "Go ahead and cry, love. God knows, we've ample cause."

"I never cry," she choked out.

Her struggle not to cry nearly tore him apart.

The air in Ruarke's counting room was so thick when Gareth entered that he could have cut it with a knife—or the keen edge of the temper he'd lately discovered he possessed.

"Where's Lord Robert?" he demanded, seeing his father leaning against the stone hearth while Ruarke paced before it. His father exhaled harshly. "No doubt nursing the snub you gave him when you rushed from the room with your..."

"With the woman I love," Gareth said stiffly.

Geoffrey's eyes widened. "Love?" he exclaimed as skeptically as Alex and Lady Catherine had. "Nay, but she is not for you. True, Lady Margory may not be as comely as your..." He paused, eyeing his eldest son's clenched fists and squared jaw. "As Mistress Arianna, but the lady is gentle, and she *is* the wellborn wife you said you wanted."

"I had not met Ari when I said that. Nay, her bloodlines may not be as noble as Margory's, but 'tis Ari I love. Jesu, Papa," Gareth growled, kneading the corded muscles in his neck. "You, of all people, should understand. Did you not sneak into Wilton in the dead of night and steal Mama away when her father forbade your marriage?"

"Aye." Grudgingly. "But Catherine was my first love."

"What does that mean?" Gareth demanded, eyes blazing.

"Mama and Papa are afraid you'll make another mistake," Ruarke blurted out.

"Jesu, I am not some child to be led about by the hand!" Gareth exploded, anger flushing his chiseled features. "And Ari is not a mistake. She is nothing like Emilie."

"'Tis true," Ruarke said, wading in. "Emilie never rescued Gareth from a cave, nor burnt his food, nor tried ropedancing."

"Ropedancing?" A slight spasm of distaste crossed the earl's aristocratic face. Ruarke didn't see it.

"Aye. She's trained as a goldsmith, too. Gaby's most jealous, I tell you. Next she'll be asking for hammers and a forge of her own. And, you should see the sketch Ari did for the new tapestry. She's a talented artist."

"Ruarke, don't help me," Gareth growled as their sire's frown deepened. "Arianna is a warm, sensitive woman. She's—"

"She disrupted your brother's court, came near to starting a brawl and she called her overlord, 'the dratted earl.'"

Gareth exhaled sharply. "I'll admit she does not have a good opinion of the way we handle our vassals." He went on to describe the case of Mary and her children, pleased to note the concern that replaced his father's dark scowl.

"I certainly gave no order to put the woman out. These men who usurped her farm may not even be our people," Geoffrey observed. "They may be renegade bond tenants or laborers from another district who happened on the scene and turned the widow's misery into their own gain."

Gareth nodded. "Though we've had no trouble of that sort, I'd heard of it happening elsewhere and was suspicious. Only I was not in a position to investigate the problem then."

"Nay. Pray God we can do that soon." Geoffrey sighed. "Gareth, you know I'd not have you wed Margory if your love is truly given elsewhere, but what of Harcourt's plan to see us tried for treason? I understand from Ruarke that only Robert's offer to intervene stands between us and the hangman."

Frustration muted Gareth's anger. "If we could get our hands on Harcourt, we'd not need Robert Peverell's high-priced help."

Arianna stepped up onto the dais that evening and sat gingerly on the edge of the chair Gareth held for her. The stiff skirts of the silver-shot blue samite surcoat Gaby had insisted on lending her crinkled, echoing her own brittle nerves.

"Have some wine, dearling," Gareth urged, taking the seat to her right. "It will relax you."

"There isn't that much wine in all of Bordeaux," she mumbled, but she let the page fill her cup and took a sip under Gareth's watchful eye. "'Tis much better than that sour stuff your mother served at Ransford," she remarked.

"I'll be certain to mention that to my wife," growled the earl as he took the seat to her left.

"Drat," Ari gasped, choking on a mouthful of wine and nearly upsetting her cup. Muttering under his breath, Gareth quickly moved the cup to safety and, using his flattened palm, pounded her between the shoulder blades—with undue force, she thought miserably.

The meal went downhill after that. Though she shared a trencher with Gareth, Ari was painfully aware of every breath the earl took. The disapproval she felt radiating from him closed her throat so she couldn't swallow any of the delicious-smelling foods Gareth tried to tempt her with. The bits of sauced chicken and roasted pork he'd so carefully cut with his eating knife and placed at her end of the trencher congealed into an unappealing, accusatory mass.

Further down the table, she heard Gaby conversing with Ruarke and Lord Robert, but between Ari, Gareth and his father, not a word was spoken that didn't have to do with the business of somehow getting through dinner.

By the time the servants carried in the trays of fruit and nuts that mercifully marked the end of the meal, Ari's stomach was wound so tight she thought she might lose what little she'd eaten. Hard on the heels of the servants bustled a page, who approached Ruarke.

Ruarke came to his feet almost before the boy had finished speaking. "Gareth, we're wanted in the stables. Gray Lady is foaling, and all is not well."

"But we were to discuss the contract," Robert complained. "Can't your stablemen see to this?"

Gareth squeezed Ari's hand briefly, then rose, tossing down his linen napkin. "Nay, I'd tend her myself."

"Let me go with you," Ari pleaded.

He hesitated an instant, clearly understanding her reluctance to be left with his father and Lord Robert, but then he shook his head. "The birthing is a messy business, and no place for a lady." He stepped down from the dais and began wending his way through the hall. Ruarke took a moment to drop a kiss onto his wife's forehead, then hurried after him.

"I apologize for my sons' rudeness, Robert," the earl said, scowling at the pair of wide, retreating backs.

"The gray war-horses are valuable and very important to both Ruarke and Gareth," Gaby said defensively. "I fear Gareth's future wife must resign herself to missed meals and nights alone in bed while Gareth frets over them." Her words could have applied to Margory, but it was to Arianna she looked.

"Margory has been taught to know her place," Robert replied. *Unlike some others,* said the smug glance he shot Arianna. "Though why your sons bother with such things is beyond me," he added, turning his attention back to the earl. "Surely such low, unpleasant tasks are best left to a man's serfs and villeins, who are bred for such menial things."

Geoffrey stiffened. "I have never ascribed to that theory, as you well know. And Gareth, in particular, has always been one to involve himself deeply in every aspect of estate life."

Robert waved that aside with a soft, beringed hand. "I'd visit the garderobe, then what say we at least look over the marriage contract you've prepared?"

Arianna's stomach rolled, and she barely heard the earl's reply, nor marked Robert's departure. She had not thought—really thought—what Gareth's marriage to another would entail. Bad enough she would never see him again, never feel the touch of his hand, never see his chiseled features crack into a

smile at something she'd said or done. But the idea of his
sharing a bed with Margory, doing with her all the hot, secret
things they had done together in the dark of night, or enjoying the sweet, lazy joinings in the pale light of dawn made her
sick.

"I . . . I think I'll go my room and see how Grizel is coming
with those herbs," Ari muttered in Gaby's direction. Jumping up so quickly she upset her chair, she fled before she dis-
graced herself yet again today by tossing her minuscule dinner
onto the linen-covered high table.

"What do you think of Mistress Arianna?" Geoffrey asked
of Gaby, his thoughtful gaze following the beautiful young
woman's graceful, if hurried, progress from the hall.

"I like her. She may not be nobly born, but she is more the
lady than many I know with better claim to the title. Ari is
kind, clever and quick-witted. Nor did Ruarke exaggerate her
artistic talents. Best of all, she has made Gareth laugh again."
Gaby paused, considering. "Nay, because of Ari, he is *more*
open, *more* at ease than I have ever seen him. Except when
someone is trying to separate him from Ari. Then he's as fierce
as Ruarke."

She smiled at her father-by-marriage, knowing he was a
good and gentle man whose censure of Ari stemmed from
concern for his son and from the terrible threat the Sommervilles faced. "Were she not a special lady, do you think Sir Neil
would have agreed to wed with her? No matter what he had
promised her father."

"Mayhap not. You plead her case as a friend."

"Aye, I'd have her for a friend, and a sister," Gaby allowed. "Ransford is only a few hours' ride away, and 'twill be
lonely here when Felise goes with William to assume Sir Neil's
place at Tyneham. But come, let us go up to my solar so the
servants may clear away this mess. I'd show you the tapestry
Arianna has designed for me."

Geoffrey sighed in frustration as he pulled himself from his
chair and offered Gabrielle his arm. "I'd see Gareth as happily wed as my Catherine and I—as you and Ruarke. I admit
I had misgivings when Gareth asked me to find him a bride. A

marriage arranged solely to gain wealth or property is not for us Sommervilles. But..."

"But there is Harcourt to thwart ere Gareth is free to choose for himself," Gabrielle said unhappily.

"Aye. There is that, and knowing Gareth, he will put the welfare of his family before his own happiness."

"You should have called me earlier," Gareth exclaimed, going down on his knees in the straw beside the straining mare, heedless of the muck soaking into his fine hose and the hem of his red silk surcoat. "How long has she labored?"

"Only four hours," murmured the head stableman, his face ashen in the flickering torchlight.

"She's been hard at it, m'lord." 'Twas Sim who spoke, and the edge on his young voice told Gareth the boy had wanted to send for him sooner, only he'd been overruled by the older, supposedly more experienced men.

Just then another contraction shook the mare, and she screamed, her eyes rolling as she shuddered beneath Gareth's hand. Two of the stablemen came forward to help hold her, but this seemed to increase her frenzied movements.

"Out, all of you," Gareth ordered.

The men looked to Ruarke, who stood behind Gareth, his hands clenched helplessly at his sides. "You heard my brother!" he bellowed, and men scrambled to obey.

"All but young Sim," Gareth called over his shoulder.

The boy knelt beside the mare's head as Gareth moved to her hind quarters. Ruthlessly ripping off both surcoat and the tunic beneath, Gareth thrust an arm inside her. "Let us see what the trouble is, girl."

"Damn, I feel nearly as useless as I did when Gaby was birthing our girls," Ruarke grumbled, holding a torch nearer so Gareth could better examine the weary horse.

"Ah, hell," Gareth exclaimed, rocking back on his heels, his arm wet to the elbow. "The foal is wedged tight inside her."

"Won't her labors work it loose?" Ruarke asked.

"More like, its hooves will tear up her insides, and we'll lose them both. We must get a rope on the foal and pull it out."

It took Sim only seconds to find a rope. Twice, Gareth tried to loop one end over the foal's slippery hooves, but his hands were too big, his fingers too clumsy. He cursed ripely and tried a third time, his stomach tight with dread. Gray Lady was the best of their four mares, the foundation on which he'd hoped to base his herd. He couldn't lose her . . . he couldn't. His features twisted with grief, he sat back while Sim tried.

"'Tis no use, m'lord," the boy said after two attempts, panting with his efforts. "I can't push hard enough because o' me bad arm."

Groaning, Gareth closed his eyes. "Damn," he said softly. "I'd sooner put her from her misery than see her suffer so."

"Whatever is wrong?" Ari exclaimed, crouching in the straw and hesitantly touching the head of the shivering animal.

"Ari, what are you doing here?" Gareth demanded, whirling on her.

"I was worried about the horse." Her voice caught on his bleak expression. "She's dying, isn't she?"

"Aye. The foal is caught up inside her, and we can't wedge it loose." He shuddered as the mare strained weakly.

"Why can you not free it?" she asked. "Let me try," she begged when Gareth had finished explaining.

"You've not the strength, and 'tis mean and dirty work."

"Come, I'll take you in," Ruarke offered. "'Tis little enough help I am here."

"I'd try. My hands are small, but nimble and strong for wielding the hammers all these years. Please." She touched Gareth's shoulder, felt him tremble as the helplessness and sorrow moved through him. It wasn't the value of the mare that pained him, she realized, tapping into the silent communication they often shared. He couldn't bear to see the mare suffer so.

Nor could she. Ari tore at the right sleeve of her tunic. It was made to be removed, and the light stitches gave easily.

"What the hell!" Gareth and Ruarke exclaimed together.

Ari paid them no heed as she snatched the rope from Sim's slippery fingers and scrambled around to the mare's rump. "Show me what I must do," she demanded.

Gareth's fingers closed around hers, and she started, thinking he meant to take the rope. "You don't have to do this."

"I must, for I'd not see her suffer, nor could I bear the thought of you having to kill her."

"There are times I'm almost glad you can read my thoughts," Gareth said, dropping a quick kiss onto her stubborn chin. *God, how he loved her.* "We need to tie this rope around the foal's hind legs. 'Tis very important to get both *hind* legs—not one hind and one fore, or I'll wedge her tighter when I pull."

"I understand," she whispered. But the doing was far, far tougher than she had anticipated. Between the wet slipperiness and the mare's surprisingly strong contractions, it was hard to work her way inside, impossible to find the hooves. She'd not lost her supper upon leaving the hall. Now she feared she might.

"Leave it be," Gareth commanded, seeing blood well up as her even white teeth sank into her lower lip.

Ari groaned. "Nay, I . . . wait." Her fingers closed around something hard and sharp. A trio of tiny hooves. "I've found them." Recalling that Apollo's hind legs had a bend in them, while the front ones were straight, she sorted out the two she wanted. "Now, if I could just…get this rope…" Panting with effort, she squeezed her eyes shut and tried to force the rope around the shifting hooves. Leverage. She needed leverage.

As though he'd read *her* mind, Gareth moved in behind her and wrapped both muscular arms around her waist. "Use my strength ere you exhaust your own."

"Aye." She braced against the coiled power in the rock-hard wall of Gareth's chest and lunged forward. The loop slipped over the pair of hooves and tightened. "Done."

Gareth pulled her arm free and set her out of the way in one lithe movement. "Are you all right, love?" he demanded.

"Aye," Ari rasped, her breathing ragged. "See to them."

Gareth flashed her a grateful smile, then turned back to the mare. At first the foal refused to budge, and he feared their efforts had been in vain. Then suddenly the burden shifted within the mare, and the foal slid out in one long rush.

"You've done it," Ruarke cheered as Gareth tumbled back in the straw, his body slick with sweat, his chest heaving.

"What now?" Sim cried, but the mare had already roused herself to look at the tiny foal. He carefully removed the rope from its hooves and maneuvered it closer to the mother's head.

Wonder filled Ari as she watched Gray Lady lick and inspect every inch of her squirming babe, hovering over it as though she counted every precious breath the newborn took. Did human mothers feel the same protective urges? she wondered. She turned to share the experience with Gareth, and found him staring at her abdomen with an intensity that sent butterflies fluttering through it again. Or was it life that flickered there?

A babe. Why had it not occurred to him before that Ari might already be carrying his child? Gareth reached for her. "Ari, let me take you inside." They needed to talk. He needed to reassure her that no matter what he was forced to do to save his family, he'd protect her and their child for the rest of their lives.

"Gareth? Ruarke? How goes the birthing?" The earl stepped into the stables with Gaby on his arm.

"We'd have lost the mare and the filly had it not been for Arianna," Ruarke growled.

"Oh, Ari. What happened to you?" Gaby cried, hurrying forward. "Sim, bring water and toweling."

Gareth took the cloth Sim held out to him and waited to see that Gaby was helping Ari before turning to his sire. "The foal was wedged tight. I had no hope of saving either animal, but Ari managed to get a rope on the foal's legs, and I pulled it free."

"I'm glad your news is good." His father smiled, but even in the dim light Gareth saw it didn't reach his eyes.

Dread made his pulse falter. "What's happened?"

"Alex's messenger rode in a few moments ago."

"He has not caught Harcourt." At the shake of his sire's head, Gareth cursed ripely and threw down the soiled towel.

The earl's growl echoed his son's anger. "Alex lost the ship in the same storm that delayed my arrival here. He sent word from the port of Blakeney, where he put in to take on supplies. He's still in pursuit of Harcourt's ship. It's *The Sala-mander,* captained by Parlan Graham."

"You say the name as if you know it," Gareth muttered.

"And revile it. Graham is Hugh Harcourt's Scots cousin. A bastard in both senses of the word. Alex has reason to believe Graham is headed for Edinburgh. There to hide among his clan."

"Harcourt's cousin," Gareth said slowly, his brain churning. "Hugh called the masked man his cousin. Do you remember, Sunshine?" He plucked Ari from the straw to stand beside him.

"Aye. 'Twas in the caves where we overheard Hugh's plan."

"If this Parlan Graham is tall and blond, he must be the one Harcourt tried to pass off as me," Gareth told his father.

"He is blond," Geoffrey replied.

Ari frowned, cocking her head as she studied Gareth's chiseled features. "No one seeing the two of you side by side would mistake you for the same person." Her eyes widened. "That's it. I'll make a sketch of the two of you."

"We'll show it to Charles and the merchants from Tyneham," Gareth said, his excitement mounting. "Will that be enough to convince the court of our innocence?" he asked his father.

A shiver raced through Ari as the earl shrugged.

"Damn. You're wet and freezing," Gareth cried, wrapping both arms around her in a futile attempt to warm her. She looked as if she'd been to hell and back, her cheeks pale, her lips swollen where she'd bitten them, her clothes filthy and torn.

"Let me take you up to your chamber," Gaby said gently.

"Nay. I'd take her myself," Gareth protested, eyes flashing. "I owe her for saving Gray Lady and the foal." That was not the only reason he wanted to go with her, and all of them knew it.

Geoffrey shifted uncomfortably, unwilling to risk widening the breach between himself and his son by disputing with him.

"'Tis better I go with Gaby," Ari said gently, regretfully. *We are not alone here,* she said with her eyes.

Denial screamed through every nerve in Gareth's body, but much as he wanted to talk with her, to hold her in his arms, he grudgingly allowed he hadn't the right. She wasn't yet his wife.

Ari felt his pain, shared it. Yet she alone accepted the fact that this was the way things must be between them. Gladly had she helped bring the foal into this world. If her drawings helped save the Sommervilles, that too would make her happy.

But once this was over, she must return to Tyneham. She only hoped that when the time came, she'd be strong enough to make him understand and brave enough to leave him.

"Which way to the dungeons?" Hugh asked.

Walter leaned against the side of Wilton's kitchen building, silent and dark at this time of night, and gnawed on the cold chicken he'd purloined from within. "Below the keep." He nodded at the formidable stone tower in the center of the courtyard.

Hugh grunted. Candlelight shone dimly from a few of the upper windows, but the rest of the castle was dark. "Let's go."

"Not yet."

"Why are you stalling? Don't you remember where they are?"

"I should . . . that bitch Lady Gabrielle locked me in them fer a month afore Lord Ruarke came home. But we'll ha' a better chance o' gettin' in if we wait till everyone's asleep."

"It can't be too quick for me." Hugh darted a glance around, uncomfortable inside his enemy's stronghold.

"Aye, I'm fer getting Charlie and leavin', but afore we do either, we need hostages."

"Hostages? Whatever for?"

"They'll not let us walk into yon dungeon an' take Charlie."

"I assumed there'd be a struggle," Hugh snapped.

Walter snorted. "Ruarke didn't get his reputation fer naught. Ye saw how many men he has guardin' the place. Even wi' the key, we've had a rare time gettin' this far. The dungeon'll be watched closer'n a wagonload o' highborn virgins. And any man whot follows Ruarke'll be hell in a fight. I've no desire ta cross swords wi' them."

Hugh lifted his chin. "Man to man, I'd match my skills against any one of them, but there are only two of us."

"Aye. Two agin hundreds. So in a bit, we'll sneak inside and see if'n we can find a hostage. Mayhap Ruarke's pretty lady. I've a score ta settle wi' her. Whot's this?" Walter whispered, straightening as two women hurried across the courtyard. By the light of the pair of torches stuck in metal rings at either side of the door, he caught a glimpse of dark hair and a proud profile before they went inside.

"Ah, 'tis Lady Gabrielle," Walter murmured. "And Charlie's Arianna wi' her. I'd say our luck has turned."

Chapter Nineteen

A short time later, clean, dry and wearing an old blue gown, Arianna sat before the crackling fire in her chamber, sketching while Gabrielle combed the straw and snarls from her hair. Grizel had been gone when they'd come in, and Ari had protested when Gaby had offered to perform the menial task. To no avail.

"'Tis little enough I do after all your hard work this night," the lady had replied.

"I'm glad we could save Gray Lady and her foal."

"Aye, working with the grays was Gareth's salvation after Emilie's death. Properly trained by him, they should sell for a goodly price and bring in much needed revenues." She sighed. "I pray this is soon over and Gareth free to wed you."

Ari's hand shook, leaving a blob of ink to mar her drawing of Hugh's cousin. So would she be a blot on Gareth's life if she wed him. "Is Lady Margory...nice?"

"She's a vast improvement over Emilie, that's certain, but she's too timid, too empty-headed for Gareth. Nay, Gareth needs a wife with whom he can share his dreams, his fears, his life."

His life as an earl. Ari shivered again.

"You're cold. I'll make us some hot, spiced wine."

Ari started to object, but Gaby had already set the brush aside and taken up the poker. Thrusting it into the bed of shimmering red coals, she straightened. "Damn, I'd forgotten the spice chest is in my solar."

"Nay, 'tis here, I think." Turning, Ari spied the small chest atop the trunk she'd brought from Tyneham. Grizel had offered to replenish Gabrielle's stock and relabel some of the packets. "Grizel was working on it when I came up after dinner. She felt more comfortable here," she added lamely.

Gaby smiled her understanding. "Aye, though she avoids the hall when the men are there, Grizel has learned to relax with us, I think. She's much in Philippe's company."

"She was meeting him in the garden this evening."

"And that bothers you?"

Ari sighed. "I'd not see her hurt."

"Nor would Philippe hurt her."

"Oh, he seems kind, and Gareth speaks well of him. I didn't mean I thought he'd beat her, or rape her, but..."

"You think he'll bed her, then cast her aside?"

Ari's lips thinned. "I feel disloyal saying so, but why else would he bother with a mute maid?"

"Love." At Ari's startled glance, Gaby smiled. "At first sight, or so Philippe tells me. I must confess he knows little of courting a woman, having concentrated all his passions on furthering himself in Ruarke's service, but he has pestered me for advice on the subject since Grizel's arrival."

"But... but Grizel says he will be knighted."

"Aye." Fondly.

"Surely he could aim higher than... I mean, Grizel has no idea who her family was. No dowry but what my grandfather can spare."

"Lack of family can be a blessing," Gaby replied tartly. Then, more gently, "Are you not happy for her?"

"Of course I am." Ari sighed. "I am only concerned for her, and a bit surprised she so easily conquered her fear of men."

"I doubt it was easy, but love often gives us the strength to brave even the impossible."

If only that were true, but love couldn't make her suitable for Gareth. "Where will Grizel and Philippe live?"

"Why, here I would expect. Ruarke intends to keep Philippe in his service for some time, at least."

So, she'd return to Tyneham without Grizel or Gareth. Ari swallowed the moan that rose in her throat. "I'll miss her."

"As I will miss Felise when she and William go to Tyneham. Do you think they'll be welcome there?"

"Aye," Ari said quickly. "Felise is kind and wise, William strong, but patient, too."

"On occasion, Ruarke will miss William's restraining hand," Gaby said with a rueful smile.

"I'd travel with them when they go to Tyneham," Ari said quickly, before she could change her mind.

"But this business with the Harcourts has made Geoffrey anxious to see a new castellan in place. William may leave as early as tomorrow." At Ari's nod, Gaby's eyes narrowed. "Does Gareth know of your plans?"

Ari swallowed hard and shook her head, unable to meet Gaby's sharp gaze, knowing what she'd find there. "You've seen the way the earl looks at me—and at Gareth for wanting me to wife. I'd not come between them."

"Geoffrey wants what we all want, Gareth's happiness. Ruarke and I have seen how loving you has made Gareth whole again. Nay, whole as he never was, for he used to hold too much inside him. You have freed the self he locked away behind natural reserve and the constraints of duty. When the rest of the family comes to know you as we do, they will gladly call you his wife and Lady of Ransford," Gaby gently added.

"I am not a lady," Ari insisted, though deeply moved by her words. "If I go, Gareth will be free to save the Sommervilles."

"And Ruarke says *I* am stubborn." Gaby sighed, shaking her head. "I definitely need that wine." Snatching up the two cups Grizel had left with the flagon of wine, she started for the spice chest. "Mayhap if I get you drunk, you'll listen to—"

The door suddenly creaked back on its hinges to reveal a leering face framed in the doorway. "Well, well. Whot ha' we here?" Walter drawled, advancing on them, a huge dagger in his right hand. "Close the door, Hugh, whilst we decide how best ta use these lovely ladies."

"I will not give Ari up," Gareth growled, desperation hard as steel beneath his low voice. "I could not."

Ruarke nodded. "I would feel the same did someone try to come between me and Gaby. But—"

"But I may not have a choice." Gareth's eyes narrowed as he glanced across the study at the man who'd become his enemy.

"If Gareth will not sign the betrothal contract, I leave for London tomorrow, and the prisoners with me," Robert repeated.

"Have I tried to stop you?" Geoffrey replied reasonably.

"Don't be a fool," Robert snarled. "There are powerful men who'd use this excuse to be rid of you."

Though he shrugged, Gareth read the unease in his father's eyes. "Edward is my friend. He'll listen to my side of things and investigate the matter thoroughly ere he acts."

"Aye, you have long had the king's ear," Robert snapped. "And he might prefer to do as you say, but those who oppose his war with France would seize on this reason to withhold the monies and men Edward needs to continue his campaign. Nay, the king may not be able to save you. But I can." His shrewd eyes locked with Gareth's, the message clear.

Gareth clenched his hands into fists of denial, yet still felt his future with Arianna trickling through his fingers.

"At Tyneham Keep, you said you'd wed my Margory," Robert reminded him.

I'll wed none save Arianna de Clerc. The words burned a path from Gareth's heart to his tongue, but he knew he dared not utter them. *I will have her,* he repeated, but the vow sounded hollow even to himself. "I will honor my word if I must, but in my own way," he said in a carefully controlled voice.

"What does that mean?" Robert growled.

It means I won't sign away all hope of ever wedding Ari until my back is to the wall.

Geoffrey crossed to stand beside Gareth. "You must follow your own heart in this matter." Tears in his eyes, he laid his hand on Gareth's shoulder and squeezed gently. The gesture was meant to reassure, but the weight of his father's trust nearly drove Gareth to his knees. How could he follow his heart when it was divided by his duty to his family and his love for Ari?

"Well?" Robert demanded.

Gareth's lip curled as he eyed the cunning little man who had backed the powerful Sommerville family into a tight corner. Obviously the man had no scruples about abusing the authority given to him by the king. The bastard probably didn't even care whether the Sommervilles were guilty of counterfeiting or not, so long as his homely Margory became a countess and he gained a blood bond with the Earl of Winchester.

God rot that title, Gareth thought darkly. If not for the damned earldom, the Harcourts would not have plotted against the Sommervilles, and Gareth would not have been cheated of the wife he really wanted. The only woman he could truly love.

Ah, Ari! his heart cried out.

The pain was almost more than he could bear, and Gareth longed to repay Robert's greed by signing the contract, then defaulting on it when the danger was past. Unfortunately, he could no more abandon his principles than he could change the color of his eyes. Nor could he escape his duty.

"I'll sign the damned contract tomorrow," Gareth forced out. Ignoring Ruarke's string of curses, he walked to the window.

Robert grunted. "We'll hang the vile counterfeiters at dawn. Then I will ride to London that I may inform his majesty justice has been served. Come, a drink to celebrate."

To Gareth, the sound of wine splashing into Robert's cup was like dirt striking his coffin as he was buried alive. Inside him, everything turned to ice. He stared blindly out the window, his thoughts on Ari asleep in her chamber. When he'd composed himself, he'd go to her, wrap himself in her soft embrace and forget for a time what he'd been forced to do. They'd spend what was left of the night spinning memories as a bulwark against the pain to come in the next days and weeks...and months...and years. Ah, the empty, wasted years.

Gareth's hands clenched on the window frame. She'd not regret losing the title or the castle. She'd made it clear she cared for neither but could he ask her to abandon her reputation, too, and live at Ransford as his mistress, knowing he'd not even the protection of his name to shelter her from slander or legitimize a child they might already have created together?

"So, we meet again, Lady Gabrielle," Walter sneered. Stalking the length of the chamber, he chucked her under the chin with the tip of his blade.

"I should have let Ruarke hang you," Gaby said coldly.

Walter's eyes raked her lewdly. "Aye, ye should ha'."

Ari watched in wide-eyed terror, all her thoughts, all her fears, focused on Gaby. What little she knew of Charles's brother made her think challenging him was not wise.

"I agreed to using Lady Gabrielle as a hostage, not to harming her," Hugh grumbled, frowning at Walter.

"Whot difference does it make ta ye?"

"She once saved my sister's life. I'd not repay her kindness with ill treatment."

"You're Hugh Harcourt, aren't you?" Gaby guessed. At his nod, Gaby's expression softened. "How is she? I've often thought of her these past two years. Did she fully recover her memory? Did she—"

"This ain't a visit," Walter snapped.

"My sister is well," Hugh said, a brief smile curving his mouth before he turned a scowl on Walter. "I say we take Lady Gabrielle down with us to free Charles."

Walter fingered his blade. "An' I say we don't."

Anger flamed Hugh's face to his red hair. "Now, see here, Walter, I'm in charge, and—"

"We aren't leavin' till I've settled things wi' the lady." The ruthlessness twisting his florid face made Ari's blood run cold. She held her breath, hoping the fury in Hugh's eyes would erupt into violence. If the men fought each other, she and Gaby might escape. But something Hugh read in Walter's snarling expression caused him to back down.

"I'll keep watch at the door." Hugh kicked the red-and-blue patterned floor carpet as he walked away. "Don't take long."

"Ye needn't worry on that count. I'm near as anxious ta free Charlie as I am ta avenge meself on Lady Gabrielle's lily white self." Walter's thick lips curled in a parody of a smile as his gaze raked Gaby from face to toes.

Gaby chose that instant to move, diving for the handle of the poker. She came up with it and turned, waving the glowing, red-hot tip in Walter's face. "Lay down your knife," she demanded. A thin trickle of blood oozed from her throat where Walter's blade had nicked her, but her hand was steady, her eyes grim with determination.

On instinct, Arianna started forward, but before she could reach Gaby's side, Walter feinted right with his blade. As Gaby dodged to meet the challenge, he swung his meaty left fist, catching her in the side of the head and felling her instantly. The thwack of her head meeting the stone hearth went through Ari like a knife thrust.

Ari darted to where Gaby lay. There was blood at her temple, a crimson splash against her snow-white skin. "Nay." Ari dabbed at the blood with her skirt hem, feeling utterly helpless, wishing she'd paid more attention her aunt's lessons.

Walter calmly bent to retrieve his dagger, then pushed Ari aside and roughly clamped his hand to Gaby's throat. "She's alive," he grunted.

"We'll take Arianna as hostage," Hugh said.

Walter stood. "We're stayin' till she comes round."

Hugh argued and threatened, but Walter brushed his protests aside. While they hissed and snapped at each other, Ari crouched beside Gaby and pressed the hem of her gown to the free-flowing wound in an attempt to stanch the flow of blood.

"Take Mistress Arianna, then, and see if ye can find the dungeons by yerself," Walter said finally. "But I'm stayin'."

"How long?" Hugh snarled, chest heaving, eyes furious.

Walter rubbed a hand across his jowls, taking in the room at a quick glance. "She'll wake up soon. I'd ha' a cup o' wine while I wait," he decided. "Hot, spiced wine. None o' that sour stuff they make at The Forge. Nay, I've a need fer some o' that fine stuff the Sommervilles buy from the Frenchies. And ye'll make it fer me," he growled at Ari.

Ari's heart leaped, and her skin went clammy under his cruel, ruthless gaze. Gaby was safe for now, but when she awakened, she'd be in mortal danger, her life and Ari's precariously balanced on the thin edge of Walter's whim. If only there were some way to alert Gareth and Ruarke.

Briefly Ari considered flinging something through the window and screaming for help, but long before it arrived, she'd be dead and the two men gone. Mayhap Walter would even take Gaby with them, not caring if she bled to death as long as . . .

"Never did see whot Charlie saw in a skinny little thing like ye," Walter grumbled. "But ye'll do as a barmaid."

Ari fought down a strangling lump of fear and licked her dry lips. "I'd bind Gaby's head."

"After ye've fixed me wine, I might just let ye."

Ari swallowed her fear and nodded. She managed to put the poker back into the fire, but her hands shook as she reached for the cups Gaby had been about to fill herself only a few moments ago. The memory brought tears to Ari's eyes, but she blinked them away just as quickly.

Squaring her shoulders, she took the cups with her to the spice chest. As ignorant as she was about spices and herbs, she knew she'd have no trouble identifying what she needed by smell alone. The first drawer she opened contained a small packet filled with white powder. Vividly Ari recalled Gaby's drugging of Lord Robert. Was this what she'd used?

A tiny flicker of hope warmed Ari. Shifting slightly, she moved so her body shielded her movements, then shook a goodly amount of powder into the cups before locating the cinnamon, cloves and honey. Now for the wine and the hot poker.

Unfortunately, Hugh, who had resumed his post by the door, refused the wine with a curt shake of his red head. Walter, on the other hand, barely waited for the wine to cool before pouring it down his throat, his gulps so greedy some spilled over his chin and throat. "Ah, good." He smacked his lips. *The pig.* "Ye can tend ta Lady Gabrielle, now. I'd ha' her awake and lively fer whot I've got planned."

Ari eyed him through downcast lashes. Drat, why hadn't the drug started to work? Had she chosen the wrong powder?

The door to Ruarke's study flew open as Grizel burst in. Gasping for breath, she frantically searched the room until her gaze hit on Gareth. Her eyes widened, the fear in them like nothing Gareth had seen before.

Something terrible must have happened. 'Twas Ari... he knew it. "What is it?" Gareth cried, starting toward her.

Uttering a garbled moan, Grizel met him halfway, her fingers sinking into his arm. Her mouth moved, but no sound emerged.

"What is the meaning of this intrusion?" Robert exclaimed. "Can not you see we are busy?" He made a grab for Grizel's arm.

Gareth shoved the man aside. "Let her speak," he commanded.

"Speak? She's a damned mute."

Gareth silenced his lordship with a glare. "What's wrong?"

Ari, she mouthed, and something else he couldn't understand.

"Water?"

Grizel shook her head and tried again, her pale lips mouthing a word that seemed like...

"Beck?" Gareth guessed. "Walter Beck is here?"

At her quick nod, Ruarke demanded, "How could that scum get past my men? Is Hugh with him?"

Grizel shrugged and looked imploringly at Gareth, who cried, "Where? Where did you see Beck?"

She pointed to the floor above and Gareth's heart plunged as he pieced together her message. Walter had somehow gotten inside Wilton. "Is he in Ari's chamber?" Gareth's blood ran cold with fear as the maid grimly nodded.

"What would they want with her?" Robert muttered. He spoke to thin air. The Sommervilles had raced from the room.

"I think I hear voices below," Hugh whispered, turning from the door.

Gareth? Ari straightened fractionally as hope rekindled.

"Got to leave," Walter mumbled. Throwing down his empty cup, he heaved his bulk from the chair. The strangest look crossed his face, and he swayed where he stood. "What the hell . . . ?"

Arianna held her breath and prayed.

"Walter, come, I say," Hugh hissed.

"I . . . I can't . . ." Walter's eyes rolled back in his head and he collapsed into a heap beside Gaby.

"Bloody hell." Hugh raced across the room and kicked Walter in the ribs. "Up, man!" he commanded.

Walter didn't even groan.

"On your feet," Hugh ordered, waving his sword under Ari's nose. "You're coming with me." She had thought Harcourt soft, but the savage gleam in his eyes promised murder and mayhem as surely as did the length of naked steel he held over her.

The tower had been built as a fortress, and the stairs were part of its defenses. Narrow and steep, they allowed only one man passage at a time. In time of attack, it slowed the advancing enemy, allowing the defenders poised on the landing above ample time to deal with each man in turn.

Today, their roles were reversed, and Gareth had no idea what awaited them above. He didn't care. Ari might be in danger, and he was going up. Sword at the ready, he climbed quickly. The landing came into view...then the chamber door. Was Ari within?

Gareth's gut clenched. Patience. He tried for patience but, with every second precious, found he had none. "I'm going in," he mouthed to Ruarke, who stood behind him. Below on the stairs, waited Robert, Geoffrey and ten of Ruarke's men. The rest, under William's command, were busy searching the grounds.

"Right behind you," Ruarke whispered.

Gareth slipped up to the door, stood to one side and lifted the latch. He tensed, expecting a counterstrike that failed to materialize as he pushed the door open. His frantic eyes swept the room, took in Walter laid out on the floor before the fire, and Gaby a foot away.

Roaring an oath, Ruarke pushed past Gareth and threw himself on the floor beside his wife. "Gaby...? Oh, God, she's dead." His voice was raw with pain.

Gareth knelt and searched for a pulse, drew hope from the faint beat his fingers found. "Nay, Ruarke, she lives. Send someone for Felise," he commanded, coming to his feet. His joy at finding Gaby alive tempered by growing concern for Ari, he scanned the room for her again, hoping against hope to see something he'd overlooked in the first rush.

"Walter lives," Geoffrey said to him. "He's unconscious, yet there isn't a mark on him."

"Have the men tie him securely and lock him in the dungeon," Gareth replied with the small part of his brain that wasn't focused on Ari. "Hugh must have been here and taken Ari with him, otherwise she'd not have left Gaby," he reasoned. Had there been time between Grizel's warning and their arrival for Hugh to have escaped? If so, in what direction?

William de Lacy strode in carrying a shield and sword, but like the others he'd been in too much of a hurry to don full armor. "No sign of them below." He turned to Ruarke for orders.

Ruarke never looked away from Gaby's face. "I should have killed Walter two years ago when Gaby discovered he'd been cheating me, but Gaby didn't want his blood on my hands. If something happens to her, 'twill be my fault, and none other's."

"Ruarke?" William said gently. "What shall we do?"

"All my fault," Ruarke said, his voice a whisper.

Gareth blinked, momentarily stunned by his brother's reaction. He had always assumed Ruarke the great warrior to be above such mortal concerns as fear and guilt.

"Gareth, what shall we do?" William asked.

Do? Without hesitation, Gareth assumed command. "Hugh didn't come down past us, so..." He looked up. "What lies above?"

"The tower room. 'Twas badly damaged in an attack years ago when old Roger de Rivers was lord here. Now it's full of lumber and tools because Gaby's just set men to repair it. 'Tis a big task, for there are gaping holes in two of the walls where a catapult sent great rocks through them.''

"Is there any way down other than the stairs?"

"Nay, wait, the stonemason's scaffolding is set up on the outside. But they take the ladders away when they leave so the children won't be injured climbing on them."

"Good, we'll have him trapped, then."

Dark as sable, the night sky yawned boundlessly just beyond the holes in the garret's stone walls. A brisk wind whistled through the openings, tugging at Ari's unbound hair where she crouched behind the flimsy concealment of a small pile of building timbers.

Dread iced her skin as she stared across the debris-littered floor at Hugh. Like a deadly spider, he skulked close to the doorless entryway, a waxen stream of moonlight glinting off his ready sword.

Shuddering, Ari prayed Gareth would *not* come.

From the darkness beyond the open doorway came the whisper of footfalls. Her heart leaped into her throat as she strained to pierce the black void. Between one blink and the next, a figure materialized. Somber clothing blended with the night so the pale face, hair, and the length of gleaming naked steel seemed to float into view.

Instinctively Arianna knew it was Gareth. "Gareth... beware to your right!" she cried.

Gareth turned quickly enough to avoid a killing blow but did not escape unscathed. Ari gasped as the wind whipped his grunt of pain past her ears. A dark, malicious stain blossoming high on his chest, Gareth staggered back a step, then rallied, lunging forward, his sword up to parry Hugh's next blow.

But Hugh had fled, his curses bouncing off the ruined walls as he dragged Ari up by her hair. "You'll pay for that," he whispered in her ear. "Not another step, Sommerville."

Gareth skidded to a halt. Dimly he heard his father and the other men move in behind him. Vaguely he felt the sticky wetness trickling down his chest inside his hastily donned tunic and knew the wound he'd taken was a deep one. All these things were secondary to the sight of Arianna standing like a marble statue in the moonlight. Alone and vulnerable to Hugh.

"What now, Harcourt?" Gareth rasped, swaying slightly.

Hugh dragged Ari's head back so her neck arched. He smiled, the tip of his sword flirting with the pale curve of her throat. "Lay down your weapons and leave. All but Gareth."

"Release her, and I give you safe passage," Gareth retorted.

Hugh only laughed, the sound low and ugly. "Think you I'd trust a Sommerville? Away, I say, or she dies."

Gareth growled an obscenity and shot a quick, helpless glance at his sire and William as he dropped his sword, but there was nothing any of them could do without endangering Ari.

"What now?" Gareth muttered when the men had filed out.

"The girl and I are leaving. You'll give orders to the men hiding on the stairs to have two horses saddled and the drawbridge lowered."

Gareth shivered, fighting the debilitating wave of dizziness that washed through him. He had to stay conscious, had to find a way to save Ari. "Let her go and take me instead," he offered.

"Nay, Gareth, you'll bleed to death," Arianna breathed.

"Better that than risk you." Gareth's eyes blazed hatred at the man who held her, but there was more: his heart, his soul.

"How interesting," Hugh said slowly. "You almost make me believe you care for this maid."

Gareth regarded him in stony silence, unwilling to put so potent a weapon in his enemy's hands. "My offer still stands," he said quietly. The pain in his chest was nothing to the ache of longing. He wanted to take Ari in his arms, comfort her. Yet he also wanted to shake her for constantly putting concern for others above her own safety.

Hugh lifted his chin as though scenting the air, his foxy features lean and mean in the moonlight, his eyes glittering. Madness? Nay, the sick fear of a cornered animal, Gareth thought, knowing he must tread carefully.

"You'd not get far with that wound," Hugh reasoned.

Ari suppressed a moan. Frightened as she was, she was more terrified by Gareth's pallor and the way he swayed, as though he hadn't the strength to resist the wind scouring the tower.

"I'll last until you're safely away from here, and even throw in a ransom to sweeten the offer," Gareth said, his soft voice at odds with the tension Ari felt radiating from him. Shadows cast his taut features into a grim mask of determination and concentration. He was waiting; she felt it. Waiting for that brief instant when Hugh's attention wavered.

"Ransom." Hugh smiled grimly. "Aye, only I want everything you Sommervilles own. And the title . . . can't forget the title. 'Tis the only thing my father has hungered for and not gotten. Aye, his face will turn green when he sees I have bested him."

There'd be no reasoning with Hugh, twisted as he was by his obsession. Ari read Gareth's thoughts as surely as though he'd spoken them aloud. Read, too, his intention to fight back.

Ari stole a glance at the man whose sword still waved in the air as he babbled about his plans. He stood only a few inches taller than herself, his wiry frame silhouetted against the sky beyond the gaping hole. All his energy was focused on Gareth, the weak woman clearly forgotten until he needed her again.

She smiled at Gareth across the small space separating them to let him know she was going to act. He frowned, but then, he'd never understood her as well as she'd understood him. No matter . . . she had his attention.

"Now!" Ari shouted, ramming her elbow into Hugh's stomach with all her strength.

The air whooshed out of him on a satisfying grunt of pain, and he let go of her hair. Before she could run, he had her by the arm. "Bitch," he cried, and shook her so she bit her lip.

Through fresh tears of pain, Ari saw that one good thing had come of her ploy—Gareth had a sword in his hand.

Gareth instinctively assumed a fighter's crouch, grimacing as he struggled to rally his torn and flagging muscles. "You may kill me," he said, low and soft, the voice he'd use on a wild thing, "but you'll never leave this room alive."

Hugh's eyes widened with comprehension as they flickered to the men massing behind Gareth.

"Let Ari go and yield to me," Gareth continued in the same coaxing tone. "I vow to turn you over to the king unharmed."

"To stand trial? To be ridiculed as a failure by my father?" Hugh's voice rose an octave as he backed up, dragging Ari with him till they stood at the very edge of the floor, their bodies framed by the dark, starry night. "Nay, I'd sooner face death unshriven than my father's scorn." He squared his shoulders. "I'd fight you. I'm accounted a good swordsman, but against all of you," he gestured at the men behind Gareth, "I doubt I'll prevail. Aye, I'd die in combat."

"None here will raise a weapon against you," Gareth assured him. "So lay down your sword..."

"Not fight me? Aye, my sister claims you Sommervilles are decent men, but I think you'll fight me." Hugh smiled nastily, his eyes gleaming with unholy glee. "Aye, I'm counting on it." Before Gareth's horror-struck eyes, Hugh pushed Ari through the gaping hole and out into the nothingness beyond.

Her scream died under Gareth's roar of outraged pain and shocked disbelief. Without thinking, he charged.

Hugh raised his sword to parry Gareth's blind thrusts, but he took no offensive moves. Even wounded, the fury behind Gareth's strokes quickly numbed Hugh's arm. The clang of steel and the harsh rasp of labored breathing drowned out the mournful cry of the wind that cooled their sweat.

Gareth fought on instinct alone, hatred fueling blow after blow as he backed Hugh into a darkened corner. Then he saw it, the opening he'd been looking for. Steel shrieked down steel as he slipped in under Hugh's guard and flipped the sword from his enemy's hand.

Hugh smiled triumphantly, hands lowered, head tilted slightly back, baring his throat for Gareth's coup de grace.

Swaying where he stood, blinded by hatred and exhaustion, Gareth rested the tip of his blade in the hollow where Hugh Harcourt's lifeblood beat, marshaling for the quick slice that would obliterate Ari's death cry.

Only it wasn't Hugh he saw, it was Alex...and their father...and Ruarke and Gaby...and all the Sommervilles whose lives would be hostage to Hugh's mad scheme if he died without confessing his crimes.

Ah, Sunshine. Damn him, he wanted to avenge her; but he couldn't.

Gareth lowered his sword.

Hugh screamed something at him, but Gareth lost the words as a black fog enveloped his senses and his knees buckled.

Chapter Twenty

Gareth opened his eyes to the soft gray light of early morning and the unexpected sight of his sire sitting vigil, head bowed nearly to his breastbone as he dozed in a chair. Gareth's mouth was dry, his tongue swollen. "Papa?" he managed in spite of them.

Geoffrey jerked upright, revealing pale, haggard features and lank hair. "Gareth." He smiled, tears of relief welling in his eyes. "How do you feel?"

"Like Apollo ran me down...and stomped on me. My chest hurts like hell, but my head feels clear. How long was I asleep?"

"Two days. Can I get you anything?"

Ari. Gareth flinched, the pain inside him as sharp and white-hot as though another blade had rent his flesh. Nay, he couldn't think of her, not yet, mayhap not ever, or he'd go mad. Shuddering, he wrenched his mind free. "Water," he rasped.

The watered wine didn't wash the taste of ashes from his mouth, but it loosened his tongue and warmed the ice in his veins. "I ... I didn't kill Hugh, did I?"

"Nay, Hugh lives, and has confessed his crimes to the Bishop of London." At Gareth's exclamation of surprise, his father set the cup aside and continued. "Harcourt nearly went insane when you refused to kill him. Fearing he might do himself some harm and cheat us of the victory you had fought so hard to win, I sent Ruarke to fetch the bishop. He and I had ridden out from London together, so I knew he visited his brother at Rawlings and could be here in a few hours."

Relief washed through Gareth. At least it hadn't all been in vain. "The bishop is well respected. Not even our enemies would accuse him of lying to save us. 'Twas well done, Papa."

Geoffrey's jaw clenched. "Aye. Especially since young Harcourt tried to hang himself in his cell not an hour after the bishop and his clerk had left him."

"Nay. Jesu, 'tis a twisted sort of justice. But what will Edmund Harcourt think?"

"Fortunately the bishop was still here when the guards discovered what had happened and came running for me. Hugh survived, but his throat is damaged so he can scarcely speak, and his neck is scarred where his hose cut into it. The bishop has offered to explain the matter both to the king and to Harcourt." His father sighed deeply. "There was no love lost between sire and son, but Edmund will surely add this to the list of wrongs he thinks we've done him."

"Even their deaths could not repay me for the loss of Ari," Gareth said grimly.

"Ari!" Geoffrey smote himself on the forehead. "Curse me for a fool, here I am prattling on about Harcourt, with you still thinking Arianna died. Nay, but she did not. She fell five feet to the mason's scaffolding. Granted, she was a bit bruised, but she is whole. Despite our objections, she refused to leave your side until Gaby determined you were going to recover."

Sweet, dizzying relief stole Gareth's breath, his thoughts. All save one. *She was alive. Ari was alive!* "I'd see her." He tried to sit, but the burning in his shoulder and the weakness of his limbs kept him flat. Clenching his teeth against the waves of pain, he rasped her name.

His father hovered over him, eyes deeply worried. "Jesu, Gareth, lie still or you'll tear out all Gaby's handiwork."

"I want Ari."

"She is unharmed but for a few bruises," his father assured him. "I swear it. She sat with you all that first night, and yesterday as well, refusing to leave you long enough to eat. Gaby swears she counted each breath as you took it."

"She ever puts the welfare of others before herself. She'll make a fine countess if she can learn to guard her tongue." Gareth allowed his gritty eyes to close, but he couldn't rest easy. Something was wrong. Something prickled at the back of his mind, only he couldn't quite grasp it. "For a moment…when I thought she was…dead, I wanted to kill Hugh more than I wanted my next breath, but…" He opened his eyes, fixing them on his father's troubled expression. "But I thought about what would die with him…our chance to clear our name, and I couldn't. Not even to avenge Ari."

"There is no shame in *not* killing, my son." His father's voice quavered.

"Nay. No shame," Gareth said slowly. "I thought so at the time, but now I realize 'twas a good thing. Do you see?" He smiled faintly. "If I couldn't kill Hugh for Ari, I couldn't have killed Alex over Emilie."

"I am glad you are at peace with yourself. Now rest, my son," Geoffrey murmured.

Gareth's smile faded. "What is it? What aren't you saying?" He searched his father's eyes. "It's Ari, isn't it? There is something wrong, something you won't tell me."

Geoffrey raked both hands through his graying hair and sighed. "I know of no way to ease the truth. She's gone."

"Gone?" Gareth's heart stopped beating. "You lied to me? She's dead?"

"I did not lie to you," Geoffrey insisted. "She is well, only she left this morn for Tyneham. Gaby tried to persuade her to remain, but…"

"Tyneham?" Gareth struggled to breathe. "Name of God, why? Nothing stands in the way of our being together now. Unless…" His gaze narrowed. "Did Robert threaten her?"

"I don't think so. Robert has hardly spoken to anyone since it became clear he couldn't blackmail his way into our family. Today Ruarke and I are escorting him and the prisoners to London to face the king's justice. Arianna went with Felise and William to Tyneham," he added. "So you need not worry for her safety."

"Safety!" Gareth began clawing at the covers. "When I get my hands on that little witch she won't sit safely for a week."

* * *

A few hours after they'd left Wilton, the sky darkened ominously and the wind turned chilly again.

Riding in the cart with Felise's maids, Ari pulled her cloak more closely around her and cursed the unpredictability of early June weather. How nearly the season seemed to mirror her life.

Ah, Gareth. I love you. I miss you. Ari clutched the cloak tighter, struggling to subdue the waves of longing that struck her. She'd get over him. She would.

Behind them, a horn sounded, and close on its heels came William de Lacy's order to halt. Ari craned her neck to see what was going on, but the cart was hemmed in by a wall of soldiers.

The ground shook as a double column of mounted men thundered by, their banners whipping smartly in the wind. Ari's heart leaped as she recognized the red banner with the gold lion running rampant on it. *Sommervilles.*

Nay, it couldn't be Gareth, she told her racing pulse, but it refused to be stilled.

"Mistress Arianna?" growled a deep baritone.

Her guard parted to reveal a big man in full armor astride a brown horse, his helm lowered to obscure his features. The proud bearing, the width of the shoulders could have been Gareth's, but she knew in her heart it wasn't him. "M'lord earl?" she hesitantly asked.

Lord Geoffrey nodded curtly.

"Oh . . . it's Gareth, isn't it?" she cried, leaping to her feet. The cart tilted, and she gripped the side for balance, ignoring the maids' startled squeals. "What's happened?"

"Gareth has not worsened, but I'd ride apart and speak with you in private, mistress." Geoffrey kept his voice low, conscious of the curious stares fixed on them.

Ari scrambled from the cart and raised her hands to the earl, who grasped them and swung her up before him as easily as Gareth had done. What did the earl want with her?

It seemed a hundred years passed while the earl guided his horse to a line of trees several lengths from the road. Pulling off his helm, he ran a weary hand through his thick hair, then stared down his aristocratic nose at her.

Unconsciously Ari stiffened her spine.

"I've come to ask for your hand in marriage."

Ari's mouth dropped open. "Pardon me?" she croaked when she had control of it again. "B-but you're already married."

A wry smile twisted the earl's lips. "Aye, so I am. And lest you think I'm playing my Catherine false, 'tis not myself I'd have you wed."

"Thank God for that," Ari blurted out. Then seeing Lord Geoffrey lift one mocking brow, she realized what she had said and hastily covered her mouth. "Oh, drat," she moaned softly.

"'Tis Gareth," the earl said gently. "If I don't have you back at his bedside by evening, he'll likely kill himself attempting to come after you."

"He what?"

"When he found out you'd left, he...he went a little mad. Fortunately, Ruarke was in the stables when Gareth staggered in looking for a horse."

"Oh, no," Ari gasped. "Is he all right?"

"Gaby assures me the young fool's taken no permanent hurt," the earl grumbled. The midnight eyes so like Gareth's searched her face with an intensity that might have frightened her if she hadn't realized he was more afraid than she was.

"I'll go back, of course. And stay till he's well, but..." Ari stared blindly out over the green hills. "I can't marry Gareth. Surely the difference in our stations—"

"Difference be damned!" he growled. "We Sommervilles have always wed for love and not given a fig what anyone thought."

"You have? But I know nothing about being a great lady."

The earl released a pent-up sigh. "Twenty years in the service of my king, and accounted a silver-tongued orator by peers, yet here I sit unable to convince one stubborn girl to wed my son. Though I know she loves him as he loves her."

"You do?"

"'Tis in your eyes when you look at each other. Nor is it solely a thing of the flesh. Gareth sees beyond your beauty to your kindness and your compassion." He smiled at her shocked expression. "You may not be cast in the usual mold of countess, but times are changing, Arianna. Though my fellow lords refuse to see it, the vassal will not long keep his place, serving his master in exchange for a roof over his head and a scrap of land to work so he may enrich his lord's coffers."

Geoffrey shook his head slowly. "I thought myself above such men because we've always dealt fairly with our people. Yet in my arrogance I was as bad as they, mouthing words like fairness and justice, but burying my nose in my books and my peace proposals, doing nothing for mine own people. 'Twill be up to you and Gareth to keep our estates profitable, yet improve the lot of our vassals. I know they'll be in good hands," he said, taking one of hers between his palms.

"I don't know what to say," Ari murmured, moved nearly to tears by his words.

"'Aye,' would be most welcome," the earl quipped. "I smell rain on the air, and I'd return to Wilton ere we're drenched."

"You . . . you aren't going to disinherit Gareth?"

"When you come to know me better, you'll realize I'd sooner cut off my right arm than lose one of my sons for any cause."

"But . . ." A fat raindrop landed on the tip of Ari's nose.

The earl slanted her a pleading glance. "Could we not discuss these 'buts' of yours whilst we ride back to Gareth? If I return his precious Ari all cold and wet, 'tis likely *he* who will disinherit *me.*"

"Aye." Suddenly Ari's throat was so tight with emotion she couldn't say more.

"Arianna?" Dame Cicily pushed open the door to the chamber she and her niece had been sharing this past week at Ransford. "Oh, there you are, child. We've been looking everywhere."

Ari started and turned from the window in a whisper of azure silk. "I've been looking at the improvements you've already made to the gardens and trying not to get wrinkled. Is it time?"

"Nearly," her great-aunt soothed. "You can relax. I've found her," she called to someone over her shoulder.

"Is she all right?" demanded a deep baritone.

"Gareth." Eyes sparkling, Ari started forward.

"She's nervous and excited."

"I'd see her."

"You'll do no such thing." Slipping inside, Dame Cicily closed the door just as Ari reached it.

Pressing her cheek to the smooth oak, Ari called, "Gareth, when did you ride in from Wilton?"

"Last eve, but they wouldn't let me see you then, either," came the disgruntled reply.

"She was busy getting ready for today. And 'tis your own fault for insisting on wedding in such haste," Dame Cicily scolded, but her eyes were warm.

"Is your wound healed?" Ari asked anxiously.

"Healed enough," he promised in a low, husky voice that sent fresh shivers of anticipation racing to stir Ari's pulse points.

"That's enough of that," Dame Cicily interjected. "She's wound tight as a top as it is. Off with you, Gareth Sommerville, you'll see her at the chapel door, and not before."

Ari sighed and turned from the door as Gareth's footfalls faded away. Was it only ten days since the earl had brought her back to Gareth? Her life had changed more in those few days than in the eighteen years that had gone before. Was she strong enough to face the challenges that lay ahead?

"Aye, you'll do just fine," Dame Cicily decreed. "You've your father's determination. Alys, much as she was the daughter I never had, lacked the courage to fight for what she wanted."

"There's so much to do . . . so much to learn."

"Take each day as it comes, and remember, every journey begins with one step."

Ari threw her arms around her aunt. "I love you. When I grow up, I want to be as wise as you are."

"My dearest child, you *are* grown-up."

"Then why do I feel like a baby about to cry?"

"'Tis just nerves. You'll be fine."

"Don't you look beautiful," Catherine murmured, entering ahead of Gaby and Grizel.

Ari started to curtsy, but the countess took both her hands and raised her, planting a kiss on her brow. "Such formality from my newest daughter? I thought we'd become friends."

"Oh, we have," Ari said in a rush. "That is, you've been so kind and helpful. I'm just nervous," she added lamely.

Catherine smiled. "It must be contagious. My usually patient eldest son is pacing before the chapel. If you don't appear immediately, he threatens to come up after you." She shook her head. "After getting to know you, I agree you're the perfect wife for him, but why such haste?"

"Oh, I think I have a pretty good idea why," Gaby mused.

Ari blushed, thinking of her own restless nights and too-vivid daydreams. "I'm for the chapel," she announced. And not a moment too soon. Halfway there, they met Gareth hurrying in the opposite direction.

"The last week seemed like the longest year of my life," he murmured as they finally stepped into the candle-lit chapel.

"I missed you, too."

Staring deeply into Gareth's midnight eyes, Ari knelt with him before the Bishop of London. The words of the mass flowed around her. With all her heart, she vowed she'd be the best wife, the most diligent lady, in the whole world.

Barely had Gareth's lips touched hers for the kiss of peace than the boisterous Sommerville relatives pounced on them. Borne along on a wave of laughing, cheering people, they were swept back across the courtyard and into the hall.

Ari stopped in the doorway, her eyes round with wonder. Gone were the blackened walls, the stench of mildew and smoke. Now the scent of sweet rosemary rose from the fresh rushes, and the walls gleamed under a coat of whitewash. Even the tattered banners hung from the ceiling timbers fluttered more proudly. "Is this Ransford?" she gasped, tempted to go back outside and make certain they'd entered the dark, forbidding castle.

Gareth grinned and urged her toward the raised dais. "You've Gaby to thank."

"She did all my work?" Ari didn't know whether to be pleased or miffed.

"Just the hall . . . and one other chamber," Gaby said, winking at Gareth as she took her place beside Ruarke. "Think of it as my wedding gift to you."

Speaking of wedding gifts reminded Ari of the key Catherine had pressed into her hand moments before they'd left for the chapel. "'Tis Geoffrey's and my gift to you *personally*." Mayhap it unlocked a trunk full of clothes suitable for a lady. She smiled. Or a tapestry of the family history she was expected to finish? Frowning at that idea, Ari turned to question Gareth, but a flourish of trumpets blasted through the hall.

Grizel herself preceded the two menservants bearing the boar's head. While the guests exclaimed over the presentation, Grizel stopped before Ari and Gareth. She clasped both hands over her heart and smiled warmly. Through a mist of tears, Ari saw her curtsy and walk confidently to the place Philippe had saved for her.

Philippe had been Ruarke's gift. Next month, following his knighting, he would join the ranks at Ransford. Soon after that, he and Grizel would wed.

"You aren't eating," Gareth prompted.

Ari looked down at the choice pieces her new husband had cut and placed on her end of the trencher. *New husband.* In spite of the knot in her stomach and the lump in her throat, she picked up her knife and attacked the food.

Gareth frowned. "Haven't they fed you this week?"

"Oh, I'm not hungry," Ari said, swallowing hastily. "In fact, I can't taste a thing," she confided in a small voice so neither Grizel nor Mary, who had come to be Grizel's assistant in Ransford's kitchens, would hear. "But the sooner we finish eating, the sooner it will be time."

"Time?"

"You know, *time.*"

"Ah, Sunshine." Gareth threw back his head and laughed, drawing surprised glances from the guests and fond smiles from his parents, Ruarke and Gaby.

Seated across from Philippe and Grizel, Dame Cicily grinned at William. "I told you things would work out."

"Aye, you did," William mused, watching his granddaughter smile. "But I never dared dream she'd come to this." His gaze took in the beautiful hall, the magnificently dressed guests and the host of servants passing efficiently among them, offering the twenty or more dishes that made up each of the eight courses. "'Tis good to see her happy."

"All this food!" Ari cried in dismay. "I'll grow fat as . . . as Gray Lady."

Gareth eyed her abdomen. "I'm looking forward to it."

After dinner, came the entertainment—provided by Ransford's resident troop of players. While the acrobats tumbled and the dwarf cavorted, the ropedancer bowed to Ari and Gareth from a rope strung across one end of the hall.

Ari absently drummed her fingers on the linen-covered table.

Gareth picked up her hand and kissed each impatient finger. "I understand our vassals have some mimicry they'd offer as their gift. As anxious as I am to have you to myself, we can't disappoint them."

Our vassals. "Do you think they'll accept me?"

"I think you'll find they already do," he said with such assurance she nearly believed it. *Nearly.*

The first piece the vassals performed depicted Gareth as the overeager bridegroom. Gareth laughed so hard there were tears in his eyes. Watching him, Ari thought how little he resembled the hard, cold, remote man she'd first met. But then, she had changed, too, from a self-centered girl to a woman well aware of the world around her and determined to make it a better place in which to live. If she could.

"'Tis obvious from your serious little face you're not paying attention, love," Gareth murmured to her.

Ari looked up to find a man wearing a wig of long pale straw trying to master ropedancing. *He was supposed to be her.* His antics had the crowd roaring, but when he jumped down from the rope, his expression changed from smiling to furious. Tearing across the hall, he rescued Janie and baby Rupert from the specter of starvation, played by a masked man draped in a sheet. The people cheered even louder as the straw-haired "Ari" went on to right all sorts of wrongs.

Shouts of "Long live Arianna! Long live our new lady!" rang from the rafters.

Lord Geoffrey, who had been silent throughout the presentation, leaned past his wife to whisper, "I would join them in welcoming you to our family, Lady Arianna."

Ari smiled shyly. "I will do my very best to make a good lady." But a small, traitorous part of her wondered if running the estate would overwhelm her. Would Ari the person become lost in Ari the Lady of Ransford?

"This seems a good time for us to escape," Gareth murmured.

"Escape?" The hopeful look Ari slanted him made his heart leap. He'd never thought to find a woman who made him feel as happy, as complete, as his Sunshine did.

"Come. Ruarke promised me a head start." Grabbing her hand, he jumped down from the dais and led her out through the buttery door. "I'd not have any but me see you naked," he explained when she asked why they went this way.

Agreement lent wings to her feet. Behind them, Ari heard the howls of the guests who'd realized they were about to be cheated of the bedding ceremony, but Gareth knew the castle well and brought Ari through the kitchens, up the little-used back stairs to the lord's chamber.

Panting with exertion, he dropped the bar across the door and leaned back against it, Ari wrapped securely in his arms. "Damn, we nearly didn't make it. That's the most work I've done in ten days' time."

Impatient fists pounded on the door. "Let us in!" called a male voice. "This isn't fair," cried another.

"Go away!" Gareth shouted. "This is not a first marriage for either of us, and I vow I'll not repudiate her come morn."

The pounding continued until Ruarke's bellow drove them away. "Gaby's and my compliments on a neat escape," he growled through the door. "And we're both happy for you."

"Not as happy as I am." Gareth called back, wiping beads of sweat from his brow.

"Are you certain you're recovered enough for...? That is, we could just *sleep*...." Ari said as the hallway grew quiet.

Gareth's expression sobered. "Nay, after thinking I'd lost you." His eyes darkened with pain as they did every time he thought back to that terrible moment when Hugh had pushed her from the tower. "And then being separated from you this week, my spirit is willing enough to overcome anything."

"Just being with you, feeling your arms around me and knowing we're really, truly married is enough," Ari assured him. *Well, almost enough.*

As though he'd read her thoughts, Gareth shook his head. "Not quite, love. If I run out of strength, I'll let you do most of the work."

"You will?" Frowning.

Gareth grinned. "Papa tells me you are interested in learning to ride."

Her frown deepened. "Aye."

"I'd be pleased to give you your first lesson." He dropped a quick kiss on her pursed lips, forcing himself not to linger when they parted on a heartfelt sigh. "What do you think of our bedchamber?"

Ari turned to look where he pointed, and kept turning in a slow circle, her eyes wide with wonder. The walls had been hung with pale yellow silk, so the room seemed to wrap her in sunshine. The silk draping the bed had been parted to reveal white sheets sprinkled with lavender. Her grandfather's silver dolphin candlesticks sat on the table beside it, shimmering in a wash of golden light. Ari's lower lip trembled. *I am not going to cry and ruin my wedding day,* she vowed.

"'Twas Gaby's doing," Gareth said, smiling tenderly at her efforts to control her tears. Tears of joy, yet she would not shed them, either.

"I see your hand in the color of the silk, and..." she eyed the overlapping furs covering the floor and wiggled her eyebrows at him "...I've a mind to do some sketching this eve."

Gareth couldn't stop the flush that warmed his cheeks, didn't even try. "Not just yet, Sunshine. Have you the key my mother gave you?"

"Aye." Ari took it from the purse at her waist. "She wouldn't tell me what it opened."

"They left that for me." After making certain the coast was clear, Gareth led Ari up to the next floor. The key fit the door at the top of the stairs. "This is yours," he told her.

Ari warily opened the door and was immediately enveloped by the sharp, familiar scent of metal. "What . . . ?" Stepping past Gareth, she entered. The undulating light from a pair of torches revealed her grandfather's scarred workbenches and, laid out on them, the tools of his craft. Beneath the benches, draped in shadows, sat the banded strongboxes holding the metals.

"Oh . . ." Ari's eyes opened wide, trying to take it all in at once. Whirling back to Gareth, she stared up at him, tears in her eyes, her trembling hands clasped to her heart. "Thank you! My grandfather will be so happy working here."

"So he may." *For the time he has left.* "In this room my father kept his most precious books and the treasures his grandsire had brought from the crusades. He gives it to you, now, that you might have a place to retreat from the pressures of being lady here and do what you love best."

Arianna burst into tears.

She cried while Gareth locked the door and helped her down the stairs, his arm wrapped securely around her. She was still crying when he peeled her out of her wedding finery and tucked her between the lavender-scented sheets. The sobbing lessened as he stripped himself and crawled in with her, but started up again when he held her close and stroked her back.

"I know you have a lot of tears stored up," Gareth murmured into her wet ear, "but I fear you'll make yourself sick ere you don't stop soon."

"I was afraid this would happen," she choked out between sobs. "I—I am just like my m-mother."

"You are crying because your life is ruined?"

"N-nay. I am crying because it is too much. Everyone has been too kind. Your mother, your father, your . . . our vassals." She sniffed. "And because you insisted on getting wed so quickly, I have no gift for you."

Gareth smiled, touched by the small voice, the sad red eyes looking up at him. "Aye, you do. 'Twas because of your gift that I insisted we wed as soon as possible."

"It was?"

Very solemnly. "Aye." Very slowly, very gently, he reached his left hand down and splayed it across her abdomen.

The babe? Ari gasped, tears forgotten. "But...but how can you know when I'm not even certain yet?"

"I know." He smiled tenderly. "I suspected the night you saved Gray Lady's foal, and when my father brought you back to me, I knew."

"You did." Her lashes fluttered as he wiped the tears from her cheeks. "You can read my mind, too?"

Gareth shook his head. "Nay, I leave that to you and Aunt Cici. 'Twas not your thoughts...it was your face and your eyes. You glowed, Sunshine, as though the sun truly was inside you. Just as I remembered Gaby had glowed when she carried Cat and Philippa."

"But..."

"No buts." He caressed her still-flat belly, making her insides quiver so she nearly believed his child—their child—did shelter there. "I know," he repeated, his low, deep voice stroking her senses as his hand did her body. "It's a boy, and we're going to call him Richard."

"Oh." Ari felt a fresh wave of tears welling, but blinked them back as she cradled his beloved face in her hands. Now was definitely not the time for tears...even tears of joy. "I love you," she whispered against his mouth.

"And I you, my Sunshine Lady. With you beside me, I can do anything." He kissed her with every ounce of pent-up Sommerville possessiveness and determination.

"We," she amended when he let her up for air.

He hesitated only a second. "We," he agreed, sealing the vow with a lingering kiss rich with the promise of more.

A dozen, a hundred kisses later, Arianna discovered that riding was a good deal like being a lady, a bit of work, but satisfying. Very satisfying.

* * * * *

Look for KNIGHT'S HONOR *later this year,
the exciting story of middle brother
and ladies' man Alexander,
in the third book of Suzanne Barclay's Sommerville
knights trilogy.*

ROMANCE IS A YEARLONG EVENT!

Celebrate the most romantic day of the year with MY VALENTINE! (February)

CRYSTAL CREEK
When you come for a visit Texas-style, you won't want to leave! (March)

Celebrate the joy, excitement and adjustment that comes with being JUST MARRIED! (April)

Go back in time and discover the West as it was meant to be . . . UNTAMED—Maverick Hearts! (July)

LINGERING SHADOWS
New York Times bestselling author Penny Jordan brings you her latest blockbuster. Don't miss it! (August)

BACK BY POPULAR DEMAND!!!
Calloway Corners, involving stories of four sisters coping with family, business and romance! (September)

FRIENDS, FAMILIES, LOVERS
Join us for these heartwarming love stories that evoke memories of family and friends. (October)

Capture the magic and romance of Christmas past with HARLEQUIN HISTORICAL CHRISTMAS STORIES! (November)

WATCH FOR FURTHER DETAILS IN ALL HARLEQUIN BOOKS!

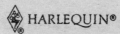

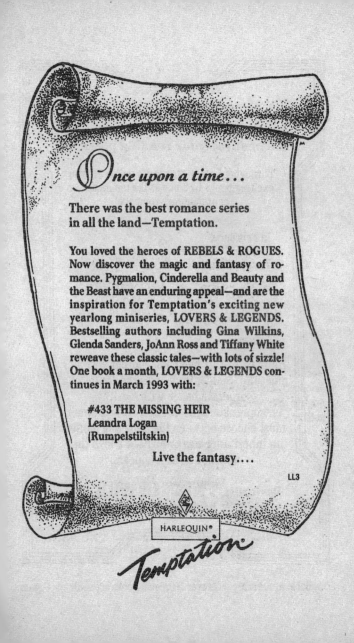

$\mathcal{O}$nce upon a time...

There was the best romance series
in all the land—Temptation.

You loved the heroes of REBELS & ROGUES.
Now discover the magic and fantasy of romance. Pygmalion, Cinderella and Beauty and
the Beast have an enduring appeal—and are the
inspiration for Temptation's exciting new
yearlong miniseries, LOVERS & LEGENDS.
Bestselling authors including Gina Wilkins,
Glenda Sanders, JoAnn Ross and Tiffany White
reweave these classic tales—with lots of sizzle!
One book a month, LOVERS & LEGENDS con-
tinues in March 1993 with:

#433 THE MISSING HEIR
Leandra Logan
(Rumpelstiltskin)

Live the fantasy....

LL3

HARLEQUIN®

Temptation